UNBOWED

UNBOWED

A Novel

by
LESTINE

FIRST YND PRESS EDITION, JANUARY 2021

Paperback	ISBN	978-1-7349660-0-8
eBook-EPUB	ISBN	978-1-7349660-1-5
eBook-Adobe PDF	ISBN	978-1-7349660-2-2
eBook-MOBI	ISBN	978-1-7349660-3-9

Fourth Edition Rev. date 1/3/2021

Library of Congress Control Number: 2013914768

LESTINE

YND Press is an imprint of
Yogi Next Door Publishing.

Also visit: www.unbowedthenovel.com

Dedicated to the Universal Presence in all of Us,

to the memory of my mother, Henrietta Johnson, who always

inspired me to reach higher and be better,and to the memory of the
real Basma.

A Cacophony of Echoes,

Silence in the Wind

I brave the icy landscape

Oh, to rule my day!

—Lestine

And years later, when her mind had finally evolved to be able to examine itself, she wondered how such concepts as fear of her thoughts, shame of her own body—the vessel that nature fashioned, and her soul adorned—had arisen at all. When had her body become something alien, separate from her? How could it be something that threatened the honor of the family, something about which she had to be vigilant? Yet at the same time, it was supposedly sacred, meant to be cherished, to be covered, protected, something powerful enough to reduce male devotees of God into lust-drooling fools poised for attack?

When did her form become something that stripped her of her humanity? A thing to be used for the pleasure of others, but never begetting her own. How else could she explain how a man can grab an unknown woman, force himself into her and not allow the woman a voice? The act ruins her for life. Her family wants her dead, yet the man is free to live unashamedly, mostly unpunished for his terrible deed.

Awareness had come suddenly, like flashes of lightening, illuminating those dark un-traversed regions of her mind, revealing ideas, forms and images hidden amongst reminders to clean this and shop for that. As she sat calmly behind the stage waiting her turn to speak, knowing full well it could cost her her life, she recalled those days when alien concepts like liberty and choice sauntered brazenly past the most pious of thoughts : 'Remember to keep every strand of hair corralled'.

She recalled the years she had navigated the world cloaked in a long black shroud, as if mourning her own womanhood. But all that came many years after her family's antiquated beliefs about honor led to the nightmare that would haunt her dreams for the rest of her days.

Basma was only eleven then, and Nature was still the laudable piper leading her young on journeys of endless discovery...

Part One

CHAPTER 1

The land was parched that day, like it had been every day that summer. Before long, the fact that water could pour from the sky seemed a myth. Yet coffee beans thrived on terraced plateaus, and rugged mountain ranges, the color of muted earth, sprawled out lazily beneath an azure sky.

High up on one of the slopes overlooking a small Yemeni village near Al-Hajjarah, a sheepherder watched his sheep graze on tufts of dried grass. Well, he was supposed to be watching, but he had long since dozed off.

About a quarter of a mile below him, three children sat around a large tree stump giggling. Basma Al-Goul was eleven years old; her cousin and best friend, Aisha Rahim, and Rafiq, a neighborhood boy, were thirteen. Both girls wore the traditional covering called hijab, the head scarf, and the abaya—a dark brown robe-like dress. Each child broke off tiny specks from a piece of unleavened bread and watched a team of ants carry the bread into crevices along the stump.

Later, Basma, Aisha and Rafiq, who always remained at Aisha's side, walked along the dusty road back toward their individual houses. It was close to dinnertime. Basma gazed up at the blushing sun sneaking behind sienna hills. The magenta sky was streaked with iridescent ribbons of gold. Jasmine shrubs and the white flowers of coffee plants infused the air with their rich fragrances. She smiled broadly and inhaled.

The children continued to giggle and chat softly as children often do.

Suddenly, Basma spotted something lying on the road right at their feet. It was shiny, and she pointed to it. Aisha immediately sprang into action. With her wide curious eyes, she squatted down for an inspection. It was a jagged four-inch wedge from a broken clay pot. Bright red, black, yellow and teal glass stones surrounded what had probably been the brim of the pottery. She picked it up, and all three children examined it by running their small, sunburnt fingers over the glass stones.

"It's so pretty. The black ones look like momma's eyes," Aisha commented.

She then handed the pottery wedge to Basma, who smiled happily and clutched it to her chest, as they continued walking.

For Basma, this was a particularly good day. She had been to school— one of her favorite things. When she was asked by her teacher to write a few lines of poetry, an integral undertaking of the tribesman, she was elated. Poetry had become a recent addition to her list of favorites, along with eating lamb fatah when her mother, Sumera, could afford it, or honey and butter fatah that had become more frequent after her father, Murjid, had passed away.

Then there was playing with Aisha. That thought made her glance over at her cousin, who was now grinning broadly at Rafiq. But what really made the day a particularly good one for Basma was the lack of pain in her right foot, usually caused by the head of a protruding nail that held her shoe together. Sometimes the nail would loosen, bore right through the inner sole and scrape the skin off her heel sending a shooting pain all the way to her head. One time, her foot bled.

Her mother, Sumera, had promised new shoes months ago, but Uncle Khalid had come up short with their allowance. That morning, Basma had gotten the idea to fold up small squares of paper she found in the streets, and put them in her shoe. Remembering all this made Basma especially pleased with herself, so she swung her arm more deliberately as she walked alongside her companions, still clutching the chunk of pottery to her chest.

When they approached the town, the first row of shops was already in the process of closing. At the shoe stall, the shopkeeper was removing shoes from a display box. One pair was Mary-Jane style, made of canvas in bright pink with a purple pansy flower on the toe. It immediately caught Basma's eye. She stopped to stare longingly.

"They would look so beautiful on you," Aisha pointed out, aware of the loose nail in Basma's shoe.

"Do you think your father will have enough money next month?" Basma inquired.

"I don't know. Maybe. Let's hope." Aisha gently pulled Basma away from the shoe stall and they continued along the narrow sidewalk occasionally stepping to the side when passing an elder.

And then, one fateful moment later, Rafiq reached over, innocently, and, for the first time, took hold of Aisha's hand, as they walked.

***

The following week, Basma, unhappily, missed several days of school to help her mother with her two younger brothers.

In the two weeks after that, it was so hot out that most of the children played indoors where the stone walls kept the air cool.

Basma began to miss seeing Aisha, who lived on the other side of the souq—an outdoor market—and had a later class schedule. She made a mental note to wait the extra hour for Aisha after school the next day. With that decided, she reached into her school bag and pulled out a book of Yemeni poetry given to the female students by one of the teachers. Sitting cross-legged on the floor, she rested the book on a low rickety table her father, Murjid, had constructed for her. He was never very good with a hammer. Like Basma, Murjid preferred to wander, to daydream, and—if he had known how—to read. She paused a moment to reflect on her father, missing him, missing his attempt at crafting things for her and failing miserably. She missed his face, framed in that black, wiry beard, lighting up whenever she entered the room. Murjid had spent time with Basma. He listened to her incessant questions on hundreds of topics and, though illiterate, provided his own carefully thought-out answers. But, mostly, it was Murjid's love she missed. For that, no one else had even come close—not even her mother, Sumera.

Opening the book, Basma had settled into reading passages aloud when she heard noises in the distance.

The scream was electrifying. Heads turned every which way, trying to find its source. Then they saw her: little Aisha Rahim, running, her face stricken with fear. Alarm and fascination ripped through the open market.

People turned to see from whom Aisha was running.

Her pursuer was lean and fierce.

He chased her with an anger that reached far beyond his twenty years. He chased her with passionate determination fueled by insane loyalty.

People, goats, and everything else that moved scurried out of the way, as they passed. Mothers covered the eyes of small children.

A hundred yards away, Sumera chopped vegetables in her kitchen while Basma's oldest brother, nine years old, squatted next to his mother, fiddling with a homemade toy. Her baby brother sat on the floor sipping goat's milk from a metal cup. Hearing the commotion, Sumera rushed to the window and looked out into the courtyard. Astonished, she covered her mouth with both hands, turned frantically, grabbed the arm of her nine-year-old and pushed him to the front door, yelling:

"Go! Hurry! Get out!"

At the back of the house, little Basma gripped her book. The indecipherable sounds coming from the front made her look towards the closed door with curiosity. In the kitchen, Sumera scooped up the toddler. Milk splashed from his cup as she hurried out behind her other child.

Suddenly there was silence. Basma leaped to her feet and dashed to the window. She saw nothing from where she stood.

Not far from the house, Aisha continued her run of terror— her face contorted, her garment flapping wildly in the breeze. Dust balls swirled up like little twisters as her bare feet pounded the unpaved road. Her chest heaved up and down, her lungs struggling for more air. Her heart pounded more determinedly, as if sensing its own end.

She glanced back at her relentless assailant and, for a moment, it all seemed like a horrible dream. Surely it was. She would wake up when she got to her cousin's house. It was just up ahead. She could see the open door from where Aunt Sumera had just appeared. Behind her, he was closing in. With sheer desperation, Aisha burst into the house, heading to the back. Basma, alarmed, ran across her bedroom to the door. As she reached for the knob, she heard someone else charge into the house... and the nightmare began.

***

Three months from that day, following custom, Basma's cousin, Sirhan, was released from jail. The family gathered to celebrate his return.

On the top floor of the four-story Rahim family home, traditionally crafted from mud and reed and punctuated with colorful stained-glass windows, the atmosphere was dense and low key. About fifty men, all wearing their best white and green turbans, sat on cushions shoulder-to-shoulder along the circumference of the mafraz, a large rectangular room carpeted with goathair rugs. As was the custom, also, they wore western-styled jackets over long white robes, and the ubiquitous jambiyah—a curved dagger with ornate handles signifying male honor and social class—hung vertically from the center of their belts. Down the middle of the room, several dozen platters of rich meat stews, millet and eggplant, prepared by Tayseer Rahim and her two older daughters, were being enjoyed communally as the men tore off pieces of flatbread and scooped up the contents of the platters.

While the men munched heartily and engaged in mundane chatter, Tayseer's son, Sirhan, attempted to bask in the celebration of his homecoming. The occasion was fitting considering the filth and squalor he had endured during those months in a cell.

His father, Khalid, patted him on the shoulder proudly, as they stood in the doorway. After all, Sirhan did what had to be done for the family— for the tribe. To them, honor was greater than love. Without honor, how could there be respect? A dishonored family was not welcomed into respectable people's homes. Their children would run away from your children. No man would ask for any of your daughters' or sisters' hand in marriage. Without honor, fruit vendors would claim to have run out of apricots, dates or pomegranates while you stood there staring at mounds of them. Even the butcher would refuse you the scraps of meat that had fallen to the ground. Therefore, a man's family had to command respect. So today, Khalid displayed the utmost respect for Sirhan.

"You have saved our family a lot of torment, my son," Khalid announced. "Now, people are speaking to us again." He raised his voice so that all could hear. "...and selling to us." A flurry of turbaned heads bobbed up and down, acknowledging the significance of Khalid's words.

Sitting a few feet from where Khalid and Sirhan stood, a man with black bushy eyebrows above unkind eyes, with a thick solid body was biding his time. He was Shafal Abseh, a thirty-eight-year-old jambiyah merchant.

Like Basma's uncle Khalid, family honor was primary to Shafal Abseh. He wore it on his face. The laceration that began at his left temple and ended just above the corner of his lip was the result of a fight he had with two boys who had looked unfavorably at one of his sisters. To Shafal, the scar was his warrior's trophy—an instant reminder to any man to respect his sisters.

Everyone knew that Shafal's passionate defense of his sister was more about his own standing in the community than any real concern for her feelings. Like many of the men in the room, Shafal had never developed any meaningful connection with any of his three sisters. In fact, he rarely spoke to the girls.

Feeling the time was ripe, Shafal got up from the cushion and approached Sirhan with clasped hands and bowed respectfully to him.

"And now there are plenty of work offers for you, too, Sirhan." Shafal added with penetrating eyes, hooking his thumbs on his belt.

Sirhan smiled back and returned the bow and, as Shafal had hoped, Khalid took extra notice of him and the expensive dagger on his belt with a handle made from rare rhinoceros ivory.

The international ban placed on the export of rhino ivory many years before had elevated Shafal's status in the village since all jambiyahs were now crafted from bullhorns, or the bones of animals—including the ones that Shafal sold in his popular shop.

***

Meanwhile, in a darkened corridor that separated the men's side of the house from the women's, little Basma squatted on a mat in the corner nibbling absently on a piece of flatbread. Her ghostly eyes with their blank stare watched the scene before her. While the smaller children ran between the rooms having great fun, her baby brother, bored and restless, began to cry.

Sumera peered out through the partition that hid the doorway of the women's quarters, and gestured for Basma to come in, get her brother and take him outside for a walk.

The moment Basma left through the partition with her brother in tow, her eyes met those of her cousin Sirhan. A shiver ran through her. Saliva caught in her throat. She looked away quickly without acknowledging him.

"How are you, dear cousin?" Sirhan called out. "Why are you acting so mysterious toward me?"

She did not respond. She couldn't. Lifting the whining child in her arms, she hurried down the stairs.

Sirhan's surprised expression soon turned to indignation at his cousin's rebuff, especially in front of the jambiyah merchant. He started after her, but Khalid grabbed his arm and shook his head.

"She is young, she does not understand," Khalid said, assuming this would explain his niece's actions.

"And she just disrespected me," Sirhan replied, unsympathetically.

Upon reaching the bottom step, nearly out of breath, Basma put her wailing, brother down, took hold of his hand and pulled him along the litter-strewn road.

Villagers smiled or nodded to her approvingly as she ambled timidly along. Yet, Basma was only able to return their greetings with her now habitual, vacuous stare born of shock and horror.

***

Two years later, thirteen-year-old Basma had grown more distant, aloof and virtually silent.

When she wasn't being the obedient daughter running errands or cleaning to help Sumera, she kept to herself. She had long given up her love of books and poetry and watching ants carry bread.

Sumera tried everything she could think of to get Basma to at least smile again. She'd ask her, "What's the matter with you? Come on." Nothing worked.

It was times like these Sumera missed Murjid the most. His passing had been a major hardship for them all. He had taken the time to help feed Basma's curious mind, as inadequate as he may have been, and a deep bond had grown between them. After his accident, Basma surprised Sumera by healing from it. Then, Aisha had to... How on earth, would Basma heal from that?

***

"You will grow to love him, Basma. He has ambition," Sumera said, out-of-the-blue one afternoon, while Basma sat cross-legged staring at nothing in particular. Khalid, who was standing next to his sister, Sumera, walked over to her.

"It's the best thing for you, dear niece. Be happy," he said sternly. "This man could have his pick of young girls, but he wants you."

Sumera moved closer to Basma as well and kneeled before her clasping her tiny hand.

"He is an honest man, Basma. If your father were alive, he would agree. He earns good money and someday he hopes to go to America!"

Assuming this last disclosure would cause a response, they both watched anxiously. Basma merely continued her stare into nothingness.

Exactly one month later, it was her wedding day.

For the village, a wedding was always a wonderful celebration that lasted four days. It was a time for music, traditional Bar'a dancing for the men, and the quat parties where women chewed a euphoric stimulant, drank sweet milky tea, and socialized away from the men. In their gender-separated and male-dominated society, this was the women's only outlet.

Basma's family had spent weeks preparing for the occasion despite having little money. Days were spent just in food preparation. The groom presented Sumera with two well-crafted jambiyahs to give to her sons when they each turned fourteen. He also paid her family the customary bride price, which was then spent to adorn Basma in lots of imitation gold and silver jewelry.

On the last evening of the four-day wedding celebration, Shafal Abseh, now forty years old, greeted his thirteen-year-old bride, Basma, for the first time. Around them, everyone nodded approvingly, including her cousin, Sirhan. However, Basma looked more like a doll than a bride in her traditional white wedding dress. In addition, she could barely look at this stranger, her husband, whose half balding head made him appear as a very old man to her.

Throughout the entire day, she had been despondent. So much so, that Sumera asked her several times:

"Basma, when are you going to smile, huh? This is your wedding day. I didn't know your father either when I married him, but I ended up with three beautiful children. I had someone to take care of me for many years. All I had to do was be a woman to him. Today, you are a woman, Basma."

Sumera waited for Basma to show she was listening—any response would have been appreciated. But Basma merely stared back at Sumera with bewilderment. Because, for the past two years, Basma could not understand why Sumera, or anyone else, had not said one word about Aisha. It was as if Aisha had never existed. All references to her had been erased. Even so, Basma remembered Aisha well— especially her laughter and her generous spirit. Now, it was as though everyone had wiped her image from mind. Yet, some things could not be wiped away so easily. Sumera found that out. She had scrubbed and scrubbed the floor, the walls, the door, and Basma's white hijab for days. Basma could still hear the sounds exploding in her ears; she could still see the images that caused her to wake up night after night in a cold sweat calling out to Sumera. And today they expect her to feel gratitude that a man she had never even seen before was now her husband?

Khalid watched Basma closely. Then he decided to offer his own words of wisdom for his young niece, lest she suffer a similar fate as her cousin.

He walked over to her and placed his large, hairy hands on her narrow shoulders, and made his portentous statement.

"Always remember Basma," he said, in that thunderous sounding voice of his, "a family's honor lies between a woman's legs."

Basma stared up at him, not comprehending what he meant, but the menacing glare from his proud piercing eyes was enough to assure that those words—whatever they meant—would stay indelibly in her head.

After, during the long walk on a dusty road to Shafal's house, Basma felt her breath began to slip away. The layers of white fabric were too much in the oppressive heat. Sirhan and Shafal walked up in front of her. Behind, her family and guests followed. When they reached Shafal's house, he turned and stepped ritualistically on her foot, a custom that meant he would rule the house.

She felt abandoned in the house of a stranger, never mind that this was her house as well. Sumera had left her.

For a long while, Basma stood at the grimy window watching her mother walk back to the village with the others, and away from her. When she could no longer see Sumera's form beyond the glass, she turned her attention to the window itself. Its shutters were yellowing with age. She noticed that the wood of the sill was splintered, and a reddish-brown ant was crawling out from one of the crevices. She fixed her eyes on the ant. Shafal fixed his eyes on her. He knew she was trying to avoid the inevitable, but he was a patient man. He had spotted little Basma years before he had approached her uncle, Khalid, and asked to marry the child.

The ant seemed to have been searching for something. Suddenly, it turned and headed back into the crevice. Silently, Basma begged it to stay, but it had already disappeared between the sill and the window.

Her eyes scanned in search of something else to absorb them. She could feel the old man's eyes on her back, but she couldn't bring herself to face him. It wasn't that she was afraid because she was too young to know what it was, she had to fear. She simply did not want to live with this old man. Why did she have to?

When his patience had run its course, Shafal calmly removed his jambiyah, belt, turban and robe, laying each on a cushion against the wall. He went to the window, took hold of the child's arm and led her to his mattress on the floor.

She knew that husbands and wives slept on the same mat as her mother and father had done. That was the extent of her knowledge.

Sumera, against her sister-in-law, Tayseer's, suggestion, decided not to make matters worse by educating her daughter on the duties of a wife. She felt it was best to keep Basma ignorant until the moment came. So, when Shafal pressed his thick body down heavily on little Basma, she panicked—pushing back at him wildly, to break free. But what match can a child be against a man's strength? He yanked up her wedding dress. Basma once again found herself gasping for air. Something seared into her, ripping her flesh. She froze, paralyzed with fear—her body filled with such excruciating pain she thought she would die. What was happening? What had she done wrong?

She cried out for her mother, and then gagged from the scent of lavender water Shafal had used to slick back his hair. She felt something leave her—something vital—then her eyes glazed over and all traces of light in them, dimmed.

The next morning, to Basma's amazement, she was still alive. Outside, she could hear the cackle of chickens and the hesitant hooves of sheep testing the hilly terrain. Then, the stranger ordered her to make him breakfast.

Sumera, her Uncle Khalid, Sirhan and Tayseer arrived and seemed pleased at the white sheet the stranger had hung on nails next to the bedroom door. At the center of the sheet was a reddish stain. And for the rest of the day, villagers paraded in and out to see the white sheet with the red spot.

Four years later, Basma Abseh was a mother of two boys, Abdel and Ahmed, and living in America.

CHAPTER 2

NEW YORK

There were times, during their first decade in America, when Basma sat for hours just listening to the unfamiliar sounds of jets flying overhead. She had never encountered the sounds in her childhood back in the small Yemeni village. Shafal said they were lucky to live so close to an airport. It was good for business. To her, every husband in that part of Queens, New York, drove a cab. She didn't know it was one of the most common jobs for immigrants of Arab and Pakistani descent to land when they arrived in New York City. Even so, the work was hard—grueling, even. Shafal said it was often dangerous. Although, he never explained to her how driving a cab could be dangerous. Unfortunately, he rarely explained anything to her. Consequently, her understanding of the world outside their apartment was ascertained through half sentences, a brief comment or a grunt here and there. That was the extent of his communication with her in general. Without Aisha in her life, she felt friendless, but her twenty-four-year marriage to Shafal Abseh had left Basma psychologically marooned.

It was early evening on what had been a cold, cloudy day in January. At the Ridgefield Nursing Home in Forest Hills, Queens, where Basma worked part-time, the day shift had just ended. Wearing a bone-white woolen hijab that also draped around her shoulders and chest, a black woolen coat over a long-sleeved, loose fitting print ankle-length dress, Basma clocked out and headed for the exit. All around her, other staff workers were coming and going. Few acknowledged her. Outside, on the busy Queens Boulevard, Basma walked alone. Her demeanor was pensive. At thirty-seven years old, the muscles surrounding her eyes and mouth had already started to droop whenever she stayed up late going through her family's clothing checking for loose buttons or to see if anything needed mending.

"Basma!" someone called. She turned to see thirty-year-old Kensasha Lewis, in her black high-heeled boots, walking toward her, smiling broadly. Kensasha, an African American part-time doctoral student of Sociology at Columbia University, earned her living as Director of Patient Services at Ridgefield. Basma was a member of her staff, so when she finally caught up with her, they two comfortably together.

Basma always liked the way Kensasha wore her lambswool beret over an elaborate dread-locked hair design, but hadn't a clue how she got her hair that way—and would never ask.

"I forgot to tell you: I won't be in until late tomorrow afternoon," Kensasha said, in her rapid-fire style. "I have a meeting with the board, but I left you a folder of instructions."

"Okay," Basma replied, softly.

As they approached a bakery, Kensasha stopped abruptly. "I have to get something in here. Come with me." Basma hesitated. "It will only take a few minutes. I promise. Come on." She shrugged and followed Kensasha.

Inside, the bakery was energized with trendy young people— mostly female. To the right of the door, customers were sampling cubes of assorted breads from white saucers on an antique table graced with a fresh bouquet of flowers in a round crystal vase. Opposite the door was a long, white marble counter with large silver platters at both ends filled with assorted miniature quiches and a two-tiered silver stand with muffins of every kind. However, the shelves of crusty loaves of varying shapes and sizes were the Chappelle Bakery's main attraction.

As Kensasha waited her turn, Basma huddled, demurely, near the door, absorbing everything around her.

13

Some of the customers who entered gave Basma a look of surprise as if she were an oddity misplaced. Most looked right through her. Basma wasn't sure which attitude was worse.

Moments later, Kensasha paid and they left.

Back outside in the frosty air, Kensasha tightened her collar and continued to instruct Basma about the following day.

"I want you to watch out for that Martha Cohen. Don't let her dump work on you. Tell her that I left you plenty. Okay?"

Basma managed a tiny smile. Martha Cohen, the office manager at Ridgefield, had targeted Basma to be her flunky. Every chance she got, Martha pushed some menial task off on Basma, knowing full well that Basma was Kensasha Lewis' assistant.

When they got to the crowded bus stop, Basma slowed down. Kensasha felt a twinge of guilt for delaying her.

"You know, there's a new Pakistani restaurant up the street. I'd like to treat you."

"I would like very much. I never had this food. But I must do the shopping for dinner," Basma replied regretfully,

"I know," said Kensasha. "Just thought I'd plant the seed." Basma stared back at her. "Sorry, I mean give it a try."

This time Basma smiled with appreciation.

"Now, get home safe," Kensasha said, waving goodbye. Then she headed off to the subway for her long ride home to Brooklyn.

Basma got off the bus on a bustling main street lined with Middle Eastern, Indian and Pakistani-owned businesses. The tight muscles of her shoulders began to relax as she moved amongst other women dressed like her. Most of them were from Pakistan, but they were Muslims, nonetheless.

She headed straight into her favorite store that had all types of exotic produce, arranged more for convenience than aesthetic appeal. She picked up a wire mesh basket and began to stroll up and down the aisle leisurely, filling it with various vegetables: eggplant, tomatoes, onions, cucumbers and bags of dried fava and garbanzo beans. In the cooler, she found plain yogurt into which she would add bread and hawayil—a spice blend to make shafoot, a dish from South Aden. This was always on the dinner table. The final item was a large, rectangular-shaped flatbread wrapped in plastic. It reminded her of sha'eer, the bread she used to make each morning before she had a job to go to—the same bread her mother made every morning in their small village.

With three shopping bags and a purse weighing her down, Basma continued another four blocks to her three-story apartment building sandwiched between two family houses.

For years, a rich assortment of immigrants had managed to live peacefully in Jackson Heights, and other parts of Queens. Flushing, for example, was home to Chinese, Pakistanis, Hindus and Puerto Ricans.

It was notable given the perpetual tension surrounding international relations in the world. However, that was something Basma preferred to ignore; instead, she concentrated on her own duties and responsibilities—all of which involved her family or her job. Besides, Shafal made it quite clear he didn't want her filling her 'tiny brain' with things that didn't concern women. She found this very puzzling because, to her, everything in the world seemed to concern women either directly or indirectly.

She recalled the time Shafal had stopped by the apartment one slow afternoon, years before, and caught her attempting to read one of Abdel's magazines: Popular Science. She had merely picked up whatever was available, to practice her English. It was a homework assignment. The articles were completely incomprehensible to her, but Shafal didn't want to hear any explanations. He snatched it from her and ordered her not to read anything outside of the English textbooks they had provided at the language school.

That event left a strong impression on her. Not so much because of the rude way he yanked the magazine from her; she was used to that. It was something else. Something she had seen behind his anger and rudeness. It only lasted a moment, but she saw it: fear. She was sure of it. But why? Why would Shafal be afraid of her reading a—? She pushed it from her mind.

The last flight of stairs was always a killer, even without three bags of groceries. Breathing heavily, she sat one of the bags down and reached into her purse for the keys.

As soon as she pushed the door open and hobbled in, Shafal charged towards her with one of his shoes in his hand and shoved it in her face.

"What is this? Huh?" he scowled. "I told you yesterday… the shoe menders! You can't remember your family with that tiny brain, but you can always remember that little job you have, right? Right?"

"I… I thought that was this morning," she replied, timidly. "I did not want to be late…" her voice trailed off for a moment. "I will do it for you tomorrow. I can be a few minutes late tomorrow."

She eased around him, and continued into the kitchen and began carefully unloading her packages with intense concentration lest she dropped something. Shafal followed her in, hovering closely behind. It was a familiar tactic of his. Basma calmly maneuvered around him to the refrigerator and then the sink, avoiding eye contact. Still, Shafal wasn't about to let her off so easily. He moved in closer.

"When you stayed home every day, then you were a wife," he said, with intimidation. "But now… now you think you are …"

Suddenly, Basma turned to face him. "I am sorry, Shafal," she said, sincerely. "I will not forget your shoes tomorrow."

She turned back to the sink and began to wash rice before taking off her coat. Shafal, unable to come up with a clever insult, gave her a disdainful look and left the kitchen.

Later, at dinner, Basma quietly put dishes of shredded goat meat, vegetables seasoned with fenugreek on the table beside a platter of red rice and the shafoot. They blessed the food.

As always, her sons, Abdel and Ahmed, were first to spoon food onto their plates. Shafal, still annoyed about the shoe menders and Basma's job, ripped off a piece of the flatbread with a hint of violence and shoved it in his mouth. They all ate in silence.

The next morning, Basma took Shafal's shoes to be repaired, and then walked several long blocks back in the opposite direction to catch her bus to work. January was never her favorite month. Today the cold breeze was cutting. Icy patches along the pavement made walking treacherous. She squeezed her coat collar tightly together and pressed her large brown handbag close to her body as if the act would protect her from the next burst of frigid air.

When her shift ended, again she proceeded straight for the bus home as she always did. Hers was a life of routine and order. She liked it that way; needed it, even. This time, however, when she passed the upscale Chappelle bakery that Kensasha had practically dragged her into the previous day, Basma encountered the intoxicating aroma of fresh bread, baked apples, vanilla and cinnamon. Following the scent with her eyes, she spotted crusty loaves in the window. Before she knew it, she was inside.

Now, white lilies graced the antique table near the door. Basma glanced at them, then looked around for the bread she had seen in the window. The two salespeople were busy with other customers, so Basma patiently waited her turn. Her mouth, watering at everything she saw, made it more difficult for her to decide which scrumptious loaf she'd buy.

During her wait, she wondered what she was doing in that bakery, alone, in the first place. Was she crazy? She'd better go. She'd miss the bus and then…

One of the servers, a young man with soft clear skin, sparkling greenish-blue eyes, and his light blond hair pulled back in an elastic band, walked over to her.

"What can I get you?" he asked. She pointed to the shelf behind him. He turned. "The tomato and olive?" She nodded. "Good choice."

He reached for the bread, wrapped it carefully in white tissue paper, and placed it in a shiny burgundy and gold bag with white roped handles. She took out cash from her 'card-free' wallet.

So, fancy, she thought, when he handed her the bag.

"That will be $6.25," he said, politely.

At first, Basma assumed she hadn't understood him. "Excuse me?"

"$6.25," he repeated.

Her eyes widened and her mouth opened, but no words came forth. Her face flushed. My God! Six-dollars-and-twenty-five-cents, for a loaf of bread? How can that be? She didn't earn much more than that for a full hour of work.

Nevertheless, she put the three dollars she was holding back into her wallet and fumbled around a moment before pulling out a ten-dollar bill and reluctantly handing it to the young man. He gave her the change. She turned and walked unsteadily to the door, impulsively reaching in the bag to get a feel of this extravagant item, expecting its hard crust to give way to a soft fluffy interior. Instead, her hands encountered a dense heavy mound. Frowning, she turned back abruptly and marched right up to the young man who was already serving someone else. And then, totally out of character, Basma called out to him ignoring the man he was serving.

"Please, Mister."

The young server, immediately disengaged from his other customer, politely, and began to walk toward Basma.

His male customer sucked his teeth. "Hey, can't somebody else help her?"

The young server paused. "This will only take a moment," he replied. "But if you want to leave then be my guest."

Taken aback, the now irate male customer looked around for someone to complain to, as the young server strolled calmly up to Basma.

"Is there a problem?"

"The bread is hard," she announced adamantly. The other customers turned to look at her.

"Is it? Oh, I'm sorry about that." He sounded sincere. "Let me have it back."

She handed the bag to him and bowed her head feeling somewhat embarrassed at all the attention she was now receiving. The young man returned with a fresh loaf and squeezed it in front of her. Reaching into a basket labeled cranberry walnut, he pulled out a log shaped loaf, and cut it in half.

He quickly wrapped both in fresh white tissue paper, handed the bag back to Basma apologizing once again. She avoided those greenish-blue eyes, but gave him an equally warm thank you and left.

Now her gait was more determined and assured. With the gold and burgundy bag dangling from her wrist, she continued the two blocks to the bus stop feeling a natural shelter from the cold. An unusual lightness overtook her and the formerly drab, mundane world she was familiar with had suddenly, unexpectedly, transformed itself into an array of sumptuous possibilities.

Later that evening, Basma was busy preparing dinner when Shafal arrived home in an irritable mood. He went straight into the kitchen and began to examine the pots on the stove.

"You just started the meal?" he asked, annoyed.

"No, I just added some more vegetables. They will cook quickly."

Shafal shook his head, got a glass and walked over to the sink. He spotted the burgundy and gold bag lying on the counter. He sat the glass down and began to examine the bag.

"And what is this?"

Basma turned around. She looked worried. Hesitant.

"Some... ah, American bread. From a bakery near my work."

Shafal scrutinized her and the bag. "They use such a bag just for bread? Why do you buy this?"

Basma thought for a moment. "Because I... it looked... very good... and the smell... I, I thought you would like it."

"I see... and how much did it cost?"

"I do not remember exactly," she replied, pretending to be absorbed with stirring the vegetables. "But it wasn't much more than our bread."

Shafal pulled out the bread. He saw the extra half loaf that the server had added.

"Why is one loaf only a half? Did you eat the other half already?" Basma stared at it, her face blank, and then she remembered.

"Oh no, the boy gave me that for free."

This sounded suspicious to Shafal. "For, free? Why?"

"I don't know. They let people taste the bread there for free."

Shafal glared at her for a moment. With no choice but to accept her explanation, he grunted and left the kitchen.

At dinner, after everyone had filled their plate, Basma nervously cut a few slices of the crusty olive and tomato bread and served one to Shafal. With indifference, he bit off a piece and chewed. His eyes widened and he nodded his head approvingly, though without any hint of warmth.

Abdel, their oldest son, held the cranberry and walnut bread to his nose, smiled, then pulled off a piece and ate it.

"This is good. It's different," Shafal said, not looking at her. "Get more next week." Her eyes lit up. Finally, Shafal felt she had done something right for the family.

Consequently, the following week, when Basma and Kensasha left work together and approached the Chappell Bakery, Basma stopped and said, "I need to buy bread here."

Kensasha gave her a surprised look then accompanied her inside.

As usual, the shop was busy. Kensasha headed straight for the muffin tray and stood contemplating which one to buy. Basma's eyes scanned the bread shelves in search of the olive and tomato bread. This time there were several salespeople helping the customers, but she looked for the young man who had served her previously.

He was leaning against the wall off to the side having a flirtatious exchange with a young salesgirl. The girl, about twenty-two, was doing everything she could to enchant him. She batted her eyelashes, repeatedly finger-combed her hair away from her face, and then tilted her head so the hair would fall over her eye again. She nervously vacillated between seductress and ingénue. The young man, on the other hand, pretended not to notice what she was up to. Clearly, she was the aggressor yet the young man encouraged her all the way. He was the tease.

Kensasha decided on the golden blueberry and pointed at it. When the counterman reached to get it, Kensasha turned in time to see Basma staring at the young man and the girl. At that moment, the young man slapped the girl on her bottom, playfully. She feigned shock, while trying to fight off the giggles. Basma felt her face grow red hot having witnessed this. She lowered her eyes.

As if some invisible hand tapped him on the shoulder, the young man looked over and saw Basma waiting. He immediately whispered something into the girl's ear and strode confidently over to Basma.

Still in a playful mood, he took a tiny pastry off the silver tray and gallantly presented it to Basma.

"Try this." Basma was startled by the young man's informality. She hesitated.

"Go on, tell me if you like it," he coaxed, seductively.

She glanced at the pastry. The center was filled with lemon custard and topped with red raspberries and powdered sugar. It looked much too pretty to eat. She glanced over at Kensasha who had been watching the whole time.

The young man used the moment to study Basma's fine, pleasant face with its thick un-tweezed eyebrows, long black eyelashes, strong angular nose and generous lips. Her skin was a deep olive with touches of cream. But in his expression was subtle distaste mixed with intrigue at the tightly pulled headscarf that framed her face, and curiosity at what she was hiding underneath.

Kensasha nodded for Basma to go ahead.

She looked back at the pastry as if it possessed a power far beyond the superficial one of taste. Then, without looking at the man, she took the pastry from his hand, brought it to her mouth and slowly let her teeth penetrate the firm cake-like outer layer. The rich creamy custard within oozed out onto her tongue. She closed her eyes to fully enter the experience. The young man watched as if sharing every sensation along with her.

Another bite and fresh raspberries added moisture and texture. Her mouth was alive with sensation. She could not recall food ever having such an effect on her. When she had swallowed the last bit, she opened her eyes and nodded her approval.

"I knew you'd like it," the young man commented, staring directly into her eyes.

She blushed and quickly glanced down at her hands that were now clasped together.

He took another mini custard tart from the plate then went to get the olive and tomato bread without even confirming with Basma if that was what she wanted.

This time, Kensasha walked over to the door to wait. Basma handed him the money for the bread and the extra pastry. He shook his head and returned some of the money.

"The pastries were on the house," he said.

Basma squinted, confused, so the young man waved it away. She gave him her usual gracious nod, followed this time with a hint of a smile, and she and Kensasha left.

21

Outside, Kensasha stared at Basma curiously. Basma, immediately assuming it was because Kensasha had not received free pastry, reached into her bag for the other one.

"Here, take this," she offered with sincerity.

"No, no. That's okay. I bought one of my favorite muffins." Basma slipped the pastry back into her bag, and they took a few more steps. "Basma, I know it's been difficult for you at Ridgefield," Kensasha continued. "People have their prejudices. But I feel fortunate to have such a conscientious worker like you in my department." Basma stared back at her. "Sorry. You speak English so well, I often forget that—" She tried once more to pay Basma a compliment. "You are such a fine worker and a good person. I am very happy Imani Sadawi told me about you."

Basma was quickly overcome with emotion, her eyes filled with tears. She simply didn't know how to respond to a rarely received compliment. Kensasha saw this as an unusual reaction. She grabbed hold of Basma's hand. "Look, I don't know what's going on in your life. I do know that there's a serious war right now in your homeland. If you have family over there, I hope they are safe, and if you ever need someone to talk to… I'll be happy to listen. That's what I do. Okay? So, if there's anything you need to tell me or express…" Again, Basma stared back vacantly.

She had overheard Shafal debating with his friend Tariq Tali, who had a different view of the situation in Yemen. She knew to stay out of such matters in order to keep the peace.

Kensasha sighed and placed her hand gently on Basma's shoulder. "Enjoy your evening, Basma."

Basma smiled modestly and continued to the bus stop. And, for a long moment, Kensasha watched her before going down into the subway.

Evergreen boxwood shrubs, perennial plants and rose bushes lined the walkway leading to Basma's apartment building. New light fixtures in the hallway, freshly painted doors and clean, carpeted stairs made the interior equally inviting. Aside from her landlord's primary residence directly across the street, their apartment complex was the most desired on the block.

Living on the top floor provided a sense of privacy for her, and having all three of the bedroom windows at the back of the building lessened the noise from the street.

In the master bedroom, Basma and Shafal's twin beds were placed a distance from each other with Basma's closest to the door, just the way she liked. All in all, it was a decent set up, except in the winter when the landlord, hating the cold, kept the thermostat around seventy-eight degrees.

That night their bedroom was particularly warm and sticky. Shafal tossed and turned, trying to make himself comfortable. When he could not, he got up and walked over to Basma, who was nearly asleep. He tapped her on the shoulder. Eyes groggy, she turned to look up at him. Although he merely stood there saying nothing, his silhouette carved by a shaft of moonlight, the message was clear. She rolled onto her back and Shafal lifted the blanket to lie down beside her. She pulled her long-sleeved thick cotton nightgown up to her knees and turned her head away from him. In a clumsy manner, he climbed on top of her and pushed the gown higher. He fumbled a moment with the opening in his pajama bottoms before thrusting himself inside her. Her back arched violently from the irritation, and then she collapsed like the dead.

As Shafal pushed and pumped harder, she stared at the faded green wall, the cracks in the plaster. Then her eyes focused on a distant memory. Often it was the countryside back home with its burnt sienna mountains where sheep grazed lazily and the scent of coffee blossoms filled the air, or the wheat-colored fields where children could be heard giggling while ants carried breadcrumbs along the stump of a tree.

Spent, Shafal rolled off her and shuffled back to his own bed. In all their years of marriage, never had he tried to give her pleasure—not once. It simply never crossed his mind. She lay there a while, listening to his breath shifting patterns, growing heavier and deeper. Then she got up wearily and headed to the bathroom to wash.

***

The weeks that followed unfolded as usual: Basma helped the patients with their puzzles and games in the recreation hall, filed folders for Kensasha, did the laundry on Sundays while Shafal read the newspaper and Abdel and Ahmed either talked on the phone or surfed the Web.

Once a week, the Abseh family attended the local mosque. After, the women would congregate outside to greet each other and exchange local gossip. Basma liked being amongst the women, but rarely did she say much more than the polite "hello" and "how is your family?" She wasn't accustomed to spending time with anyone just to converse, because there was always something she needed to take care of for her family. It was for that reason or excuse that Basma had no close female friends to confide in. Of course, there was her landlady, Imani Sadawi, who had been a godsend for Basma, especially in the early years when they had first arrived in America, and who had gotten her the job working for Kensasha Lewis. But Mrs. Sadawi was more like a mother figure than a friend.

Then, there was her weekly bread run, with the same young man always handing her a cookie or a pastry with a bright smile. She would not have admitted it to herself, but this was the high point of her week. For her, the bakery and the young man symbolized a touch of the exotic in an otherwise bland existence.

Continuing her weekly routine, Basma stopped by the bakery one late afternoon on her way to the bus stop. This time, however, a woman came over to serve her. Basma pointed to the tomato and olive bread, and the woman got the bread and wrapped it. As Basma handed the woman the money, she caught sight of the young man who usually served her. He was standing in a doorway near the back talking to an older man. It seemed like a confrontation, with the older man doing the talking while the young man stared at him with open contempt. When the older man had finished the heated discussion, and returned to the kitchen, the young man noticed Basma watching him. And for a moment, it was as if he didn't recognize her. His expression was ambiguous, frosty and distant. He stared at her. She couldn't look away. Slowly, he nodded and forced a polite, if less friendly, smile. Basma responded with her customary nod. However, this time, she was aware that she had desired his gaze. Flustered, she took the bread self-consciously from the saleswoman and hurried out.

A week later, Shafal and the boys sat talking at the table while waiting for their dinner. Basma brought out the food then sat down as they began to serve themselves. But Shafal paused when he saw a plate with unleavened Middle Eastern bread and glanced up at Basma frowning.

"It is Tuesday, where is the American bread?"

"Yeah, Ma?" Ahmed added with disappointment. All three men stared at her, waiting.

Basma remembered the feeling she had when she was just about to enter the bakery earlier that day. She should not be there. That was what she felt. Now, whether that feeling was from within her or projected toward her from the staff and customers inside the shop was something Basma would have never contemplated. Nor would she have contemplated whether her reluctance to enter had anything to do with her eagerness to see the young man and his cool reaction toward her the week before.

"It is costing so much to keep buying it every week," she finally said, awkwardly. Her reason surprised Shafal.

"Didn't you say it was only a little more than this bread?"

"Yes, but..." she lowered her eyes.

"You are working, so you can afford to spend a few more pennies once a week," he replied, with a sardonic smile.

What excuse could she possibly give now to get out of it? She had no other choice but to return to that bakery.

The wintry sky was deeply overcast the next afternoon when Basma left work. She paused to take in a deep breath as she reached the block with the bakery. Outside the door, she hesitated a moment, checking her hijab, and she reached into her handbag to take out her wallet, holding it in her hand so she could pay quickly.

Feeling naked and obvious, she walked in, headed straight to a saleswoman and pointed to the bread she wanted. While the saleswoman wrapped the bread, Basma struggled to keep her attention focused on retrieving money from her wallet. Glancing neither to the left nor the right, she paid and left.

There was a larger crowd than usual waiting at the bus stop. Traffic had backed up for some reason and she couldn't see a bus in sight. The sky was growing darker by the minute. A few drops of rain

25

wet her wrist. She quickly repositioned the bread bag closer to her body with the handbag on the outside. A swift wind passed, sending a chill straight to her bones. Now, every passenger faced the same direction hoping to detect some outline of a bus. Teeth chattering, Basma checked her watch. The bus was now twenty minutes late. Now, she was behind schedule for dinner.

Just then, a group of people paraded past the crowd already waiting at the stop. Some moved aside to allow the throng to get by. As a young couple weaved through the crowd of waiting riders, the boy said, "Hey everybody, the bus is not coming. There's a bad collision about half a mile back. They're rerouting all the buses until they clear the streets."

"Yeah," said the girl, "better to take the subway if you can."

"Or start walking," the boy added.

"Oh, damn!" exclaimed a passenger. Others cursed under their breath.

There was a moment of confusion while people contemplated alternate means of travel. Some did head to the subway station three long blocks away. Some looked around for livery vans, hoping to flag one down. Then a few more pellets of rain hit the pavement and, in no time, the crowd of passengers had dispersed in all directions, leaving Basma alone, still straining her neck, in the hope she'd catch sight of a bus.

Unlike the other riders, she couldn't take any of the trains on Queens Boulevard to get home. And she wasn't up to walking the ten miles or more in the freezing rain. Even if she could find a public phone and call Shafal on his cell, how long would it take him to get to Queens through stalled traffic?

She checked her watch again and looked up at the sky. Now it had turned charcoal gray.

Traffic crept along. Tempers became heated. Car horns blared in a cacophonous symphony. She heard a loud thump. A cab had just gotten rear-ended on the opposite side of the boulevard. The driver leaped out, forgetting his passenger, and headed straight for the car behind him, yelling at the top of his voice, and shaking his fists. The other driver was poised for an explosive confrontation.

Lightening streaked its way across a sky growing darker by the minute, followed by a grumbling roll of thunder. The two drivers clashed, hurling insults at each other.

As Basma stared at them, dumbfounded, a brand-new red car pulled up in front of her. The driver honked his horn. Basma ignored it. She kept her eyes fixed on the two men who were nearly at blows. Again, the driver honked.

"Would you like a ride home? It looks pretty bad out there."

She looked behind her, expecting to see the person that the driver was talking to. But she was alone.

"Come on, get in. I'll take you home." The familiarity in his voice caught her attention. She leaned forward to see who it was. The young man from the bakery grinned at her. Startled, she stepped back.

It started drizzling.

"It's going to come down hard," he warned.

She looked down the block for the bus that would never come. Once again, she peered into the car. The young man was still smiling. It was a sweet, kind smile. One might even say… trustworthy. Even so, she couldn't possibly get into a strange man's car—Muslim woman, or not. She wasn't suicidal. Besides, what if someone saw her? That would be worse.

Suddenly, there was a blinding flash of lightening.

"I'll take you straight to your door," he tempted. She chewed her lip a moment and glanced at the traffic stalled back several blocks.

The next great boom of thunder settled it for her. She got in.

CHAPTER 3

Fastening her seat belt, Basma leaned back. It was toasty inside. The first thing she noticed was the plush black leather on the seats. As soon as the car began to move, heavier raindrops splattered against the windshield, obscuring her vision, but the activated wipers, moving like an inverted pendulum, created a half-moon-shaped opening. She let out a loud sigh of relief. Through the cleared front passenger window, she watched people running for cover from the ensuing downpour.

"Th—thank you. I live in Jackson Heights. You can make a right turn when we reach the place for the gas. You know where it is?" He nodded. "You can let me out near the big factory for the car tires. I will show you," she added eagerly.

"I said I'll drive you straight to your door. It's not a problem."

Basma took her eyes away from the street scene and focused on her hijab, smoothing down its folds.

"For a Muslim woman, it is a big problem." Feeling a little uneasy now, she began to wring her hands. It was bad enough that he wasn't a relative. "There was this accident and the buses had to go another way," she informed him and shifted her focus. "I hope the people are okay.

"Yeah, me too," he said, and glanced over at her.

She still hadn't looked his way since getting into the vehicle, and now she returned her attention to the pedestrians along the main thoroughfare.

Finally, she said, "I didn't know what to do and I have to make dinner for my family," She turned to steal a glance at him. His expression had become serious.

"This is getting far from your work. I am sorry."

"No, it's fine. I'm not going back there today," he remarked, with a hint of distaste. Basma looked over at him with great concern. As if he knew what she was thinking, he said: "I'm not going to lose my job over this. Getting fired is the last thing I have to worry about." It was sarcastic.

Earlier that day he had another run-in with Alfred Chappelle, the owner, and now it flashed across his mind. Absorbed in his own thoughts, he forgot Basma was there.

From the corners of her eyes she watched his hands on the steering wheel. His nails were well manicured, unlike her own. His sandy blond hair, now free of the elastic band, grazed the top of his shoulders. It was a designer cut. His bomber-style brown leather jacket lined with shearling, over the white tee shirt and white Jeans, looked as though it came from a store where the price tags equaled the average person's weekly pay. It certainly wasn't bought with the wages of a bakery sales cashier.

When his attention returned to the moment, he became aware of her eyes on him. He smiled to himself and took a few quick glances her way. She focused her eyes straight ahead while twisting the roped handle of the bread bag around her fingers. It caught his attention.

"So, you really like that bread, huh?" She nodded as she looked down at the glossy burgundy bag and her fingers entangled in the braided white handle.

"My husband… he enjoys very much this bread. And my boys like it too."

"That's a long way to go to buy bread," he replied, curiously.

"Oh, no, I work on Dillard Street. There is a nursing home there."

"I see." He looked over at her again. "So, tell me… where did you learn to speak English so well?"

Basma perked up. "You know, for seven years, I don't speak it. Then Mrs. Sadawi tells my husband that I must learn it. Her husband owns the building where we live. She took me to a place where many people from different places come to learn English. It was so hard for me because I didn't finish school and…"

The car slowed down. The man rose up as if to see what was going on.

Basma settled back. She knew Shafal would be annoyed that dinner wasn't on time, but at least she was on her way home, finally.

She needed more rice, yogurt and fresh mint for tea, but the store was too far to walk back from in this downpour. Well, she thought, if I use that leftover rice and just added it to the sautéing meat along with a lot of onions, the canned lentils and coriander leaves. Of course, Shafal won't like the canned lentil beans. They don't taste nearly as good as the dried. Mrs. Sadawi often uses canned beans and spices them so well that—

"It doesn't look good up ahead," said the bakery guy, interrupting her thoughts. "I know a short cut."

He turned left at the next traffic light off the main road and opposite to where Basma lived. The car sped further and further away from the populated areas. It all happened too fast for her to utter a word. Then, on a deserted stretch of a rundown industrial street, he stopped the car.

Basma surveyed the area quickly and frowned. She was puzzled. Was he lost? The man turned off the ignition and leaned back, tapping the steering wheel without looking at her.

Rain pounded on the roof.

Just as she was about to speak up, he turned toward her, allowing his eyes to crawl up and down her body. She, in turn, continued facing forward, all the while watching him out of the corner of her eye. Then he slid closer to her. She clutched hold of her bag, avoiding his eyes. Her mouth watered. She gulped repeatedly. Not knowing what to say or do at this point, she remained silent, her body stiffening, while her eyes blinked rapidly. Think! Think!

"So… how do you like those extra treats I give you?" he asked in a soft silky voice, leaning so close, she could hear him breathing. "Huh?" He put his left hand to the right side of her face and firmly

30

turned it his way. With eyelids lowered seductively, he pressed for an answer. "You like them?" She gave him a painful nod and shrunk back. His thumb glided slightly across her bottom lip.

"P-please take me home. My h-husband will... I have to make his... his dinner. The time is... there is so much to..."

The young man put his finger to his own lips to silence her. But she persisted, as her throat became dry.

"You do not understand. This... my husband will... Why are you...?"

"Hush..." He had said it softly yet the undertones sounded deadly. He yanked her hijab back to reveal one thick braid of hair entwined in an orange elastic fabric. "You have beautiful hair, why do you hide it?"

"It is my religion. I am not hiding it," she responded, timorously, as she tried to pull the fabric back up over her head. "I only cover it." Unconcerned with her reason, he placed his hand on her thigh and squeezed it. Basma gasped, loudly.

He leaned in closer and slowly ran the back of his fingers over her breast. She shrunk back again as far as she possibly could. But he misread her paralyzing terror as an approval. His fingers slipped in between the buttons of her coat attempting to reach skin. Basma closed her eyes. Her breathing stopped. Her trembling hands now clutched the handle of the bread bag so tightly the fingers swelled. A tear escaped down her cheek. He didn't notice. But the moment his hand slid out and boldly reached down between her legs, she heard a great booming voice in her head: Remember, Basma, family honor lies between a woman's legs. Her body jerked as if struck by a lightning bolt.

"No!" she yelled with such force it startled them both.

He pulled his hand away. They sat staring back at each other.

"And what was that?" he asked, bemused.

She had never, ever reacted so powerfully before, except when Shafal...

"I am married!" she reminded him.

"So, what? I've been with married women before."

Tears welled up in her eyes. She wiped them away. "You do not understand."

31

"What's there to understand?" He leaned back in his seat. "Look, I know you like me. And you're not exactly thrilled about being married, are you?" he teased. "You just want to do your wifely duty and make the man's dinner. Am I right?"

She looked at him, helplessly.

"Oh, fuck it," he mumbled to himself and started the ignition.

Fifteen minutes later, he brought the car to a halt at the side of a tire factory a few blocks from Basma's apartment building just like she had asked. The street was usually empty at this time of day and the storm guaranteed it.

Still shaking with fear and not caring about her disheveled appearance, Basma immediately reached for the handle of the door. The man grabbed her arm and squeezed so tightly, she winced.

"Hey, hey... not so fast." He leaned closer. "Aren't you going to say goodbye?" He released her arm. Basma stared at the sheets of water cascading down the windshield.

The man took out a red pack of Dunhill cigarettes from the glove compartment, and lit one up.

"This game you're playing... hard to get. I like it," he said, nodding his head. "It's different. Usually, I'm the one being seduced." He said this matter-of-factly, without boast. He took a long drag of the cigarette. "I want to see you again," he announced, casually, exhaling a puff of smoke into the air. "And I don't mean at the bakery." She was at a loss for words.

"Meet me around the corner from the bus stop. Say... next Thursday? Between two and two fifteen." It was an order.

Basma shook her head forcefully, but her voice quivered when she finally spoke.

"No! I cannot do that."

The bakery guy remained silent for a moment. His pleasant expression grew darker, his voice sinister.

"Look, I said I want to see you again. Now... uh... what do I have to do to make that happen, huh?" He waited. She didn't respond. He leaned over until his mouth was right at her ear. She felt his hot breath on her skin. "Do I have to threaten you? Is that what you want? Huh? You want me to say, 'I'll hurt you.' Would you like that?" He began to nudge her, teasing her. "I bet you'd like that." He grinned.

Repulsed, she turned away from him.

"Or I could find a way to let your husband know about us." Terrified, Basma jerked back to face him.

"You do not know my husband. You don't even know my name. You can't…"

"I know you work at that nursing home. The rest is easy to find out…. trust me," he smirked, taking a long drag on the cigarette. When he looked over at her, she was ghostly pale.

"I will tell the police," she threatened, bravely, but missed the moment of alarm on his face.

"I doubt that," he replied, firmly, "… because then… everybody would know that you and I—"

She buried her face in her hands, and then tried again. This time she pleaded for sympathy.

"You cannot talk to my husband… he will have me killed."

Man, what an absurd exaggeration. Did she think he was that gullible? But he used it for leverage. "Then be there," he said, forcefully. "It's that simple."

He allowed her to get out of the car. In the pouring rain, she hurried down the street to her apartment building, all the while adjusting her clothes and shoving strands of hair back beneath her hijab, which was already soaked. She glanced around to see if anyone was watching. Thank God for the rain.

As it turned out, there was enough rice. She hastily opened two cans of lentils, drained away the water and dumped the beans into a pan of sautéing lamb and tomatoes. Her every move was dictated by the clock. One minute to check the rice and stir the vegetables. Two minutes to throw away the empty cans, taste and check the meat.

Hmm… a little more coriander and a pinch of salt. Stay focused.

The doorbell rang. She nearly leaped out of her skin. If she didn't move… if she remained silent maybe-

"Basma! Are you there?" It was Imani Sadawi. Walking hesitantly to the door, she adjusted her clothes unnecessarily, then paused a second before opening it. A tall, regal, Egyptian woman of fifty-three stared down at her with great concern.

"Basma, are you, all right? I have been calling you all afternoon."

"There was an accident," Basma replied in a monotone. Mrs. Sadawi walked in passed her and looked into the kitchen noticing pots simmering on the stove.

"Yes, I heard about it on the TV. I was very worried about you. How did you get home?"

Basma turned away from her and hurried back into the kitchen, picked up a wooden spoon lying on the counter and began stirring the meat and lentils.

"Basma? How did you get home? Surely you didn't walk all this way in that rain?" With arms folded, she walked over to Basma, closing the distance between them and waited for a response.

Basma rubbed her middle finger across the back of the spoon to catch some of the pan juice, then she put her finger into her mouth and pulled it out quickly.

"Basma!"

"It took a very long time." Though the words were simple enough, they came out with enormous effort each accompanied by a string of images. She felt her face heat up and kept her head lowered to avoid any eye contact. Imani had seen Basma act this way before and knew that it was useless trying to get anything more out of her.

"Well, at least you are home safe. Do you need me to help with the dinner?"

"No."

"Are you sure? I know how Shafal gets when—"

"Everything is fine," Basma said, finally looking up at her emphatically. But Imani only saw fear in her eyes. Something she had also seen many times before. "Okay. I just…"

"I have very little time," Basma added with haste.

"Yes. Yes, I know. All right then." Imani turned to leave. "Now remember the women's prayer group is meeting tomorrow. I will come to pick you up around 8 o'clock."

When the door had closed behind Mrs. Sadawi, Basma let out a sigh of relief. She knew Imani Sadawi would be the hardest person to fool. Shafal was easy simply because he rarely paid close enough attention to her. All that was necessary was having his dinner prepared when he got home, his clothes laundered, and having the house clean. She didn't have to worry about how she may come across in conversation because he rarely spoke to her. Now the boys may pose a problem but, surely, if she could deflect Mrs. Sadawi, she could avert them, too.

Feeling a little more confident, she checked the rice and glanced at the clock. Shafal would probably be the first to arrive. She'll explain how the accident and the weather slowed her down and…

Both Abdel and Ahmed were already seated at the table when Shafal did arrive home. Basma was bringing plates of food to the table when he entered. He headed straight to the bathroom without a word. After washing up, he came back and sat down heavily.

"This had to be the worst day of my life," he said with irritation, "I spent most of the time in traffic jams trying to get to the airport. And you know… the customers always blame me for not being able to fly the cab."

Abdel, the oldest, smiled and looked across at Ahmed who was focused on the steaming bowl of lamb stew Basma had just placed in the center of the table.

"Are those lentils, Ma?" Ahmed asked reaching for the serving spoon. She didn't respond.

There was a strange burning sensation arising in her chest. She sat down demurely. For a few minutes, hands moved toward and around each other in sort of a dance as each of the men scooped food from the various bowls. Basma watched, but did not attempt to join in.

Shafal picked up his fork. "At least now I am home and I can eat decent food." He was more cheerful. Then he looked around the table and frowned. "Where is the bread?" He looked over at Basma angrily. "I told you to buy that bread. Where is it?"

Basma stared at the table surprised that it was not there. Until that moment, she had completely forgotten about it. Oh God, she left the bread in the bakery man's car. She glanced up at Shafal and back down at the table so quickly, he missed the look of terror on her face. But Abdel caught it.

"I… I must have left it in the bus," she replied, her voice quivering. "There was… the… the accident and so much confusion. People…" her voice trailed off. "You know… the weather and—"

"So, tonight we eat without bread?"

Abdel and Ahmed watched Shafal as he glared at their mother. They readied themselves for the usual outburst.

Surprising everyone, Shafal merely threw up his arms in defeat. He leaned back in his chair, stared off for a moment, grumbled something under his breath, and then he began to eat. The boys relaxed.

"Ma, can I have a Coca-Cola?" Abdel asked shoving the lamb concoction into his mouth heartily.

With efficiency, Basma went into the kitchen and returned with a jar of pickled condiments, handed it to Abdel and sat back down. The three men sat staring first at the jar then at Basma as if waiting for a punch line. But Basma hadn't realized what she had done. Shafal brought it to her attention.

"Are you *that* stupid? This is not Coca-Cola." He pointed to the jar.

She felt her body shrink in size. She got up hastily hitting against the table causing a few teaspoons of tea to spill from their cups. She became tearful. "I'm sorry. I'm sorry. I'm sorry," she repeated, burying her face in her hands.

"It's all right, Ma." Ahmed got up and put his arm around her shoulder. "You didn't *kill* anyone."

Abdel went to get his own soda and when he sat back down, he glanced over at his father in time to see how disgusted he was with Basma.

For the remainder of the evening, Basma sat on the edge of her bed staring into nothingness.

She had managed to clear away the dishes and put everything in its place. She hadn't eaten a single mouthful of food and she still wasn't at all hungry. The burning in her chest and the churning in her stomach made sure of that. Had they noticed anything different about her, she wondered. That boy... he had put his hand on her breast. How could he do that? He had no right. He was not her husband! He was a stranger. On the other hand, neither did Shafal have the right—when he married her. Wasn't he a stranger to her, as well?

When she heard Shafal's footsteps just outside the door, she leaped to her feet and hurried past him to the bathroom, closed the door and locked it.

Inside, she stood still for a moment, and then turned on the faucet in the tub. Slowly, she began to disrobe.

That night was fitful, she couldn't fall asleep. Her head was flooded with memories of every single word and gesture. She could still feel the man's hand on her. The burning sensation in her chest had made her nauseous.

Exhausted, the next morning she phoned Ridgefield Nursing Facility explaining impassively that she wasn't feeling well and wouldn't be in. She also phoned Mrs. Sadawi to inform her that she was too sick to attend the women's prayer meeting. The rest of her day was divided between sweeping, dusting and sitting on the couch waiting for some unknown thing to happen.

Basma was masterful at shutting down, blocking out sensations. It was a skill cultivated over the twenty-six years that had passed since her childhood nightmare. A skill that rendered her as conscious in her day-to-day life, as a somnambulist in a dream. Even the birth of her two beloved sons hadn't been enough to bring back her old self. The duties and obligations of domestic life were carried out efficiently, yet mindlessly, as any routine or ritual. But now, this... this awful experience with that boy had jarred something inside her, something subtle and foreboding.

It was all that meddling Mrs. Sadawi's fault. She was the one who said working would make her life richer. She and her husband nagged and nagged Shafal until he finally gave in to it, but he had never forgiven either of them—nor Basma for that matter. Now, she could see that Shafal had been right all along. Women belonged in the home, where they can be safe. There were too many terrible people out there in the world. Life was much easier when she had been afraid. The walls protected her. Washing baby clothes and folding towels absorbed her. What more did she need... money? The few extra dollars she earned working certainly weren't worth losing her life over.

But what should she have done? Stood there waiting, getting drenched in the rain? Should she have attempted to walk the ten miles home? She could have returned to the nursing home, called Shafal, and then waited there until he made his way from Manhattan to the airport, with a passenger, through stalled traffic, dropped them off, and then drive over to get her—again, through stalled traffic. It would have taken hours. Even so, Shafal would have delivered her home safely—with *her honor intact.*

***

The advantage of being home all day was having all the dishes prepared and the table set in record time. She took some rice then waited until the men had served themselves before she poured a ladleful of stew over her rice. She lifted her fork and stared at the food.

"What's the matter with you? You didn't eat last night and now again you don't eat?" said Shafal.

She pushed some beef cubes around her plate. "I'm just very tired."

"If you are so tired you can't eat, then you need to stop going to that job."

She knew Shafal was preparing to argue the point. She had no defense this time. She really shouldn't go back there. What could that boy do anyway? He couldn't find her. Could he? Could he? She really liked her job.

"The work there is not hard, Shafal. The ladies are really no trouble for me. And, you know Miss Lewis is very kind to me."

"But you are not a strong woman, Basma," Shafal insisted. "That is why you are all the time tired. You belong in the house." He was emphatic—not because he was genuinely concerned about her health, but because he wanted to affirm his own convictions: that a woman's place should be at home and not extended beyond the family.

She yielded. "Maybe I will not go back." Shafal's face brightened.

This time, Ahmed, the more sensitive son, was the one who glared back at her with suspicion. She had given in too easily. "You love going to work, Ma. Why would you want to sit in the house all day like you used to?"

He had a point. Even Shafal realized that. They stared at her, puzzled.

Continuing to push food around on her plate, she tried to come up with a reasonable justification, other than the truth, for her sudden change of heart, but nothing came to mind.

38

***

Every day Shafal drove to the cab garage, a large two-story brown brick structure in Long Island City, where the drivers came to pick up and drop off their cabs. Cabs always lined the streets. Most of the men were Pakistani, with quite a few Sikhs, Hindus and a handful of Russians. The garage was a place where cabdrivers had the opportunity to socialize. Several groups of three and four casually congregated just to the side of the entrance as Shafal pulled up. He got out of his cab and headed into the noisy building.

The head manager was inside the office talking on the phone. About six other drivers lingered around the doorway watching the news on an old 19" TV that was mounted on the wall.

Walking past the office on his way to the restroom, Shafal peered up at the TV. On the screen was a woman reporter. Whatever she was saying upset the Pakistani men who were watching because they all began to talk and wave their fists almost in unison.

When Shafal exited the restroom minutes later and walked back past the office, he saw the woman reporter was still on the screen. Curious about the commotion she was causing, he stopped to listen. Just then, the image of the woman reporter dissolved to video footage of the same woman reporter accompanied by another woman: an American writer. It had been videotaped a month earlier. They were sitting in the small, cluttered office of an attractive Indian woman in her mid-sixties. Her name was Dr. Neelam Sethi. She was sitting be-hind a desk and the two women sat opposite, interviewing her.

"So, the purpose of my trip to America," Dr. Sethi said, "is to expose the extent of this vile practice called 'Honor Killings': young women are being murdered by their own families. It is horrible! And I hope to set up a meeting at the United Nations. I will bring women who have..."

Shafal didn't want to hear any more. Like the rest of the men, he, too, was upset. He walked back out to his cab.

LONDON

Dr. Neelam Sethi was an OB/GYN who had received her medical training in England. Over the years, she had become deeply saddened by the common practice in certain countries of devaluing women's lives to the point of infanticide. A female baby was killed by its own parents or aborted by a doctor simply because it was female deemed, therefore, to be a burden on the family.

Thousands of women, all over the world, had been tormented and abandoned by their husbands when they did not bear sons. Why hadn't the medical establishment informed these people that it was, in fact, a man's sperm cells that determined the sex of a child, not the egg cell.

Dr. Sethi had heard of brides in Indian villages being killed by their in-laws because the bride's family couldn't come up with more dowry money. Investigators were told the bride's sari, her dress, caught fire. Supposedly, all these women were getting too close to the stove.

When had seemingly normal human beings become so callous, merciless and disrespectful of life? Dr. Sethi wondered. What would you have to tell yourself to make it all right to take another's life and continue living your own? Is it ever all right to kill an infant? A child? How about a woman whose parents can't afford to pay out more money? It's okay to kill her? Or, better yet, a woman who is touched by a man? Or raped? How do you justify her life being taken by her own family?

For Neelam Sethi, the psychology behind these acts was much more worrisome than the psychology of the common sociopath. After all, these people were supposed to be law-abiding, Godfearing citizens with a conscience.

Gradually, Dr. Sethi became one of the most outspoken crusaders for the rights of women from her native India, as well as Pakistan and the Middle East, after the Daily Mirror newspaper quoted her as saying, "Sane people do not treat a daughter or wife like a farm animal. A female is not some irritating fly that you swat." When *In Our Time* magazine printed one of her speeches, it caused a lot of controversy, which sealed her popularity.

Now, two American women journalists were in her office interviewing her for an investigative report to be aired on American television. One of the women, Amy Stein, listened and jotted things down on a small notepad every few seconds. The other, Courtney Goodman, questioned her, while a cameraman adjusted the focus ring on the lens. The red light on the camera remained steady. Dr. Sethi found herself staring at this red light while responding to the questions.

"Dr. Sethi," Ms. Goodman announced. "I'm going to read the speech that was printed in Our Time Magazine for our American audience, and then have you comment.

"An autonomous woman has a whole new reservoir of experiences to add to the collective.

"An autonomous woman is any woman whose identity is not characterized by having or not having a man, nor by being a mother—but by self-actualization and manifestation, independence of finance and of thought and, most importantly, the power to act.

"An autonomous woman is self-defining.

"Every woman must be recognized as a Human Being, first and foremost, then as an Individual. An Individual with Rights. The Right to Life, to Love and to pursue Happiness, whatever form it may take for her.

"Every woman has the innate right to freedom. Freedom to be and to think whatever she wants to think. Free to question authority in all of its forms: political, ideological and religious. Husband and God.

"Free to decide for herself if she even believes in a god, after all.

"The same exact freedom afforded any man in a democratic society.

"How she wants to live her life is up to her and her alone.

"Who she wants to be sexually intimate with is entirely up to her; it's her choice only. It is truly a matter of choice. There is no 'I' without choice.

"These questions have echoed all down the centuries: Why have women been subjugated? Who benefited? Why the violence? And more importantly: Why have women allowed it? These questions must be answered. In South Asia and parts of Africa, specifically, women still participate in the subjugation of other women: their daughters and granddaughters. But now, how do we put an end to it?"

"So, Dr. Sethi, would you please tell us more about this philosophy of yours and whether or not you've found any answers to your questions?"

The cameraman pivoted around and zoomed in on Neelam Sethi, but the telephone rang before she could respond. She raised her hand for the cameraman to stop recording, and waited until she saw the green light come on before she answered the phone.

As she listened to the caller, the journalists saw a look of alarm cross her face, and then fade.

"Yes. Yes, I know," she said, nodding quickly, and then hung up.

The women's curiosity was palpable. Dr. Sethi nodded for the cameraman to continue. The red light returned.

"What we are trying to do is to let the world know what is going on in these countries and to gather all the resources necessary to help these women. We ask people to volunteer their services. We have lawyers, doctors, educators and ordinary people giving us their support, their time and, most importantly, their homes, and to do so can be quite dangerous for them. I tell you, these men are relentless."

"But surely the authorities in these places don't just sit back and..."

"Yes, they do!" Dr. Sethi responded abruptly. "Honor killing has been going on for a long time. Twenty thousand women a year die this way and recently, this practice has spread to European cities and to North America."

"America? I find that hard to believe," Amy Stein said. "No government anywhere condones murder of innocent women and children!"

Dr. Sethi found herself growing impatient. Apparently, the two journalists did not know that the practice of killing women to protect family honor was not relegated to a handful of isolated cases, until now.

"You have to understand that to these people it is not murder, it is retribution," Dr. Sethi explained. "They think they are saving the family from the shame and ostracism imposed by the community."

A knock at the door interrupted their exchange. The tall thin woman who entered had an air of authority about her.

"This is Enid Statham. You may know of her husband, Terrance Statham, he's connected to people in the Parliament. We have been working together on this."

The American women acknowledged Enid Statham and she them, and then she turned to Dr. Sethi.

"Everything going well, so far?" Enid Statham asked. Before she got a reply, the reporter cut in.

"I refuse to believe that governments are allowing this to go on."

"It's not that they allow it to go on. It is much more complicated and crosses class lines. The well-to-do are just as guilty, but most of the people are from the villages—uneducated, and—" Frustrated, she said, "Perhaps, I can talk with you again during my trip to New York in a few months, or you can continue this with Mrs. Statham. She knows as much as I do about it."

NEW YORK

Later that evening, Shafal sat at the table carefully counting out his tips. In the middle of the table, a gray metal box, about a foot long, was open, revealing stacks of one- and five-dollar bills. Basma, meanwhile, walked through the apartment adjusting and wiping things absentmindedly. The little noises she made doing this disturbed him.

"Can't you do that before I get home?" he shouted and then he commanded her to sit down.

She eased down on the couch, and folded her arms.

Shafal put the money into the metal box. "Do you know what I saw today? I saw an Indian woman doctor on the television actually condemning our…" his voice trailed off as he looked at Basma. Staring off, she hadn't heard a word he said. Vexed, he got up and carried the metal box into the bedroom.

Thursday was a brisk sunny day with February temperatures higher than normal. Outside Ridgefield Nursing Facility, the staff members relished the warmer weather by mingling on benches or strolling up and down the landscaped walkway.

A clock on the chapel-like structure across the main street read 1:57 p.m. With her hijab tied extra tight, Basma walked out toward the gate as if her shoes were made of lead. She strained to appear calm, but she was fighting terror. It was in her eyes.

Kensasha left the building a minute later with two other people, all walking quickly.

"We're going to that restaurant, Basma. Why don't you join us for a late lunch?" she called.

Basma shook her head. It was all she could manage at that moment.

Kensasha expected as much. "You never say yes. It doesn't hurt to break a routine and try something different. That's how you grow," Kensasha urged, lightheartedly.

Basma managed a feeble smile, and then clammed up. She suddenly looked overwhelmed and Kensasha moved closer to her and asked in a hushed tone:

"Are you still feeling sick? If you need some more time off…"

"No, no, everything is fine. I have to go," Basma replied and continued down the path and out of the gate, moving slowly and methodically.

She passed the bakery without regard. Ahead, people gathered at the bus stop. Many were the same ones who had waited with her two days ago—before the red car pulled up and changed everything. When she finally reached the bus stop, she slowed and stood amongst the crowd for a while, feeling protected. Half of them were talking into cell phones, while the other passengers either bopped to their playlists, or stood transfixed by their social media feeds, thumbs scrolling and texting, frantically.

With her back hunched, she clutched her purse tightly to her chest. A voice in her head screamed out, "Help me," yet she couldn't make it audible. She swallowed hard. They ignored her, all of them. Just like at Ridgefield. She was invisible. Well, wasn't that the intention behind hijab—the abaya, the burka and the chador: invisibility, to not be seen? These people were merely being accommodating. She understood.

A second later, an old memory flashed in her mind as quick as lightening: Aisha's face. It jolted Basma to a new level of fear.

When the bus finally pulled up, everyone around her scrambled to get on. Suddenly, she found herself being pushed and jostled along until she was the only one left at the curb. The driver looked down at her waiting for her to step on. Basma only gazed at the steps.

"Come on, lady. Make up your mind. I'm on a schedule. Are you getting on or not?"

She heard a man's voice in her head, "I'll tell your husband."

Basma looked up at the driver with intense regret, then turned away and headed to the corner as if walking on eggshells. When she reached it, she slowed her pace down to a tiptoe. She gulped as she turned the corner. There was the red car, waiting. Tears welled up and hope drained out of her. She mumbled a few words of prayer as she inched towards it. Hands trembling, she fumbled with the passenger door, unable to open it at first. Soon she managed to get in, gingerly, pulling the door shut. The car was still, for a moment, and then it pulled away.

CHAPTER 4

Inside, the radio was blasting music from a contemporary jazz station, the DJ's banter seductive and melodious. An open can of Red Bull was in the cup holder and a half pack of red Dunhill cigarettes lay next to the energy drink.

Basma may have been naïve enough to get into a stranger's car, but now she was fully cognizant of her perilous situation. Recalling the sweetness of his smile in the bakery, she wondered if he could really hurt her… or worse. Where on earth was he taking her?

The Bakery Guy reached down for his drink, took a sip, changed lanes and sped up. He glanced over at the woman who had not spoken one word nor looked his way since getting into his car. He sensed her fear and, for a moment, was reluctant to continue with his plans. She soon changed his mind back, though, when she announced firmly, "I must be in my house by 4 o'clock. No later than 4:30."

He gazed back at her, totally surprised at her presumption. "Oh, let me guess… to make dinner for your husband?" he asked.

"Yes. Of course," she replied, with a touch of haughtiness. He smirked and took another swig from the can.

A few minutes later, when they left the expressway and pulled into a motel parking lot near Kennedy airport, her fear returned. With a confused expression, she studied the Bakery Guy then the row of motel room doors. He gave her a cocky smile, leaped out of the car and disappeared for a few minutes. He returned waving a magnetic card for her to see. Basma could only stare at it perplexed. After all, she'd never been to a motel before in her life. He reached over the seat for a white paper bag and two more cans of his energy drink, and then motioned to her to get out of the car.

She followed him along a row of numbered doors, stopping at the second from the end, room 128.

She watched him put the key card through a slit near the knob, pull it out quickly and a little green light bulb flicked on. He pushed open the door, stepped aside and gestured for her to enter.

Basma peered into the half-darkened room and then proceeded as if she expected something to leap from the shadows.

The first thing she noticed was the faint odor of stale tobacco that no vacuum cleaner could remove. It clung to the walls and was em-bedded in the carpet. The second thing was the cheap soundproofing that did little to muffle sounds of cars and trucks zooming past. A queen-sized bed situated between two end tables along the left wall dominated the room. Next to the front door was an upholstered chair with a low round table in front of the window. The only other furni-ture consisted of a dresser with a TV sitting on top. The bathroom was opposite the entrance. Her eyes went to the blue and white striped wallpaper and the yellow floral-patterned bedspread. Not a very good match, she decided.

The Bakery Guy closed the door behind him. He scanned the room then walked around her to the nearest bedside table and put down the drinks and whatever was in the white paper bag. He took off his brown leather jacket and flung it across the chair, then plopped down on the bed. For a moment, he stared at Basma who had re-mained just inside the doorway. He beckoned her over to the bed. She couldn't move. He got up, walked calmly over to her and tugged at her hijab.

"Take this off." Suddenly aware of his power over her, he said: "On second thought, take off your coat and your blouse." Seeing the shock on her face, he repeated it. "That's right... your blouse... now!" She blinked repeatedly. Her lips parted to speak. He stared at her, waiting.

Whatever she had imagined was going to happen, it wasn't this. Awareness of the bed alone was enough to scatter all thoughts of reason. When he demanded she undress before him, her first instinct was to run. Get out of that door quickly and run. But a second thought followed swiftly after. Where could she run to? The motel office? How would they help her? Call the police? Then what? How would she explain being there in the first place? What exactly would she tell Shafal? No, she couldn't run.

She was trapped, and it was her own fault. Now, the only questions were how far was he planning to take this, and would she make it home alive?

She sighed and allowed her purse to slide off her shoulder to the floor. She unbuttoned her long brown coat and slid out of it. The Bakery Guy reached and took the coat from her and slung it over the chair on top of his own. This made her pause.

"Go on," he said.

She took in a deep breath and began fumbling with the buttons of the blouse. When she finished unbuttoning the last button, she turned away from him and slid out of it as well. Underneath, she wore a plain white cotton slip and an old-fashioned white bra with pointed cups. She clutched the blouse in front of her.

"No, no. On the chair."

Placing the blouse on the chair as directed, she stood with her back to him rubbing her bare arms.

"Turn around," he ordered. She obeyed. "Now the skirt. Take it off."

Her eyes grew misty as her trembling hands unhooked and unzipped her long skirt. Its loose fit allowed it to fall to the floor. She stepped out of it, turned her head away and continued to rub her arms, which had never been exposed in front of a man other than Shafal.

He noticed the thick, dark stockings she wore, suitable for a very old woman.

"Now, the stockings." Not understanding the word, she didn't respond. "Look at me," he commanded.

She turned his way avoiding his eyes. He pointed to her legs. She tried to slide the stockings down without having to raise her slip.

"Come on, just take them off," he ordered, impatiently.

No choice left, she slid them down and stepped out of them.

He let her remain standing in her slip and hijab for a few minutes. But, for him, there was nothing remotely erotic about the situation. She was much too frightened for that, and he was much too confident in his own sexual prowess to be aroused by a woman's fear. He was simply satisfying his own curiosity about this woman, her odd dress and strange mannerisms.

He studied the shape of her body with its wide hips, and the hair on her legs. She wasn't much different than the old, widowed women living in those villages in southern Europe where his mother had taken him. Without husbands, these women stopped grooming themselves and always wore black clothing, black stockings or thick socks with unshaved legs. While every woman he'd ever been with had their legs, and most other body parts, waxed.

Neglect. That's what he saw.

"All right, now the slip and the…"

"No! Please, please," she implored, covering her face with her hands. "I cannot…"

"Sure, you can," he replied dispassionately. "And the sooner you do the sooner you can go home."

Hearing that he planned to take her home made the next moment bearable, she took off her slip and let it drop to the floor. The bra was much harder to let go of. With nothing left but her cotton underpants and headscarf, her body began to tremble. Tears streamed down her cheeks.

He didn't show an ounce of empathy. Instead, he stood silent, gawking, while she shriveled up and died of shame right in front of him.

"Why are you crying?" he asked, with genuine sincerity. "I haven't even touched you. Come over here," he said calmly. This time Basma didn't obey so readily. "You act as though my eyes are hurting you. What? You think I'm judging your body, your flaws? Well, I'm not, so come over here."

After what seemed like an eternity, she walked slowly toward the bed with her arms shielding her breasts from view. She flinched when he pulled off her scarf. He found her modesty absurd.

"The way you cower, I thought you'd be hideous under all that." In a naïve attempt to reassure her, he added, dispassionately: "Don't worry, you'll get used to it."

Suddenly, he grabbed her wrists, forcing her arms apart. Her face reddened. She closed her eyes and turned her head away. He started to touch her breast, but stopped. Jumping to the other side of the bed, he commanded that she lie down. She lay on her stomach, with her face turned away from him. He snickered, and slowly traced his fingers along her bare back from the shoulder over to the spine then down to her buttocks. She winced, shutting her eyes tightly.

"Hey, I think you forgot something," he teased. Curious to know what he meant, she finally turned her head towards him. He tugged at the elastic waistband of her underpants. "Take these off."

Her eyes widened. This was one order she would not obey. So, he got up, straddled her and began sliding her pants down. She muffled her protest in the pillow, but he continued to pull them slowly towards her feet until they were off. He stroked her thighs a moment, and once again laid back alongside her propped up on his elbow.

"Turn over," he commanded. His voice was soft, but something in its tone alarmed her.

Slowly, she turned over, cringing, covering her breasts with one arm and her pubis with the other. Her eyes were squeezed tightly shut.

This time, when he pulled her arms away, he cupped her breast. She stopped breathing.

He felt aroused and kneaded it slowly.

She gasped for air.

He fondled her other breast.

Her lips tightened. A natural reflex caused her body to stiffen.

He let out a frustrated grunt and got up abruptly.

Basma's eyes flew open to see what he would do next. He stood by the bed staring down at her, thinking. Wondering. She quickly folded one arm across her breasts, and the other covered her below.

Seeing this, he frowned, looked away. His original eagerness was waning fast. He seemed puzzled by the way the situation was unfolding. 'You're a real challenge,' he mumbled.

Suddenly, the Bakery Guy reached his hand into the back pocket of his white jeans and pulled out a Swiss army knife. He sat back down on the bed glancing at her with an ambiguous, threatening gleam in his eye, and then he flipped open the blade.

She jumped and cowered at the edge of the bed. His grin was more disconcerting as he scanned her body. She watched the blade, transfixed, envisioning horrible outcomes. The Bakery Guy grabbed the white paper bag on the nightstand and pulled out a large mango. He peeled back the pale greenish-yellow outer skin. Inside, the orange-colored pulp was soft and laden with juice. He cut a slice and offered it to her. She shook her head timidly. He insisted on putting it to her lips. She took it in, but some of the juice dripped onto her neck and chest. He leaned over, slowly, and licked it up seductively with his tongue and finished with his face very close to hers. He gazed, lustfully, into her deep brown eyes, and hungrily at her moist full lips, all the while her eyes darted everywhere but into his enigmatic blue ones.

Still grinning, he flashed his perfect white teeth then cut another slice from the mango and put it to her mouth. Again, she refused. So, he ate it.

After that, he began to cut each subsequent slice slowly, methodically, and ate them while Basma looked on in sheer absolute terror. When all the loose flesh was eaten, he licked the pit and each of his fingers as the juice ran down, all the while, looking on her nakedness with his blue-green eyes, twinkling.

Moments later, he disappeared into the small bathroom. She heard water running and immediately yanked the bedcovers across her body and over her head, instinctively curling into a fetal position, expecting the worst.

When he emerged from the bathroom, the knife back in his pocket, and saw her quivering, he let out a loud sigh of disappointment.

She peeped out from beneath the cover. Their eyes locked for a second.

"Get dressed!" he ordered.

Thirty minutes later, the car came to a stop just down the street from Basma's apartment. She got out as fast as she could.

But as she closed the door, the Bakery Guy, looking straight ahead, said, "I'll pick you up on Tuesday, same place." And, without a glance, he sped away.

She watched the car with her mouth gaping. She watched until he was out of sight.

There was no time to bathe, to wash away his scent. The meat had to go into the oven first. Onions and tomatoes had to be peeled and chopped.

Did she really have to endure all that again? At least, she was home safe for the second time. Thank God. But would he let her go safely the next time? How far did he plan to take this? What did he want from her?

But there was no time to think about any of it. She couldn't afford to. Instead, she mindlessly sifted through the mail, and then left it on the small table in the living room for Shafal and the boys to see.

There was no inner dialogue, no self-talk. At least, not a conscious ongoing one. If there had been, she would have questioned how it was possible to feel fear and excitement at the same time, loathing and desire. This man had seen what her own husband had never seen: her nakedness.

***

Abdel arrived home first. Basma was somewhat relieved. She didn't have to make conversation with him, so she remained busy in the kitchen. Abdel entered and gave her his usual gentle kiss on the cheek.

She patted his face, affectionately. They looked at each other with great tenderness. Of the two boys, good-natured Abdel was her heart.

When he was only three years old, he would ask her why she was crying. Was it because of him, he wondered? He would then twist up his mouth or cross his eyes to make her laugh. The funny thing was, during her entire marriage to Shafal she had never actually cried. There were never any tears, at least not physical ones. She began to wonder if Abdel, alone, could see her soul.

Ahmed appeared soon after with a girl about seventeen years old, wearing a head scarf pulled extra tight causing her face to puff out. Unlike Basma, the girl's attire was fashionably stylish while keeping with the dress code. She had bright curious eyes. Basma welcomed the girl and managed to be congenial until Shafal finally arrived home.

Shafal greeted the girl excitedly then headed straight to the kitchen carrying a few bags. Without greeting Basma, he crossed to the counter near the sink.

"I wish we had more notice that he was bringing home a guest. You could have made some special dish," Shafal said, as he began unpacking the bags at the sink. "What time did you get in today?" Basma was standing over the stove stirring the cubed lamb pieces. "I called you several times."

She stopped stirring.

"I must have been in the tub with the water running. You know how loud it is."

She hated having to lie. Avoiding eye contact, she walked over to the fridge and opened it. As she bent down to see what was in the bottom bin, Shafal reached into the bag again, pulling out green grapes.

"Why were you taking a bath in the middle of the day?"

Basma took out a dish of previously chopped tomatoes, to add to the lamb sautéing with ginger, garlic and onions. She had to think quickly.

"I felt so warm on the bus because there are always too many people."

Gripping the dish of tomatoes, she walked back around the table, positioned between the stove and the refrigerator.

Shafal, took out the oranges. "Well, Ahmed reached me in the cab to ask me if it was all right to bring that girl home for dinner."

She poured the tomatoes into the heavy iron pan containing the lamb.

"I wanted to tell you. And, to tell you to buy that special bread."

Basma paused at the stove. Her throat tightened. She turned to place the empty dish on the table behind her. Simultaneously, Shafal took the remaining item from the bag, and turned to the table. "Well, it was okay. I remembered you said it was near your work. So, I went there and bought it myself." He put the shiny burgundy and gold bag on the table just as Basma was about to put the dish down. It slipped from her hand, hit the table, shattered and the pieces crashed to the floor startling everyone.

"What's the matter with you?" Shafal lashed out, immediately, "How can you miss a table this big? You need glasses or something?"

For a moment, Basma wasn't even aware of the shattered plate, nor Shafal's angry voice, only that he had actually entered that bakery.

Shafal started to say something else, then remembered their dinner guest. He gave her the evil eye instead. Basma sheepishly gathered up the broken pieces from the floor.

CHAPTER 5

When Shafal decided on Basma as his wife, he expected her to bear him the sons he wanted and to be the kind of wife worthy of a successful merchant. Mostly, he wanted someone who was docile, the polar opposite of his first wife, Naife, whom he married two years before he married Basma.

Naife had had difficulty conceiving. At twenty-two, many of the villagers believed it was because she was too old. But Naife wasn't too old. She just did not want to be the mother of Shafal Abseh's children.

Like Basma, Naife's mother, and all the other women in their village, Naife had no say in the wedding or in the marriage. Naife grew to believe Shafal was incapable of having real feelings for her because his primary concern was for her to bear sons for him.

"Make me proud," Shafal would say to her, repeatedly.

So, Naife used a strong tea made of roots that disrupted her cycle and told Shafal the special tea increased her fertility. When it finally came to light what she was really doing, Shafal was livid and humiliated. At first, he thought about returning Naife to her family, which would've been scandalous enough. Instead, one day, he took her on an excursion high up into the rugged Haraz Mountains, driving along a rough, perilous road of dirt and loose stones. When the treacherous path narrowed, Shafal forced Naife, who was ill prepared, to hike with him on foot another quarter mile. Finally, he left her there.

Unable to make her way back on foot, it took approximately six days for Naife to succumb to exposure and dehydration. Her family knew not to ask questions about her or her whereabouts and Shafal omitted any mention of her from all his communications.

***

On Tuesday, Basma found herself in the same motel—different room—standing before the Bakery Guy with her head lowered, while he sat calmly on the bed watching her.

"Come on… you know what I want. Don't take all day."

She hesitated. Her reluctance increased. It stemmed more from anger than fear of what may come. After all, he hadn't physically hurt her… yet. She began to believe he wouldn't.

"All right, I'll make it really easy for you."

He pulled his white tee shirt up over his head and tossed it. Her eyes followed the shirt's trajectory. Startled, she looked back at him as he sat bare to the waist. He smiled to taunt her. She looked away quickly. He leaned over, took off his ankle boots and socks, and then he stood up and unzipped his jeans. Basma gasped and swung around.

With his jeans and briefs removed, he sauntered up behind her and whispered in her ear: "Your turn."

She stepped farther away surprising him. He quickly moved in front of her. She covered her face with both hands. He pulled her hands from her eyes and backed away. His body was striking, perfectly formed and he was quite comfortable in it. He spread his arms out to the side.

"You can look at me. I want you to."

Breathing heavily, she looked everywhere but at him.

"Ah, come on," he said, with a silky voice, "do I look that bad? Huh? My body may not be as beautiful as yours but…"

The unexpected compliment made her look straight into his eyes. Then her eyes, suddenly—with a mind of their own—drifted down to his muscular chest. He grinned. Flustered, she took in a deep breath and inadvertently glanced at his manhood. He became aroused. She flushed, clasped her hands back over her eyes and stumbled toward the door. Bakery Guy quickly grabbed her arm, pulled her back and swung her around to face him. Frightened, Basma struggled to break free. The Bakery Guy lost his patience and shook her hard.

"Stop it!" he yelled. "What the fuck's the matter with you? Do I have something you haven't seen before?"

It was an attempt to calm her. Yet, his physical aggression only frightened her more. Realizing this, he let go of her arm abruptly, walked back to the bed and sat down heavily—, frustrated that things still weren't going the way he wanted.

He looked up at her with no expression on his face. She stood perfectly still, holding her breath.

"Come here and lie down," he commanded in a gentler tone. Spooked by his previous outburst, Basma obeyed immediately.

He stretched out on his side in an amorous pose, his head propped up on his elbow looking down at her. Breathing heavily now, she stared up at the ceiling. He leaned in until his face was just inches away from hers.

"Sorry if I was a little rough," he said, softly.

She ignored him.

"Okay… look… you don't have to take anything off. And… I won't touch you." She visibly relaxed. "But" he continued, in an even softer tone. "I want you to touch me… anyplace you want to."

She glanced at him. Why would I want to? she wondered. And was just about to say that, when he said, "I've already touched you, so…" He followed it with a sly grin and then laid on his back with his eyes closed in anticipation.

She didn't move a muscle. She couldn't. Did he really think that she would…? That she could…? How absurd. Why would she want to?

But, after a long moment, she found herself actually resisting this strange impulse.

Anyplace you want to, he had said. He was giving her permission to touch him, but she hadn't given him permission to touch her—he just did it; like there were no boundaries between them; like he didn't care about her feelings, her humiliation.

Fact is, he hadn't really noticed. Sure, he saw the tears, the shivering, but he wouldn't have recognized it as humiliation. His narcissism wouldn't permit that.

Apart from his good looks, how was this man any different from her husband, Shafal, who climbed on top of her whenever he wanted, without once asking how she felt or what she desired?

It didn't matter that she had never ever been aroused, had never felt the stirrings of sexual desire. Shafal could have, at least, gotten her consent.

Basma watched the Bakery Guy's chest—with its little tufts of golden-brown hair—move up and down. Then without thinking, she gingerly placed her hand on his shoulder and felt the warmth of his creamy smooth skin. She held it there pressing firmly. She allowed her fingers to gently trace the curves of the muscles of his arm.

He opened his eyes to watch her hand. An almost imperceptible look of delight formed on her face. She had no idea what compelled her to do this—to actually touch this man. Was it because no one would know?

But hadn't he betrayed her trust by bringing her to this motel against her will? Hadn't he already humiliated her by staring at her nakedness? And, he had touched her! A married woman at that. Her death was assured. Yet here she was, touching him, the man from the bakery with the white teeth, and secretly enjoying it. This was suicidal.

Still, Basma allowed her hand to glide along the top of his shoulder and down to his chest. Her heart sped up as her fingers played with the golden-brown tufts of hair. When had she ever done such a thing? Never!

Now, both of them watched her hand, wondering what it would do next, where it would go.

The hand inched down and stroked even smoother skin just above his navel. Her breathing intensified. Bakery Guy glanced at her with amazement and anticipation, and he, too, began to breathe heavily. But when the hand came to a halt just below his navel, he grabbed it and pushed it towards his groin. Basma resisted and managed to yank it free, then placed it back on his chest and continued to stroke him, this time tentatively.

He studied her intensely for a moment. She looked into his eyes then quickly looked away. Frustrated, he cupped her hand and said, "That's enough."

He sat up without looking at her, and then he got up and strolled over to the chair where he had tossed his clothes and began dressing. While he did so, Basma remained on the bed reviewing in her mind what she had just done. She simply couldn't believe she dared to touch a nude man. What on earth had possessed her? Surely, this was some kind of evil possession. Something wicked had been awakened inside of her.

Dressed, the Bakery Guy walked to the door and opened it. Basma quickly sat up. He didn't say one word. He just stood there with the door wide open glaring at her.

She jumped up, grabbed her purse and walked awkwardly toward him with her eyes averted. She passed by him out the door, neither of them looking at the other.

As they crossed the parking lot, Bakery Guy finally glanced over at Basma who was a few feet was away. She was clutching her purse close to her body and she walked looking at her feet alternating from left to right.

"You're a strange one," he said, shaking his head.

He pulled a set of keys from his pocket. When they were back in the car, he hastily inserted a key into the ignition, shifted into reverse and checked the back window. It was all clear.

"I mean," he continued, "you've seen your husband naked, so…"

"No," she said, correcting him.

"No? What do you mean no?"

"My husband does not undress in my presence," she said, pursing her lips and shifting her body nervously.

Bakery Guy began to back the car out. "But he has his clothes off when you're having sex, so you must see him naked sometimes."

"No, he does not." She lifted her head slightly, appearing more dignified.

Amazed, Bakery Guy slammed on the brakes and turned his whole, upper, body ninety degrees towards her.

"Wait, are you telling me you've never seen your husband without his clothes?" She nodded. "Why? Is that some religious thing?"

Still facing forward, Basma shrugged. "I don't know."

"But why would you keep your clothes on when you're having sex? I could see if you were outside on a beach... in a hallway... or a car. Yeah." Appalled, she jerked around and glared at him. "But why at home?" He pressed, "All the time? I mean, that's crazy!"

"That is our way," she said curtly. His familiarity exasperated her. "I do not want to talk of this."

"Fine," he said, with a sulk. He took his foot off the brake and the car eased out of the space. Shifting into first gear, he circled to the exit, and then headed out to the main highway.

They drove half the way back in silence. Basma stared out of the passenger window at the rows of motels and fast-food restaurants lining the highway. Until last week, she'd never seen, let alone been inside, a motel. This was an entirely new experience for her—new and dangerous. So was touching him. And what about seeing his... his.... She felt heat rise to her face. She could barely swallow at the thought.

There were no intimate friends to share this with.

Finally, Bakery Guy broke the silence. "Why did you marry him?"

No one had ever asked her that. She'd never considered she had an alternative. The images were vague, hazy. They had surrounded her.

Uncle Khalid and her mother, Sumera. She could only recall a few words here and there. Something about being chosen and going to America.

"I had to," she responded, looking down at her hands.

He smirked. "Oh, I get it. You were pregnant."

"What is that?"

He reached over and put his hand on her stomach. "A baby?"

Mortified by the insinuation, she jerked his way, frowning. "My mother told me to marry him," she said, defensively, in a loud voice.

Bakery Guy smirked again. "And you assume mothers are always right?" he chided. She gave him a frosty stare. Their eyes locked. He pressed on, "Well, was your mother, right?"

Basma faced forward. After a while, she said, "My husband is a good man."

She smoothed out her coat and tugged at the sleeves. Then she stiffened her back causing her head to rise in an effort to regain at least a few ounces of decorum. "He works all the time for his family," she began, her voice firm, yet quivering with emotion. "He works so hard. He is a good man and he... he wouldn't do this," she spewed with venom. It was a tone new to her.

Now, twice in one day, she had done something totally out of character that shocked her. She waited for him to assail her, but the Bakery Guy didn't respond. He coolly reached over and turned on the radio.

From the start, there was something about the way he looked at her and spoke to her that both infuriated her and, at the same time, allowed her the luxury to feel infuriated, to express infuriation. It was a feeling far more empowering than her usual one of fear. It had awakened something she couldn't yet define. Like touching him— that too gave her a glimpse of a side of herself that she never knew existed.

His intrusiveness was maddening and that too awakened all kinds of strong emotions.

"What is your name?" she asked, yielding to this familiarity.

"Why do you want to know my name?" he replied, with irritation. "Are you going to tell me yours?" She thought about it. "No names!" he said with finality.

The car left the highway at the next exit and soon entered her neighborhood. As they approached the tire factory, she began to grow uneasy.

"Do I have to come again?" she asked, timidly.

Bakery Guy slowed the car and gave her a sly grin. "Do you want to?" Startled, and unaware that it was purely a rhetorical question, she attempted a response. "You don't have to answer that," he said, dismissively, and turned off the radio. The car approached the drop off point. She looked at him, waiting. He stopped the car and leaned back, thinking to himself.

Basma rubbed her thumbs together and twisted the strap of her handbag. She checked her watch. She had no time left.

"Hmm, I don't know… I don't want a repeat of what happened today. That was a real bummer, you know?" He drummed on the steering wheel. She waited. He glanced over at her with lowered eyelids. "But… now that I realize I'm the only man you've seen naked…"

Her cheeks flushed. When she swallowed, the saliva caught in her throat and she had to cough to clear it. Amused, he turned away, stared out the window, and then continued: "I like you. You're different from the girls I usually… date. I wouldn't mind seeing you one more time. Next Thursday." His tone was soft, but this was definitely an order.

She ignored the queasiness in her stomach and quietly got out of the car. Up ahead, a cab slowly crossed the intersection.

As Basma turned the corner to walk the long block to her apartment building, she heard someone calling her. She turned to see Shafal in his cab driving to their apartment building. She stopped, frozen in her tracks.

"Get in," he yelled through the window.

Cheeks still flushed, she walked hesitantly to the cab and got in. Hands shaking, she fussed with her clothing to avoid Shafal's ever scrutinizing eyes. As expected, he noticed her demeanor a moment before speaking.

"Where are you coming from? Shouldn't you be home already?"

Basma took in a deep breath and quickly searched her mind for a suitable reply. "I went to look in some shops on the other street," she responded, trying to keep her tone light. "Don't worry your dinner will be ready in time," she added. "Why are you home so early?"

"This is my fourth trip from La Guardia," he replied. "I have to go to the toilet and I prefer my own instead of those filthy gas stations."

"You come so far to go to the toilet?"

"Basma, it is not far."

Shafal stopped the cab in front of their building. She hopped out quickly and went straight in without waiting for him to park. Wasting no time, she hurried into the bathroom to check her face and clothing, washed her hands, and was back in the kitchen grabbing food items from the fridge when Shafal finally entered.

He went directly to the bathroom. She poured two cups of millet into a colander, turned on the faucet and began to rinse the tiny grains.

"Do you need me to buy anything for dinner?" Shafal asked passing the kitchen on his way out.

"No, I have everything," she replied, her back to him.

She heard the door close. For a moment, she just watched the water cascading down and encircling the little grains cleansing them of all manner of dirt and grime—purging them of any transgressions. Easy for them.

CHAPTER 6

T he next afternoon Basma got off the bus one stop sooner. Walking the extra blocks gave her a chance to clear her head a little. The pressure of keeping up the appearance of normalcy weighed heavily on her. She thought about Shafal finding out about the boy from the bakery and what he would do. She thought about the stormy afternoon at the bus stop and how different this present moment would be if she hadn't gotten into the car, if she'd returned to work and waited for Shafal to come and get her.

Passing a kosher butcher, she decided to buy a leg of lamb for roasting with onions, potatoes and herbs. It was a French dish she had seen prepared on TV at Ridgefield, around the Christmas holidays, and thought now was the time to try it; anything to keep her mind off of her problems.

At the supermarket, she bought the herbs and potatoes, and left carrying a lot more groceries than she'd planned for the extra distance.

By the time Basma reached her street laden with four bags of produce, the handles were already cutting into her wrists.

Imani Sadawi was standing just outside the apartment building casually conversing with a stout woman around fifty years old who was dressed in a stylish brown abaya—a full length coatdress with a high embroidered neckline and long sleeves. As soon as Imani saw Basma approaching, her face lit up.

"Ah, Mrs. Abseh, good to see you!" she exclaimed. "You are looking quite well these days. I knew that job would be good for you. Do you know Mrs. Jazeer?"

Basma set down her bags and nodded at the Jordanian woman whose opulent frame she had seen many times coming and going but to whom she had never said a word.

"After the prayers Friday night, Mrs. Jazeer is having another gathering for the women. Why don't you come this time?"

Mrs. Jazeer nodded without enthusiasm and both women waited for Basma's reply.

Knowing Basma needed a little persuading, Imani placed a hand on her shoulder and said: "All you do is go to work, come home and cook." She glanced down at the grocery bags and shook her head, "You have to have fun, too, Basma. It's good to meet other women."

Basma looked at the ground and replied awkwardly, "If it is okay with my husband, I will come."

"Oh, don't worry," said Imani, excitedly, "I will talk with him."

***

That Friday evening, eight women originating from Turkey, Syria, Yemen, Egypt and Jordan gathered in Mrs. Jazeer's cramped living room.

Assembled in small groups, the women wore varying styles of traditional Islamic dress. Some were in full flowing black abayas— long loose-fitting dresses—having just left the mosque; others wore only the hijab and long skirt. The women who usually wore the niqab face covering had removed it because only women were present.

Mrs. Jazeer rushed about in her colorful flowing kaftan, making sure everyone had enough to eat and drink. Though considerably overweight, she had a lot of nervous energy and enjoyed entertaining.

Three heavy-set middle-aged women in dark gray abayas sat on the couch sharing the latest gossip and giggled away.

Basma stood in a corner alone. She offered an occasional polite nod to the women but couldn't think of any other way of connecting beyond that.

In the middle of the room, surrounded by a number of women, the extremely popular Imani Sadawi was engrossed in a conversation about Dr. Sethi, the Indian woman who had been on the news.

"I don't care how my husband feels about it," Imani Sadawi announced in a serious tone. "I am going to write a letter to that Dr. Sethi and ask her to come here and talk to you women." This caused a slight commotion, and Mrs. Jazeer looked over at the group with concern. She put down her serving platter and joined them.

"Imani, do you know what the news people will do?" Mrs. Jazeer asked. "They already think all our men are terrorists. Look how hard it has been for us since that awful attack here over twenty years ago." Her emotions intensified. "Remember our husbands and sons were taken from us for weeks and some were gone for months, even years!"

"And they were never charged with any crime," added one woman.

"Yes, and my sister and her husband and his parents were all deported, and they didn't do anything wrong," another added and then wiped a tear from her cheek.

This incited more commotion as the women recalled those tense chaotic weeks and months following September 11, 2001, and the continuing surveillance and repression of Muslim communities by the authorities. Did they really need another negative issue pinned on them? But Imani Sadawi was not dissuaded.

"This is about women and girls. Our women and girls. We all know someone or heard about someone. It just happened again in Iraq and in Florida. Shouldn't we try to stop it?"

"It cannot be stopped," said another woman, as she reached over for a sweet from Mrs. Jazeer's idle tray. "These are very old practices. This doctor talking about it on American television cannot stop what's happening in those villages, or in Iraq or even here in America. It is foolish to think so."

Basma, like everyone else in the room, was now aware of the discussion, but she remained silent with a faraway look in her eyes.

Mrs. Jazeer nodded at the woman, and again addressed Mrs. Sadawi. "She is right. And it will make more trouble for us. People will think we are some kind of barbaric—"

"To me, it is barbaric," countered Imani Sadawi. "And so is setting a wife on fire because you can't get more money from her parents. That is what they do in India! If Dr. Sethi can get the media to shame people into stopping, then—"

"Those people don't read newspapers, Imani!" Mrs. Jazeer retorted even more upset. "Even if they did, do you really believe they would stop because of what is in American newspapers?"

The women surrounding Mrs. Jazeer nodded and mumbled in agreement. Basma, who had been sitting by herself all along and hadn't tried to engage any of the women in conversation, got up discreetly and headed for the bathroom.

When Basma reentered Mrs. Jazeer's living room, she was pleased to see that the crowd around Mrs. Sadawi had dispersed. The tension of the heated discussion had subsided and the women had returned to a more mundane discourse while they nibbled on Mrs. Jazeer's famous delicacies.

Visibly disappointed at the discussion's outcome, Imani Sadawi half listened to the woman who had sided with Mrs. Jazeer.

Basma strolled over to Imani and gave her a pacifying smile. Imani sucked her teeth and shook her head in annoyance, then looked around for Mrs. Jazeer.

Minutes later, Mrs. Jazeer was handing Imani her shawl, while trying to coax her into staying.

"But it is still early and your husband..."

"You know, I am fed up with such narrow minds," Imani said, uncharacteristically. "Look at what the young people have done in my country because they want a better life. I am so proud of them. And it is happening everywhere. People are waking up. Yes, there are still many problems, and they will solve them. But here, we never do anything but go to the mosque or shopping."

Mrs. Jazeer's eyes widened and she puffed up her chest. "I have a family to take care of and so do all of the women here, Imani. And we work hard to do that. Money is not coming like before. Your children have their own families. Your husband lets you do whatever you want. You are college educated. Many of these women haven't gone to school. So, it is not easy for the rest of us. And this is not Egypt."

Imani let out a deep sigh, and replied, "All right, I guess I will have to do it alone." Reaching over to hug Mrs. Jazeer she added: "I do hope I didn't ruin the gathering by talking of unpleasant things."

Mrs. Jazeer returned the hug and said, "Don't worry about it."

Imani opened the door and stepped out into the hallway saying, "I'm very tired, please tell everyone goodbye for me."

"Of course, I will, Imani." Mrs. Jazeer said and closed the door.

***

On the Thursday following the gathering, Basma exited the service door of Ridgefield Nursing Home and headed straight across the lawn. Her stride was quick and light with a little bounce. It was one of those glorious sunny days with low humidity. Many of the staff workers were standing about smoking and chitchatting. Just as she reached the front gate, she saw Mrs. Sadawi entering and was startled.

"Leaving so early, Mrs. Abseh?" Imani asked in an unusually formal tone. Basma hesitated, lost for words.

"Uh… you have come here to visit with me?" Basma asked, attempting to hide her uneasiness.

"Oh, no, no, no. What would be the point in that? I have come to see Professor Lewis."

Basma stared back confused. "Professor Lewis?"

"Yes, Kensasha Lewis, your supervisor. Remember? I got her to hire you." Basma nodded then waited curiously for a further explanation. "I spoke with her about contacting Dr. Sethi. You remember all the resistance I got last week at Mrs. Jazeer's. And you never said a word."

"I was in the bathroom."

"Not the whole time. But it is okay. I know that Shafal would never let you get involved in anything that might give women a voice."

Basma knew this was true, of course, but she didn't like Imani's constant criticism of Shafal. She grew defensive.

"My husband is a good Muslim. He works very hard." Then she added proudly, "And, he lets me come to the women's group." Imani waved her hand in disgust.

"That was because I told him to let you come."

Annoyed that Imani always had to shove that in her face, Basma walked away without saying goodbye. Imani stared after her a moment, and continued to the front entrance of the nursing home.

Kensasha was just finishing up a call when she heard Martha, the office manager, directing Imani Sadawi to her office. She went to the door to greet her and they embraced. After, Imani took a seat at the table Basma used to sort out files. Kensasha closed the door and swung her chair around.

Imani put her purse on the table and removed the shawl that was lightly draped over her head. All night she had practiced what she'd say to Kensasha in order to enlist her help, since none of the women at Mrs. Jazeer's were eager to pursue the matter. She had anticipated the questions Kensasha would ask and worked out persuasive responses. But now, sitting face to face with Kensasha, who was perpetually absorbed in her own work or her studies at the university, Imani felt as though she was complicating Kensasha's life with one more distraction.

"Okay, so how do we approach this?" Kensasha asked folding her arms across her chest. She saw Imani's eyes light up when she said "we".

The two had met three years earlier, during a talk and interview with an Islamic scholar at Columbia University, where Kensasha attended class. Imani was seated next to her. They struck up a conversation and found they were of like minds. A friendship developed, though Imani was twenty-four years her senior. For Kensasha, it was about having someone in her life with a worldlier perspective who was a Muslim as well. For Imani, it was about connecting with someone besides the domestically minded women in her community.

The day before, Imani had been under the weather, not sure about her choices in life. She was bored with everything and everyone and couldn't get out of bed. Long ago, she believed the world to be her oyster, and she intended to taste every morsel. But just when she was about to venture into her chosen career path as an engineer, her parents pressed her to marry Azad Sadawi, a very bright, kind man, who everyone knew always had a warm place in his heart for her, and she "should not let him get away".

"I'm sure this Dr. Sethi has many requests to speak all over the world," Kensasha continued. "What makes you think she'd take us up on ours?"

"If we craft a letter with the right tone and point out the advantages of speaking to the women here, how it may help save a woman's life, I am sure Dr. Sethi wouldn't refuse us."

Kensasha wasn't convinced and expressed as much. Nevertheless, she turned to her computer and said, "It won't hurt to give it a try." She began typing: Dear Dr. Sethi...

***

By the time Basma slid into the passenger's seat of the Bakery Guy's car a few minutes later, she was the one distracted mulling over what Mrs. Sadawi had said.

He took her to a better-quality motel with the wallpaper, carpeting and bedding colorfully coordinated. This room had a custom-built cabinet for the TV, a writing desk and two armchairs.

When they first entered, she sensed a change in him, a different air. He was much more unpredictable with little to say. His altered behavior crystallized when, after ordering her to undress, he stripped to his briefs and lay beside her without touching her. Had he lost interest in her? Now, she huddled beneath the sheets assuming this was the very last time she'd have to see him.

Before long, he began a tirade on geopolitical issues, the people's revolutions reportedly happening all over the Middle East, where they failed to bring about what the people expected, their possible connections to U. S. government conspiracies, and who was really behind the terrorist attacks in Europe. He seemed very serious about the topic.

"Have you noticed that the media hardly mentions global warming, anymore? Now, it's climate change," he said, fervently. "I wonder why that is."

Basma, meanwhile, was preoccupied with planning the dinner menu and watching him. His scent filled her nostrils. It wasn't displeasing. She studied the folds of his ear, and noticed a thin scar on the side of his cheek. His voice was rich in its tone, confident in its phrasing. Was he talking to her, or to himself? She wasn't sure. Shafal never talked to her about such things.

Then he turned to face her.

"Am I right? Don't you think an alliance between North Korea and China would be a major threat? She stared back with that vague expression.

"What's the matter with you?" he sneered. "You didn't have a problem speaking up the first time we met." His words didn't upset her because she couldn't understand what he expected of her.

"Look, I've seen that spunk in you. 'Excuse me, this bread is hard'," he said, imitating her voice.

"But it was hard," Basma responded, naively.

"I know, but that's not my point." He let out a loud sigh and sat up. "I just want to know what you think, that's all. I was hoping we could have a proper conversation. So, in your opinion, what are the most pressing problems in the world today? How about Russia invading the Ukraine? Election tampering? Refugees? Questioning science? There's no right answer." He waited, impatiently.

Basma's doe-like eyes shift around in their sockets in response to the thousands of neurons firing rapidly in her head. Could it be something in a newspaper headline she may have caught, or perhaps it was something she had overheard Shafal mentioning to Ahmed. They loved to talk about such matters.

"Do you have a brain or what?" he asked. It was cold and callous, done intentionally to ignite something in her. Even so, Basma didn't understand that. She stared back perplexed. "What's the matter with you?" He lashed out. "Can't you think for yourself? You act like a stupid child! But you're an adult. I don't get it. It really pisses me off."

"Wh... what is it that you want me to say?" she asked, trembling. "Tell me. I will say it."

He nearly blew a fuse. His fist slammed so hard against the wall above her head, the lamps on the tables shook. Basma burst into tears. At this, he threw up his hands in defeat. He got up off the bed and reached for his clothes. "I can't take this anymore," he said, shaking his head. "Get dressed, I want to get out of here, now."

Afraid he might retaliate in some awful way, she remained on the bed wiping her eyes and sniffling.

"I said, GET DRESSED! I'm sick of this shit. I can't even have a normal conversation with you."

When she didn't move, he calmed down and sat on the bed with his back turned. Moments passed in silence. He reached for his pack of cigarettes on the nightstand, put one to his mouth and lit it. Taking a deep draw on it, he exhaled a cloud of smoke into the air like an actor he'd seen in an old Hollywood movie. Then he turned to look at her. She was quivering like a hurt animal. He carefully placed the lit cigarette on the edge of the nightstand, and leaned over to look into her eyes. She stopped shaking. He pulled back the sheet and sucked her nipple. Her eyes blinked slowly. He buried his face in her bosom while caressing her body. Something stirred inside of her. She could feel a warm sensation spreading from her belly down to her feet.

Slipping beneath the covers, the Bakery Guy climbed on top of her. Immediately, her body locked up and, once again, terror-filled eyes stared back at him. He ignored it and pushed his knee down between her thighs to pry them apart.

"Please, please. You cannot do this!"

Proceeding with force, he managed to spread her legs apart and was preparing to thrust himself inside her. But the look of horror on Basma's face at that very moment made him go limp. There was no possible way he could continue. Angry at defeat, he rolled over and got up adjusting his briefs.

Trembling now, Basma finally leaped from the bed, pulling at the well-tucked sheet in the hope it would envelop her. Yet she was unable to loosen it without considerable effort, so she used her arms to hide her body from him as she rushed into the bathroom shutting the door.

For a moment, the Bakery Guy just stood there with his hands on his hips staring at the closed door. Suddenly, he scooped up her clothes in a huff, trotted over to the bathroom, thrust the door open, threw her clothes at her and slammed the door shut.

She dressed quickly, but took her time washing her tear-stained cheeks and securing the hijab on her head.

It was a good while before she mustered up enough courage to face him. There was no doubt in her mind that this was the last time he'd want to see her. She felt relieved. She'd go back to her normal routine life and would never ever go into that bakery again. Shafal will never know about any of this, and she would live.

Looking at her reflection in the mirror, a new calm came over her as she realized she had survived once again. But when she finally exited the bathroom, the Bakery Guy had disappeared.

A new terror gripped her. Now, she was stranded in a motel room on a highway, and she didn't know where she was.

Grabbing her purse from the chair, she ran across the room to the front door, yanked it open, wildly, and stumbled out. She backtracked along the row of rooms and made her way to a familiar staircase at the far end. She gripped the metal rail and began descending rapidly, skipping steps. But her pace was so frantic she missed a step and nearly tumbled to the bottom. She cried out. Luckily, no one heard it.

By the time her feet touched solid ground, Basma was so out of breath and crazed, she could barely take another step. Why did he do this to her? Why?

Tearful, she hobbled out toward the parking lot dotted with cars, not really knowing where she was going. Beyond the parking lot, cars and tractor-trailers zoomed left and right along the four-lane highway. Overhead, the sun was much lower in the sky than it had been the other times, when they left the motel. Shafal would surely be home before her. What on earth could she possibly tell him? More lies, of course. After all, she wanted to live.

Delirious with fear, she plodded aimlessly behind three parked cars and then turned left cutting between a blue Honda Civic and a large black SUV. Maybe the office could call her a cab. Shafal would have to pay the driver. It was hopeless.

When she cleared the last car, she spotted a red car with the rear lights on. Familiar music drifted out from a half-opened window. Was she imagining this? Tears blurring her vision, she hesitated towards it as if it were a mirage that would surely disappear. Yet there, in the driver's seat was the Bakery Guy, nonchalantly sipping his favorite drink.

An overwhelming sense of relief engulfed her. With joyful tears, she jogged the remaining few yards.

"I'm sorry, I'm sorry!" She fell in beside him.

Bakery Guy cocked an eyebrow and holstered the can in the cup-holder. He stared at her, still vexed. She looked away, self-consciously. She wanted to say, 'thank you for not leaving me', but remained silent.

He also started to speak, but instead, he seized hold of the gear-shift and forced it into drive.

***

That night, while Shafal worked the late shift and her boys visited with friends, Basma settled her mind by securing loose buttons on Abdel and Ahmed's white shirts. She replayed her adventure with the Bakery Guy in her mind while repairing the frayed cuffs of Shafal's old blue zippered parker.

She was amazed at how relieved she had felt when she saw the Bakery Guy's car waiting for her. He hadn't abandoned her after all. Never mind that she had run into the bathroom to get away from him minutes earlier. Never mind that he didn't apologize or say one single word to her the entire trip back. She had been relieved to be in his car and she had hesitated before getting out, expecting him to say "Thursday" or 'next week" or, more likely, "Don't bother to come again". However, he said absolutely nothing. She had fumbled noisily with the door handle reinforcing the fact that she was about to leave. He continued to remain silent, focusing straight ahead.

The walk to her apartment had seemed mercilessly longer. And when she unlocked the front door of the building, she caught a glimpse of her reflection in the pane. Her eyes were sad and swollen, her hijab too tight. Shafal barely glanced her way when he did arrive thirty minutes later. Dinner wasn't ready, but instead of throwing the expected tantrum, he decided to take a long shower. When had he ever done that?

And so tonight, Basma was feeling particularly grateful being home, being safe. She gladly settled into her wifely duties stitching and mending. Her mind was clear as she gripped the needle firmly. Then, out of nowhere, it came: a memory.

She's lying on a bed, hands are touching her, stroking and caressing. She wants to scream out, to push away the hands. Only, a warm sensation floods her body, arresting her attention.

She struggles against it, determined to take refuge in her head, as she had done since her wedding night, but the warm liquid sensation coaxed her back down into her body and once again she experienced something entirely new: a tingling between her legs. It wasn't unpleasant... in fact it... Then, he was on top of her and...

A loud thump startled her, followed by banging at the door. She placed the needle safely in a fold of fabric and laid the garment aside. As soon as she opened the door, Tariq Tali wobbled through supporting Shafal around the waist. Shafal was conscious but groggy and there were bruises on his face. For a moment, Basma was too stunned to speak, having never seen Shafal in a vulnerable position before.

Tariq helped Shafal into a chair in the living room. Basma snapped back, rushed over and began stroking his swollen face.

"What has happened? Was there an accident?" she asked.

Tariq answered for him. "Some young boys tried to rob him."

"Oh no... they hurt you," she gasped, covering her mouth with both hands. Shafal shook his head.

"I hurt them," he said defiantly.

"That was a very stupid thing you did," Tariq threw in, obviously annoyed. "You know those boys could have killed you."

"I cannot just give them money I work for," he responded angrily, more at the situation than at Tariq.

"When it is your money or your life, you give up the money."

"Not without a fight."

Tariq shook his head, exasperated, and walked back to the front door.

"Don't come in tomorrow or Thursday. Just rest... I will pick you up on Friday morning."

That was an order.

Tariq Tali was Shafal's only friend. They had met at the mosque when their children were still in kindergarten. Tariq had helped Shafal get the job as a cab driver in the first place. And, for the first half of the week, they shared the same cab. Shafal drove it during the day till 5:30 p.m., and then Tariq would work the night shift finishing around 3 a.m.

Sometimes, Shafal worked out of a Brooklyn garage on night and weekend shifts. So, it was Tariq he called after the thieves had run off. The blows he had received to the head made him dizzy.

"Shafal, you have to stop working nights," Basma demanded, when they were alone. "Now I understand why it is so dangerous." She became more emotional, "And why do you have to fight with these people? Huh? They are crazy! What if they would have killed you? Huh? What then?"

Shafal rubbed his bruised face. Basma jumped up and rushed out of the room then returned shortly with a small bottle of peroxide, cotton balls, and a cold wet cloth. She proceeded to dab Shafal's bruised face with the peroxide and press the wet cloth to his forehead, tilting his head back to rest.

He allowed his eyes to close for a moment, then with bitter satisfaction, he said: "They ran away with nothing!"

***

The following week, the recreation room was crowded. Basma hastily packed up the craft kits. A commotion on the news caught her attention. She stopped to watch. On the screen, a large group of young Syrian men ran through the streets of Damascus yelling angrily at American soldiers. Some picked up small stones and threw them at the soldiers, who practiced restraint throughout. The scene then cuts to the President of the United States who explained that "Having a few boots on the ground in the capital, at this time, is merely a precautionary measure. There are no plans to invade. I repeat, there are no plans to invade."

Basma was captivated. When the story ended, she became thoughtful for a long moment. Yes, there were many things happening in the world around her, but her sphere of awareness was limited. If it didn't impact her life directly, why should she care? She did worry about her mother and siblings, back in Yemen. But what could she, a woman, do about it, anyway? Perhaps, she could discuss this with the Bakery Guy.

She began a dialogue with him in her head where she imagined asking thoughtful questions about what she'd seen on the news and he would answer in a way that she could understand. This new inner dialogue continued throughout the repacking of the box.

At that very moment, in the Chappelle Bakery, three blocks away, the bakers were busy removing hot bagels and bread from hot trays. In the adjacent corridor, the Bakery Guy leaned up against the doorframe of Alfred Chappelle's office, his mouth curled with disdain at another lecture.

Al was a tall muscular man, except for his exceptionally large girth. His employees often joked that he had sampled too many of his own bagels, but that wasn't the case. He never liked bagels much. His preference was Kobe steak and plenty of ale from the tap to wash it down.

He sat comfortably with his legs stretched out on top of his desk, wearing his usual silk print shirt over a white tee and tailored brown pants. Behind him on a counter was a stainless-steel espresso machine. Hot steam rose from a tiny cup of the extremely strong liquid, which he managed to down about six times per day. He was on his fourth.

"Look, Vincent," Al said, gesturing with his hands for emphasis. "I give the orders around here, and when I tell you I want something done a certain way, you do it that way. Got it?"

Vincent, the bakery guy, nodded his head, glancing at the floor intermittently.

"Now, you're supposed to be the smart one around here, college and all," Al continued, "but why weren't you smart enough to know that the club you managed was owned by a crook? That guy was only good at making other guys disappear. The cops knew it, but not you. No, you were too busy messing around with the ladies."

Vincent peered back at the bakers as they put the piping hot bagels onto sparkling silver platters. There was tension in the air. They appeared to be absorbed in what they were doing, but their ears stretched to catch every word Al said. It was known that none of the men cared much for Vincent. He was cocky, too sure of himself, especially around the female employees and the female customers. Also, they resented the fact that he rarely listened to anything Al said and still had a job.

"That fancy club was a front. See?" Al went on, picking up the hot espresso. "That's why you got in trouble." He carefully raised the cup to his lips, blew on it and sipped. Vincent watched with loathing.

"Now here," Al said smugly, "you're just sales help. A server, that's all. But you still have an opportunity to—"

In a huff, Vincent gave Al 'the finger' and stormed passed the bakers out through the back door, leaving both Al and the bakers stunned.

Half an hour later, Vincent pulled up to the usual spot around the corner from the bus stop. He turned off the AC, rolled down the window and rested his arm on the door. As he waited, he drummed on the steering wheel appearing confident that the woman would show up and on time, even though he hadn't ordered her to.

Then, like clockwork, she opened the door, got in beside him, pulled the door shut and looked straight ahead waiting for him to drive off. As usual, she didn't acknowledge him and he couldn't think of anything to say to her, so they just sat in silence.

He had always acted as if he were in complete control of the situation, now he appeared to be having conflicting emotions. He wasn't sure why, and he wasn't the type to process any of it. For that reason, he was as confused, uncomfortable and insecure, in that moment, as Basma was.

Finally, he turned and gazed at her with such fierce intensity that Basma could actually feel the energy pouring from his eyes engulf her. She struggled to maintain her composure by sitting upright. When she couldn't take it any longer, she faced him.

"What?" she inquired uneasily. Their eyes locked in a long moment, but the fire in his was too much for her. She looked away, flushed and began to fidget with her fingers. "Did I do something wrong?" she pressed with concern. At that, Vincent let out an exasperated groan and clutched the wheel with both hands. He thought for a minute or two before slowly turning on the ignition.

He cast another look her way and said, "Fasten your seat belt."

CHAPTER 7

I t was one of those unexpected, blissfully hot days in mid-March, and nobody wanted to work. Winter had faded fast, and spring was wide-awake. Global warming, no doubt.

Foregoing the motel excursion, Vincent ended up taking Basma to a newly landscaped park that was alive with energy. Everywhere, young women had shunned tanning salons to lay bareback on the grassy fields. On the bike path that encircled the park, cyclists weaved around joggers, baby carriages and people on roller blades. Picnickers dodged the occasional Frisbee, children ran around screaming with delight while birds chirped and lovers whispered to each other.

In the midst of it all, Basma looked awkward traipsing along in a dowdy brown sweater and her ankle-length, floral polyester dress. This time, however, she wore a pastel orange silk hijab instead of the usual black or white one.

Vincent walked several steps ahead of her. Over black jeans and white tee shirt, he had thrown on a khaki zipped jacket, rolling up the sleeves to his elbow in the hot weather.

As they walk, Basma became distracted by women skating, jogging, riding bikes in shorts and skimpy tops or sunbathing in bikinis. Under a tree, she spotted a couple lying together kissing and stroking each other—in public! Her face flushed and she turned away. How could people do something like that outside and with other people around? She wondered. Then she saw toddlers playing near the smooching couple and "My God!" sprung from her lips.

Oblivious to everything except what was churning in his own head, Vincent, too, let his thoughts become audible.

"And that jerk!" he exclaimed, to no one in particular, "I hate taking orders from him. On second thought, I hate taking orders from anybody. He's worse than my mother," he said, then paused. "He's gonna tell me how to treat customers? It's not a five-star restaurant. It's a fucking bakery, for Christ's sake!"

Basma, walking just a few steps behind, commented, "You can leave."

"Oh, I intend to!"

Suddenly, he jerked his head around, surprised, as if he'd forgotten she was with him. He slowed his pace. She caught up and fell in alongside him. "Look," he said. "A while ago, I got into some... something happened." He shot a quick glance her way and saw that she was eager for more. "I... uh... did some time... you understand?"

She gave him no indication whether she did or not. She was too captivated by his vulnerability. She didn't recognize it as being that and certainly couldn't have articulated it that way, but for the first time, she'd lost her sense of ineptitude.

"Anyway, he gave me this job as a favor for my stepdad." Then Vincent mumbled angrily to himself: "He's definitely not doing anything for me. But that's okay, soon I'll have my own place." The thought seemed to lift his spirits a little and he smiled at a row of yellow and purple pansies along the edge of the pavement.

They walked a few more yards and discovered a secluded bench overlooking a duck pond. Vincent gestured for Basma to sit down and he followed. She watched him pull out his red pack of cigarettes, flip open the top, remove one, put it to his lips and return the box to his pocket.

Assuming she was judging him, he said: "I know, I know. It's a bad habit."

Actually, Basma had more curiosity than judgment about smoking. None of the people in her family smoked. Kensasha Lewis didn't smoke, nor did Mrs. Sadawi. She continued to watch his ritual: taking out the lighter, flicking the top, guiding the flame carefully to the tip of the cigarette and then inhaling. She saw his body relax for the first time that day.

"I started when I was thirteen," he confessed, exhaling smoke into the air. "I wanted to be like my father." He leaned forward, resting on his thighs and stared off.

Basma, with her demure posture, was uncertain what to do next—so she closed her eyes, tilted her head up toward the sky. A subtle fragrance of apple blossoms filled her nose and her face took on a serene child-like glow.

After a while, Vincent looked her way. He observed how the sun's rays were illuminating her dark olive skin and smiled. But he still appeared somewhat troubled inside. Finally, he asked, "So... uh... how have you been?"

Basma slowly opened her eyes, looked down, shyly, at her hands folded in her lap. "Fine."

He waited politely for her to elaborate. When she didn't, he ran his fingers through his golden blond hair several times—a gestured often done habitually when he needed to repress strong emotion. And then, noticing the unconventional color of her hijab and the floral-patterned dress, he attempted a new strategy.

"You look pretty today."

She glanced at him, surprised at the compliment and at the sincerity in his voice, and lowered her eyes self-consciously.

He grinned. "Is it for me?" Was it? she wondered. He saw her thinking it over, so he threw up his hands and said, "Just kidding!"

Their eyes met, blue green to sable brown. Something shifted. The air surrounding them turned sweeter.

Basma was the first to look away. She smoothed out her dress— unnecessarily. A warm breeze happened by and slipped up under her hijab, tugged it back exposing the top of her head. She reached up quickly to readjust it securely around her face. Vincent watched, and then he took hold of her hand and examined it, stroking the top skin with his long-tapered fingers.

"Umm, I didn't notice before... you have strong hands for a woman... they're nice. I like them." He stroked her palm. "You work hard."

Basma looked on curiously as if the hand he held didn't belong to her. Yet, she was very aware of the feel of his much softer skin against her own.

When he let go, she stretched her hand out before her face as if seeing it for the first time. Vincent observed her.

After a while, she began to twist and fold the sleeve of her dress nervously, while taking unfocused glances at the duck pond and quick ones at Vincent.

Hesitant, she finally asked, "Wh-why are we here?"

"Because it's a nice place. My father brought me here when I was as a kid. He was a musician, you know, late nights in the clubs on weekends, so we came here during the week." He saw her staring back at him "What? Don't you think this is a nice place to be?" She nodded, but still waited. "Oh, so you want to go, is that it?" Without waiting for a response and trying to hide his disappointment, he said, "All right, I'll take you home. Come on." He stood up quickly.

Startled by the abrupt change, Basma lingered.

Vincent grabbed her hand to pull her to her feet.

"No!" she exclaimed. "I don't want to go home… now. There's more time." He let go of her hand and studied her face a moment.

"What are you saying?"

"I want to stay… longer. But… if you don't want to…" She looked up at him with innocent eyes, waiting.

"No, I thought you wanted to go." She shook her head. He sat back down.

"Is your father still working in the clubs?" Basma asked.

"No, he's dead," replied Vincent, matter-of-factly. "Drug overdose."

"My father is dead, too," Basma informed. "He liked poetry."

Vincent smiled and took a long drag on the cigarette. He tilted back his head and coolly exhaled and then he extinguished it.

Once again, she watched this Bakery Guy from the corners of her eyes, as they sat in a pregnant silence—each taking in the lushness of nature all around them.

***

Spring arrived officially that Saturday.

On a busy main street, Basma and Imani Sadawi strolled amongst families of varying Arabic and Indian ethnicities, all engaged in their weekly shopping rituals. Always regally dressed, Imani Sadawi stood out amongst the crowd. Her long salt and pepper hair was pulled back into a twist, and her black sheer headscarf was loosely draped around her head revealing long ornate gold earrings. She talked rapidly—flitting from one subject to the next—while getting distracted by the wares on display. Basma, on the other hand, barely listened to Mrs. Sadawi; instead, she observed the couples passing by.

Mrs. Sadawi spotted a fabric shop and pulled Basma in. The store was crowded with women. Several large bins were piled with yards of colorful fabrics. In the hectic crush of women scrimmaging over the piles of cheap material, Basma felt claustrophobic. She began to breathe heavily.

Panicking, she squeezed and pushed her way back to the front door to wait for Mrs. Sadawi outside.

Embarrassed, she stood awkwardly just beyond the entrance until the moment her eye caught something directly across the street. It was a bouquet of tulips! The color resembled a blazing flame, a juicy ripe mango, and the hijab that the Bakery Guy liked. She dashed for it.

Later, when Mrs. Sadawi exited the fabric shop holding two large bundles, she looked and down the street for Basma.

"Where is that girl?" she mumbled.

"Mrs. Sadawi!" Imani looked in the direction of the voice. She saw Basma crossing the street carrying two bunches of bright, fiery-orange tulips and a few other packages. Her face was beaming. As soon as Basma was next to her, she opened up one of the packages. "Look, Mrs. Sadawi!" she exclaimed. "Nice lotion. And very pretty flowers." She hugged them.

"Oh yes, they are quite nice," Imani replied. "Basma, I didn't know you liked flowers so much. I never see them in your home."

Basma lowered her head. "I never thought to have them before," she replied, amazed. "I want to make the walls different colors. The rooms are so dreary now. Is it okay?

"What? Painting? It is your apartment," Imani responded. "You need to ask Shafal if it is okay."

Basma sighed at that reminder, but she was undeterred.

They continued to walk along the congested boulevard. Up ahead of them was a row of street vendors. One sold scarves, baseball caps, T-shirts and socks. Another table was laden with various fragrances of incense, incense holders and miniature statues of Hindu Gods. The seller was a petite Hindu woman. Right next to her was a large African woman with a traditional head wrap sitting behind an elaborate earring and bracelet display.

Basma left Mrs. Sadawi's side and walked over to the earring table. She pointed to a pair and asked, "How much do you sell these for?"

The African woman stood up, leaned over the display to see which ones. "Ten dollars," she replied.

Basma looked thoughtfully at the other table of wares.

Imani soon joined her at the vendor's table. "Why are you interested in these things? No one will see them, you are always covered."

Basma, absorbed in thought, glanced up at Imani, but didn't actually hear the question.

"Do you make these?" Basma asked the African woman.

"Some of them I make," the woman replied with a heavy accent.

"How much money do you spend to make one pair?" The African woman stared back at her.

"Basma!" Imani said, discreetly. "That is not a proper question to ask. That is her personal business. Basma, genuinely surprised that her simple question may have been inappropriate, replied, "I only wanted to see if this is a good business to have."

The African woman studied her a moment and determined that Basma was being sincere.

"I buy most of these in large quantities at a very low price." The woman returned to her seat behind the table. "It is a good business if you are in the right location. Manhattan is very good. More money. But my husband couldn't take me in the car today. Are you from Sudan?"

"No, I am from Yemen. Are you from Sudan?" Basma then asked.

"No, I come from Senegal." Basma nodded and smiled. She couldn't remember ever talking to a stranger as casually as that. Imani joined in.

"I am an African too. I come from Egypt," she informed them, proudly.

The African woman nodded and smiled at both of them.

"Okay, bye-bye," Basma said, and turned away.

Imani looked at the woman awkwardly as Basma began walking down the street. Irritated, she called out: "Wait! Basma." Then she looked closer at the earrings. With her arms were full of packages, Imani struggled to try on a pair as Basma continued walking. "I'll take these," Imani concluded.

Minutes later, when Imani caught up with Basma, she was standing in front of a women's dress shop, absorbed in the window display. Basma immediately turned to her grinning excitedly, but Imani did not smile back.

"Basma! I just do not understand how you can spend all that time talking to that woman and not buy anything."

Basma stopped grinning. "Why do I have to buy?"

Imani sucked her teeth, dumbfounded.

Resuming her excitement, Basma announced: "I am thinking about making a business. But there are so many different kinds. What do you think is the best business for me?" Her innocent child-like eyes widened with expectation. Imani studied Basma as if she hadn't really seen her all day.

"I can't answer an important question like that, now, Basma," she said, awkwardly. "I need to think about it." Shaking her head again, "You are full of surprises today."

Basma looked up at the powder blue sky, and exclaimed, "It is a beautiful day!"

Imani raised an eyebrow. Basma grinned back and tugged at the older woman's arm, affectionately, and they continued down the bustling thoroughfare, weaving their way in and around the Saturday afternoon crowd.

That evening, when Abdel opened the front door of the apartment, it was quiet inside. He proceeded, casually, through the living room but halted halfway. His eyes scanned the room, widening with surprise. He smiled to himself. Four glass jars of orange tulips were placed around the room. Their faded brown-paisley-velveteen couch had been revived with colored pillows in purple, lime green, orange and pomegranate.

At dinner, Shafal talked about how wasteful it was to buy such flowers.

"They serve no purpose whatsoever," he reasoned. "It is a ridiculous expense. They just sit in water for a few days and then die. Who has time to sit and look at flowers? Don't you ever do that again," he ordered.

However, Basma had felt so much happier having fresh flowers around her that once again, she did something out of character.

"The room looks warmer with the flowers," she pointed out. "If you are worried about them dying too quickly, maybe I should get the ones in the pot. They will last very long. All I have to do is put water on them."

Shafal stared at her. Abdel and Ahmed stared at Shafal, waiting for the explosion.

"Did you hear what I just said?"

"Of course, Shafal, you are right." Basma replied, cautiously, "But the ones in the pots are much cheaper and…"

"What is the matter with you?" he screamed. "What is this obsession with those stupid flowers?"

She forced herself to remain calm. "I see other women buying flowers for their families," she continued, unyielding. "And… and I just wanted to make our home look better too."

"I don't want you to spend one penny of my money on that stuff. You want flowers—you use the money you work for." He figured that would put an end to the matter since Basma barely had enough spending money left over after giving two-thirds of her salary to him.

"Can we paint the living room?" she asked.

***

Wearing a brand-new powder-blue hijab on her head, Basma got into Vincent's car again. However, this time, she looked over and smiled at him. He returned the smile, and immediately, they both looked away attacked by a sudden bout of shyness. Then Basma's elbow brushed against a bag on the cup holder between them, making a crackling sound.

"Oh yeah, that's for you. The bread and…" He picked up the bag and took out a tiny custard tart with strawberries and blueberries surrounding a tiny mint leaf in the center. "If I remember correctly, this was your favorite." He handed it to her. Her eyes widened with delight. Reaching into the bag again, he said: "But in case I'm wrong, I brought this one too," and pulled out a baby blackout cake with a tiny cherry on top. Basma cupped her mouth in surprise.

"But it is so much," she said, softly. "Thank you." She took a bite from the custard tart. "Umm," she moaned. Then, holding the tart up to his lips, she said, "Here, you have some too."

Vincent shook his head: "No, it's for you."

"But it is too much. You have some."

He put his hand up to block her. "Look, I can have that every day. I just… got it for you. You can take the other one home." Basma yielded and took another bite of the pastry.

This time, Vincent splurged on a room at a four-star motel near La Guardia airport. Then, instead of ordering her to undress, he began to undress her himself, slowly.

She watched him trustingly as he removed her head covering and kissed her neck. She closed her eyes while he gently unbraided her hair and combed it loose with his fingers. He pulled it over her face, playfully. She responded by pretending to be disinterested. She no longer felt self-conscious of his hands or his eyes on her. And when had anyone played with her hair?

Since that day in the park, she had looked forward to being with him again. Being with him had somehow morphed into a secret adventure for her, never knowing where they were going or what to expect. She knew this was wrong. Dangerous. Dishonorable. But what could she do about it now, not show up?

He removed her dress, stepped behind her and planted quick kisses across her back. Each time he exposed a part of her body he kissed it and told it how beautiful it was.

She let her head fall back, rapturously, as Vincent removed her full white cotton slip. He knelt before her navel and pudgy stomach.

"Oh, belly button, you are so beautiful!" he said in a playfully, seductive tone.

She giggled at the word: belly button.

He moved his lips to her stomach and said, "Oh tummy, you are so…" His lips tickled and she jumped, struggling hard to suppress another giggle.

When he slid her underpants down to her ankles, and continued kissing her, she became breathless. Her self-consciousness returned. Even so, Vincent proved to be skilled in pleasuring a woman.

He carefully led her to the bed, kissed her face but not her mouth. He made love to her ears, her neck and her shoulders with just the touch of his lips and his tongue. A whole cadre of sensations she never knew existed, suddenly awakened inside of her and for the first time in her life, she actually began to moan with pleasure. Her ability to shut down, to disconnect from her body, had ceased.

The moaning grew deeper. Louder. Suddenly… Vincent stopped.

Startled, her eyes flew open. She wanted more of whatever that was.

Instead, Vincent rolled onto his side, and just lay there watching her. Embarrassed, she tried to cover herself. He grinned, victoriously. Then, he pulled her hands away from her breasts and caressed them playfully.

"You know your heart is beating very fast," he teased. Alarmed, she gave him a worried look. "Are you really that naive?" It was caustic.

Basma didn't understand the word: "naïve", but was hurt by his tone.

She sat up and pulled at the sheet to cover herself. He tugged at her shoulder to pull her back down, but she resisted with an expression of sadness, disappointment, and confusion. One minute, he was making her body come alive using words that made her feel beautiful, special— even loved—for the first time. All in spite of her expanding hips and her disregard for the American obsession with hair removal, and the next minute he was insulting her.

"I want to go home!" she announced dolefully.

"Oh, come on… we got a few more minutes," he said, hugging her from behind.

"I want to go home, now," she demanded and wiggled free. Taken aback by the firmness in her voice, he said, "Fine."

***

Of all the varying job responsibilities Kensasha had assigned her at Ridgefield, Basma's favorite was helping the female patients make art projects. At 10 a.m. each morning, she and another assistant would begin placing various games and craft-making supplies on each table. It was rare that Basma and the other attendant would exchange words. In fact, Basma never initiated casual conversations with anyone. But on this particular morning, she was especially aloof. She was staring right through the box of crayons that she had just laid on the table, when Kensasha Lewis appeared in the doorway and headed straight for her.

"Excuse me, Basma." The agitation in Kensasha's voice made her stiffen, she turned slowly to see her beloved supervisor's eyes piercing a hole clean through her.

Kensasha hesitated a moment, when she saw the fear on Basma's face. Then she remembered why she had come and relinquished her need for diplomacy.

"Do you recall the Nichols' file, the one we couldn't locate?" she asked, her hands on her hips. "Well, I just found it." She didn't sound pleased.

Basma put a board game back in the box hastily and headed out of the recreation hall to Kensasha's office.

Kensasha followed behind her briskly. "I also found quite a few folders in the wrong drawer."

This caught the ever-listening ears of Martha Cohen whose bright pink lips curled with pleasure.

When they reached the office, Kensasha stationed herself in the center of the room, and lifted her arm. "Take a look in that cabinet over there," she ordered, pointing to a white file cabinet that was separated from the rest.

Basma shot her a worried glance, and then hurried over to the lone cabinet, pulled open a drawer labeled M-P, and fingered through the hanging files. Suddenly, she stopped and looked back at

Kensasha with embarrassment. Behind a folder labeled 'Mackenhei-mer' was one labeled 'Nichols'. Fighting back tears, Basma pulled out the Nichols folder and handed it to Kensasha.

"I am sorry, Miss Lewis. I… I don't know—"

"Well, at least it's found, and I don't have to keep apologizing to Dr. Wexler." With the folder under her arm, Kensasha proceeded to the door, but paused and turned just enough to insure Basma could hear her and said with an unusually stern tone: "Go through that cabinet right now and make doubly sure that all of the folders represent only the patients who are deceased.

In the stillness of the room, Basma stared at the single white cabinet, and at the row of gray cabinets assigned to the current patients, and was baffled by her own actions.

She ended up staying until 3:30 p.m. going through all the file drawers twice to make sure each folder was where it belonged. Of all people, Kensasha was the one person she most admired and wanted to please. Apart from Imani Sadawi, Kensasha was the only other person who had always shown her kindness and respect and treated her more like a friend than an employee.

Still shaken by the upset as she exited the building, Basma fumbled through her handbag in search of her Metro card in case she'd have to run for the bus. When she reached the front gate, she happened to look up and there was Shafal leaning against his cab. Her footsteps faltered.

He frowned and checked his watch the moment he spotted her.

"I've been waiting since 3," he said. "Why are you late coming out?"

She couldn't answer him right away. She was too busy trying to figure out why he was there in the first place. He hadn't mentioned anything about meeting her. This was the first time he'd shown up at her job unannounced. Thank God, it wasn't Tuesday or Thursday.

After a while, she responded, "I had extra work to finish for Miss Lewis and…" her voice trailed off, "No one told me you were waiting."

Shafal noticed that she wasn't particularly pleased to see him. "I didn't call. My last fare from the airport was a few minutes from here. I can drive you home."

He was aware of Basma's emotional swings: one day she'd be sulking around withdrawn, the next day she'd have sudden bouts of euphoria. Her recent obsession with wasting money on flowers and wall painting was a perfect example.

Lately, she wouldn't look him straight in the eye—instead, whenever their eyes met unexpectedly, Basma would quickly turn away and find something with which to occupy herself. Now, he wasn't a stupid man, but for the life of him, he couldn't figure out what was going through that bird brain of hers.

She walked around to the passenger's side of the cab and opened the door to get in.

"Wait," Shafal said. "I think I want that bread since I'm here." Basma cleared her throat. Shafal ignored it and continued, "Let's walk so I don't have to worry about parking." She closed the door and rejoined him on the sidewalk and together they strolled to the Chappelle Bakery.

If she was shaken earlier, this topped everything. Heart pounding, she prayed all the way that the Bakery Guy would not be there.

When they arrived at the bustling establishment, there were five servers behind the marble counter, each rushing to fill orders, but no Bakery Guy. Believing her prayers were answered she mumbled a thank you to herself.

While waiting to be served, Shafal took a curious interest in the shop's layout. With his hands behind his back, he paced up and down studying the interior design of the space in a discerning manner, as though he had suddenly transformed into a man of culture. Next, it was the many varieties of bread and pastries, which attracted his attention. He wandered over to the sampling table with its vase of fresh cut sunflowers and its china plates with cubes of assorted breads that a staff person was busy replenishing. Squeezing past the other customers, Shafal sampled cubes from every saucer with the air of a gourmet before deciding which he preferred.

All the while, Basma waited by the counter, her teeth clinched, staring at the hardwood floor, praying to be served next so they could get out of there.

Shafal rejoined her and offered her a bread cube. She shook her head and kept it lowered.

When more customers came through the door, one of the counter personnel shouted, "We need more help out here!"

Someone came from the back and asked, "Who's next?"

Shafal raised his hand and said, "We are."

The server maneuvered through the other servers to get to the customer with his hand up and asked, "What can I get… for you?" Hearing that voice, Basma raised her head and saw dazzlingly handsome Vincent, The Bakery Guy, standing before her, causing her breath to catch in her throat. He looked puzzled—unnerved—while the stupefying effect of having him and Shafal inches away from one another nearly stopped Basma's heart. She had a sudden urge to urinate.

"I like this one," Shafal said, shoving his hand with a bread cube in Vincent's face.

Avoiding Shafal's gaze, Vincent glanced at the cube, then at Basma and said with a blank expression, "That's our rosemary and onion focaccia. Very popular."

"Okay, we will have that" Shafal said with an air of importance and glanced at Basma who was playing the well-behaved, pious wife—just like he wanted.

Vincent turned to get the focaccia from the shelf. The next moment Shafal called out, "Wait! I want another bread too." He scanned the shelves and then asked Basma, "What's the name of that bread you always get?"

"Olive and tomato," Vincent responded, before Basma could.

"Yes, yes," Shafal said, pleased they were recognized as regular customers.

Steadying his hands, Vincent carefully wrapped each loaf with intense concentration taking twice as long as he normally would have. Then he handed Shafal the burgundy and gold bag and said, looking from one to the other, "$11.75." Her eyes still averted, Basma immediately withdrew a twenty-dollar bill from her purse to hand to Vincent.

"What are you doing?" Shafal scolded. He looked humiliated. "You think I need money from you?" He handed Vincent two ten-dollar bills instead, and Vincent went to get the change.

"But I always buy the food…" she responded, timorously.

"I let you so you can feel useful." Shafal continued angrily oblivious of their surroundings. "I provide for this family, not you!"

Vincent returned with Shafal's change and handed it to him with a disdainful expression that Shafal missed because his attention was focused on the money, which he counted carefully and pocketed.

"Okay, let's go!" he ordered Basma, grabbing her arm.

They moved to leave as Vincent gave his attention to another customer. But he glimpsed them, just moments before they cleared the outside window, in time to see Basma turn back with a rueful expression on her face.

CHAPTER 8

For months, Kensasha Lewis had been trying to coax Basma into breaking her routine of rushing home to make dinner for Shafal and have a late lunch with her instead. Why anyone would need to spend that long making a meal baffled her. She was aware Basma usually left work around 2 p.m., shopped for groceries and then went straight home to begin that long preparation just to please a husband who came home after 6pm. It was absurd. No wonder she was misplacing files! Surely, once in a while, the man wouldn't mind her picking up something already prepared. Why not just eat out? The things women do for men. Well, she was determined not to become one of those women. Her mother had been one, but she certainly wouldn't be.

Kensasha found herself intrigued by this woman, Imani Sadawi had suggested she hire. In the eight months that Basma had been at Ridgefield, not one employee had developed a friendship with her and Basma did little to change that.

At first, Kensasha assumed it was because of the whole 'niqab wearing' incident that occurred a while back when the elderly patients began to get frightened of Basma's attire, and she was subsequently asked not to wear the abaya, the black robe-like dress with the niqab or face covering, during work. But Basma had put up little resistance to all that. Actually, it was her husband who blew the

94

whole thing out of proportion, by threatening a lawsuit because he saw the nursing home's dress code as an attack against his religion. However, even with her hijab and white lab coat, they marginalized her. Of course, if this had bothered Basma in the least, no one would know it. In fact, Basma displayed little more than a need to blindly serve and obey.

In doing research for her doctoral dissertation called 'Women and the Psychology of Victimization', Kensasha had visited numerous women's shelters. Most of the women she interviewed didn't have an ounce of self-esteem because their husbands, boyfriends or fathers had beaten or insulted that out of them. They were the women who had returned home immediately after being released from a hospital and later, just barely escaped the morgue. She had no doubt that Basma was that type of woman: one who has no self-identity outside of the familial structure— no self, without a husband and children. Having a husband secured her purpose and her worth.

Still, for some reason she liked Basma. Basma didn't take up a lot of space—physically or emotionally. She didn't intrude or impose her problems on anyone. But it wasn't Basma's shy, coy, almost maidenly demeanor that Kensasha found intriguing, because she'd seen that amongst the women at the mosque. No, Basma had something else, a quality she couldn't yet define, but was determined to discover.

Now, finally, Kensasha found herself sitting in a bistro opposite her clerical assistant, Mrs. Basma Abseh.

Mortified by the bakery incident and still recovering from her mishap at work, Basma could barely concentrate on anything, let alone trying to restore Kensasha's confidence in her. Her head was spinning with thoughts and images of Shafal talking to the bakery guy. Did that really happen? Had Shafal noticed anything inappropriate between her and the Bakery Guy? Was he suspicious in the first place and that's why he wanted to go to the bakery with her?

Ever since her whole entanglement with that man, she'd done everything she could to be an even better wife and mother. The house was never cleaner. The meals had never tasted better. What more could she do?

"This is my first time in a restaurant," Basma informed with a childlike voice.

"Your husband never takes you out to dinner?" Kensasha asked, feigning surprise.

Basma shook her head. Kensasha let out a grunt, reached for her glass of water and sipped it. Basma, meanwhile, looked around sheepishly at the other diners, then back at Kensasha.

"Miss Lewis, I am very sorry about Mrs. Nichols' file. I don't know why..."

"Don't worry about it. We all make mistakes sometime." She smiled warmly at Basma and they continued waiting quietly for their order to arrive. Kensasha had taken the liberty and suggested a 'real' American meal for Basma to try. A cheese & mushroom burger deluxe. Basma, of course, complied.

Stealing a glance at Kensasha, Basma wondered how long it took to get her hair into so many tiny braids. She wouldn't dare ask. Then another more pressing question flitted through her mind. She attempted to say something, hesitated, and then tried again.

"Miss Lewis, why you are not married?" It was framed with genuine curiosity—after all, Kensasha was a very intelligent attractive young woman. Still, Kensasha was caught off guard, not by the directness of the question, but by who had asked it. Until that very moment, Basma had never asked her or anyone at Ridgefield, for that matter, anything that opened up personal communication. The innocent curiosity in the question required a sincere answer.

"Because... uh... God, there are so many reasons. Where should I begin?" She laughed to herself. "Umm, well, I guess it's because I haven't fallen in love with anyone that I want to spend my life with... yet. I am dating a very intelligent, attentive man right now. I doubt if I'll marry him, though." Kensasha paused to contemplate.

The only men she'd ever fallen for were either dead icons, like Malcolm X, or characters in a novel or, more so, the novelist, himself, or the poet, the philosopher—but a regular flesh and blood, nine-to-fiver, simply didn't excite her one bit. The Sundays watching football, or baseball or golfing-with-the-boys-kind-of-guy, didn't interest her. A money man, someone who just worked for money like a Wall St. trader, financier or banker—but who didn't create, produce, or manufacture anything or save anyone's life—could never interest her as a mate. After a while, she added: "You know, I may never marry. And that's okay with me."

Basma's mouth actually dropped open in shock. "But how will you have children?"

"I don't need to be married to have a child, Basma." It was unintentionally brusque. "Surely you know that. Besides… I don't really want children."

This baffled Basma even more. She replied, "But it is a woman's duty to have children."

"Well, I certainly don't believe having children is a duty. I believe it should be a conscious choice. A desire. And if a person doesn't want them, they definitely shouldn't have them."

Basma stared back, dismayed, at the much younger woman who had always treated her with kindness and protected her from Martha Cohen—, yet she often felt incapable of holding a conversation with her. Now, for the first time in her life, Basma had the compulsion to debate.

After taking a moment to ponder Kensasha's statement, she said: "But you are Muslim."

"Yes. I am. By choice." Kensasha knew where this was going. "And I'm also an American."

The waiter arrived with a tray and carefully placed their orders on the table. Kensasha continued talking as he did so.

"You know all Muslim women don't share the same views. Imani says she wishes she'd never had children, even though she's always rushing to her daughter's side whenever she calls."

Basma's eyes widen with surprise at this disclosure about Mrs. Sadawi. Then she felt her heart sink. Mrs. Sadawi was her role model; someone to aspire to. Well, maybe not in the self-assured way Mrs. Sadawi related to Mr. Sadawi, but certainly in the way she put her children first and how she managed her home. Everyone knew Imani Sadawi, and they all listened when she spoke.

Kensasha reached for the pepper and sprinkled it over her broiled fish. She opened two small packets of butter and added that to a side of baked potato and broccoli.

Basma, still mulling over what Kensasha said about Mrs. Sadawi, hadn't even looked down at her food when Kensasha began to eat.

Leaving her mentor by the wayside, Basma proclaimed proudly: "I believe all women should be married and have children."

"Do you?" Kensasha replied, patiently. "Or is that what you were raised to believe?" Basma stared back. "Anyway, all women can't have children, nor should they." She noticed Basma hadn't touched anything. "Is there something wrong with your food?" she asked, "It smells delicious."

Only then did Basma look down at her plate. She peeked beneath the hamburger bun. What she saw was very appetizing. She reached for her knife and fork and began to cut into the burger. Mushrooms blanketed with melting cheese oozed out from the bun, and several fries tumbled off the plate. Basma became flustered trying to organize the mess. Kensasha smiled knowingly.

"It's best to just pick it up with your hands and bite it," she offered. "That's the way we eat it."

Basma was relieved to hear this. She lifted the burger, delicately, and took a bite. Then she nodded with approval.

Kensasha studied her for a moment then grew serious.

"Many cultures put a high price on marriage just to continue the bloodline or gain wealth and position. They also force women to marry so they won't be a financial burden. But I can't see having sex with a man I don't love and who doesn't love me—married or not." Basma choked on the burger and began to cough discreetly, while Kensasha calmly placed a fork full of potato into her mouth.

After a while, Kensasha continued, "Look at arranged marriages. They force women into loveless and passionless sex with a stranger or worse—their cousin!" She glared at Basma who found herself unable to swallow. "And those people believe a moral woman is not supposed to enjoy sex. Can you believe that? It's a bizarre form of prostitution, isn't it? Women trade their bodies for food and a roof over their heads, or some twisted stamp or code of honor, instead of becoming autonomous."

Blood drained from Basma's face. She swallowed hard and almost dropped the burger. She felt her face heating. Her heart sped up.

"I read somewhere that marriage without love, or at least affection, is far worse than being alone." Kensasha added, nonchalantly.

Basma put the burger down. She began to breathe heavily, biting her lip while Kensasha resumed eating heartily.

On the verge of exploding, she finally blurted out: "Marriage is to make a family. The families hold the village together... the world together!"

Kensasha calmly finished chewing before responding.

"So, what are you saying, Basma, that love doesn't matter? Women shouldn't enjoy sex?"

Flustered, Basma still hit back. "Love is for our children and our parents. And... and for Allah."

Kensasha leaned forward and asked: "Have you ever been in love?" Basma blinked slowly and then lowered her head, feeling bruised. Kensasha put down her fork and patted Basma's hand comfortingly.

The waiter came over to refill their water glasses. He noticed Basma hadn't eaten much of her food and that Kensasha seemed almost finished.

"Should I clear this away for you?" he asked, addressing both of them.

Kensasha waited for Basma's response. She looked at her food then nodded. He cleared the table. Kensasha felt a little guilty at the way the conversation had gone.

"Sorry, if I got a little passionate. Women and marriage is part of my dissertation. Did I spoil your appetite?"

Basma shook her head. Of course, it was obvious she had. The waiter brought them the check.

Kensasha, still on her soapbox, stated, "I believe our duty as women is not to have children. Our duty is providing the best care for the children we have—whether we give birth to them or not."

Diminished, Basma attempted a smile. Kensasha reached for her purse and Basma reached for hers. Kensasha waved her away.

"I'll get this."

"No, no," Basma said.

Ignoring her, Kensasha plopped her credit card on the table, and said: "Well, did you like the burger?" And then, as an afterthought, "You never touched your fries."

***

By the time Basma was with Vincent once again, all of her doubts and fears had multiplied. At first when Vincent climbed on top of her, she wanted to fling her arms around his neck and pull him close, to seek refuge in him. He began kissing her ears and her neck as before, but this time her thoughts were so distracting, she turned away from him.

"I am married," she reminded him.

"Yeah, I met the guy, remember?"

"I am sorry. I did not know he was coming."

"You've explained all of that, now I'd like to forget about it." He nibbled her ear.

"This is not... To my family this..."

"But I thought you liked this?"

She started pushing at him. Amused, he clasped hold of her wrists and pushed back. When she yielded, he resumed kissing and nuzzling her neck gently. She closed her eyes, pretending to be disinterested, shutting him out. Undaunted, he continued kissing and caressing her body until he felt her relax beneath him. Placing his hand firmly on her thigh, he parted her legs. Her body stiffened. He began stroking the soft inner skin until she relaxed once more—her body waking slowly but surely. Soon, something ignited within her, and she was engulfed in ripples of pulsating damp heat. She swooned and moaned with pleasure.

When he finally entered her, it was slow and gentle—so much so, that she hardly realized it until he was deep inside. Then she gasped. Her body arched and, again, that voice resounded in her head: "Remember, Basma, family honor lies between a woman's legs." Panic stricken, she began to struggle against him, violently.

Vincent did not understand what was happening. He attempted to calm her by brushing her hair back with his fingers—remembering how much she liked that. But tears streamed from the corners of her eyes.

"Come on stop that," he whispered. "It's okay... it's okay. Relax. Just feel it. Feel me." He kissed her again. "Can you feel me?" he asked.

She looked up at him and nodded slowly, needing so much to trust him in that moment.

"Am I hurting you?"

She shook her head, feeling defeated by her body's new appetite for sexual pleasure, and little by little, she drifted into a kind of death-like state, resigned to her present fate and its future consequences.

Vincent moved in and out, cautiously, methodically, while continuing to stroke and caress her breasts.

"I think you're a beautiful woman. I just want to make you feel good, that's all. You have a right to feel good, don't you?"

Aroused by his voice, and the feel of his hot breath on her neck, she gripped his shoulders wanting to press herself into him, merge with him. She bit down on her lip to hold back the sounds. But as waves of intense pressure started rising and expanding throughout her whole body, she couldn't keep silent any longer. Her moans of sensual pleasure rose to such a feverish pitch that Vincent was both mesmerized and aroused by it. He pushed faster and harder and the bed creaked and their breathing grew heavier and suddenly, her eyes flew open, wildly, as if startled, and her body began to arch and jerk out of control.

"Oh, oh, oh no. No," she uttered breathlessly, "What's happening to me? What is happening! Oh… am I dying?"

She clutched at the sheets, her body contracted. Vincent thrust harder and there was blood throbbing, and fire and tears, and flashes of lightening. There was this exquisite tension that erupted into a crescendo of intercepting melodies, and bands of rainbow colors exploding. The ground dissolved and she was soaring through space, higher and higher. Spinning… floating… dissolving… into… a delicious… excruciating ecstasy.

For a long while, they lay entwined, hearts thumping against each other, and the sounds of the motorway returned to their conscious mind.

Eventually, Vincent rolled onto his side, propped up on his elbow and stared at her.

"What was that about?" he asked with curiosity. "You're not a virgin."

"What do you mean?" Her body still tingled.

"You heard me. You're a married woman. You have kids."

Still breathing heavily, she stared back at him, puzzled. "Yes, yes?"

"Well... you and your husband do this, obviously." Embarrassed, she turned away from him. "Well don't you?" She nodded reluctantly. "So... why did you act like you didn't know what was happening? I don't get it."

"I do not understand what you mean. I... my husband... it is different. I never felt that."

"Never felt what?"

Excited, she sat up, eager to share what she just experienced. "I could not stop my body from shaking. And I felt like I was high on a mountain, then I was falling and I thought I was dying but it... it..."

"That's called an orgasm!" Vincent replied, instructively. "Are you saying you've never had an orgasm before?"

"Or-g-asm?" she pronounced, innocently. "No, I have not felt this orgasm before."

"But that's impossible!" Vincent replied, dumbfounded. "That's frightening!" He sat up and stared at her with disbelief. "Wait, are you screwing with me? I mean... are you serious?"

She looked over at him, perplexed. "You are surprised?"

"Surprised? Try speechless!" His eyes widened and he began to laugh out loud. "I knew it! I knew there was something different about you. But... believe me, I never suspected that you... Man, I don't know what to say."

He paused, and then shaking his head slowly, he said, "Your husband is a real prick."

All she could do was to stare back, pondering his reaction.

Vincent grinned, leaned over and put his lips to her ear. "So, did you like it?" he whispered.

Basma's eyes brightened, her face took on a radiant glow and with great intensity, she replied, "Yes! Very much."

Disinclined, she prolonged getting out of the Bakery Guy's car and then proceeded down the long block to her house, as she had done so often. Only this time she barely felt the sidewalk beneath her feet and kept looking down to reassure herself the ground was still there. The trees were a richer shade of green, the sky a deeper blue than she'd ever remembered. He told her she was beautiful and he kissed her with tenderness. It was strange and new, his mouth on hers. She'd never been kissed, and now this man kissed her everywhere. Imagine!

For twenty-three years, her body had instinctively assumed the likeness of wood anytime Shafal was within three inches of it.

As she walked up the path to her front door, heat rose to her cheeks at the thought of that amazing feeling she'd just experienced with the Bakery Guy. So, that is what she had been deprived of all these years and didn't even know it: an orgasm.

***

The kitchen window was now filled with yellow and purple flowering plants framed by new white lace curtains. On the stove, three pots of varying sizes had steam seeping from beneath the edges of the tops. Basma placed the last one, a large frying pan, on the front burner, adjusted the flame and wiped her hands on her apron. She poured in some peanut oil. Taking a bowl filled with cubed spiced meat from the counter, she added it to the heating oil. As she did so, her mind's eye filled with images of the Bakery Guy's chiseled form on top of her—his blue-green eyes smiling down.

She put the cover on the skillet and wiped off the countertop. She washed up a few plates and knives and put them on the dish rack.

Another image imposed itself. She and the Bakery Guy lying in an embrace with legs and arms flung around each other. She's stroking his cheek and running her fingers through his golden locks.

She reached for the bar of soap in the soap tray, but only a tiny thin sliver of a grayish-white mass remained. Tossing it in the garbage, she headed to the bathroom, opened the cabinet below the sink and took out a new bar. Her eyes fell on the perfumed moisturizer, which she had bought impulsively while shopping with Mrs. Sadawi weeks ago. It was called Honey Vanilla Crème.

She washed her hands and began to apply the moisturizer. Bringing her hands to her nose, she took in a long breath. The fragrance was heavenly. She poured another drop into her palm and spread the lotion on her neck slowly. Then she slid her right hand down into the top of her blouse to her left shoulder and began to caress it. With eyes closed, she slowly brought her fingers back up to her nose and gently allowed them to slip down to her lips, brushing over them the same way that the Bakery Guy did, and instantly he appeared.

His hot breath warmed her ear. He takes her hands in his and plants little kisses on each of them. She wiggles one hand free and brushes her thumb across his lips and across his cheek affectionately while staring unflinchingly into his eyes. His arms encircle her waist and he begins to...

"BASMA! BASMA!" Someone called out with alarm. It was Shafal.

She heard a door slam shut, and then a more fearful voice calling out:

"Ma! Ma! Where are you?"

Her eyes flung open. Frightened now, she ran from bathroom to see what was going on. The living room was filled with a thick gray smoke. Abdel, coughing, rushed from window to window opening them, wide.

Basma hurried past him into the kitchen. Abdel turned and when he saw her, he let out a deep sigh of relief.

"Oh... thank God! You are okay," he said, and followed behind her.

In the kitchen, Shafal, quite angry, tried to salvage some remains of his dinner. Basma was completely stupefied. Not only was most of the food inedible, two of her pots were ruined.

Shafal's glare cut right through her. "What were you doing?" he asked struggling to suppress his rage. "What? What?" he demanded. Basma's body started to tremble and she burst into tears. "What happened to your nose? Didn't you smell the smoke? Huh? Huh?" he yelled.

She shook her head, feebly, and tried to squeeze by him to get a closer look at the damage. Shafal blocked her as he swung his arms up gesturing as he spoke:

"All day I wait for the time when I can have real food... our kind of food. All day! Now look." He pointed to a few miserable teaspoons of rice and one cube of browned meat that he rescued from the blackened pan. "That is my dinner!" he spewed with disgust. Basma, who had become completely unhinged at this point, looked at the scraps and nearly laughed.

Exploding, Shafal struck her hard against the side of her head. She cried out. Abdel winced. Shafal's arm swung again for a back-handed slap, but Abdel yelled out:

"Let's order pizza!"

Distracted, Shafal's hand halted inches from the other side of her face and he stared at Abdel. He let his hand fall to his side like a heavy weight and with a dismayed look at Basma he slowly headed to the bedroom.

She called out after him, "I will make you something else."

Abdel took her hand, tenderly, and added, "I'll help." She stroked his face, appreciatively.

Why, is it, she wondered, that Abdel is always the only one present whenever Shafal hits me?

***

In previous years, Abdel had thought nothing of his father slapping his mother around. He just accepted that that is what people do—they fight. Children fight. However, at school when one child struck another child, whether boy or girl, they usually struck back, except when scared. His mother never hit back, never defended herself. That was the part he could not understand.

Even though his father had stopped beating on her years ago—until today—Abdel knew she frightened easily. He recalled that day from his childhood.

He was just able to stand and take a few steps before tumbling over with giggling fits when it happened. Basma made it all the way to the playground with him in a stroller without anxiety attacks and hurrying back to the house.

The temperature was warm and humid so it must have been mid-summer. Basma was sixteen and pregnant with Ahmed.

The playground was swarming with children dangling from colorful iron beams, sliding down poles, or playing tag while their mothers, Indian and Pakistani alike, conversed in small groups.

Another group of mothers were dressed in brown or black abayas, similarly to Basma's, and they all sat together. Some mothers gently rocked carriages as their infants slept.

Basma crossed to the other side of the sandbox and sat down on an empty bench not far from a large tree. Placing Abdel on her lap, she ran her fingers through his coarse black curls and repeatedly kissed his chubby little cheeks.

He spotted something flying in the air and landing on a tree branch.

He pointed to it. Basma looked up and saw a bird with a red underbelly. She didn't know what it was called, so simply said: "Bird."

Abdel repeated, "Ba... ba... ba..." and stretched out his tiny hand to touch it. Realizing his arm was too short, he tried to wiggle down from her lap and run over to the tree. Instantly, Basma's arms encircled him like a harness. He began to squirm and whimper and she tried to distract him by pointing to a child who was bouncing a ball.

"Look... look, Abdel." But he wasn't interested in that child, he just had to touch the bird so he began screaming and continued to squirm and clutch at the air.

When Abdel's actions caught the other mothers' attention, Basma became flustered assuming the women were judging her. The more Abdel screamed out, the more attention she received. Releasing one arm from around him, she reached inside the pouch at the back of the stroller and pulled out some sweet honey cake. He took advantage of this moment by jutting backwards until his body was vertical and then slipped through her arm almost to the ground.

"No... no," Basma reprimanded. "Stop it." She yanked him back up into her lap as he bawled. "Here, here... see what I have for you. See what I have?" She put a piece of the sweet cake into his mouth. He stopped wailing for a moment as the sweetness found his tongue. She wiped his nose. He looked up at her with his big brown eyes still moist with tears. Basma grinned and got him another piece of sweet cake. It didn't satisfy. Abdel wanted the bird.

He grabbed the cake from his mouth, flung it on the ground and began to squirm once more. Basma decided the best thing to do was to put him back in the stroller. He continued sobbing for the bird that had already flown away.

Basma sat back down glancing at the women. After a while, the women returned their attention to each other. Relieved, Basma brushed crumbs from her lap and began to reposition the stroller so that it faced away from the tree.

"I will buy you a bird when you get older, okay?" she said, reassuringly. She gripped the sides to wheel it around. Her eyes caught sight of the sweet cake Abdel had thrown to the ground. It was now covered with ants that were pulling off crumbs and carting them into crevices beneath the bench. All of a sudden, Basma stopped wheeling, and stared transfixed at the ants.

Abdel glanced up at her when the stroller came to an abrupt halt. He saw a look he couldn't have possibly interpreted at such a young age, but he always remembered it, because it was after that look that his mother leaped to her feet and pushed the stroller frantically toward the exit. All of the other mothers stopped chatting when they saw Basma hurrying back past them as if fleeing from someone.

She spent the rest of that day sitting on the couch half staring off and half watching him as he tried to make her smile again.

When Abdel grew a little older, he realized that the look on his mother's face that day was fear. It seemed from that time on, Abdel had felt responsible for his mother's fear and he wanted to be her protector. This was clarified for him at the age of twelve.

That particular evening when his father began to hit his mother, Abdel stopped him by grabbing his arm. Horrified, Shafal shoved Abdel to the floor. Ahmed heard the thump and came running into the room in time to hear Shafal yelling at Abdel:

"Don't you ever disrespect me like that again. I am your father. Do you hear me? Stay out of what does not concern you."

His mother had stood by, quietly watching, a piteous look on her face.

CHAPTER 9

D espite feeling profound guilt and shame after burning her family's dinner and receiving a brutal slap from Shafal, Basma still looked forward to her meetings with the Bakery Guy. She couldn't help it. Each time, she was transported to a realm of sheer bliss where she felt such intense overwhelming pleasure it caused her to cry tears of joy. It was as if she'd brushed against eternity.

One day, weeks later, when she slid into the passenger seat beside him, he marveled how serene she looked. When he leaned over an inch from her face and stared into her eyes playfully, she smiled back at him.

"Motel?" he asked.

Basma nodded. "Good choice."

The burgundy carpeting was plush, and the writing desk was pure oak. Pulling off her shawl, Basma immediately went over to the bed, sat down, removed her hijab and began unbuttoning her blouse. Vincent followed, sat down behind her and slipped one arm around her waist. He lifted her hair off her shoulders and kissed the nape of her neck—it smelled like vanilla and honey. She leaned her head forward in surrender.

A second later, Vincent got up off the bed. "I left something in the car," he announced excitedly and rushed out of the room. Basma grinned and shook her head at his erratic behavior.

While he was gone, she let her blouse fall to the bed and unhooked her bra in anticipation.

He returned carrying a package under his arm, elegantly gift wrapped in a royal blue metallic paper with a large gold voile ribbon, with a stunning bouquet of yellow roses in his hand. He strolled over to the bed.

Basma grabbed the flowers first, buried her face in them and moaned.

Grinning from ear to ear, Vincent presented the package to her. Her mouth opened but nothing came out. She stared up at him with surprise.

"Go on, open it!" he ordered impatiently.

She laughed girlishly, put the flowers to the side, and grabbed the package like an excited child. First, she ran her hand across the smooth surface admiring the color. Vincent knelt down on the bed facing her as she slowly untied the gold-colored ribbon, not wanting to damage it. Vincent let out a sigh when he saw how long this was going to take.

Finally, with the ribbon put aside, Basma carefully unwrapped the metallic paper to keep it from ripping and revealed a box. Immediately, Vincent became intrigued and delighted. Even though he knew she was much older than he, her childlike manner was, at times, enchanting.

She lifted off the pearly white lid, parted the gold tissue paper and pulled out a full-length sleek purple satin nightgown fit for a Hollywood star. It looked very expensive. The silky fabric beneath her fingers made her swoon. She'd never owned anything this glamorous. Overwhelmed, she clutched the gown to her chest and rubbed it against her cheek. As Vincent watched, his face took on a warm caring glow, and he seemed caught in a wave of emotion.

Basma glanced over at the yellow roses and then up at Vincent—, his blue-green eyes glistening. All of a sudden, she paused and a dark expression crossed her face.

"What is this?" she asked, suspiciously and then raised her voice: "We are not lovers! You make me do this. I never really wanted to be here. I was afraid of you."

Vincent just stared at her. She began to rub her temples trying to organize her thoughts and put things in perspective. Somehow, it seemed important. It was a moment of clarity.

"I am married... married. You made me come here... remember?" She waited for validation.

But Vincent was so stunned by her abrupt shift in attitude that he couldn't respond. When he continued to remain silent, she became indignant.

"You threatened me! Remember? Remember?"

"What?" he said, at last, with increasing anger. "That was a long time ago. You come here now because you want it."

She ignored him. "I come so you won't tell my husband. He would kill me if he knew."

"Oh really?" Vincent replied, baiting her. "Oh, it's your fear of your husband that keeps this whole adultery thing going?"

"Yes! Of course," she responded with unusual detachment. "So, do what you came here to do and we can go."

Her remark stunned them both. A long awkward moment passed with Vincent staring at her with a pained expression that soon turned to confusion. She was right. He had forgotten. He felt utterly foolish, now, giving her the gifts.

A moment later, he got up and said in a distant voice: "Well, guess what? It's over! I'll leave you alone."

He pulled up to the usual drop off point with Basma staring straight ahead. Neither had spoken a word since leaving the motel. With Vincent also staring ahead, not saying a word, Basma stalled getting out of the car.

"I wasn't going to tell your husband," he said, still upset. "Why would I do that? It was just a threat to get you to show up".

She searched for something to say to him, a way to apologize for her behavior. Then she gave up and opened the door. As soon as she was out of the car, he slammed his foot hard on the gas and the car bolted away.

Suddenly, it screeched to a halt and reversed noisily back to where Basma still stood. He rolled down the window on the passenger's side and flung the box with the purple gown through it. As it landed, the silky negligee tumbled to the ground. Next, he tossed out the long-stemmed yellow roses, which came loose from the wrapping and spilt all over the sidewalk. Then the car took off again at break-neck speed.

Her eyes followed the car until it was out of sight, then she looked forlornly at the flowers, the gift box and shimmering gown scattered over the grimy pavement.

Four young children ran over to get a closer look. Afraid of un-wanted attention, Basma smiled at them, nervously, and offered the flowers for them to take home to their mothers.

Delighted, they grabbed them up carefully, and ran off in differ-ent directions. Basma then picked up the gown, stuffed it into her handbag, scooped up the gift box and tissue paper, turned and walked sadly toward her house. When she reached the corner of her block, she put the box into the trash.

***

A few days after her breakup with the Bakery Guy, Abdel was the one bringing a girl home for his parents' approval. Her name was Nya and she was fine-boned, petite with intelligent eyes and a pleas-ant smile. Basma was in the kitchen filling serving bowls. It was a very hot day and Basma was under the weather, lightheaded even, but she wanted to support Abdel. The girl came into the kitchen and offered to help. Basma handed her the serving platters and told her to arrange them on the big table in the living room and then they all sat down to eat.

"When we get married," Abdel began, "We can live at Nya's par-ents' house until I get transferred to the Virginia branch." Nya sat quietly eating, letting Abdel do the talking.

"Why do you want to live so far from your family?" Shafal asked. "Be like your brother."

"Virginia is not far. And they need computer experts down there."

"And you are an expert?" Shafal asked, with a hint of resent-ment.

"That's what my boss thinks." Abdel returned modestly.

111

Shafal glanced over to Basma for support. She was staring at the wall, lost in her own thoughts for a moment.

"Don't you have anything to say about this?" Shafal asked her.

She came back to the present, realizing she had missed some of the conversation.

"Abdel knows what he wants and that is what's important."

"But he should stay close to his family, like Ahmed," Shafal added, firmly. "Family is what is important."

Basma's response was equally as firm. "He is not a child, any-more. Soon, he will have his own family and they are what is important." She nodded towards Nya in an accepting gesture.

Early on Tuesday evening, Basma decided to change her white top before preparing dinner. When she tried to pull another blouse from an overstuffed bottom drawer, she spotted something and stopped. Her hand came out with the purple silk negligee that she buried so Shafal wouldn't find it. She examined it a moment, and then slowly began to unbutton her high neck, long-sleeved blouse and shake her twisted hair a loose.

Standing before the full-length mirror nailed to the closed closet door, she shut her eyes and slipped the purple gown over her head. It floated down around her in cascading ripples. She opened her eyes and gazed at her reflection: it was sensuously feminine.

At first, she didn't recognize the woman in the mirror as herself. But once she did, her face lit up with amazement.

"That's me," she whispered, captivated by her own reflection.

By Thursday, the temperature was already 80 degrees by noon. One full week had passed since the breakup. Basma had counted the days, the hours and the minutes. All morning her stomach churned as she helped to set up the recreation room and file papers for Kensasha. Presently, it was a few minutes before two o'clock and she was minding a patient in a wheelchair.

Normally on the days that she met with the Bakery Guy, she would be in the locker room changing at this time. And ten minutes later, she'd be beside him in the car. It had become a secret escape from her ordinary life—a life without change, a marriage without love or sexual satisfaction.

It was the Bakery Guy's lovemaking that she looked forward to most—even if she wouldn't admit it to herself, now it was over. But hadn't she also wanted it to end? Wasn't she tired of lying? How long could it have possibly gone on? So, today she would return to the safety of fidelity. The danger of discovery was also over.

At the end of her shift, she would simply ride the bus home, shop, cook, and clean up, and sleep and come back here tomorrow and do it all again—just like before. Before the Bakery Guy's touch forced her back to life, before his lips seared her skin, branding it forever.

Her head began throbbing and the muscle near her left shoulder tightened so fast and completely, that it actually stung.

She glanced up at a clock. It was two o'clock. Anxious, she pondered for a moment what to do. Was it even possible? She wheeled the patient onto a balcony and waved goodbye.

Minutes later, upon leaving the locker room and proceeding down the long corridor toward the front of the building, she heard a loud thump, followed by a groan. Then she heard a woman's voice say, "Oh, no!"

Shortly after, a woman wearing a nurse's uniform rushed from a room just as Basma approached.

"Please, come and help me," she begged Basma, concern in her eyes. "Mrs. Nichols has fallen." Basma hurried back into the room with the nurse and they both struggled to pick the husky woman up off the floor. Basma glanced at the watch on the nurse's arm. It was 2:12 pm. Her stomach churned.

At the very same moment a few blocks away, Vincent pulls up to the curb.

After a few more attempts, Basma and the nurse were able to get Mrs. Nichols to her feet. Disoriented, she flung her arms about and hit a food tray that was on castors sending it crashing to the floor. The commotion brought orderlies who began to pick up the scattered food dishes. But the elderly woman began to cry at this latest affront to her independence.

Basma patted her back in an attempt to console her.

"Everything is fine. The doctor will come soon. It is okay." By then, several people had entered the room to assist.

She looked at her watch and saw that it was now 2:17.

113

"Oh no!" she mumbled to herself, then turned to one of the orderlies and the nurse who had asked for her help. "I am very sorry, but I must leave now."

"Thank you so much for being out there and helping. I'll remember that," the nurse replied, touching Basma's shoulder.

Basma hurried toward the door.

Vincent checks his watch, and then stares ahead solemnly.

Back in the corridor heading for the front once again, Basma walked right into Kensasha who was just coming to see what had happened.

"Is anyone hurt?" Kensasha asked, concerned.

Vincent sits contemplating.

Kensasha listened to what Basma reported, then tapped her on the shoulder for her to take off. Basma hurried down the hall toward the front door once again with Kensasha watching her curiously.

Outside, finally, Basma took the same route to the bus stop as always.

But with each step, her anxiety increased.

Vincent puts his hand on the key to start the engine.

Reaching Queens Boulevard, Basma eyes a clock up on a steeple. It's now 2:27. Her eyes began to tear. She panics. Clutching her handbag to her body, and holding up her long skirt, she breaks into a jog.

She makes it to the corner just in time to see the red car pull away.

He did come!

Vincent's foot presses on the gas. In a flash, he sees a hand grab frantically at the passenger door handle and yank it. He slams the brakes, startled.

Basma yanked the door open and jumped in, completely out of breath, and slammed the door shut.

Totally disheveled, her hijab nearly around her neck, she sat holding her chest, gasping for air. She wouldn't look at him, couldn't look at him.

Slowly, Vincent grinned and he let out a big sigh.

He eased back down on the gas pedal while Basma leaned into the soft black leather, relieved.

They drove onto a highway. Basma was a little concerned initially, and then relaxed again.

She decided to just trust him. He showed up, didn't he? Besides, he knew what time she had to get home.

He chose a stretch of highway with little traffic and continued on it for a few miles before turning off onto a smaller roadway that climbed higher and higher.

***

Nature's stillness is like a pregnant pause—filled with so much possibility.

With eyes closed, Basma could still see… see with her ears… her nose… even her skin. In the silence, she could identify where the flowers were. Her ears caught the chirping sound of birds, insects crawling along a blade of grass—the flying kind flitting from petal to petal. Her skin recognized the summer breeze. All this abundance around her, she saw with her eyes closed.

Ah, but what wonders can the open eyes see?

She raised her eyelids slowly and the first thing she saw was an expanse of blueness. Rapt in wonderment, she turned to the right just in time to see an orange spotted butterfly landing on a pink flower. She sat up in slow motion, keeping her eyes fixed on it.

It was then that she remembered she was outside without hijab! The Bakery Guy had taken her to a remote, wooded area high above a main thoroughfare.

How amazing the fresh clean air felt on her legs—her arms. Intoxicated by nature's beauty, she turned on her side and looked down at the Bakery Guy lying on his back, dozing. Unlike her, he had removed all of his clothes.

This man! How can he be so free and comfortable with his body? She smiled warmly as she watched him. Then she leaned over and kissed him on the lips ever so gently. He didn't respond but turned his head away, still asleep. She stared at his body, taking in every inch of its beauty, enjoying this new freedom to look.

All of a sudden, an impulse overtook her. She wanted to touch it— the source of so much pleasure. He was still fast asleep. So, she stretched out her hand and moved it closer. His pubic hairs tickled the palm of her hand. She started to breathe heavily, but pulled her hand away before she could feel skin. Putting her fingers to her lips, she grinned with self-conscious delight at this unusual act of boldness.

Wearing just her slip, she got up and walked to where the butterfly danced from flower to flower. She walked further, arms outstretched, surveying her environment. She allowed herself to wander around exploring all this magnificence, without a hint of shyness or a moment of self-consciousness at being in her underwear out-of-doors. Even though there was no one around to witness it, for the first time she felt as fearless as a small child.

Reaching the edge of a cliff, she looked down. The drop was steep—at least a quarter mile. Across the way, there were green flatlands.

She closed her eyes and inhaled, hoping to transfer all this lush abundance outside into her own body. She inched a little too close to the edge but kept her eyes closed, listening, sensing. It was fun.

Several feet behind her, something or someone was moving toward her—quietly. It was a subtle awareness. Then, the distance shortened. She sensed their approach. Her heart started pulsating faster. Was it a bear? Or... Then she knew, and chose to surrender to whatever happened.

A man's hand reached toward her, but she didn't hear anything. Instantly, he grabbed her around the waist—startling her. But then he buried his nose into her hair.

"Hey, beautiful Eve," he said. "It's very late. I've got to get you home."

This time, as they sat outside the tire factory, Basma was much more reluctant to leave. They sat quietly for a moment, keenly aware of the irony of the situation.

He turned to her. "Tell me, how did you know I would be waiting for you today."

She looked over at him, surprised. "I didn't."

"Hah," he responded, surprised as well, and then he very tenderly cupped her hand and squeezed it. "I'll see you next Thursday."

This reminded her that they would indeed be together again. It wasn't over after all. She gave him such a caring smile that he leaned over and kissed her sweetly on the cheek.

"Have you ever been in love?" Kensasha had asked her.

She got out of the car and walked away like a smitten schoolgirl.

CHAPTER 10

Most of the women present at Mrs. Jazeer's that Friday were the same ones Basma had encountered at her previous gathering. There were a few new faces as well. However, Imani Sadawi was conspicuously absent. Apparently, she was in the process of connecting with Dr. Sethi and bringing her to America.

Basma, wearing a bright green blouse with matching head covering, strolled over to a table that had cups and a tea dispenser and poured herself a cup of tea. She stirred in a spoonful of sugar and had just put it to her lips to sip, when a woman walked over to her smiling and looked her up and down. Basma recognized the woman as Khadija Tali, Tariq's thirty-nine-year-old wife.

"It is so good to see you here, Basma. How is Shafal? Tariq told me what happened. Is he still working those late nights?"

Basma told her that Shafal had cut down on working the Friday night shift and asked her about her family and if she was a grandmother yet.

When Ahmed and Abdel were still toddlers, Basma used to accompany Khadija, and her children, to the park several times a week. Their conversations, at that time, were always about the children or food. Occasionally, Khadija would offer some intimate tidbit about Tariq, but Basma never spoke about Shafal. She knew that Khadija, for the most part, had been satisfied with the man her parents had chosen for her.

On the day that Tariq Tali went to his future bride's house to meet her, he wore a double-breasted brown pinstripe suit with very wide lapels, cuffed trousers, a white shirt and a tie that had red and black polka dots.

Khadija, then seventeen, was immediately attracted to his tie. During his whole visit with her and her parents, she kept her attention on the tie and how well it matched his Western-style suit. This is what she told Basma.

Tariq turned out to be a decent husband and father. He was never abusive to her and he loved his children. What more could she ask for?

However, with their children now grown up, the two women rarely saw each other. Basma liked Khadija because she smiled easily—a trait Basma had difficulty with.

"My daughter is expecting. I hope it is a boy."

"Yes, I hope so too," Basma agreed, excitedly.

"Thank you," Khadija said, still smiling. Then she leaned in closer.

"Basma, you are looking very well. Maybe you can help me to get a job, too? It is good to get out of the house, huh?"

Basma considered what Khadija had said and was delighted to have someone to converse with.

Mrs. Jazeer was in the kitchen adding a few more mini cakes to a plate when she heard a swell of surprised laughter, shrieks and giggling coming from the living room. Relieved that the tension, which had plagued her gatherings ever since Mrs. Sadawi's last visit, had obviously subsided, she hurried back into the room to see what was going on.

Over by the tea table, she saw that a group of women had Basma surrounded. Some of the women had their hands over their mouths as they listened to Basma, who was in turn excited and absorbed in whatever she was telling them. Two of the women looked positively shocked.

Mrs. Jazeer hurried over to them carrying the plate of little cakes.

Grinning curiously, she asked, "What are you ladies taking about now?"

There was immediate silence. Then Khadija Tali giggled and some of the other women laughed. Eager to know exactly what was going on, Mrs. Jazeer closed in on them.

"Come on, ladies, what is it?" she inquired.

"Orgasm," Khadija clarified, in English.

Mrs. Jazeer looked from one face to another. "What?"

One woman, loving this gossip, replied in Arabic, "Basma has discovered orgasms and she described them to us."

Mrs. Jazeer glanced at Basma, perplexed. Basma returned a look mixed with slight embarrassment, as well as the enjoyment of being the center of attention.

Khadija Tali naturally assumed Basma's newly discovered orgasms were the result of something Shafal had done.

"You see," Khadija said to the other women, "some men take their husbandly duties seriously. They want to please their wives, also." And, then to herself, "I think I should have a talk with Tariq."

Some of the women nodded, agreeing they must talk with their husbands. Mrs. Jazeer finally caught on, raised her eyebrows and stared at Basma—shocked at such unusual candidness. Even so, Basma, her eyes twinkling, returned a look of pure innocence.

Later that night, Basma easily drifted off into a sound sleep. In the darkness, Shafal stood over her, watching her breathe. Often, through the years, she would be turning from one side to the other. Now, she slept like a baby. He had noticed her lighter moods, and felt sudden desire for her. He pulled back the cover, unzipped his pants and lay next to her. He began to pull her gown up to her thighs. She awakened just as he rolled on top of her. With almost the same feelings of disgust and revulsion she had felt on her wedding night, almost twenty-three years earlier, she winced and her body stiffened.

But Shafal was used to his frigid wife and proceeded to enter her anyway. Without thinking, Basma impulsively put her hand between her thighs, blocking his entrance. Tonight, it was Shafal's turn to be mortified. Mortified and humiliated. So much so, that he didn't even attempt to remove her hand. Instead, he got up off her and stared back at her, waiting for an explanation. She felt cold ice water ripple down her back. Her eyes flitted from side to side searching her brain, wildly, for an excuse. Anything would do.

"I have my monthly and it is very heavy today," she said, apologetically. She pushed her gown back down over her knees avoiding his eyes. Shafal still felt humiliated at what she had done.

"Why didn't you just tell me that right away?"

"I was half sleeping… maybe. I don't know."

He had no choice but to accept her explanation as he walked to the bedroom door. "It is always something," he said, with irritation. "You haven't been a wife to me for a long time."

Basma rose up on her elbows and stared after him.

***

The girl behind the counter at the beauty supply shop was speaking Spanish into her pink iridescent cell phone while straightening up a line of square plexiglass containers filled with emery boards, nail clippers, tubes of Chap Stick and miniature bottles of hand lotion—all products positioned for that impulse buy. Obviously, the manager had stepped out.

Basma wandered up and down the aisles, amazed at the volume of stuff women put on their faces. How did they know how to use all this? She looked back at the cashier, whose own eyelids were a light purple, and just under her eyebrow, the girl had added copper—between these two colors was a deep indigo. Her lips had an extreme shine with a hint of plum. Every inch of her smooth, young skin was covered with something. Why so much? She is still young.

Rhinestone-studded eyelashes encased in plastic boxes were positioned close to boxes of false fingernails and bottles of polish and removers. Fascinated, Basma picked up a box and turned it from side to side causing the rhinestones to sparkle. Returning the box to its perch on the rack, she picked up a box of false nails and studied it. She pondered the use of extra nails. Couldn't they fall off into the food?

The opposite wall contained all the hair paraphernalia complete with synthetic wigs and falls. She ran her fingers through one with long orange-colored tresses and chuckled.

She spotted what she came for, but didn't know which to choose. The girl seemed nice enough, but Basma was much too shy to ask for help. For a good twenty minutes, her eyes flitted from one color to the other. The variety of methods one could select to apply color had increased to include tiny pots to dip fingers in, tubes for squeezing, wands for spreading or that stick you twist.

Should it be a reddish-pink or a reddish-brown? Should it shimmer with gold or be satiny? Pearl, or flat? She wanted to try them all. But some were so bold—they screamed. Some shouted while others whispered. She decided to choose one that whispered. It was a sheer peachy brown in the traditional stick form. She liked the way it looked on her olive skin.

Was she really going to buy this?

Basma presented her selection to the cashier who was utterly disinterested as she rang up the sale. In the few seconds that the transaction took, Basma became aware of the great divide between them. Could this young girl even remember the first time she had bought lipstick? Probably not.

This simple lipstick purchase was the second most bold and rebellious act in Basma's entire adult life so far. The first one had been walking in the woods wearing only a slip!

Then again, the lipstick purchase was truly, her own choice—no one brought her here—so this action was independent of peer pressure. She told herself she had the right to get it. After all, Mrs. Sadawi wore lipstick… occasionally. And didn't Miss Lewis wear it all the time? Yet, she had never given lipstick any consideration, whatsoever, until now. Why would she? Guilt began to engulf her. She peered around coyly at the other shoppers, and then shoved the lipstick into her handbag as if it were contraband.

***

During the busiest hour at Chappelle Bakery, the call Vincent had been waiting months for finally came. He was in the middle of helping a customer when Al called out to him. Apparently, this person had already left a message on Vincent's cell phone but it was turned off. Asking another staff member to relieve him, Vincent hurried to Al's office.

Al sat back down behind his desk and watched as Vincent nodded excitedly and grinned incessantly at whatever the caller was saying.

"That's a lot of money, man." Vincent said, his excitement increasing. Then, adopting a more serious tone, he said, "Okay, sure. Of course, great! Whatever they want, right? When do we sign the contract?" Al watched Vincent's happy face turn to concern.

"Why so soon?" Vincent asked the caller. "Hmm… I see."

Al's curiosity was piqued, but he knew this was none of his business, so he reached for a letter on his desk in which to absorb himself.

"Sure," Vincent said into the phone, "But I have a few things that I need to take care of and…" The voice cut him off. His mood changed back to happiness. "Yeah, yeah, you're right, of course. It is a great opportunity. Okay then, I'll uh… see ya soon."

When he hung up, Al glanced at him. Vincent's smile faded again. He stared at the floor, contemplating for a moment, before shrugging off whatever was going through his mind. He thanked Al and returned to the front of the store.

Later that evening, Vincent found himself outside the tire factory feeling like an absolute fool. How on earth did he let himself get involved with this woman anyway? He knew she was into this whole religion thing—definitely not his type. The way he had gone about it was criminal, even if she did want him.

He looked up and down the street not knowing in which direction to drive. Why hadn't he asked for her name? The price of secrecy. Slowly, he began to drive in the direction she'd always walked.

It was a very humid evening. Many people had come out of their hot apartments to socialize on the streets. He cruised around hoping to spot her.

He saw a man playing with his children on the lawn and thought he resembled her husband. Four teenage boys were shooting hoops on the side of a building. Maybe those are her boys. She had a couple of them, he remembered. Once, she had told him: being a mother was her only purpose for existing. He knew lots of women who could argue that point. But he didn't comment at the time, because she so rarely disclosed anything about her thoughts and feelings to him.

A door opened at one of the houses as he passed. A woman rushed out wearing a colorful scarf loosely draped over her head and shoulders and a tunic with matching pants. Vincent immediately jerked his head in that direction. But she was a Hindu woman. She picked up a child's toy from the lawn and returned to the house. He continued to drive hoping to find Basma.

After two more blocks of this, he reached an intersection and took a random turn, pulled over and stopped. He lit up a cigarette and leaned back in deep thought. An older, short, stocky man with Arabian features crossed the street in front of him. Their eyes locked. The man gave Vincent a dark intense stare.

Maybe that guy was her husband and he recognized him from the bakery. Vincent glanced away self-consciously and rubbed the ridge of his nose.

What if she walked by right now with her husband or her boys? What exactly would he say to her? He hadn't prepared anything. His feeble attempt to contact her was a failure; their relationship deserved more. But what choice did he have? He had to be on that plane tonight.

Maybe it was for the best. The adventure really was over. Now, she could forget about him, stop worrying about her husband finding out and dedicate her life to having his dinner ready on time.

Vincent let out a regretful sigh, flicked the cigarette out of the window and drove away.

***

All day long Basma waited for that moment when she could hop into the Bakery Guy's car and be carried off to another erotic adventure. After her free-spirited romp, practically nude under the open sky, she felt she had the courage to take on anything—to try anything. Now that the Bakery Guy was in her life, she was like two distinct people. He had forced her to step way beyond any idea of a comfort zone, and venture to the wild side with his arrogant, brazen, sometimes cruel, yet always sensuous seduction. But the self, that part of her that had been awakened and evolved from the experiences with him, was very much a stranger to her; someone she never knew existed. Now, she was eager to encounter this other Basma again. Would he like her in lipstick?

Just before leaving, she had slipped into the visitors' restroom on the second floor to apply it. After, to insure she wouldn't attract any attention to herself, she exited through a side door walking with her head down. She passed the bus stop expectantly and turned the corner.

For two full minutes, she stood at the curb staring at an empty spot where the Bakery Guy's red car should have been. She was simply unable to process the fact that it wasn't there.

This is Thursday, she said to herself. She checked her watch. Yes, it's 2:15.

She looked down the street, and then nervously adjusted her clothes a few times by tightening her shiny blue hijab tucking loose strands back beneath it, and moistening her newly painted lips. Assured of his arrival, she straightened her back and lifted her head high and waited. No Bakery Guy.

Maybe he is sick. Or maybe the car broke. Yes, that must be what happened.

She turned around and headed back to the bus stop, disappointed that she wouldn't see him that day.

Tuesday, she bought the bread as usual, but Bakery Guy was nowhere in sight.

The following Thursday, wearing her orange hijab and peach lipstick, Basma approached the corner anxiously, and turned. Again, there was no car. She continued walking slowly to the spot, anyway, stunned that he wasn't there. She waited for half an hour. And then for three consecutive Tuesdays and Thursdays, she showed up and waited for him to appear. She tried different days.

One Tuesday was so muggy she almost passed out. Even so, she managed to wait a full hour. On the Thursday, it rained and still she waited.

Finally, on the sixth week, her initial resolve had given way to depression. So, she decided to cast all pretense of fidelity to the wind and return to the bakery—not for bread but to demand to know what happened to this man.

The place was as busy as ever. She looked around for a moment. A counterman finished up with his customer and came over to her.

"What can I get for you, miss?"

Basma glanced at the pastries almost in a daze. Emotions began to well up inside.

"Where is… umm… what happened to, to—"

The man stared at her impatiently. She couldn't finish her sentence. She was so overcome with the absurdity and unbearable shame of asking the whereabouts of a lover whose name she did not know that she spun around and rushed out of the store.

***

Just as Kensasha had anticipated, Dr. Sethi declined their invitation. Both she and Imani had come to the same conclusion: if they couldn't persuade Dr. Sethi by mail or the telephone to come to Queens, when she visited America, then Kensasha would have to persuade her in person. It was exciting and bold. And, even if Dr. Sethi still said no, it would be a great opportunity to meet her, connect with some of the women she sheltered, and see London all at the same time.

Kensasha had spent the entire afternoon making the final arrangements for her upcoming trip. By pledging her commitment to assist Imani, Kensasha had, inadvertently, pushed her regular responsibilities as head of a department into second place. To make matters worse, she still hadn't found a suitable replacement to delegate decisions while she was away on sabbatical. She wished Basma was more competent in handling administrative duties. This thought made her conscious of Basma at the filing cabinet across the room.

It seemed for a while there, Basma had grown more enthusiastic and eager to learn, but lately she had become sullen, distant and preoccupied once again, and Kensasha didn't have the time or energy to pry the reason out of her.

Her flight booked and the confirmation form printing, Kensasha began a separate search for accommodation. With the economic crisis still plaguing Europe following the global shutdown, London had become very expensive and she hoped to find a clean comfortable B&B close to Dr. Sethi's office in Grosvenor Square.

The website displayed five possibilities. One, in particular, caught her attention. As she reached for a pen, Basma let out a loud groan of frustration. Kensasha turned around and saw that Basma was having difficulty stuffing a file into an already jammed cabinet. Exasperated, Basma gripped the file and began to shake it violently.

Kensasha dropped her pen and watched with stupefaction. The papers spilled out onto the floor. Basma squatted immediately to pick up the papers, but her body began to shake uncontrollably and she started to hyperventilate. Kensasha rushed to her aid.

Back at home, Shafal and Mrs. Sadawi stood near the doorway with Basma now lying in a fetal position on the bed. Shafal, with stubble on his chin and his shirt carelessly tucked into his trousers, repeatedly rubbed his balding head and began pacing the floor.

"If she wasn't around all those old sick people, she'd be fine," he complained. "She is a very delicate woman. I told you I didn't want Basma to work. She belongs in the house with her family. Now look, her health is bad. This is your fault."

Imani wondered if he was right. Was this indeed her fault?

Attempting a defense: "But she was doing so well for a time," Imani reminded him. "And she was looking so much better. Surely you noticed that?"

Of course, he'd noticed. In the past two months, Basma was glowing and he had almost witnessed a smile on her face. Shifting blame away from Mrs. Sadawi, he said, "They took advantage of her in that place. Worked her like a dog." He gestured with both hands for emphasis. "She doesn't know how to say 'no'."

At that, Imani Sadawi walked back to the front door and then called out, "I will bring you dinner tonight and if you need me for anything else, just call. I will come."

For several days, Basma remained at home, mostly in bed with Imani assuming the dinner responsibilities for the household. After everyone had left for work, Basma found herself sobbing repeatedly. Shafal thought her red puffy eyes were due to an allergic reaction to something and offered to take her to the hospital, but she refused to go.

But this particular morning, she felt sharp pains ripping through her. Clutching her stomach, she barely made it to the bathroom before blood gushed down her legs. She screamed out at the sight of it and collapsed on the floor.

Hours seemed to have elapsed before she regained consciousness and she realized she had just miscarried—fortunately without anyone discovering her there. It took amazing effort but she used the side of the tub to pull herself to her knees and then grabbed hold of the sink to get to her feet. That's when her frantic cleanup began.

She yanked down towels from behind the door and blotted up the blood on the white floor tiles, then rinsed them out in the sink. She continued this process with lightning speed until there were no obvious signs of blood left.

There was no time to think or to feel. No one must know about this. Now, she had to dispose of the... the... She stared at the mass of tissue and blood, and a wave of nausea overpowered her. She bent over the toilet and heaved violently. She clutched the sides of the tank as another wave of nausea made her heave again. Tiny beads of sweat oozed from her skin and once more, she began to hyperventilate.

No! She mustn't pass out again. This time Shafal would surely discover her here and her life would be over. After months of derailing his conjugal visits, there was no possible way she could explain her pregnancy—except by claiming an immaculate conception.

She pulled herself together by taking deep breaths, and flushed the toilet. Gripping the edge of the sink to steady herself, she stood up straight and stared back down at the fetal mass that floated in a red pool on her new blue and white bathmat. Well, she'd buy another mat just like it. Simple enough.

As for the life that would have been—the Bakery Guy's child— she couldn't possibly face that now.

She heard the front door open. Her heart nearly leaped from her chest in fear. She grabbed a wad of toilet paper and scooped up the fetus and quickly flung it into the bowl and flushed. She rolled up the bathmat, and hid it in the tub behind the shower curtain, intending to dispose of it later.

Shafal hurried to the bedroom to check on her. When he didn't see her, he sensed something was wrong. He immediately noticed some blood on the bed and rushed to the bathroom calling out to her.

"Basma! Are you all right?" Before he got to the bathroom, Basma came out, her skin frightfully pale, clutching the doorframe. When he looked at her, she felt her face heat up. When she saw how worried he was, she tried to comfort him.

"I am fine, Shafal."

"But there is a lot of blood on the bed," he announced with great concern.

"Oh, again my monthlies are very heavy. And because I have been so weak all month, it makes me feel worse."

Shafal took hold of her shoulders, helped her to the bedroom and over to his bed, instead. He pulled back the covers, she climbed in and he sat on the edge watching her with growing concern.

"I should get you to a doctor. You are looking very bad."

She patted his hand tenderly, "I will be fine, Shafal. Stop worrying. These are women's problems."

Unfortunately, there is no balm for heartbreak or shame, both of which erode the spirit. Neither Advil, nor antibiotics, are a match for a defeated will. In a month, Basma had deteriorated. Her face had become thin with dark circles under the eyes.

She was sitting in the living room wearing a drab house robe, practically catatonic, with Mrs. Jazeer busy brushing her hair, when Khadija Tali entered from the kitchen carrying a tray with hot food and set it down on a side table. Mrs. Jazeer finished braiding Basma's hair, and formed it into a coil at the nape of her neck. Then she stood back admiring her work.

Khadija got a chair from the dining area and sat down in front of Basma. She took a fork full of food and attempted to feed Basma. Each time Khadija put the fork to Basma's mouth, Basma turned her head away.

"What are you doing? Do you want to die?" Khadija yelled out in frustration.

Did she deserve to live?

Mrs. Jazeer put her hand on Khadija's shoulder to console her.

"Don't you care about Abdel and Ahmed?" Khadija continued.

"Of course, she does," replied Mrs. Jazeer. "Don't you, Basma?" she asked, leaning over. Basma managed to nod once. Again, Khadija offered her the food. She took a few mouthfuls and then refused any more. Khadija sighed forcefully and stood up.

"I'm only trying to help you, Basma. We cannot keep coming here every day with food if you will not eat it. It is not fair."

"She is right," Mrs. Jazeer concurred. "You are so weak you can barely wash yourself. And Imani has her hands full trying to clean and shop for you. It is too much." She patted Basma's shoulder. "You must try to get better."

Khadija took the tray of food back into the kitchen then called out, "I will leave this on the stove in case you change your mind."

Just then, Shafal arrived home early. The two women greeted him reservedly. Basma remained silent. Mrs. Jazeer immediately noticed that Shafal's eyes were twinkling. He beckoned her to join him in the kitchen with Khadija. Feeling his excitement, she quickly moved her portly form.

"I found a solution," he whispered. "I know what she needs. But I will tell you when it is certain. All right?" Mrs. Jazeer was clearly disappointed, but Shafal reassured her that she would know soon enough and they both stared at him with curiosity. Neither had seen this almost playful side of Shafal before.

Khadija gathered up her things and asked: "Do you still want me to come tomorrow?"

"Yes, yes. My plans will take some time. So, for now, I will still need both of you and Mrs. Sadawi's help."

The two women nodded and left together.

With his confidence and manhood restored, Shafal walked over to Basma and squatted before her. She showed absolutely no acknowledgement of his presence. Undeterred, he leaned in close and said: "I know what you need."

Part Two

CHAPTER 11

LONDON

When Kensasha Lewis first met Dr. Neelam Sethi, she was amazed at the older woman's vitality. Every day there were people calling her from all over the world, people coming to offer their support, and then there were those secret calls in which Dr. Sethi spoke only in a code. Yet, she always kept her focus.

That morning, they hadn't been at the office for more than an hour before another one of those special secret calls came in.

A half hour later, Kensasha, conservatively dressed in a gray tailored suit and pumps, was following Dr. Sethi out of a side entrance of her office building on Grosvenor Square and into the back seat of a black non-descript car. At the front of the building, the usual slew of foreign journalists were camped out, hoping to get an interview or a photograph.

As the car sped down the highway heading north, Kensasha rechecked her briefcase to make sure she had what she needed. The British driver said little and kept his focus on the road. Occasionally Dr. Sethi, looking a little weary, checked the back window to see if they were being tailed.

"I can't believe how quickly time flies. Just two more weeks left," Kensasha said, reaching over and cupping Dr. Sethi's hand. "You'll see that it is a good decision to speak before the United Nations and to the local women in Queens. Nothing beats international support."

Dr. Sethi sighed and looked away. "Yes, usually, that is true," she replied. "But I worry this can make more problems. And, I do not have someone to take over while I am in America."

"It'll only be for a week, two at the most. Although, I understand what you mean. Maybe you should consider having a full-time assistant. I'm sure the person wouldn't be as dedicated as you are. But then... they don't have to be."

Dr. Sethi turned and looked out the window in contemplation.

After an hour, the car turned off the highway in Surrey and entered a small suburban neighborhood, the kind where people walking their dogs often stopped to chat.

The two women got out of the car and hurried up the walkway of a house surrounded by tall thick hedges and hydrangea bushes. An Indian woman opened the door, delighted to see them.

Eight women of various nationalities, religions and backgrounds gathered in a large, open, well-furnished living room. Dr. Sethi greeted them and was led down a hall into a bedroom by one of the women. Kensasha followed.

Inside the room a young African girl, around six years old, sat on a bed sipping water and eating a sandwich. She looked up at the doctor with weary, frightened, yet determined, eyes.

Another African woman, husky and in her thirties, wearing the traditional Tanzanian dress, approached Dr. Sethi and took her hand.

"Thank you, Doctor," she said graciously, with a thick Tanzanian accent.

Dr. Sethi nodded humbly and walked over to the bed. "Hello, my name is Neelam Sethi. How are you feeling?"

The girl didn't understand so the older woman translated in Swahili.

"She say she feels weak."

Kensasha pulled a writing pad from her brief case and immediately began taking notes. Dr. Sethi sat on the edge of the bed to examine the girl. Kensasha decided to return to the living room.

Some of the women were sitting and waiting. There were a few mulling around in the kitchen. One woman talked on a cell phone while another typed on a laptop in an alcove. Everyone looked tired or overwhelmed. Kensasha found an empty space on the couch and opened her briefcase; she pulled out a digital voice recorder and put it on the coffee table. She surveyed the room for a moment.

"Okay, who wants to go next?"

An Arabian woman wearing a black abaya sat in the kitchen area with a sad distracted look on her face. Her name was Nasima Khatami, a twenty-two-year-old from Saudi Arabia. Kensasha spotted her.

"How about you over there?" Kensasha inquired, pointing in Nasima's direction. The woman looked up. Kensasha gestured for her to come into the living room and take a seat near the recorder. Nasima hesitated before coming over.

Two women, sitting on one of the couches, made room for her. A third woman joined Nasima on the couch. She was a twenty-four-year-old political science graduate student, originally from Iran, who also spoke Arabic and had volunteered to translate for the group. She stayed at the house one month out of the year.

Kensasha pushed the record button. "Okay, you know what to do. You don't have to say your name."

The translator repeated this to Nasima. She nodded, and looked around at the other women. They had all stopped what they were doing and moved in closer to listen. The young woman was not used to having so much attention placed on her. She cleared her throat and adjusted her veil. Then she lowered her eyes and stared off for a moment. When the first words came, they sounded like they were coming from someone who was just learning to speak. Each word was a surprise to the speaker. The translator repeated it all in English.

"My family is very angry with me because I refused to marry the boy that they chose for me. I told them that I wanted to marry another boy that I knew for a long time." Her voice began to crack. "...and I love him. But... they say it is not possible."

In the Khatami household, Nasima had attempted to talk with her parents but they dismissed her. She didn't know that the financial arrangements had already been finalized with her future husband's father. The only thing her parents were interested in was making the wedding preparations. So, in the subsequent days, Nasima witnessed the members of her family involving themselves in a wedding that she did not want. Because of her impending bride status, she was kept close to home.

"I cannot see the boy I love. Each day I get more sad. When I tell my family I will not marry this boy they chose for me, there is a big argument."

The shouting had escalated to such a feverish pitch that Nasima ran to her bedroom. But this didn't stop them. All evening she could hear her father and brothers expressing their indignation at her refusal to marry.

"Their anger got so bad, I became scared of them. I ran away to the house of a friend. Everyone was talking about it. My family is well respected in my city. Then people stopped talking to them. Everyone was against me. It was so hard. Then my friend made me leave because my family threatened to damage her home. And her parents didn't want me there at all."

When Nasima left her friend's house, she was aware of the shift in attitude on the streets. Those people who recognized her either turned their heads away or they shouted something ugly at her. Even people she'd known since childhood turned from her. So, she drew the thick fabric of her niqab up to cover most of her face and walked in the shadows. Where could she possibly go now? After walking the streets for hours, her stomach demanded food.

"I wanted to go to my boyfriend's, but I was afraid people there may try to hurt him. I thought of going back home and marrying the boy they wanted me to, and making everyone happy. Then I telephoned my boyfriend." Nasima paused and swallowed hard. "When I heard his voice, I knew I could not marry anyone but him. He told me, 'We will be together soon.' She paused again to wipe her tears.

Kensasha, intrigued so far, couldn't help but ask: "How did you get all the way to England?"

"I heard that my family said they were going to kill me for doing this to them. I had no place to go, so I left my city and walked many miles to a small village to hide. I was there for many weeks. I stayed close to the people who made the streets their home. They shared with me what little they could. It took time, but Omar, my boyfriend, got friends to help me.

Against the backdrop of jagged mountains and parched earth, Nasima, face covered, found herself riding in the back seat of a weather-beaten car. In the front were two young men she didn't know. The men had decided that an older model was best because it was known that only the well-to-do had access to the channels of escape, and the wherewithal necessary to see it through. Still, the men were worried. They knew they could be thrown into prison trying to smuggle a woman into another country. Regardless, she was too exhausted to worry at this point. After so many nights sleeping on the pavement, the torn brown vinyl seats of the car felt like a plush mattress. The car, occasionally spewing out puffs of white smoke, continued along the dusty highway, stopping only for the passengers to relieve themselves or to change drivers. Nasima slept for most of the journey.

"It took a long time, but we finally crossed the border to Jordan, then to Egypt. They hid me under the back seat at the check points."

Hearing this, Kensasha clasped her hand to her heart, taken in by Nasima's dangerous trek. At that moment, Dr. Sethi entered and took a seat.

"Those men were good friends. They risked their lives for you," Kensasha said, shaking her head and jotting something down on her pad. The interpreter translated what she said back to Nasima, who lowered her head in contemplation.

At the same time, one of the women dressed in a floral printed tunic over matching pants, her waist-length hair in one braid, walked over to the couch with two cups of tea on a tray and offered it to Nasima and Kensasha. Nasima took one and immediately sipped it. Kensasha gestured for the woman to put hers on the side table. As the woman did so, she noticed that Dr. Sethi had returned to the room and immediately went to fetch a cup for her as well.

Every woman in the room had her own special connection with Dr. Sethi, because Dr. Sethi made it a point to meet personally with every woman upon their arrival in England. To most of them, she was the only person who really understood their plight.

Eager to get to the England part of the story, Kensasha asked, "So, how long did it actually take you to get to England after you got to Egypt?" The interpreter conveyed this and Nasima contemplated for a while.

"I was there maybe seven months. Omar wanted to come, but the people who helped me said it was dangerous and I should remain in hiding. Then a rumor spread that my family found out I was in Egypt. The people who helped knew of Dr. Sethi so they sent me here. It was another long journey but at least I am alive and free." She looked over at Dr. Sethi and smiled demurely.

Stopping the recorder and picking up her cup, Kensasha sipped it thoughtfully. She looked at the faces of the women, each in different cultural attire.

"What amazes me the most, after coming here these past few weeks and hearing your stories," she said, visibly moved, "is that you are all running from your *own* families. That is so hard for me to imagine. And, you've come so far and still you have to fear them."

The women who understood English looked at each other. The ones that did not understand looked at the others questioningly. Kensasha put down the teacup, stood and walked over to the Arabian woman with her hand outstretched.

"Thank you for telling me your story," she said shaking the woman's hand. "I hope everything works out for you." Kensasha returned to her seat and asked Dr. Sethi, "How is she doing?"

"Considering the alternative, she is doing very well", Dr. Sethi replied. "Her aunt is here with her. And someday, when she marries, she will be able to experience sexual pleasure with her husband, as is her right," Dr. Sethi added, emphatically.

Dr. Sethi felt that the women sitting around her needed to hear that. They needed to know that an educated woman, a doctor, agreed with what they felt in their hearts. They had rights. Of course, none of them had actually voiced this to anyone. As for the new arrival, she was too young to even contemplate such a thing as having rights. She was just fortunate to have an aunt who loved and respected her enough to be willing to do whatever it took to rescue her from the brutal practice of "pharaonic circumcision"—a form of genital mutilation that rendered the women in her country as *sexless as male eunuchs*. Although they had ovaries, they were devoid of sexual desire. Why any mother would believe her daughter's genitals to be so ugly and abhorrent that they should be cut off or else the daughter was unfit to marry, was beyond her. Didn't these women realize its purpose was to usurp their power, guarantee fidelity, make them docile, obedient slaves, the property of their husbands and unable to ever truly compete with the men for status or resources? Nevertheless, this heinous act was widely practiced.

Before immigrating to England, the girl's aunt, Uhuru, had looked after the child for a few years following her mother, Nkaela's, death. Nkaela, who was twenty-five years old at the time, had just given birth to her fifth child and was once again undergoing the procedure that would restore a pencil-size opening to the anterior part of her vulva. As had happened when Nkaela was seven—and Uhuru also—her clitoris was cut away and the labial walls of her vagina were excised, then the raw skin surfaces sewn together. Her legs were tied to allow the wound to heal. In time, it was supposed to heal back to a smooth surface. But this time, with the fifth child, the old woman, *the gedda*, who had cut Nkaela, neglected to sterilize the knife, causing an infection.

Uhuru knew it wouldn't be long before her mother and grandmother back in Tanzania would be preparing her little niece for the same misogynistic rite following her seventh birthday. She decided to persuade her mother and grandmother to let the girl come visit with her in England a few months before the birthday. A Kenyan friend in London was planning a visit to Dodoma, the capitol of Tanzania, and could bring the child to London with him upon his return. Uhuru was to send her family a roundtrip ticket and they could then apply for the child's visa.

But the old matriarchs, who had greatly resented Uhuru's departure in the first place, though they accepted the money she sent every month, flatly refused. They informed her that they were not interested in going to all the trouble of getting a visa for anyone and that they "could use that money you spend on those aero planes".

Uhuru called Dr. Sethi several times before she finally received a return call from an unidentified assistant of Dr. Sethi. Uhuru then explained how important it was to her to rescue her niece and wanted to know what she was up against legally and the consequences.

"First of all," the assistant informed her, "We have no connections in Tanzania. Secondly, you would be committing a serious crime, since the child did not ask to leave her family." The assistant went on to say that the consequences depended on her family and the legal system in Tanzania of which, the assistant admitted, she knew nothing. But the assistant did add that they had a contact in Nairobi.

Consequently, acting on her own initiative, Uhuru orchestrated an elaborate kidnapping of her six-year-old niece from a small town near Kondoma, Tanzania, and had her smuggled into Nairobi where a Hindu couple, associates of Dr. Sethi, then worked hard to get the girl to England.

The teenage boys hired for the kidnapping were paid very little money but were happy for the adventure.

Fearing the child would be terrified, Uhuru told her contact, a man she knew from church, to urge the boys to be discreet and not draw any attention to themselves. The boys, two fourteen-year-olds and a sixteen-year-old hung around the streets most of the time doing nothing except hassling people for money.

Uhuru's contact had called his brother in Kenya, who then arranged everything else from there. He said he would only talk with everyone involved by public telephones and would have a friend transfer the instructions and money to the boys in Kondoma through an older boy he knew who traveled there monthly from a border town in Tanzania.

This older boy was a familiar sight in the villages where he sold an assortment of odds and ends that the people living there did not have access to. Everyone in the border town knew the boy and they trusted him. The boy, in turn, would never know the person giving him the money or instructions. That way, if any of the boys became cocky at any time in the future and told what they did, the contact's brother and older boy wouldn't have much to say.

It was easy, really. The grandmother was busy conversing with the other elder women while the mother was in the hut with Nkaela's three-year-old. The niece was playing with children completely out of sight of the grandmother. One boy watched the child until she wandered away from the view of the other children. He simply walked up to the child and spoke to her then asked if she'd like to ride on his bike. He led her away from the village and then helped her onto the bike and rode quickly to Kondoma.

Once there, he took her to an old shack where he and the other boys often hung out drinking beer, laughing and listening to hip hop music from an old beat-up boom box. His friends gave the child Coca-Cola and chocolate bars to keep her calm and then waited for the older boy to show up with the rest of the money he promised them. Each kept reminding the other to speak politely to the child so she wouldn't become frightened.

Before long, the older boy arrived carrying jeans, a pair of socks, a T-shirt, and a colorful book for the child, as per instructions. He paid the boys $15 each, which seemed like a fortune to them, and pulled out a bag full of lunchmeat sandwiches for everyone.

When the child finished eating her sandwich, she said she wanted to go home. The older boy told her not to worry. He would be taking her back home on a bus.

The child had never been on a bus and was fascinated by the whole journey. But when he carried her from the bus in the border town and put her into the back seat of a car driven by the Hindu woman, she began to cry uncontrollably. In the end, her auntie's voice on a cell phone, which the Hindu woman held to her ear, stopped the tears.

***

Again, time had pushed the sun clean across the sky. Now the blood-red disk hovered just above the horizon. In the suburban house, each woman was involved in either dinner preparations, or sleep arrangements for the new arrival. Kensasha and Dr. Sethi had long since departed.

The Arabian woman, Nasima, slipped out of a side door when no one was looking. She walked several blocks to a fairly busy main street in the quaint middle-class town.

People strolled about, absorbed in their own affairs, yet they smiled at one another when passing.

Looking around cautiously, Nasima hurried along the street. Some people eyed her, but most ignored her. In the last decade, even small towns like this one had seen a considerable number of foreign-attired women in the shops and on the buses.

When she spotted a mailbox, she reached into the pocket of her abaya, pulled out a letter, and quickly dropped it in and then continued down the street. Every few steps, she cautiously glanced over her shoulder again.

Twenty minutes later, she slipped back into the house through the side door she had left ajar. No one noticed.

***

NEW YORK

Basma eased out of the bathroom, holding on to the wall for support. As she entered the living room, the front door opened and both Abdel and Ahmed entered carrying very large packages. They passed her and continued toward the bedrooms.

Abdel, not stopping, said, "Hi Mom."

Ahmed added quickly, "Shouldn't you be in bed?"

Not waiting for her reply, they disappeared for a few seconds, and then rushed back past her to the front door. Puzzled, Basma stood watching the front door close behind them. Before she could take another step, Shafal came in carrying groceries.

"Why are you out of bed?" he asked, taking the groceries into the kitchen. Basma ignored the question and followed him.

"Shafal, why so much shopping?"

Again, the front door opened, and the two boys returned with more large packages from Costco and J.C. Penny. From the kitchen, Basma stared after them as they traipsed by towards the bedrooms.

"What is happening here?" Shafal called out to the boys. Basma gave him a puzzled look.

"I guess now is the time to tell you," he responded, as Abdel and Ahmed walked over to Basma. Abdel smiled at her. She stared back at them both and then at Shafal, mystified.

"What?"

"Tomorrow, your mother and your Uncle Khalid will arrive here to take care of you."

Hearing this, Basma's legs turned to jelly. Both boys reached for her, but Ahmed was the first to catch her. Shafal smiled, assured Basma was overcome with joy.

The following day, when Basma heard the commotion in the outside hallway, her first instinct was to adjust her white hijab. She was dressed in a long floral skirt and long sleeved, high collared blouse. As she shuffled to the front door, she inspected the living room and sighed when she spotted her once luscious plants on the windowsill now in varying stages of decay.

She nervously adjusted a lamp, and was straightening a pillow on the couch when the door flung open and Shafal practically tumbled in carrying several tattered pieces of luggage. Her mother, Sumera, followed, covered head-to-toe in black with just a tiny slit for her eyes. This startled Basma, for a second, but Sumera's eyes sparkled through the slit when she spotted her daughter, and Basma ran to her.

The feel of her mother's arms was too much. She burst into tears, and the two women held each other in a long emotional embrace, while the rest of the group continued to file through the door.

Uncle Khalid, wearing a grey tweed sleeveless tunic over a floor-length white robe, entered carrying an old suitcase and a faded satchel covered with a Persian-styled carpet material. His stern face was much older now. His salt and pepper beard had turned snow white. A thin young woman, with a poised erect posture, followed, also wearing the abaya with her face covered. Right behind her, but out of Basma's line of vision, was none other than her cousin, Sirhan, now in his forties. He was the only one wearing western-styled pants and shirt. He carried a few bags, and was still handsome despite that intense, perpetually serious, expression. And, finally, Tariq Tali, Khadija's husband, stumbled in dragging a hefty cardboard box of handmade gifts, tied with thick rope.

Basma broke free of the embrace with her mother to wipe her eyes. Then she focused on Khalid who loomed over her like a mad holy man. She bowed to him politely. He scrutinized her as if trying to ascertain the cause of her supposed illness. Then he frowned when he looked at her clothes. Basma lowered her eyes. Her mother reached for her hand.

Khalid turned to Shafal, "You send your wife to work to make money? But that is a man's duty." All eyes stared at Shafal. Khalid continued, "A respectable woman should not work outside the home unless it is in the family business. If a woman makes money, she becomes like a man. Then how can you control her?"

Shafal glanced sheepishly at Tariq Tali following Uncle Khalid's rebuke in front of everyone. Khalid continued, unconcerned with whom he might offend.

"Well, it is a blessing that you now have a chance to be around one of the most obedient women in our village." He turned and gently pulled Osha forward to meet Basma. It was in this moment that Basma saw Sirhan. She felt sick to her stomach, her head started spinning and her body gave a perceptible swoon. She began hallucinating. The sound of their voices became distorted, jarring, and the faces of Khalid and Sirhan merged into each other like some monstrous beast. A blood red liquid poured from the beast's eyes and then… darkness engulfed her.

When Basma finally regained consciousness, she found herself lying on her bed with her mother, Sumera, sitting on the edge pressing a cool wet cloth to her forehead. The younger woman sat in a chair scanning the bedroom with great interest. Both women's faces were now unveiled, since Tariq Tali had already departed, and Basma was delighted to finally see her mother's face.

Sumera sighed with relief and asked, "Are you feeling better?" Basma nodded, trying to remember what happened. "Too much excitement all at once, huh? We were all so happy to see you that we forgot how sick you have become."

Basma tried to sit up. Sumera helped her. The young woman stood up politely. Sumera beckoned her over to the bed.

"Basma, this is Sirhan's wife, Osha." Osha bowed toward Basma and Basma returned a smile. "He took her as his wife only five months now," Sumera informed. "She has fit in with his other wives and the children all love her."

Basma nodded pretending to be impressed.

"Very soon she will add more children to the family," Sumera predicted.

Osha smiled demurely.

Basma glared back. Rubbing her temples, she said, "I think I should rest here a little while longer. You can take Osha to get settled in." She lay back down.

"I do not mind sitting here with you," Sumera said with renewed concern. "It is a great pleasure for me just to look at your face. I have not seen it since you left for America."

Basma took hold of her hand, "Now you will have many days to see my face and I will have many days to see yours. But you have had such a long journey. It is better you go and get some rest yourself." Sumera yielded to her suggestion and led Osha out of the bedroom.

***

By dinnertime, the house guests had settled in somewhat. Now, the men sat in a group around the couch talking softly while the food was being prepared to serve.

Earlier, Basma's tidy little kitchen had been in chaos. Sumera and Osha had labored for several hours trying to cook up enough food for everyone, while learning to use all the unfamiliar appliances and gadgets that Shafal had proudly handed them, but both became intimidated by all the multi-functioning buttons, switches and speeds offered. And who could read the instructions? Finally, Sumera gave up and resorted to what she knew. She took the rice cooker, the food processor, an electric can opener, and a few other strange looking metal contraptions and put them on the floor in the corner. Armed only with a couple of knives and a few large spoons, the two women reproduced a delicious looking array of Yemeni cuisine.

Sweet and pungent aromas wafted through the apartment. They lured Basma from her bed. When she arrived at the doorway of her living room, she paused a moment staring at its transformation. A large white sheet had been spread on the floor in the middle of the room. The couch and table had been moved to the front entryway making room for the sheet. She stepped gingerly around Osha, who was kneeling down to place the sahawig—hot sauce—and condiments—like houlbah—on the sheet. And she eased passed the men, choosing not to disturb their intense conversation.

Sumera was in the process of pouring the contents of a big pot into a large aluminum tray when Basma entered. The kitchen table was already crowded with other aluminum trays, each filled with food.

"Mother! This is... I cannot believe you have done all this!"

"Osha is a great help," Sumera replied, modestly. "She does whatever I tell her to do, and very fast." Osha returned in time to hear the praise and smiled modestly at Sumera.

Basma eased closer to the table and surveyed the array of dishes.

"These are some of my favorites!" she noted. "I have not made them in many years."

"Well, maybe now you will eat something and stop looking as thin as a skeleton," Sumera replied.

Just then, someone came through the doorway. Before Basma could see who approached, he was next to her.

"Cousin! I did not have a chance to greet you earlier, "Sirhan announced, dispassionately. "Are you feeling better?"

Basma instinctively recoiled, but caught herself, and pretended to be excited to see him.

"Yes, thank you," she responded with difficulty. Continuing to focus on the food, she said "I... I am grateful that you have left your successful business to come so far because of me. Umm," she faltered adjusting the trays. "I am happy to have you... and, and your... Osha here," she nodded at Osha, her voice trailed, "... staying with us." Then, as if aware of her awkwardness, she shifted focus. "And look at all this food Osha has helped my mother prepare." She gestured toward the table excitedly.

Sirhan, like his father, was always economical when it came to expressions of pleasure or happiness. He managed what could have been considered a smile and moved closer to Osha. Basma pointed to a platter filled with aseed—tiny dumplings topped with gravy.

"Remember this one!" she asked Sirhan, her eyes focusing on a distant point in space. "We would all play that game: who could eat the most in one minute. And you and... and," the name caught in her throat as a face filled the distant point, little Aisha, grinning and giggling. "W-would always..." Her voice dropped to a whisper. "win."

Sirhan stared at her.

Did they all forget? What are they doing here? Why is it so hot?

Osha sprung to Basma's side. "You are feeling bad?" she asked in the sweetest voice.

"Maybe I need to eat something soon," Basma suggested, her head throbbing.

"We can take food in now," Osha exclaimed.

"Yes, yes. Everything is ready," Sumera added. Instantly, there was a lot of movement as the two women began to carry the large aluminum platters into the living room. Basma reached to take one, but Sirhan stopped her.

"They have come to help make things easier for you. Let them do it," he commanded.

Basma nodded, obediently, and walked with a concerted effort into the living room to take her place around the sheet.

***

The next morning, Shafal coaxed a very jet-lagged Sirhan and Uncle Khalid out of bed. They breakfasted on eggs cooked with tomatoes and onions, and homemade fateh mixed with butter and honey. Osha had prepared food at the crack-of-dawn for Abdel and Ahmed. No bagels and coffee from a donut stand near the subway for these boys today.

Does the girl ever sleep?

With pride, Shafal drove Khalid and Sirhan into the busy garage so they could see where he worked. Khalid still wore his traditional robe and tunic. Feeling superior, some of the Pakistani drivers distanced themselves from the newcomers in the same way city folk distanced themselves from country folk. But most of the drivers were quite friendly. Sirhan, with his own air of superiority, scrutinized everyone and everything.

By late afternoon, Shafal did what he spent each day doing: weaving in and out of bumper-to-bumper traffic, trying to get across the Queens Borough Bridge. Sirhan and Uncle Khalid in the back seat of the cab watched as the highly captivating energy of New York City swirled all around them, their glances darting from tall skyscrapers to billboards to women in shorts and low-cut sleeveless tops. Shaking their heads at the disgrace, both continued to look.

As the cab crossed 60th street, Khalid leaned forward to talk with Shafal through the open panel in the partition.

"You see these women, Shafal?" asked Khalid. "They are like men. They do what they want. The men here are not real men. They let their women walk around uncovered for other men to stare at. See that!" he pointed out a young woman leaving a restaurant with a man on each side. She laughed, and grabbed one man's arm, playfully, and she pulled the other man along in a familiar gesture.

Sirhan sneered and looked away mumbling, "Women having sex with any man they want?" He shook his head in consideration. "Who can marry them? They are already used."

When the cab finally reached 57th Street and 7th Avenue, heading south to Times Square, a wall of neon lights and mega billboards swarmed up on both sides of the street. Three-storied posters with scantily clad women and men were on display for all to see. Uncle Khalid and Sirhan scanned the scene all around them with fascination and contempt. Shafal peered through the rearview mirror at them.

"Now you understand how hard it has been for me to raise my family here and keep them decent boys. Tomorrow, I will take you to Ahmed's office. He just got a job on Wall Street," Shafal informed them with pride. But the news was lost on them, since neither had ever heard of Wall Street.

The cab careened left on 42nd Street while the men continued their critique of the Big Apple.

***

Shafal decided that the women would sleep in Ahmed's room. Basma spent the morning assisting her mother in making space for the extra luggage. Now she was busy helping Osha—who seemed to be an unstoppable workhorse—unpack and arrange a few more things. She was squatting between the bed and the chest of drawers putting clothes in neat piles when the men were heard returning.

Sirhan stormed into the bedroom agitated, eyes flaring but was instantly relieved when he spotted Osha. Basma's body grew rigid.

"I don't want you outside—only to the Mosque," he commanded his wife, as if they were suddenly in the middle of a war zone. "This means no shopping!"

Osha's serene face dropped. Sirhan ignored it.

"This place is not for a respectable Muslim woman like you. You'll find plenty to keep you busy inside." He stormed back out. Basma looked at Osha, her face now serene once again, who had resumed taking items from a suitcase, and her face grew dark with anger.

"You must be very disappointed?" Basma asked, compassionately.

"My husband knows what is best for me."

Basma lowered her eyes and grunted, then walked over to the window and gazed out.

"When we first came here, I was afraid to leave the house. Shafal and the boys had to buy all the groceries. I would just sit most of the day afraid of all the noises outside. So many cars and planes and words I could not understand." She walked back to the bed and sat down. "One day, Mrs. Sadawi... her husband owns this building, you will meet her... she came here one day and made me come shopping with her." Lost in revelry, Basma smiled to herself. "It was funny because I was so scared. But after, I was okay. I wanted to go out shopping every day. But Shafal was very angry. When I wanted to go outside, he did not want me to go."

"So, you never go outside?"

"Of course, I go... I used to go outside. I even had a job and..."

Basma delighted in telling Osha all about going to work on her own, and eating in a restaurant. However, she did leave out some of her exploits.

One afternoon, a few weeks later, Sirhan and Uncle Khalid sat conversing on the couch when Basma entered from the hallway. Her neck muscles tightened, as they always did, at the sight of him. Why was he here, in her house? Feeling overwhelming defiance, she walked right past them and began to rearrange the wilted plants on the windowsill, deliberately making a racket. Sumera rushed from the kitchen, put her arms around Basma, and led her back towards the bedroom.

"You don't need to do that now. Go and lay down. We will take care of everything for you. I am making the food. Osha can take care of that for you. Don't worry yourself."

In the days that followed, Basma wondered how much longer she could endure being treated like an invalid, or worse, like she was feeble-minded. This was her house after all, wasn't it?

CHAPTER 12

LONDON

Dr. Neelam Sethi's third-floor flat with its high ceilings was located in the Southwest section of London. Kensasha had been staying there to save money at Dr. Sethi's suggestion. The four-room flat had tall arched windows at one end of a large central room flanked by white walls covered with paintings from local artists. Dr. Sethi had replaced the plain wood or chrome frames with elaborately carved oak and mahogany ones that were themselves works of art. Along one wall, opposite the bay of windows, stood five bookcases, each ten feet tall and packed solid with books on Asian and European political science, sociology, and medicine, with a special section devoted to novels and non-fiction written by women.

Although the furniture was purchased merely for functionality, an armoire hand-painted in the classical style of Mughal India, was both a thing of beauty and function.

A few feet from the armoire was Kensasha's favorite: a comfortable reading chair wide enough to curl her legs under her or stretch them over the arm—when Dr. Sethi wasn't around.

One evening during Kensasha's stay, Dr. Sethi decided to host a small gathering of her close friends and supporters to meet Kensasha Lewis.

With her long braids pulled back and twisted into an elegant chignon, Kensasha tried on several outfits she'd brought before settling on a wine-colored silk blouse and a simple black pencil skirt. She then joined Neelam in the kitchen, where they prepared everything together.

Half an hour before the guests were due to arrive, Kensasha unwrapped two flower bouquets and began arranging them in vases to go on the white linen-covered buffet table, between an assortment of wines, and scented yellow candles.

In the kitchen, Neelam placed samosas—little pastries filled with spiced potatoes and green peas, on a large platter, and unscrewed jars of mango, tamarind and onion chutneys to go over the samosas.

During most of the preparation, they kept their conversation to a minimum. When they did speak, however, it was just to convey information about the food or instructions on placement of the furniture. When there was little left to do, Kensasha engaged Dr. Sethi in another of their many discussions.

"I still don't understand why those women continue to wear those black robes in a free country. Their families aren't around."

Neelam stopped what she is doing. The statement confused her.

"Perhaps, because it is a free country," she replied in a clipped tone.

Kensasha reached for another flower and stuck it into the vase. "But they are not oppressed here," she commented. "They do it in America, too, outside of the mosque. It's so strange to me."

"Oh… so you, a Muslim, think covering is oppression?" Neelam asked, diplomatically, while spooning condiments into ornate silver bowls.

"Of course, it is," replied Kensasha, adamantly. "It has nothing whatsoever to do with Islam. I say they do it because they are afraid. Afraid of what the men will do if they don't. Remember years ago, in Afghanistan, some women were badly beaten for not wearing those awful burkas? Soon after the Taliban were ousted, many women began to show their faces. Now, the Taliban have returned. The situation there will likely get worse for women once the last of the American soldiers pull out."

"But those are two different things, Kensasha." Neelam sighed heavily, and brought out the platter of pastries and condiments and placed them near the wine and candles. "A woman who covers her head is one thing, denying women their natural human rights are another."

Kensasha stopped the floral arranging abruptly and looked over at Neelam. "Forcing women to cover is denying them their identity, their individualism, their humanity. It's the same thing, Dr. Sethi."

"No, it is not!" Neelam replied, maintaining composure. "Mandating or forcing a woman to cover her head and body is not the same as a woman wanting to do it. It is quite different, Kensasha."

Kensasha gathered up the paper, loose leaves and broken stems from the bouquet. "But they don't really want to do that. They're just trying to—"

"You are wrong," Neelam interjected. "I know women who are doctors like me. I know women who will become professors like you, and they cover their heads whenever they are in public. Very independent women, I might add. Some live here in London, and they are not afraid. They want to do it. Covering the hair is a part of their culture that they like. It is not part of your culture, so it is strange for you."

The doorbell rang. Dr. Sethi went over to the intercom and spoke into it, waited, then pushed the buzzer. She returned to the kitchen to get another dish to add to the buffet table.

"Listen," she continued, softening her tone. "This is a very complicated matter. There is a lot of confusion surrounding this. Many old traditions, including Christianity and Judaism have women wearing scarves on their heads also, remember?"

After positioning the food next to the vase of flowers, she went over to the mantel to get a box of matches and lit the candles.

"In Africa, the women do it," Neelam went on. "You've seen it. In my culture, they do it. I used to do it all the time. Now, not so much, but I liked it. I felt very feminine. But I was never forced to wear the veil." There was a knock at the door. "Anyway," she added, smiling, as Kensasha went to open it. "I would not have done it if I was forced."

Several guests entered together: two men and three women. One of the men and two of the women, who both wore colorful saris with flowing sheer scarves draped over their heads and shoulders, were Hindu. The other man and woman were British. They were all very cheerful and chatty, so the energy shifted towards attending to the guests. The doorbell rang, again.

It was weeks later when Kensasha and Dr. Sethi returned to the house in the suburbs of Surrey for Kensasha to complete her interviews before flying back to America.

As before, all of the women were drawn into the sitting room even though some of them could not understand English or Arabic. Simply knowing that each had shared the common experience of abuse, had had their lives threatened or worse, and had miraculously found their way to this free country, made them comrades.

This time it was a fifteen-year-old Pakistani girl who entered the living room and sat opposite Kensasha. The same Iranian woman interpreter came in and sat next to the girl. This interpreter had only a few more days left in her stay before another volunteer would arrive to assist in interpreting the many dialects of the Indian languages, Farsi—the modern Persian language, Arabic and Urdu.

Kensasha pulled out a small notebook from her briefcase, the digital voice recorder, then searched her handbag for a pen to take notes on the girl's story.

NEW YORK

Finally, the apartment was quiet. Basma knew her uncle was most probably still around, but she could not stay cooped up in her bedroom a moment longer. She headed to the kitchen to make a cup of tea hoping to locate the tea bags without too much trouble. Sumera had decided to reorganize the kitchen her way. So now, Basma had to search the cupboards for what she needed in her own kitchen.

Uncle Khalid was at the stove trying to heat up some leftovers when she entered. She managed a thin smile.

"Is Osha still downstairs doing the wash?" Basma inquired.

Khalid grunted an affirmative.

"Is there water in the kettle?" She pressed.

"There is enough," he said, shaking it. "Now that you are here, you can make me a plate of food." He gestured with disdain at the pot and said: "This is woman's work."

Suddenly, her face flushed and her body began to tremble. The words that spilled from her lips surprised her once again.

"I'm going out," she announced, as if it were a revelation.

"Out? You cannot go out," Khalid protested. Ignoring him, Basma spun around and stormed out of the front door.

With fire under her feet, she huffed and puffed as she walked in no particular direction. Her heart pumped wildly. Her muscles finally released months of stagnant energy. How many times had she wanted to run out, to escape the suffocation?

Her chest expanded in the effort to let in more oxygen. The oxygen flooded her brain. She walked faster, harder. It was most exhilarating. It reminded her of the day she actually ran down the street to meet the Bakery Guy. The thought of him slowed her pace a bit.

After several long blocks of this, she stopped to rest at the small corner playground opposite a school. A seven-foot-high chain-linked fence surrounded the noisy park. Mothers looked on as their children enjoyed themselves climbing, sliding, swinging or filling pails in the sand boxes. It was the same park where Basma had taken Abdel when he was a baby.

She wiped away the sweat that was now dripping down her face, and walked up to the fence to look in. One little girl was engrossed in a puzzle. Basma became absorbed in the joyous faces of the children as they played.

A faint image of orange tulips flickered by. She recalled a time when her windowsills had been filled with healthy, thriving plants and when she went riding in a sleek red car along a tree lined highway. She heard a man's voice whispering and her own voice giggling. She gripped the chain-linked fence. That time was over now... gone. It had all slipped right through her fingers.

Her eyes swelled with hot salty tears but she refused to let even one fall.

Later that evening, her whole family stood staring at her. Apparently, Uncle Khalid had been greatly affronted by her unabashed act of Independence.

"...and she was very rude... she just walked out," he explained as he paced the living room floor flailing his arms in the air.

Basma sat on the couch listening with indifference. Shafal seemed ashamed of his crazy wife's disrespectful behavior toward an elder patriarch. She saw her mother and Osha eyeing her with pity.

Both Abdel and Ahmed looked on captivated by Uncle Khalid's rant. Although, neither could figure out what all the fuss was about. She went out. So, what?

Still, Sirhan's knowing expression indicated that this was indeed something very serious.

"See how this country corrupts our women and our values?" he insisted. Shafal nodded, pleased to finally have someone understand what he had always recognized. Sirhan glared at Basma.

"You cannot live here without becoming caught up in their ways. You are sick in the mind." His voice was cutting, "I do not want you talking to Osha about how free women are here." He raised his head and straightened his shoulders unconsciously and his voice took on an air of piety. "There is no freedom here. This country is for indulgence and it is corrupted; it disobeys all the laws of Islam."

While each of them silently contemplated what Sirhan had said, Basma quietly got up, went into the bedroom and closed the door. She really didn't care what Sirhan said or thought. He was less than nothing in her eyes. As for Uncle Khalid and Shafal, well, what more could she expect?

Basma had hoped Sumera would come over, and throw her arms around her and tell them all to stop making an issue over nothing. But Sumera had become a stranger. Now, obedient, pliable Osha had become her dream daughter. Not once, since arriving nearly a month ago, had Sumera taken the time to just sit, and talk, and listen to what Basma had to say. In fact, she showed little interest in the life her daughter had led since she'd married her off to Shafal at thirteen years of age.

Whatever bond Basma thought she had with her mother dissolved that day.

LONDON

With her pen in hand, Kensasha reached for her notebook just as Neelam accepted a cup of chai that had been handed to her. Kensasha pressed the record button on her recorder, and both of them readied themselves as the young girl began to tell her story.

"I am from Pakistan," the girl relayed. "I am fifteen years old. First, you must understand that women and men in my village are separated all the time. Only close family members are permitted to talk to a woman. When this girl in my village met this boy, and fell in love with him, she did not want anyone to know about it. But people in my village are always watching and talking about each other.

"The boy and girl tried to hide their feelings but people suspected something and told the girl's father. When her father found out she had a boyfriend, he was very angry and went out looking for her. That particular day, she was at the house of her boyfriend. Her father found out where he lived. In a rage, he went there, and stabbed his daughter many times, and then he cut off her head."

"Oh, my God!" Kensasha exclaimed. Some of the women gasped and covered their mouths.

The girl lowered her head a moment. Kensasha looked over at Neelam Sethi, wide-eyed. Neelam nodded back in assurance that this did actually happen.

The girl's eyes began to water as she recalled the commotion in the village when the girl's headless body was being brought out of the house. The boyfriend had vomited and had become inconsolable. His whole family had to find different shelter for weeks while the blood was cleaned from the carpets and walls.

She recalled how many villagers took the side of the father. They claimed to understand his pain of having a shameless, vile daughter who obviously did not care what affect her actions would have on her family. 'How many other boyfriends did she have?' was the pervasive question.

The Pakistani girl wiped her eyes and continued, "The man who raped me... he lives in our village. He knew I was to be married but he did not care about that. The Chief of the Police begged him to marry me to save my life and to keep him out of jail. But he did not want to do it. And I did not..."

"Wait!" Kensasha called out. "I didn't get that. You said marry?"

The translator spoke to the girl in Urdu. The girl listened, and began to explain. "In my country, if a girl is raped, automatically, she brings shame to her family. No one will ever marry her or her sisters. But if the man who rapes the girl marries her, then there is no more shame for the family. They will not kill her."

The recorder stopped. Kensasha examined it and sucked her teeth in frustration. "I can't believe this!" Kensasha exclaimed, "I forgot to charge the battery last night."

Neelam stood and began to smooth out her tunic. "Don't worry about it. You have more than enough already."

"Still, I wanted to record the rest of her story."

"You already know the rest. It's the usual. Her father shot her and left her for dead. The police chief helped get her out of the village." Neelam sighed. "There are so many of these stories. Just know that what they all have in common is that a woman's life is second to some supposed family honor. Women have no protection from their families. They have no right to sexuality and no right to choose whom to love or spend their lives with. Actually, they have no right to love. Period!

"And the problems women have are not only in Arab countries or African countries. In India, a woman's worth boils down to her dowry or how much more money her in-laws can intimidate her parents into giving them after the wedding. In the villages where the parents are too poor to come up with more money, the in-laws cast the wife out into the street or send her back home—which brings great shame—or they kill her, so that their son can remarry," Neelam concluded, heatedly, and stepped past the Pakistani girl over to a table to get her handbag.

"We have a long drive back. We should leave now," she told Kensasha.

Reluctantly, Kensasha picked up the recorder and put it back into her briefcase along with the writing pad. Rising to her feet, she embraced the Pakistani girl, and looked around at everyone. Faces, once foreign, were now very familiar. Nasima Khatami smiled warmly when her eyes met Kensasha's.

"Thank you all for sharing your stories with me," Kensasha said, with a lump in her throat. "My book will be a way to let people know what you've been through. In American culture, there is a lot of violence against women as well, but it is different from in your countries. In America, it is a crime, not an accepted part of the culture. Parents don't kill their daughters to protect the family. The mere notion of such a thing is bizarre and inhuman to us. But, still, we have a lot of violence there and women are raped and killed. In America, many of those women do fight back physically or through the courts. And often, family members will go after the rapist. But I do hope we can all come together in the future to find the real cause behind all these hate crimes against women, and all this cruelty and put an end to it forever. So, pray that we can get an international forum together, followed by a summit."

The interpreter translated all of this. The women crowded around Kensasha to say their goodbyes. Neelam, looking a little weary, moved towards the front door, paused and said:

"Now remember, that young girl must remain here for at least two more weeks without going outside of the house." The women nodded at her in agreement. She continued to the door with Kensasha following. "I will be away for almost two weeks. I caution all of you to keep indoors as much as possible." Those who could understand her listened with rapt attention. She stopped and turned around. Her expression was that of great concern and guilt. These women were her charges. How could she leave them for so long?

"Remember," she commanded, "never, ever, let anyone know where you are. This is very, very important."

***

As their mute driver focused on the road ahead, both Kensasha and Neelam tried to get comfortable in the back seat, but found it hard after having heard those stories, particularly Kensasha.

"Who would believe such a story? I'm glad it's on tape. Marrying the rapist to save your life? That's absolutely ludicrous!" declared Kensasha, feeling a wave of emotion welling up inside.

"Rape is the worst thing that could happen to these women," Neelam explained "You see, it is always their fault. No matter how young they are. They must have tempted the poor helpless man, is the excuse. Even the suspicion that a girl has been raped is enough to put her in danger."

Kensasha slumped down in the opposite corner of the car. "What do they do to the rapist?"

"Nothing usually," replied Neelam. "Sometimes the police will put them in jail for a while, but nothing severe. The man always claims it is not his fault. She aroused him. He is considered the victim."

"And people believe that?" She attempted to sit up straight, but failed.

"Maybe the worst of these is about two sisters from Yemen. One seven, the other nine. They were seen talking to two older men. That is all. The father was told about this. He believed that the men must have lured the girls off somewhere and molested them. The girls denied the men had even touched them."

Neelam paused and looked out of the window for some object of beauty to calm her, something to create distance from the horror. She found it in the lilac bushes planted outside the last house just before the car got onto the highway back to London. She rolled down the window to catch their rich fragrance.

"The father had a doctor examine the girls. The doctor found that they were still virgins. They had not been harmed. Even so, the father would not believe the doctor. After, he and one of his sons shot both of the girls, many times, while they slept. One girl died immediately. The other lived a few days, but was brain dead." Tears welled up in Kensasha eyes.

"That's insanity!"

Neelam turned to her, determination in her eyes.

"That is why we have to do all we can to stop it."

CHAPTER 13

I n the days that followed, Neelam Sethi oversaw making hotel reservations for her short visit to New York. Kensasha, on the other hand, busied herself with finding out all the pertinent information she could about who made up the network of support and how they maintained their high-level security for each other and the women.

What Kensasha discovered was that those involved never met in a group. They used the Internet for ninety-five percent of their communication and arrangements. She learned that many foundations had provided financial support, while some of the people working in small European government jobs had provided equipment to forge new documentation. Most was done in total secrecy.

With the reservations settled, Neelam turned her attention to speechwriting—her favorite pastime. Closing the curtains of her office window one afternoon, to diminish the glare of the sun, she switched on her computer and poured herself a glass of red wine.

The first meeting, with one of ten women's organizations to gather the needed political support, was scheduled after her return from New York. She didn't want to waste any time deciding what to feed the media. From the very beginning, this new women's coalition that had sprung up around her had to be taken seriously. They had to differentiate themselves from all the other women's coalitions in the past. And indeed, they could, because these women were all powerful activists from the most problematic regions in the world. They had to challenge all the social and religious tenets of every culture that continued to enable violence towards and intimidation of women—and in their own respective countries of Saudi Arabia, India, Afghanistan, and parts of Pakistan, the outright subjugation of women. Perhaps, ultimately, the forum shouldn't be just about Asian, African, Arab or Persian women, but all women who had had violence inflicted on them because of their gender—including Europeans.

How could she convince the Europeans and Americans that many women like themselves were still fettered in their minds, that much of the violence inflicted on women in the West—daily—is psychological, but violence, nonetheless? Didn't American women still hold themselves up to a standard evolved from a historically misogynistic social stratum?

Hadn't a multi-billion-dollar industry grown up around the insecurity and shame women and young girls had been made to feel about their female bodies— its imperfections—and how to improve it? Each year women all over the world spent billions trying to improve their flawed selves—whether through pills, cosmetics or surgery. All in an effort to create some ideal version of a woman—for men's desire—that Mother Nature seemed too inept to produce.

She coined a perfect term for it all. A term inspired by something she'd read somewhere: like body hatred or body terror.

She reexamined the strategy for socially conditioning the female. A strategy that supplanted natural urges, instincts and intuitive knowing with subliminal messages of inadequacy, to outright disrespect by a deluge of images of thin prepubescent looking girls with breast implants, layered in makeup and hair extensions. Images that supposedly represented what a woman should aspire to look like. And then she added to all that the constant barrage of ads about women with weight problems. If she analyzed how sexual harassment had been used to usurp a woman's voice and power in the work place, and how unbridled rape disempowered women in the military, and incorporated all the violence inflicted on the women in Africa and the Middle East who somehow violated some restriction imposed on their bodies, be it physical or emotional violence, and included the millions of fetuses aborted in India and China just because they were female—it could only be labeled one thing: "gender terrorism."

She slid her chair away from the desk, picked up her glass of wine and walked over to the window. Peering through the small slit between the curtain panels, she sipped the wine and gazed at the fashion-conscious young women strolling by. Maybe she should exploit this idea, give it a political association.

Let's see… distract women, keep them body-obsessed, worried about their looks and they would be poor competitors in the office, poor negotiators in the board room and ineffectual voices in the Houses of Parliament. Keep them oblivious to the global jousting for supremacy or corporate and political subterfuge. Yes… that's it!

Back at her desk, her fingers moved, feverishly, across the keyboard.

Terrorism means the use of violence and intimidation in the pursuit of political and religious aims. Isn't this the very thing that has been done to women all down the centuries in mostly every culture?

Three countries actually have religious police. How absurd. If only the women have to be policed to keep them from laughing in public, traveling unescorted by a male, singing or playing an instrument in public, smoking a cigarette, driving a car, or exposing any skin on their body in public, then surely that's gender terrorism.

What else explains why an exposed wrist caused one woman to be dragged from her car by a mob of offended males, and beaten to death? Why was a woman who was seen riding in a car with a man who wasn't her relative, gang raped and then arrested and thrown into jail for having sex outside of marriage with her rapists? Fortunately, that incident did catch the attention of the international press causing enough outrage against the offending country to secure the woman's release. But nothing can repair what happened to her. It was an attack on her womanhood and her humanity. And that recent attack in India, when a woman traveling on a bus with her boyfriend was gang raped, sexually assaulted with a weapon, and died.

It's about using fear to maintain control. It was pure gender terrorism.

Ah, but hasn't the subjection of women always been political? Always been about power in society? Control? Who would control the resources, the populace?

She paused, staring at the screen. There was nothing new, here. What then could she possibly say to the international community that they hadn't heard before? Or, that they didn't already know? Or, that some legislation hadn't, already, addressed? What could Dr. Neelam Sethi possibly say that wasn't already included in scathing discourses by staunch, erudite feminists down through the ages? What indeed? She clicked save and shut down the computer.

***

At last, everything was in order. They would leave for New York the following morning. Neelam had spent most of the day packing and talking on the phone to her associates across the country. Kensasha saw hope in Neelam's eyes. Something she hadn't seen before. It was hard to feel hopeful when, day after day, you heard of people going through absolute hell. Kensasha understood this, but she believed in the power of hope. We can't lose hope, she thought. Hope makes us act when the odds are not in our favor, when all thumbs point down. Hope has the power to inspire all those around us, affecting the outcome.

Now, even the London night air felt hopeful, so Kensasha took a few extra breaths. She and Neelam Sethi had just finished dining with a Mrs. Enid Statham, who worked for one of the private foundations providing major financial support, and an Indian male colleague of Neelam's, Dr. Patel.

Meanwhile, at the safe house, three of the women were in the kitchen preparing a celebratory dinner for the Iranian interpreter's last night with them. She in turn was helping two of the Arab women converse with the Pakistani girl. The Jordanian girl went over to the computer.

The next instant, a car engine was heard outside the house. The little African girl ran over to the window and peered through the thick floral drapes covering the window. She saw a man get out of a taxi and walk up the footpath. She spun around with alarm, and yelled out in her native tongue, "It is a man!"

Her aunt repeated this in English. All the women understood the English word, 'man', and stopped what they were doing. The women in the kitchen hurried into the living room and everyone stood looking at each other trying to figure out what to do. Before they could act, there was a rapid knock on the door. The women remained silent. Then another knock came. Uhuru, the African woman, older than the rest, went closer to the door and asked in a proper English accent:

"Yes, who is there?"

They all listened, but could not understand what the man said.

"Please speak louder. Who are you?"

The man spoke louder with longer sentences.

Suddenly, Nasima Khatami screamed out, jumped up and ran to the door shouting:

"Omar? Omar! Omar!"

She unlocked the door, swung it open and practically leaped into the arms of the exhausted-looking young man standing before her. For a long while, they hugged, they kissed, they laughed and cried, repeatedly. Finally, husky Uhuru grabbed them both and pulled them back into the house, shutting the door and locking it securely.

For a moment, everyone was transfixed as the two cried in each other's arms. Then some of the women snapped out of their daze and covered their faces with their shawls or their hands—out of habit.

Uhuru stood with her hands on her hips shaking her head.

Soon, Nasima and Omar composed themselves long enough to acknowledge the other women. Omar looked sheepishly around the room. Nasima bowed her head, guiltily.

"What have you done? Do you think no one will tell Dr. Sethi about this?" Uhuru blasted, rolling her eyes at both of them. With a toss of her head, she strutted out of the living room beckoning her young niece to follow.

After that, the atmosphere grew uneasy. Three of the women returned to the kitchen to continue preparing dinner.

Nasima pulled Omar over to the couch. They sat entwined, while the rest of the women looked on.

The interpreter rushed over to converse with Omar. She wanted to know his every move from the time he left home to the moment he arrived at their front door. But Omar was too tired to say much. He'd just completed an exhausting journey on top of sleepless nights ever since receiving Nasima's letter. He knew he had to get to her no matter what it took.

As he looked around at the other women who stared back at him, it was obvious that he was unwelcome. But he didn't care. All that mattered now was that he and Nasima were together again and in a free country. They could finally get married and have a wonderful life. He would find a job, maybe in an office fixing computers or sweeping the floor. What did it matter? All he wanted was to take care of her. Thinking all this, he squeezed Nasima's hand and grinned with happiness.

She looked up into his eyes with a face as radiant as the sun. He had made it. He was really, here, beside her. They were safe. Everything would be all right now. Everything. She let out a sigh of relief, as Omar lifted her delicately shaped hands to his lips and kissed them. She blushed.

Just then, a sound outside made the Pakistani girl start, but before she could take another breath, like lightning three men burst through the door, guns drawn.

With rage on their faces, they scanned the room quickly. Nasima's terror-filled eyes recognized one of the men. She shouted out something in Arabic at him while attempting to disentangle herself from Omar to go over to the man. A split second later, the men opened fire. In less than a minute, they emptied their guns into Nasima, Omar and anyone else that moved. The Pakistani girl was hit, the Iranian interpreter and all the other women in the room.

Guns emptied, the men turned, ran out the front door, piled into a car and it screeched and careened down the road.

***

During their entire dinner, Neelam Sethi had her cell turned off out of politeness. Once outside the restaurant, she turned it on to check her messages while walking to the car. Dr. Patel opened the door for her to get into the front seat. She paused holding the phone to her ear. She could barely make out what was being said. Frowning, she dialed a number and waited. Someone answered.

"Hello? Who is that?" There was commotion in the background. "Oh my God… no, no, no." She swooned. The phone began to slip from her hand. Dr. Patel grabbed it and threw his other arm around her to keep her from collapsing.

Kensasha leaped from the back seat and rushed to her shouting, "What happened, what happened?" She took the phone from Dr. Patel and held it to her ear. "Hello? Hello? Who is this? What happened?" As she listened, her body slumped. "Are they all dead?"

Somehow, Dr. Patel managed to keep his wits about him and got the women home. He and Kensasha helped grief-stricken Neelam to her bed. After, Kensasha brought in a warm wet cloth and pressed it to her forehead. Dr. Patel slumped down in a chair and closed his eyes.

Enid Statham, on the other hand, immediately took the initiative to contact the local police station near the safe house. After, she called all their supporters within ten miles of the safe house to find volunteers to go and deal with the fallout until she could get up there. Then she looked in on Neelam, who was resting, her face ashen.

Kensasha, who didn't look so good herself, was still holding the warm compress to Neelam's forehead while Dr. Patel appeared to be in some kind of meditative state. For a moment, Enid was reluctant to disturb this scene.

"Excuse me, Neelam, I just want to inform you that the police assured me that they would do everything to keep the incident out of the newspaper. And a few of our people are driving over to the house, right now, to see if anybody else, besides Uhuru and her niece, are still alive and ambulatory. If so, they will take them back to their homes. I'll drive up first thing in the morning. I have faith we will find another safe house for them in no time. Don't worry."

Neelam tried to sit up, but still felt lightheaded. "I had a feeling all day something was going to happen, but I ignored it because of the trip. Now it's worse than I ever imagined." Struggling, she rose slowly to her elbows.

Kensasha took the cloth away and helped Neelam sit all the way up.

"You should lay back down. You need plenty of rest. Remember we have an early flight."

"What are you saying? I cannot go to America tomorrow! I have to make... funeral arrangements for seven or eight... people," Neelam exclaimed. She let out a big sigh then put her hand over her eyes and rubbed them. "I must get to the hospital to see that child. Thank God, they didn't kill her too. Then I must talk to the police. Talk to Uhuru to find out exactly what happened. We don't know how many of those men know about the house now. There may be others coming to kill the surviving women. We just don't know. And I must find another safe house."

Kensasha dismissed all that. "Didn't Mrs. Statham just tell you she would drive up in the morning and that other people are already taking charge? Those people can handle the funeral. Why do you insist on taking on all of the responsibilities? Huh? Isn't it even more important now for you to start the process of getting UN support and protection for these women?" Kensasha then put her hand on Dr. Patel's shoulder and shook him gently. When he looked up at her, she signaled to him to leave the room.

During that moment, Neelam considered what was said. Of course, the trip mustn't be postponed. She just needed to trust that Enid Statham and the others in the network could take charge in her absence. But, when the reality of what just happened returned, she shook her head.

"I am not so sure, now, that we can ever stop them. They are ruthless." Then she looked up at Kensasha with greater resolve and said, "But we will try."

Kensasha walked over to the door, where Enid Statham stood, glanced back and said,

"Yes, we can try."

CHAPTER 14

E nid arrived at the safe house just before dawn. A heavy mist hung over it as if even the air was in mourning.

She had visited this particular safe house once in late summer and remembered the lush hedges and floral plants. This was a peaceful community with strong family ties. It had taken the committee almost a year to find the right house in the right neighborhood. The criterion was always privacy. A place where people minded their own business unless, of course, someone was in need. Taunton was that kind of place.

Now there were police cars, ambulances and emergency vehicles blocking the street. She had to park two blocks away and approach on foot. Clusters of people numbed by the shock of it all, stood behind police barricades sharing whatever bits of information they had with each other.

Just beyond the barricade, Enid spotted a man of about forty, wearing an ill-fitting brown tweed suit, busy scribbling notes in a small pad. She assumed he was the detective she had spoken with the night before. He was questioning a couple still in their robes and pajamas. Enid slipped past three police officers and headed toward them.

"Mrs. Statham?" he inquired. Enid nodded and offered her hand. "I'm Detective Inspector Holmes, we spoke last night."

"Yes, Detective. What can you tell me? Do you know who was responsible for this?"

"Quite frankly, madam, no one seems to know anything. The survivors who witnessed it either, don't speak English, or refuse to talk."

"So, there are survivors?" Enid asked, pretending not to know.

"Yes, madam. They were in the bedrooms and heard everything. But" he said, scratching the back of his neck, "we can't get anything out of them or the people who took them in. We do have their names and the addresses where they're staying now. I was hoping you could shed some light on all this."

Enid knew the names given were fictitious. "No, I'm afraid I can't. May I go inside?"

"I wouldn't advise it, madam. It's a bloodbath. The bodies are still in there."

"I must get the computer," she said, anxiously.

"You can't remove anything from a crime scene, madam!" he said.

Of course, Enid knew this, but she was hoping he'd make an exception under the circumstances.

"Look, Inspector, we don't know who was behind these killings. Maybe someone in this town was paid off to reveal the information that led those gunmen here. The only way that we communicate with the safe houses is through encrypted email. With the kind of technology the investigators have today, they can decode our emails and trace them back to all the people and organizations helping these women. I can't let that happen. There are too many lives and professions at stake." She gave him the most earnest look she could muster. He let out a deep sigh and adjusted his tie.

"I understand what you're saying, madam, honest I do. But I can't let you walk in there and snatch up a computer and walk out. They'll have my head."

Enid didn't hear anything after, "I can't let you". She was already searching her brain for a way to get past him. For the last three years, she had used her husband's connections in the government to inform and enlist influential people to donate their time, money, goods and services to keep these women, and others like them, alive. She was determined not to have those same people's identities compromised.

"Well, can you at least tell me where I can get a decent cup of tea?" she asked, with a smile.

"Ah, I can do that. There's a wonderful little place just up the road on the high street, but you'll need your car."

Enid Statham hated being refused, hated the word 'no'—unlike her mother who seemed addicted to the word: "No, we can't afford this. No, Enid, that's not good for you. No, luv, this is not the right time."

When they said she couldn't marry outside her social class, she proved them wrong by marrying Terrance Statham, a prominent barrister for several top members of Parliament.

She slammed her car door shut, but didn't bother with the seatbelt. A half-filled thermos of tea lay on the passenger seat. She reached over and picked it up, unscrewed the top and sipped. It was lukewarm. Maybe the café, which the detective mentioned, might be a good place to wait until things quieted down. She would come back later, she thought. That decided, she put the car in reverse and made a U-turn. A split second later, two TV news vans swished passed her. Moments later, a TV news helicopter flew overhead. So much for keeping it out of the papers. Now it will make the midday news, and the Associated Press will pick it up and carry the story internationally.

She glanced through the rearview mirror and watched the reporters leap from the vans, their cameramen in tow. More cars flooded the area like little insects swarming around a piece of bread. Cameras clicked repeatedly capturing the first black body bag to be wheeled out past the rose and hydrangea bushes.

Great care had been taken to make sure this house would not stand out from the others on the block. Any lapse in pruning or watering of the grass would have caught the neighbors' eyes. In towns like this, people valued their lawns. A lawn told a lot about its owners. So, every week a volunteer was sent to Taunton just to see to it that hedges were trimmed and pruned at the safe house, accordingly.

The "safe house"—what irony.

If she didn't gain possession of that computer before the police did, all the safe houses could be in jeopardy.

At the top of the road, Enid slowed down. Feeling like a character in an Agatha Christie novel, she parked the car and returned on foot. It would have to be lightning speed. Sneak in, grab it and run.

Avoiding the blockade and the cameras, she walked nonchalantly around the back of a neighboring house knowing its occupants were outside watching the drama. The grass, still wet from morning dew, darkened the edges of her gray suede shoes. She quickly crossed the adjacent back yard, and then slowed to a normal pace when she reached the back yard of the safe house. She was surprised to see it empty. Had this been London, the whole place would be crawling with police.

She wiped the moisture that was forming on her upper lip and smoothed back her hair. She took in deep breaths to slow her heart rate, but it didn't work.

Walking along the side of the house, she tried a door just off the kitchen. It was unlocked. That meant the police or someone else must have entered the back yard from the house. Good. She paused for another one of those deep breaths, and slowly turned the knob.

Inside the house, more cameras captured the grisly scene. If not for the body bags, one could easily have imagined this to be a new form of artistic expression with gallons of red paint splattered on baby blue damask drapes and dumped on a matching floral couch. Then, there was the smell. She gagged and clasped her hands over her mouth diverting her eyes from the living room. But the tears fell anyway. Maniacs! They must've been maniacs.

Something had burned on the stove. Diced vegetables and meat sat in a bowl putrefying. The floor was peppered with grains of rice, dried peas and a broken plate. One moment you're preparing a nice dinner the next moment you're… She had to clear her head. Now the computer would be in an alcove on the other side of the kitchen, if I remember, she thought. That was where the younger women took turns sitting for hours searching the Internet. Something they couldn't do so freely in their own countries.

From where she crouched, Enid could see a young man dusting the laptop for fingerprints. Another man emptied the contents of the wastepaper basket into a plastic bag, tied it and put an orange sticker on it. He then turned and walked over to the tall white bookcase and scanned the books. He began to jot down some of the titles. Many of them, the world's most treasured works, had been banned from the women's countries of origin.

Enid waited for the right moment to run in. It never came. More police, reporters and forensic specialists found their way into the alcove. The only way to do it was to just do it.

She stood up, adjusted her cardigan and gently pressed her palms against her tear-stained face. She thought of how Dr. Sethi had worked tirelessly—often putting her health, if not her life, in danger. She thought of the women and men of the underground network from places in the world where a woman's life was worth less than that of a goat. These people risked their own lives daily to provide temporary shelter, medical aid and transportation for women and girls escaping familial violence. And the women themselves, who had determined that their own lives meant something—that they had the right to live and the right to choose how to live. Yes, that is true courage. This is easy.

The young man had not quite finished lifting fingerprints from the laptop when Enid suddenly appeared beside him and whispered nervously:

"Uh, you're wanted in the bedroom immediately. I think they found something in there and... want you to check it for... whatever you do. An officer told me to 'Get the bloke at the computer'."

She managed an awkward grin. Several heads turned her way, then quickly went back to their searches. But the young man stared up at her. He hadn't seen her before and wondered which division she was from. He was just about to ask when the urgency in her eyes disrupted his thought. He hastily packed up his kit, and took off toward the bedrooms.

Heart racing, Enid closed the lid of the laptop, gently pulled the cord from the back, slipped the laptop under her arm and headed back through the kitchen, out the side door all in less than sixty seconds. This time she dashed across both back yards, but slowed to a normal stride when she reached the street. All those morning jogs had paid off. Almost out of breath, she kept her eyes focused on her car as she walked toward it.

The young forensic specialist stood in the hallway peering into each of the three bedrooms and wondered which one he was needed in. Every room had officers either pulling clothes from the closets, running their hands under mattresses, or dumping drawer contents on the floor. No one appeared to have discovered anything that needed his expertise.

"Umm, who needs fingerprints lifted?" he shouted, loud enough to be heard in all the rooms.

Hands shaking, Enid tried to put the key into the ignition. They slid from her fingers and made a sharp clunk sound when they hit the car floor. She noticed this because it was almost as loud as her pounding heart. She fumbled around the cramped space beneath her legs to retrieve them. This cost her a good forty-five seconds.

It took them a while to realize the computer was missing. They were too busy trying to locate the woman in the pale pink cardigan. When word got to Detective Inspector Holmes about some unidentified woman in the house, he knew immediately that the computer was gone and who'd stolen it.

On her next attempt, she made it and let out a deep sigh of relief as the engine started up. She knew they would be on her tail in an instant. She was sure that Detective Inspector Holmes hadn't seen her actually get in or out of her car. So, he wouldn't know the make of it—at least at the moment.

She banked on that.

In the back seat was her blue, all-weather, jacket. She slipped it on. Without a hat, it wasn't possible for her to hide her blond bobbed haircut, nor could she change her London license plate. All she could do was pray, and slowly pull out of the parking space.

Instead of heading straight back to the highway toward London, she decided to go to the high street, find that café and have something to eat. This would calm her nerves, she figured, and kill time. The police would assume she'd be headed home and alert the London police. She had to give the computer to someone else before they arrested her. That someone had to understand its importance and not allow it to fall into the hands of the police under any circumstances. With Neelam on her way to the United States, there wasn't anyone Enid could think of whom she could trust, and who would be willing to take the risk of being arrested, as well.

She cruised several blocks along the main street before spotting the café that Holmes had recommended sandwiched between a chemist and a butcher shop. The words Good Eats were stenciled in big red letters across its large plate-glass window.

With the laptop safely hidden beneath the driver's seat, Enid entered the restaurant, caught a waitress's eye and discreetly pointed to a vacant table near the back. The waitress, a teenager, nodded, grabbed a menu and escorted Enid to the table.

The café was crowded with people having breakfast and chatting excitedly. This was a quaint neighborhood establishment where the same customers frequented daily. Yet, it was the first time all their conversations involved the same topic: those grisly murders.

Enid leafed through the menu. It listed all her favorites but nothing appealed to her at that moment. An older waitress came over to take her order.

"What can I get ya, luv?"

"Eggs and toast, I think."

"Would you like a bit of bacon with that?"

"Ah, no. But I'd love a pot of tea."

"Coming right up."

Enid could hear snippets of the various conversations around her but tried to stay focused on what she needed to do. She hated to involve Terrance in all of this. He had turned a blind-eye to her activism concerning Third World women—his term—and she wanted to keep it that way. But now… she hadn't actually planned on stealing the computer. She really assumed the authorities would give it to her under the circumstances. After all, it belonged to her organization. Anyway, Terrance would get her off the hook. What proof was there that she was the one who took it? All they had on her was that she mentioned a computer to a Detective Inspector Holmes and coincidentally, a woman, perhaps matching her description, was later seen standing near the desk where a computer happened to be. That wasn't enough to charge her with stealing the computer. It was purely circumstantial. Right?

Maybe she could leave it with someone who didn't necessarily understand the computer's importance, but who cared about Enid herself and therefore would protect her… like… her mother.

Her mother, Edith, whose favorite word "No" might pay off. No, I haven't seen Enid in years. No, Enid would never steal anything. No, I don't know anything about computers. And it would be the truth. Now, if she could just get into her mother's house, without her knowing, and hide the computer in a place no one would even consider, her mother wouldn't have to lie for her. She could leave it there until Neelam returned.

The waitress appeared with Enid's order on a tray.

"I suppose you heard what happened?" the waitress asked, placing a steaming hot pot of tea on the table, "A shame, ain't it?" She put down a cup and saucer. Enid nodded, reached for the pot and poured the tea.

The waitress then set the plate in front of Enid.

"I ain't never seen you in here before, luv. Are you from around here?" Enid added milk and sugar to the cup.

"I was just passing through and saw your cute little establishment," she replied, stirring quickly and enfolding her hands around the cup. The heat was soothing. She lifted it to her mouth. Aaah… Holmes was right. They did make a great cup of tea. She smiled hoping the waitress would take that as a signal to leave.

"Well, I want you to know that this is a decent town. I've lived here all me life, and nothing like this has ever happened here before."

As if to confirm what the waitress had said, the conversations at each table grew louder and spilled over to other tables. In seconds, there was an active group discussion. Other waitresses were drawn in.

"See what I mean?" said the waitress, placing her hands on her hips.

Enid wanted to comment but something inside told her not to encourage the woman. Instead, she bit into her toast. Ugh. It's dry. Her eyes searched the table for those little pats of butter carefully wrapped in foil, but she saw none.

"Oh, I need butter for the bread." At that, the waitress also searched the table for butter.

"Sorry, luv. I'll get some for ya." She disappeared.

For a moment, Enid felt what she thought was relief. Her body was sinking into… relaxation? No… exhaustion. She studied the food before her. She had expected it to be the medicine needed to settle her stomach. Instead, the smell of the eggs and the red color of the tomatoes produced a more sickening feeling. Then, an enormous wave of emotion overtook her. She gripped the sides of the table.

"Here you go, luv," the waitress said, placing a saucer of butter next to the teapot. "Is everything all right?"

Enid couldn't answer. Her throat tightened and her bottom lip quivered. She needed an iron will to keep away the images that were now surfacing. The... bodies... still in the house! The curtains... the couch soaked in... She clenched her jaw, but the tears filled her eyes and cascaded down her cheeks.

"How do we know they weren't terrorists?" a man shouted. The waitress looked around to see who had spoken.

Enid snapped back. That last comment shook her.

"We don't," someone else shouted.

"That's why they were all living in that house. They were planning something," said the first man.

"You mean they were suicide bombers?" asked the second man.

"My God!" a woman exclaimed.

"So, who killed them?" a third person asked.

"They were all women," Enid's waitress commented.

"So. The women are doing it too," added an elderly woman, sitting at the table in front of Enid's.

"That's right. It could've been some undercover agents that killed them," a man added. That's a good thing, ain't it?"

"It's strange though. I've never seen Pakistanis around here," said Enid's waitress moving toward the center of the restaurant.

"You mean Arabs," the first man commented. The waitress stared back with confusion. "They're the terrorists, not the Pakis," he added, for clarification.

"What's the difference?" she said. "I still haven't seen any of those kinda people in this town. Who has?" Silence. "And they were right under our noses. Now isn't that strange? How do we know there ain't more of them living here? They could be living right down the street from any one of us," she added, with such distaste, Enid flinched.

"More can end up dead," said another man.

'Yeah, they could,' Enid thought, 'but not for the reasons you think. Maybe it would be better if these people knew the truth.

"What if they get the wrong address?" asked the teenage waitress. More silence. Enid could almost see their collective brains twisting around with what ifs. That was her cue.

"Bill, please."

***

The drizzle seemed appropriate. It underscored the murkiness of the day. Everything around Enid seemed to have slowed to a crawl—the cars up ahead, the people ambling along the sidewalks, even her own motor coordination. Now, for sure, every action was purely on instinct. There was no plan. She had always had a plan, but today, stealing the computer had changed everything. She was now a wanted criminal. What would this do to her reputation? How would she explain all this to Terrance? Should she even care about something as volatile as a reputation? What about being in a jail cell? Oh my God!

Without a thought, she got on the M25 motorway and headed east. An hour later, she turned onto the A12 for Colchester.

It was late in the afternoon when she drove down Sir Isaacs Street and ended up near the Red Lion Hotel.

Colchester was said to be the oldest town in England. Her mother knew everything there was to know about Colchester, having worked in the Castle Museum for fifteen years. Enid hoped that her mother would be at the museum until after closing, giving her enough time to walk that 2 miles to the house and hide the computer.

She parked near a pub, then retrieved the computer from beneath the seat and dumped it into a large brown leather shoulder bag she'd brought. Getting out of the car, she had the strange feeling she was being watched. But how could anyone know she would be in Colchester? She'd rarely visited her mother since getting married, and she had no emotional ties with the place at all.

The dreariness of the weather left the streets empty, which wasn't the greatest situation for someone needing to blend in with the crowd. Not wanting to bring attention to herself, she decided to keep her eyes to the ground and avoid the main streets.

She chose Trinity Street because it seldom had a lot of foot traffic during the week. She walked briskly as if to get out of the rain.

Crossing St. Mary's footbridge, she passed a man who had just left a corner building. He gave her a nod and a cordial smile. Enid returned the nod but not the smile lest he felt inclined to stop for a chat. It was a small town so it wasn't unusual that people stopped to talk with strangers.

The house her mother, Edith, lived in now was not Enid's original home. That place had long burned down. This present house was older—it had character.

As expected, the key was in the usual spot under a planter near the door. Enid slid the key into the lock then looked back over her shoulders to see if anyone was watching, and then opened the door. She wiped her feet on the welcoming mat before entering. Once inside, she took off her wet shoes and her jacket so that she wouldn't drip water through the house.

Upstairs there were two bedrooms and a bathroom. She contemplated hiding the computer in the spare bedroom—perhaps in the closet. Her mother never used it and seldom had guests that stayed the night. But if the police did decide to come out there, they would surely search the bedrooms.

She stood in the foyer contemplating which way to go. Up or down? Now the basement was a possibility. No. Not enough places down there to hide anything.

It had to be somewhere that a clever police officer would not think of and where her mother would seldom venture. She headed up the carpeted staircase to the spare room separated from the master bedroom by the bathroom. The only furniture besides the bed and end tables was an old chifforobe and a thick high back leather chair with a matching leather footstool.

As she stared at the chair, the idea came instantly. She placed the laptop on the bed, dropped to her knees and flipped the stool over. Just as she'd expected, the underside was cloth and was bolted to the wooded rim. If she could pry the bolts loose, she could wedge the laptop up inside the footstool and replace the cloth. No one would suspect it being there and her mother would never need to touch the stool.

She had to act fast. Skipping stairs down to the kitchen, she searched frantically for a flat-headed screwdriver and a hammer. Once found, she returned to the bedroom, slipped the screwdriver under the edge of the first bolt and began to pry it loose. It barely moved. She jiggled the screwdriver all around the sides of the bolt until there was a perceptible shift. A few more tries and the bolt loosened. By the time she was able to remove all thirteen bolts and a considerable amount of the cloth to insert the computer, she was drenched in sweat, had three broken fingernails, tiny cuts that were beginning to bleed, and it was closing time at the museum.

Fortunately, her mother took the bus to and from work, so it would still be a while before she actually arrived home. Even so, Enid knew she had to be completely out of the area or else her mother would spot her on the street. The only route to walk back to where she'd parked her car intersected with the bus that went to Colchester Castle Museum. She needed to get out of there immediately. But the bolts proved harder to replace than to get out. The fabric wasn't strong enough to support the computer. The weight kept loosening the bolts.

"Tape! I need duct tape!" She leaped to her feet and flew back down the stairs, searching drawers and cupboards until she found what she needed.

Back up the stairs on just fumes of energy, she taped the laptop up inside the stool, stretched the cloth over it and hammered down the bolts. Afterwards, she righted the stool and placed it back where it had been.

She waited a moment just to make sure the computer wouldn't plop out. It seemed fine. With a sigh of relief, she scooped up the tape, screwdriver and hammer, grabbed her bag and was back down the stairs in minutes.

She couldn't remember exactly where the hammer and screwdriver were positioned in the drawers, but was sure her mother wouldn't either.

By the time the bus stopped to let off its passengers, Enid had just managed to dart across the street behind the bus, therefore, avoiding being glimpsed by her mother. This wasn't the time for a mother-daughter reunion. Tomorrow she would call her mother to find out if the police had contacted her or not.

With the laptop off her mind, Enid turned her attention to how she was going to avoid arrest and jail time. The thought of jail sickened her. And wouldn't it be publicized? Wouldn't this bring unwanted attention to the computer? The good thing was that those assassins were either hired by the family of one of the women, or they were the family—perhaps the brothers and the father. So, even if they heard about a computer with important data on it, they probably wouldn't be interested nor have the resources to do anything about it if they wanted to. No. It was the authorities who worried her because whatever they learned they'd leak it to the media soon after.

On her return, she cut through Castle Park and stood for a few minutes at the Coline River, watching as a swan gracefully led her young.

Yellow tulips lined the footpath on the southern bank and the mill could be seen at the east. Enid leaned up against a stoned wall that bordered the northern tip of the river. The light rain had stopped and the park was gradually filling up with people eager for its beauty.

She listened to light-hearted chatter, saw couples in a meaningful embrace, and wanted to linger there awhile, wanted to be enfolded in their sense of safety, wanted to see the world they saw, once again. For surely, it was a world where women were an integral part, they mattered too—all women. A world where parents were thrilled to see their baby girls and would do anything to keep them safe, protected in the shelter of a mother's arms, protected within the sanctity of family.

She recalled the first time she had visited a "safe house", she was surprised to see how nurturing the women were toward one another. Each had found solace not only in knowing that the other women shared their plight, but also having met total strangers who not only provided them with food, clothing, personal items, magazines and books, but put their own welfare in danger without expecting anything in return.

After a few visits, Enid could tell immediately which of the women had just arrived. They were the ones with hollow eyes and tightly drawn lips, who kept to themselves. If you can't entrust your own family with your well-being—if they think your life is worth nothing, if they want you dead over the slightest provocation—how can you possibly believe total strangers would risk their own lives to save yours?

Some of the women were shell-shocked. But the mortar was psychological in nature, aimed at their humanity, designed to shatter self-esteem and lay waste all ideas of personal freedom, liberty, happiness, hopes and dreams. Even romantic love became a casualty.

A gust of wind swept across the north side of the river, abruptly, as if to remind people not to get too comfortable. Enid headed back to her car.

Once inside, she turned on her cell phone. The automated voice said, "You have eight new messages." The first was from a safe house coordinator who gave her a code number that represented the name of the person who took in the survivors.

The second was from Detective Inspector Holmes telling her what a stupid, thoughtless thing she had done, and demanded she return the computer immediately. He also informed her that a warrant had been issued for her arrest.

The next message was from Kensasha informing her that they had landed safely in New York and that Neelam was feeling a little more hopeful, yet concerned about the computer. The remaining messages were the most troubling. Three were from Terrance, who sounded distressed and concerned for her and two were from her mother who was, totally, baffled at having received a call from the police asking for her whereabouts.

She returned Terrance's call first. It went to voice mail. She was relieved since she hadn't worked out an explanation other than the truth and wasn't sure if that was the best thing. She left a message saying she wouldn't be returning home that night—that she would spend the night in a B&B because she was too tired to drive back safely and that she would explain everything when they spoke. It wasn't a lie. She was exhausted.

Her mother would have to wait. If she called her now, she would have to lie if her mother asked where she was. Instead, she called Neelam to reassure her that their network's personal information was safe. Then the urge to use the toilet alleviated the momentary guilt regarding her mother.

Leaving the ladies' room of the Red Lion Hotel, the aroma of roast potatoes overtook her. She followed her nose to the adjoining pub and was presented with the food and drink menu.

As soon as Enid surveyed the menu, her appetite ceased. She needed something to numb her and prepare her for that talk with her mother. She ordered brandy.

NEW YORK

One hot, humid evening five days later, about sixty-five women of various ethnic origins within Islam and Hinduism gathered in a large hall. This was a major achievement in itself, being that Muslims and Hindus rarely socialized together. The room, often used for wedding receptions by people who could not afford fancy banquet halls, had twelve white Corinthian columns gracing the circumference of the dingy steel-blue room. Opposite the four large doors of the entryway was a makeshift wooden platform, often used as a stage for a small band. The badly scuffed wooden floor creaked here and there as the women filed in.

Amongst them, Basma saw some familiar faces. She acknowledged Mrs. Jazeer and Khadija Tali. There were women who had attended Mrs. Jazeer's party, and opposed everything Imani Sadawi had said, present as well.

Tonight, was a special night. Imani Sadawi's determination, to get Dr. Neelam Sethi to Jackson Heights, Queens, had paid off. Kensasha Lewis had actually traveled back to New York with Dr. Sethi. Basma identified her immediately. She was the Indian woman with a commanding presence up on the stage conferring with Kensasha and several other people. One of the people was a white woman about Basma's age, and the other three women were obviously from India and the Middle East judging by their attire. One woman, like several in the audience, was in a black burka. Her age could not be determined, but Basma guessed the Indian was no more than a girl of fourteen or fifteen, and the other woman, who appeared confident and worldly, was close to thirty.

Dr. Sethi had brought a seventeen-year-old Hindu girl, and a nineteen-year-old Afghani woman. Imani Sadawi had found the female interpreter. The other woman was the American journalist, Courtney Goodman, who had interviewed Dr. Sethi for TV earlier in the year.

Kensasha had contacted Courtney as soon as she had persuaded Dr. Sethi to make the trip and then alerted her as soon as they got off the plane to ensure Courtney could attend the first public meeting.

Courtney Goodman, thirty-three years old, had worked free-lance for eight years and had connections with MSNBC and CNN. She immediately cancelled all of her appointments for the rest of the week in order to finally accompany Dr. Neelam Sethi around and meet a few of the women being sheltered in America. Dr. Sethi certainly wouldn't permit reporters to tag around with her in England.

Through her mesh face covering, the Afghani woman's curious eyes could be seen darting around the room, taking everything in. The Hindu girl sat gracefully with a shawl draped over her head and shoulders. Basma noticed her eyes were sad.

Basma looked over at Kensasha Lewis, whom she hadn't seen since her episode at work. Yet she took comfort knowing Ms. Lewis would have visited her if she had had the time.

Kensasha whispered last-minute instructions to a videographer hired to film proceedings. She reminded the young man that at no time would he film the faces of the women telling their stories, and she would be taking immediate ownership of the tape at the end of the evening. They planned to deliver the footage to a U.N. representative working with a committee that oversaw issues of violence toward women at an international level.

When she was satisfied that the man understood, she looked over at Neelam.

"It's all set."

Neelam gave a signal and began ushering the Hindu girl, who had a limp, over to one of the chairs at the center of the stage. The female interpreter followed and sat in another chair near to the girl.

The audience settled down and grew silent. All eyes were focused on the young girl who stared back at them.

Noticing how fragile the girl appeared up there surrounded by strangers, Basma couldn't imagine sitting before an audience like that, and everyone watching and waiting for her to speak, or having a camera pointed in her face. This girl was no Imani Sadawi or Professor Lewis.

Clearly, from the way she dressed, she came from some small, perhaps rural village in Northern India.

Neelam Sethi leaned over, put her hand on the girl's shoulder gently and spoke to her in Hindi. "You know what to do. Don't say your name. Just say where you are from."

The girl nodded nervously and Neelam walked to the right side of the stage and sat down in one of the six chairs.

Kensasha took one of the seats right next to Neelam who was then joined by Imani Sadawi and Courtney Goodman.

Several minutes into a hair-raising story—about the girl's husband's parents wanting more dowry money and her parents not having it, so somehow her in-laws tried to kill her by dousing her in kerosene and throwing her into a wood fire, and, later, claiming her sari must have caught fire accidentally—Basma was overcome. Perhaps it was the heat, she thought and slipped away to the bathroom.

Inside, she turned on the faucet full force to drown out the voices. She washed her hands repeatedly and splashed her face with cold water. Looking in the mirror, she adjusted her scarf and saw that her face was ghostly pale. She paused a moment to breathe before exiting.

Just as she was returning to her seat, the audience erupted with gasps. Basma looked toward the stage and saw the Hindu girl with her long skirt pulled up to her thighs revealing severely scarred legs from third degree burns. One leg had most of the muscle tissue burned away which was why the girl limped. Then she turned around and exposed her back and side. They both looked as though the flesh had just melted together to form one thick ugly mass of scar tissue. It had completely deformed her body.

Basma cried out at the horrific sight then quickly clasped her hands across her mouth. But the rest of the audience had been stunned into silence.

Imani Sadawi got up and rushed over to the girl and put her arms around her, and held her a moment then escorted her back to one of the chairs at the side. The women in the audience shook their heads and slowly began whispering to each other. Dr. Sethi rose slowly, and walked back to the center of the stage and waved her hands to restore order.

"There are thousands upon thousands of women with all kinds of stories like this. Many have now found their way to England and other European countries. In England, some are kept in jail cells to protect their lives. Can you believe it?" Many of the women in the audience shook their heads again. "Sometimes we house them in secret locations to protect them. Sometimes we fail." She cast a glance over at Kensasha and the two of them exchanged heartfelt emotion. Dr. Sethi swallowed hard, and then continued:

"You can't imagine the lengths some of the women's families will go to in order to see these women dead. You cannot imagine. They are fanatics. I tell you they are ruthless. Many of them will keep searching and searching for their daughters or wives for years until they track them down. They don't care if she is happy with whomever or wherever she is now, they will kill her."

She paused when she saw a few pensive looking faces staring back at her. Then she realized she didn't know who these women were. There could easily be just such people in the audience—those on the run and those who wanted someone dead. When she resumed, her voice faltered:

"Anyway… we are here… to ask you all to support our efforts to get a hearing before an International… Tribunal. You must call… and, and write letters."

The women in the audience looked at each other apprehensively. Imani got up and walked briskly across the stage to joined Dr. Sethi.

"Ladies!" she called out, confidently, "this International Forum that we hope to organize, with the help of the United Nations, will be a way to let the world know what this young woman," her right hand gestured toward the girl, "and many other women like her are going through right now." Her voice became more forceful as she continued. "There are these dowry deaths and they are killing baby girls. All these are hate-crimes against women. Ladies! We have to do something to put an end to this barbarism.

The atmosphere in the hall grew tense. An elderly Pakistani woman around seventy-years old struggled to her feet to speak.

"We have the same things happening here. One girl was choked till she died by her own father because she wanted a divorce from the man he picked out for her. And another man in Florida set his house on fire, and burned his wife and both daughters to death, because they sided with the one daughter who refused to go through with the marriage, he had arranged for her."

Another woman called out, "I know of women here who have suddenly disappeared because of the same reasons." At this, Basma got up discreetly to leave.

Dr. Sethi nodded to the women, relieved to see that this audience was filled with like-minded people.

"Yes, those are so-called 'honor killings.' That is why we have a network of people now, who provide new identity documents for some of the women in danger, to cross borders. And this is how we were able to bring these young women here to speak to you."

Dr. Sethi then gestured for the Afghani woman to come over and speak to the audience.

***

With the houseguests retired for the night, Shafal finally got his long-awaited turn in the bathroom. Abdel and Ahmed slept uncomfortably on the sofa and floor, respectively. And Basma, still agitated from the Hindu girl's deformed body, repeatedly scrubbed and straightened up the kitchen.

Then, exhausted, she sat down at the little table in the kitchen and buried her face in her hands.

Suddenly, she raised her head, jumped to her feet, and rushed toward the bedroom not caring if she disturbed the boys.

She headed straight to the closet, rummaged through cardboard boxes and a lot of old junk Shafal had stuffed in there until she retrieved a large worn wooden box. She plopped down on her bed and opened it. Inside was a colorful assortment of knick-knacks that a child would save. Basma groped through it and pulled out a wedge of pottery—the same one she had found as a child walking with Aisha.

She studied it as if it were something magical running her fingers across the different colored glass stones lining one side of it.

Absorbed by the pretty colors, she didn't notice Shafal entering the room. He saw the old wooden box and Basma's unusual captivation with something and walked over to her bed.

"What is that?" he asked. "What are you doing at this time in the night? You have said nothing all evening."

Basma continued to examine the pottery wedge as if she hadn't heard a word he said. With anger, Shafal grabbed the wedge and tried to yank it away from her. But she clutched it tighter and glared up at him threateningly. He released it and stared back at her for a moment. Getting up awkwardly, he went to his own bed and crawled in.

"I think you are getting sick again," he warned and rolled away from her.

Basma continued stroking the wedge a few more times, and then she gently laid it back into the box.

Days later, Osha placed a pile of freshly laundered clothes on Basma's bed and went over to the chest of drawers, to find a spot for them. After opening three drawers filled to the brim, she decided to shuffle the contents at the bottom drawer to one side in order to get the fresh pile of clothes in. Some of the clothes tumbled out, so she picked them up and replaced them. She went back over to the bed, scooped up the laundered pile, and began to stuff them into the space she'd made. Still, there wasn't enough space. She reached into the bottom of the drawer for a better grip, and gave another push. The movement caused something shiny amongst the, otherwise drab assortment, of garments to appear. She yanked, and out came a shimmering purple satin gown.

CHAPTER 15

Remarkably, the entire household managed to climb out of bed before a hint of daylight, in honor of Ramadan, the holiest of holidays for Muslims. Ramadan occurred in the ninth month of the Islamic lunar calendar—this time it was late July. It was during Ramadan that the Prophet Muhammad had received the first verses of the Koran. In honor of this, all practicing Muslims abstained from food and drink—including water, cigarettes and sexual relations between sunrise and sunset. Therefore, it was necessary for Basma and her family to pray and finish, sahūr—a light breakfast, before the rising of the sun.

Still bleary-eyed they drank as much juice and water as they could to stave off thirst until dinnertime.

"Tonight, my sons are bringing their girlfriends to our special, Iftar dinner." Shafal announced proudly, breaking the silence. "And I spoke with the Imam at the Mosque last week. He said he would be honored to come to eat at our house on this first night of Ramadan, before going to the mosque for Tarawih."

This was truly an honor. Expressions of surprise and excitement suddenly animated the formerly deadpan faces around him. Tarawih was the reading of 1/30 of the equally divided parts of the Koran each night of Ramadan.

"Basma why don't you do some shopping near the nursing home where they have that bakery?" Shafal suggested. No one noticed that Basma suddenly stopped breathing. "Remember that bread you used to buy?" he pressed further. She glanced away, as if trying to recall. "Well, get enough of it for our guests, and for the Imam."

"Uh, that bakery is very expensive. I will try some around here." Both Sirhan and Khalid raised their eyebrows and studied Shafal to see how he would handle what they perceived as insolence.

Shafal also interpreted her response as insolence and ignoring his command. But having her do this in front of family, especially Uncle Khalid, outright embarrassed him.

"I do not care about the price," he said, forcefully flicking his wrist, and then, he continued even louder, "It is Ramadan and we are having special guests. I told you to buy the bread. That is it!"

Basma flinched and turned away.

***

At the cab garage in Long Island City, the usual assortment of drivers stood around huddling in groups waiting to begin their shift.

Tariq Tali was just going out when he noticed Shafal arriving with Khalid and Sirhan in tow.

Shafal wanted the two men to see what the possibilities were for earning money if they happened to prolong their stay in America.

Tariq got out of his cab and walked up to greet them shaking his head and speaking in English out of habit. "This is going to be a very difficult month. Nobody wants to work during the day without food or water."

"And this is just the first day," Shafal commented also in English, wiping his brow.

"Money will be less," added Tariq.

Shafal let out a deep sigh and stared off. Sirhan gave his father, Khalid, a concerned look. Khalid nodded that he understood.

"But maybe... since this is the holy month, Khadija will stop—" Tariq looked around to make sure none of the other men heard him. Then he leaned in closer to Shafal switching to Arabic, unconcerned that Sirhan and Khalid were listening, since they were just 'country

190

folk'. "—stop talking about wanting orgasm." His voice dropped just above a whisper, "You know, for months now she talks of this." He glanced at Shafal, shyly. "And she insists on instructing me on all these different things I should do. Can you imagine how I feel?"

Although this would sound amusing to any of the other men standing around, if they could hear it, Sirhan and Khalid certainly did not think so. Shafal glimpsed over at them, uncomfortably, then back at Tariq, who rarely showed such frankness.

In an attempt to impress Uncle Khalid and Sirhan, with his high moral standards, Shafal commented, "A proper Muslim woman should not be interested in such things." Raising his head, a little higher, he added, "That is for men. You need to remind your wife of this." Tariq Tali stared at Shafal. His face reddened. He looked confused, and finally offended.

"Why don't you remind your wife?" he blurted out.

"Basma? Of what?"

Tariq pressed his lips together to control his temper. When he couldn't hold it any longer, he shouted in Arabic, "She is the one who told Khadija about orgasm… how wonderful it is, and how to have it!"

Sirhan and Khalid turned to look at Shafal with growing curiosity.

Shafal was visibly flabbergasted and perplexed. 'Basma?' he said to himself. "But that is impossible."

"You are surprised your wife speaks of such things?" Sirhan interjected. All of a sudden, he appeared to be having a revelation. "Now I know why she was sick… too much sex. You buy your wife those sexy American dresses. It is your doing."

Khalid's face darkened, and he folded his arms across his chest.

"What sexy dresses?" Shafal asked, in total bewilderment. "I have not bought her a thing. I never buy anything for her," he added proudly.

"That purple gown. Osha saw it when she was putting away the laundry," Sirhan explained. "She said the front was open down to the waist." Shafal stared back with his mouth open. "I am surprised that you spend money on such expensive shameful things," Sirhan continued.

The wheels in Shafal's head began to spin.

"How can she have something like that and I know nothing about it?" He contemplated aloud. They all looked at each other—wondering. "She cannot afford to buy expensive dresses!" Shafal informed them. "Maybe one of the old women at the nursing home gave it to her when she started getting sick."

"That gown is not something an old woman would have," Sirhan responded. "It is new style... and it is for 'sexy'," he added, with certainty.

Shafal dismissed the whole thing with a wave of his hand and walked to the garage to get his cab.

Completely disappointed with Shafal, Tariq Tali got back into his cab, put both hands together in a prayer position, gave a nod to Sirhan and Khalid, then he drove away.

Shafal, still deep in contemplation, pulled his cab up in front of Sirhan and Khalid who stood on the driver's side.

"That dress is not Basma's," he called, leaning out the window.

"Someone must have given it to her."

Now he was convinced, but still assumed it was from a woman friend. 'Maybe that meddling Mrs. Sadawi passed along some of her old clothes', he thought to himself.

Finally, with a sheepish look, he confided: "Basma does not like sex."

Khalid, the old patriarch, raised one eyebrow and asked, "Then why does she talk about such things?"

That question plunged Shafal deeper into thought about his wife's indecent behavior. Was it even possible? He glared at them and replied bitterly, "Maybe... because... she was with someone else."

Now this was a revelation. Khalid and Sirhan immediately understood what he was referring to. A storm began to brew in each of their minds.

"Get in!" Shafal commanded.

Sirhan and Khalid climbed into the back seat of the cab. Anger rising, Shafal bore down on the gas and the car jerked forward. He swerved off down the street under the gaze of the other drivers, completely forgetting about his shift.

***

Sumera and Osha spent the entire afternoon happily preparing for the celebratory dinner. Because the Ramadan fasting requirements included no liquids until sundown, Sumera moved around the kitchen slower than usual. However, Osha seemed to thrive on being busy—water or not.

Both women were in the kitchen when Shafal threw open the front door and stormed in with Sirhan and Khalid right behind him. Struggling, unsuccessfully, to contain his increasing shame and fury, he called out, "Where is my wife?"

Sumera stopped rolling out pastry dough and turned to look at him, surprised, then stated nonchalantly:

"She went out early. Maybe 10 a.m."

He looked at his watch. It was well past four. He rushed into the bedroom and searched the drawers for this infamous purple gown. When he found it, he yanked it free, held it up and was astonished at how revealing it would be on a woman. Who did she wear this for?

Intent on confronting her with it, he put it back, inadvertently, in a different drawer.

Sirhan and Khalid stood silent with their arms folded like sentry. To them, this was a matter of grave importance. And it was necessary that the husband deal with this appropriately. Never mind that Basma was their own flesh and blood, their allegiance was with the husband—and always would be.

Shafal returned to the front of the apartment with renewed determination to find Basma, immediately, and confront her. He stomped back out the front door. Sirhan and Khalid followed.

As he drove along the main street of their neighborhood, with Khalid and Sirhan in the backseat, his wild eyes flitted all around searching for Basma.

At that very same moment, Basma was standing just to the side of the bakery in Forest Hills. The customers going in and coming out gave her a curious look. After a long while, she gathered enough courage to enter.

Just as she had witnessed many times before, everyone was absorbed in either selecting items or bagging them. Immediately, that wonderful fragrance of freshly baked bread filled her with desire, and she wondered: Is he here?

She approached the counter, tentatively—her eyes lowered. Her stomach began to churn. What if he suddenly—

"May I help you?" a woman asked curtly, with a mid-western drawl.

Startled, yet relieved, Basma pointed to the olive and tomato bread she came for. "I would like three, please."

The saleswoman, a plump ash blond in her thirties was not used to serving people who looked like Basma. She replied in a rather snobbish tone: "Those are six dollars and twenty-five cents per loaf."

Basma nodded casually and waited for the woman to get the bread. The woman hesitated, and then walked over to the basket. Basma used the time to glance in the back to see if he might be there. She saw no one.

The woman packed up the loaves nicely for her, took the twenty-dollar bill Basma presented and gave her back the change. Basma put the money into her purse, carefully picked up the familiar large, shiny burgundy and gold bag with white roped handles, and turned to leave.

"Have a nice day," said the saleswoman, pleased with the sale.

Basma bowed and started for the door. Then, she nonchalantly turned back around to the saleswoman.

"Please, where is the man who works here?"

"Who? You mean Al, the owner? He's back in his office."

"No. There is a boy who works here in the front… with his hair—" She demonstrated with her hand the way the Bakery Guy wore his blond hair pulled back with elastic while working.

"Oh, you mean Vincent? Vincent Langois?" The saleswoman replied. "He don't work here anymore."

Basma felt as much. Well, at least, now, she knew his name. "Where does he work?" she asked, trying to show casual interest. But her face betrayed her.

The woman folded her arms and scrutinized Basma. She had witnessed the olive-skinned woman turning pink, then nearly the burgundy color of their bag.

After a minute, she replied, "Why, he up and moved to Boston, I believe."

"Boss Town?"

"Yeah, in Massachusetts," said the saleswoman. "Boston, Massachusetts. He's got his own place, I hear," she added with envy. Basma stared at her with anticipation. The woman looked reluctant to reveal anything further. She stroked her chin thinking to herself. Then she shrugged and headed to the back of the bakery.

A man standing just behind Basma sucked his teeth and sighed. Basma fumbled with her purse and peered back, self-consciously.

The saleswoman strolled back and said, "Le Jardin. That's his restaurant."

"Lay Hardeen?"

"Yep."

Grateful, Basma thanked the woman and left.

***

It was so hot in the apartment even the walls of the kitchen were sweating. Never had they endured such heat, even in August. But Sumera was intent on preparing a lavish feast that would dazzle the Imam. This was a great opportunity for her family to rise to a higher position in this community. Sumera, who had come from a village on the other side of the world with no mosque to speak of, was now doing prayers twice a week in a beautiful mosque—thanks to that Mrs. Sadawi. It was like a dream coming true, even though she never actually dreamt it.

And she was aware that each day, now, she felt less intimidated by all there was to know; all the things one person was expected to know how to do. Who could have thought that a food processor would become her ally? And Osha had fallen in love with a vacuum cleaner—using it every day! Of course, Khalid complained that the roar of those contraptions was driving him mad.

"Just like all the other noises in this Godforsaken land of unbelievers," he ranted.

Sumera was thinking all of this while stirring fava beans in a pot at the stove when Basma returned with the bread and a few other groceries. She seemed distracted. Preoccupied. She didn't really acknowledge Sumera, but immediately began to help with the Holy Ramadan meal.

First, she set the bread bag on top of the refrigerator out of the way, and then she removed tangerines, dried dates and apricots from a white plastic bag.

Since Sumera had no idea what was going on in the men's minds, and since she herself was preoccupied with the different dishes she was preparing, she acted normally towards Basma—forgetting to mention that Shafal had called a few times anxious to speak with her.

After checking the lamb roasting in the oven, Sumera went to the bathroom to splash water on her face and cool off a bit.

House fully vacuumed, bathroom spotless, Osha entered the kitchen to help with the rest of the preparations. She had her face covered in case any of the male guests arrived early.

Basma remained silent, but made a considerable racket getting more plates and pots out of cabinets and slamming doors. Osha glanced in her direction, but said nothing to her. Sumera returned with her face covered as well, and resumed stirring the fava beans and checking the other pots cooking on the stove.

At the sink, Basma dumped cups of rice into a large stainless-steel bowl, turned on the faucet and began to clean the rice.

"Mrs. Sadawi called to see how you are doing," Sumera offered, not turning around. "She will eat at her daughter's house in Noo Joy-see tonight. But her husband is coming here." Basma barely acknowledged that she heard her.

It was obvious that Basma was bothered about something, and not wanting to create any problems, Sumera left it at that. When Basma continued cleaning the rice, obsessively, Sumera took notice and carefully removed the bowl from her hands. With eyes wild, Basma made a frantic reach for the rice and tried to wrestle the bowl out of Sumera's hands. Sumera and Osha looked at Basma as though she were mad. Seeing their expressions made her stop and regain her composure.

"I am sorry," she said. Sumera waved it off, but remained suspicious and decided to keep a close watch on her. Osha also showed her concern. "Maybe you are not feeling well? You can lie down until dinner. We can take care of it. Do not worry," Osha suggested.

"No! I don't need to lie down. This is my house," Basma exclaimed adamantly. "I cook for Ramadan."

Sumera started beneath the thin black niqab, and poor Osha shrunk with embarrassment.

"I did not mean to—"

"I know," Basma said, regretfully.

***

It was close to sundown by the time Shafal, Sirhan and Khalid returned, eager to hear what Basma had to say about her much-pub-licized sexual expertise. They had driven all over Queens trying to track her down and had gotten to the bakery long after she had been there.

But Shafal knew it would have to wait until later when he saw the two young female guests whom his sons had brought, helping in the kitchen. In the living room, Azad Sadawi, Imani Sadawi's hus-band, was conversing with Abdel and Ahmed. Yet, Shafal did have a chance to leer at Basma—but, again, she was so preoccupied she hardly noticed his presence.

The living room became alive with kinetic energy as seating was decided and the aromas from the platters of food wafted through the air. There was a momentary dip in activity when the Imam arrived and everyone paused graciously to greet him. The Iman was a tall, very thin man with a flowing, silver-gray beard, wearing a white head wrap. After the introductions, he was shown the bathroom to wash his hands and then was immediately offered the head spot at one end of the sheet, while Shafal sat opposite him at the other end. Since Khalid was the respected elder of the family, he sat to the right of the Imam—while Abdel, the oldest son, sat to the Imam's left.

Shafal was so proud and flattered that the Imam had accepted his invitation that some of the pent-up anger and embarrassment, he had felt towards Basma, subsided.

They blessed the food and, except for Basma, they all ate with gusto. Even so, the air was thick with tension. Sirhan decided he didn't want Osha around Basma anymore. Who knew what wicked thoughts she might have already planted?

Khalid gave Basma a fierce stare, concerned about the stain she had put on the family, especially if Tariq Tali started to tell everyone what he had told them today? What if the Imam heard about it?

Sumera was pleased to see everyone eating heartily. Of course, having not eaten all day—they probably would have devoured anything. Still, she was pleased to sit and share the food she had prepared with an Imam. She found herself sitting up a little straighter and, although no one could see, the corners of her mouth were in a perpetual curl.

As small pockets of conversation sprung up, Basma stared at her plate, pushing food around with her fork. Gradually, she slipped into musings about her recent discovery, oblivious to her surroundings. Inside, she heard her own voice—strangely disembodied: His name is Vin-sent Lan-gwa. Vin-sent. Then the voice changed into the saleswoman's: 'Boss town. Vin-sent moved to…' It switched back to her own voice: He moved… he moved? How could he?

The pain was too much. She got up.

"Basma?" Shafal called out, dumbfounded. "Sit down!"

"I do not feel very well. I must go and lay down."

"You look fine," he said harshly, then glanced self-consciously at the Imam. He tried a more dignified approach. "It is wrong for a wife to leave her guests in the middle of Iftar. And we are honored to have the Imam here with us."

An awkward silence followed as Basma sat back down. Both of her sons glanced toward their fiancées with sheepish looks on their faces. Basma found herself twisting the end of the sheet. Ahmed broke the silence by addressing the men, excitedly.

"There is a good chance that in a few months I will be working for myself, helping small companies with their online systems."

A little commotion broke out, lightening the mood as the men shared his enthusiasm. The women's eyes lit up with interest, but each remained silent. The Imam looked on approvingly.

"Where will you get money for that?" inquired Abdel leaning forward, with a hint of jealousy at his younger brother's entrepreneurial endeavor.

"I have two friends who want to go in with me," Ahmed responded, and paused to get one of Sumera's specialties: meat stuffed pastries. Taking a bite from the pastry, he sat back addressing every-one. "But we need office space." Looking over at Azad Sadawi, he said: "You know a lot about real estate, Mr. Sadawi, how do we—"

"Where is Aisha?" Basma asked, suddenly, her eyes ablaze. Shock rippled through the air. Sumera, who had been watching Basma stare at the pastry, was the first to react.

"Basma may be coming down with fever," she announced, apol-ogetically, and got up to go to her.

"She should be here, too," Basma continued, oblivious to her sur-roundings. "She is family. Why is she not here?"

Sumera froze. Slowly, Basma's attention returned to the room and she began to search the faces around her. She stopped when she spotted Sirhan. He glared back with indignation and contempt, dar-ing her to utter another word.

"Who is Aisha?" Abdel inquired, confused.

Khalid, aware of the Imam, ignored his nephew's question and addressed Basma with a stern, composed, voice:

"You have broken a sacred code. Do you know this?" he admon-ished, leaning in to give what he said more weight. "Never mention the name of anyone who has brought dishonor to this family."

"Dishonor? How can a child, a child bring dishonor?"

Khalid's eyes shifted nervously. "We will not discuss that kind of thing, especially on a holy occasion," Khalid commanded.

He glared, menacingly. Both young girls flinched. Sumera rushed around the sheet to Basma, placed her hands on Basma's shoulders, sinking her fingers deep into the flesh signaling Basma to hold her tongue.

Basma continued, unflinching.

"She did nothing to shame anyone."

Infuriated, Khalid lost it: "You deny this family suffered great dishonor and shame? She was alone with a man and doing indecent things!" he scolded.

"A man?" Basma challenged, looking him straight in the eye. "Rafiq was a child, also. He was a schoolboy. He always took her hand in his because he liked her. She liked him, too. That is all." Con-tinuing, she added, fearlessly, "It is natural that human beings should touch each other when they feel affection. How is that shame? A girl is a human being. What shame is it to the family if a girl holds a boy's hands? Is it dishonorable for two boys to hold hands? Huh?"

Azad Sadawi was used to this point of view coming from his wife, Imani. He immediately sided with Basma, as did the younger ones. But not Uncle Khalid, he and the rest were mortified, absolutely, mortified.

The Imam could keep silent no longer. "You cannot speak to what is right in our culture," he said, admonishingly. "Woman, you dishonor the Holy day with this talk."

Defiant, Basma kept her eyes on Khalid. "I was only speaking about his daughter."

"You know this is forbidden," Sumera scolded. She rose to her feet then bent over and grabbed Basma's arm trying to pull her up and away from them.

Basma wrested her arm free. Her body began to shake with emotion as she closed her eyes remembering the day her childhood ended. Sumera also remembered.

As little Basma opened her bedroom door, she heard three loud pops in rapid succession. Just outside the doorway, Aisha halted in perfect stillness, suspended in time. A second later, her honey-colored eyes bulged, her mouth opened, and she collapsed heavily to the floor.

As if on cue, Sumera returned, accompanied by Aisha's parents: Khalid and Tayseer. Other family members arrived. Khalid was stone-faced. Her mother, Tayseer, eased over towards her son, Sirhan, who was still holding the gun. She watched him staring transfixed at his sister's lifeless body, as pools of blood seeped out surrounding it like a deep crimson aura.

Tayseer squatted, put her hand over Aisha's bulbous eyes and closed them.

Her own black shiny eyes, like semi-precious stones, peered above the niqab without remorse.

Tall and imposing with his great salt and pepper beard Khalid, the patriarch, stepped forward, tapped his wife on the shoulder.

"Remember, Aisha brought shame to this family. From this day on, we will not speak her name. It is forbidden!"

His voice was as stern and authoritative as his eyes. Tayseer nodded, resignedly, and rose to her feet. Khalid glanced around to make sure everyone present had heard his command. To reassure him that they did, all those gathered bowed to him, respectfully.

Seized with a bout of nausea, Sirhan thrust the gun at his father, and rushed from the house. Satisfied, Khalid, and the rest of the family, followed.

It was a good while before the police arrived, that Sumera realized Basma was not amongst them. Holding her son, she searched the crowd that had gathered outside the house, asking if anyone had seen her daughter, Basma. No one could remember seeing the girl.

Handing the toddler to Tayseer, Sumera reluctantly returned to the house despite the fact that Aisha's body was still there.

Once inside, Sumera tiptoed to the end of the hall. She paused a few feet away, fearing any vibration might resurrect Aisha's body to life. And there, just beyond the doorsill, stood Basma staring straight ahead, her body trembling, her lungs gasping for air. Her face and clothing were splattered with Aisha's blood and brain tissue; and her mouth gaped open in mid-scream.

Basma opened her eyes again. "I want to know what kind of family… what kind of people think a girl and a boy holding hands is dishonor to the family… but murder restores that honor? Huh? What kind of people?" Her breathing grew faster, heavier. Her voice quivered, but never faltered. "Aisha… I can never mention? But I must share my home with her killer?" She scowled at Sirhan. Everyone gasped—but for different reasons.

"You… you killed your sister?" Ahmed inquired, sickened.

At this, Khalid, the defender of patriarchy, lunged at Basma. Osha screamed. Food spilled from the platters. But Khalid's action was outdone by, an even angrier, Shafal—who got up swiftly and charged toward her. Ahmed's fiancé hastened out of his way. Before Ahmed could act, Abdel leaped to his feet. In seconds, he physically blocked his father's onslaught—pleading with his eyes.

Blinded by rage, Shafal felt someone pushing him back, but he could only see his target: Basma.

"Why are you doing this?" he shouted, his face beet red. "You know our ways. Why bring up past things? You cannot change them." Basma wouldn't look at him.

Sumera, still standing behind Basma, began to sob loudly with concern. The sound snapped Shafal out of his vengeful cloud. He looked at the son who stood bravely in front of him. Abdel fought back tears.

The three younger women had sat watching with terror and amazement at Basma's defiance and stupidity. 'What was she trying to do? they seemed to wonder. Then Sumera's own anger, disappointment and embarrassment pushed away the fear for her daughter.

"How can you disrespect your cousin, Sirhan?" Sumera castigated, forgetting the Imam and Azad Sadawi. "He has always made this family proud. And your uncle, hasn't he devoted his life to keeping the honor and respect people have for us and our traditions."

Basma stared down at her fingers twisting the edge of the sheet. She heard her mother, but was unyielding. It felt as if her own garment of stoicism, worn all her life as a refuge, a shield, was now unraveling, thread by thread.

"There is conflict with the family beliefs and... my own... beliefs," Basma declared.

"Conflict?" Sumera shouted, dumbfounded. "How can there be conflict? You are a part of this family. You cannot have different beliefs."

Basma swung around glaring up at her mother who seemed more like a stranger. "But that is not true," she exclaimed, adamantly. "I do not believe in 'honor killing.' I do not believe in any killing. And there are many other things that I do not agree with in our culture." She paused, aware of all eyes on her. Even Abdel turned away from Shafal to his mother.

Her eyes were wide open. Never had she been so fully conscious of a moment. This moment. And she was fully cognizant of its impact on all the proceeding moments. She had already sailed far out into the ocean alone, and now she was willing to cut the line. She paused and looked apprehensively at the Imam who returned an icy autocratic stare.

"I think… a woman… should make the decisions about things that… affect her personally—like when to marry and who to marry. No one has the right to decide a husband for her. She—"

"Shut up!" Sirhan exploded, and then leaped to his feet "You?" His finger jabbed the air between them. "You are a woman! You have no right to think. You have no right to any beliefs."

"Shafal was right," Khalid echoed in a loathsome tone. "This country has corrupted you. You defend Aisha, but what shame do you hide from your husband?"

She held her breath and didn't swallow. What was he talking about? She finally looked at Shafal for confirmation.

But Shafal was spent. He turned and shuffled back to his place and dropped down with a thud. All eyes, except Basma's, followed him. After a moment, Sirhan sat back down and gave Basma a deadly scowl.

Only Sumera and Abdel remained standing by her side. Abdel was shaken with disbelief at all the rage just vented at his mother and then, all eyes seemed to turn simultaneously, from Shafal to Basma.

"Leave the room now," Shafal ordered gravely avoiding her face. "You have brought enough disgrace to this holy night and to this family. We are all sad that you have chosen this time to talk of forbidden matters, when we have kept silent about what you have done." Beneath his sorely tried reserve, he was seething.

Basma glanced around at everyone, purposefully meeting each eye. Some held her glance with disgust, like Khalid, Sirhan and Shafal. The Imam's was one of distaste, while the often-silent Azad Sadawi managed a look of compassion. Suddenly, they were all strangers to her. Not one person spoke up in her defense. She knew Azad Sadawi understood her, but in the presence of the Imam, he wouldn't dare show dissent. Nor would Ahmed, who glanced down when she looked at him, and then turned to his father. Hadn't he heard her say that Sirhan killed his own sister?

The timid young girls completely shied away from her, and they were the women her sons wanted to marry?

Sweet forgiving Osha, though shaken by the allegation that her proud husband might be a murderer, refused to meet her eyes.

Feeling totally defeated and abandoned, Basma struggled to her feet. There, standing face-to-face with her was Abdel. His eyes were moist, but behind them, she saw his love and admiration for her. The effect was so palpable, her knees buckled. He reached to catch her. She gestured that she could manage on her own. She squeezed his hand discreetly, and then, ignoring Sumera who had been standing behind her, she moved past Abdel, rushed to her bedroom and quietly closed the door.

***

The guests had long since departed for the mosque by the time Sumera and Osha finished washing the dishes and cleaning the food stains off the rug. After what had happened, the family couldn't possibly participate in Tarawih. Neither said much to the other.

Compliant as usual, Sumera resigned herself to accepting any decisions the men made regarding Basma's fate. For her, nothing could remedy the humiliation she felt in front of the Imam. Khalid was right, they had to do whatever was necessary to repair their family's image. As she turned out the light and closed her eyes, she told herself that she had done her best and now all was in the hands of Allah.

However, in the living room, Shafal, Khalid and Sirhan were taking matters into their own hands. In hushed tones, they were deciding Basma's fate, even though each man seemed to have lost a little confidence—in his own way.

"It must be done," Khalid demanded.

"Yes, but who will do it?" Shafal replied, leaning forward resting his forearms on his thighs. "Things are different here in America. To them, it's a crime." He began to rub his palms together. "I don't want to spend the rest of my life in an American jail. Do you?"

Khalid actually thought about it, for a moment. Maybe it would be worth it. The Imam… everybody would respect him the way they do Sirhan. What's a couple of years in an American prison in exchange for respect?

Sirhan leaned up against the wall with his arms folded and stared off, still heated with contempt. He could almost feel his hands around his cousin's throat. Never had he heard a woman criticize, let alone denigrate, the very tenets that had not only governed his entire family for centuries, but had given him the fortitude, the dignity, to continue his own life. How else could he have survived all those seconds, minutes, hours and years after blowing his beloved sister's brains out?

Agitated and absorbed in thought, Shafal got up and began to pace back and forth, then stopped.

"We could pay someone," he suggested, dispassionately. "They do this all the time here in America. But my sons— especially Abdel —must never, ever know. Understand?"

***

In the dimly lit bedroom, Basma waited for hours hoping, praying someone would peek in to see how she was. She understood why Abdel might have found it difficult. He had already defied his father. But where was Ahmed… or, her mother?

By 3 a.m., the men were in a sound sleep. She remained seated on her bed with her unfocused eyes replaying every detail of the evening in her mind.

Before long, she grasped the precariousness of her situation. She began to pace the room, wringing her hands. Afterward, she walked over to the window and looked up at the small sliver of sky hovering between the buildings. She listened to the silence. And, somehow, she knew what they would do. It made her sick to her stomach. How will it happen? When? Who? Sirhan or Shafal?

Her breathing became audible and tears gushed from her eyes. She hurried across the room, tiptoed out to the bathroom and quietly closed the door.

She ran hot water in the sink, unbuttoned her dress and washed up quickly. She brushed her teeth without feeling the pressure of the bristles or the taste of the gel. She unplugged the sink, pausing to watch the water drain, then took her toothbrush and wrapped it in the washcloth along with a bar of soap.

She hurried back to the bedroom, closed the door, gingerly, got her big handbag from off the dresser and stuffed the washcloth and soap into it. At the chest of drawers, she took out her passport from a manila envelope and put it into the bag, along with several under-garments.

Dashing to the closet, she pulled out a coat, flung it across the dresser and took the metal box from the corner of the top shelf. It was always unlocked, so she grabbed a handful of ten-and twenty-dollar bills and returned the box to the shelf.

She knelt on the floor of the closet, pulled out the tattered wooden box, took something from it, and put that and the money in her handbag.

Despite the warm weather, she slipped on her coat, lifted the strap of her bag onto her shoulder and then went over to the nightstand next to her bed and picked up the Koran. Holding it to her chest, she looked around the room for the last time. Satisfied, she walked to the bedroom door.

Suddenly, she halted, spun around and rushed back to the chest of drawers. She placed the Koran and handbag on the floor and opened the bottom drawer. Her hands pawed through the clothes, upsetting Osha's neat little arrangements. She paused a moment, puzzled, then pawed again. She opened the next drawer up and re-peated her search. Not finding what she wanted there, she frantically opened still another drawer and searched through it as well. Then she stopped abruptly, and with a sigh of relief, pulled out the purple silk gown and stuffed it into her bag—perplexed.

"I know I put it in the bottom drawer," she mumbled. She real-ized it had been discovered. She picked up the Koran again and hurried from the bedroom.

Back out in the hall, Basma could hear the men snoring in the living room. Walking softly holding her breath most of the time, she reached the bedroom where her mother and Osha slept. She opened the door slowly and peered in at her mother.

Sumera rested peacefully, as if there wasn't a care in the world. Basma watched her for a moment, and then closed the door.

The next was more difficult and precarious—but she had to do it. Regretfully, she slipped her head in and looked at her sons, her babies, for a long moment. Her heart wrenched, and once more tears gushed from her eyes. I can't, I can't go. But she knew she had to try.

When she got to the doorway of the living room, she saw Shafal asleep on the couch. Both Khalid and Sirhan were asleep on the floor.

The room was dark with the curtains drawn. But a thin sliver of light above the curtains illuminated the ceiling enough for her to see that there was a two-and-a-half-foot wide pathway between the couch, where Shafal slept, and the place on the floor where Khalid and Sirhan slept.

She clutched the big bag to her chest for support and took a large step forward and waited. She took another one, paused and listened. Another step. Silence. Then, out of the blue she heard a commotion. Someone was yelling. But it was in her head. Little Aisha was yelling.

Basma shook her head hard to stop the hallucination and took another step forward, then listened again. The silence was only pierced with snoring and dreams of atonement.

Another step and she would be three quarters of the way past the couch where Shafal laid.

Again, the desperate screams of Aisha running from Sirhan filled her head.

Seconds later, Shafal's arm slid away from his body and blocked her path. She nearly screamed out in panic, but his loud wheezing reassured her and she squashed her own scream. Side-stepping the arm, Basma continued along the narrow passage towards the front door.

In her head, the sounds of rapid footsteps pounding on hard dry earth. She took a giant step—paused, her heart thumping wildly—then another big one and cleared their bodies.

Just then, Sumera, groggy-eyed, came out of the bedroom and turned on the light in the hall. Basma was at the front door, now. She reached for the lock. Sumera walked right past the living room opening on her way to the bathroom just as Basma unlocked the door.

CLICK. It seemed loud enough for the entire house to hear, but Sumera didn't hear it and continued into the bathroom, while the men merely stirred a little. Opening the front door slowly, Basma hears *panic-stricken Aisha bursting through that other door*. She slipped out. The murderous footsteps of Sirhan, as he also bursts into her house, filled her mind and she saw her child-self getting up and hurrying to the door to see what was happening. Sirhan takes aim. He fires. Bullets soar through space directly at her.

She closed the door.

CHAPTER 16

It was daybreak by the time the subway roared onto the elevated platform in Jackson Heights. She hadn't been on a subway since she stopped going to the language school ten years earlier. And that trip was only two stops away. Now she was taking the train all the way into Manhattan.

Choosing a seat in the far corner of the subway car, she sat with her arms folded. The four men that were in that car each glanced her way. It wasn't because she was a woman traveling alone at such an early hour—they had all seen that before. It was the fact that she was a Muslim woman, traditionally dressed, and traveling alone by subway at dawn, that made them notice her.

Three hours later aboard a Greyhound bus, tired and emotionally spent, Basma's weary eyes tried to catch some of the beautiful scenery that zipped past her.

At the bus station in Boston, Basma walked over to a female employee leaning against an information booth chatting with the attractive male employee inside.

"Please… I want to go to a restaurant called Lay Hardin."

"We don't have no Lay Harden in here, honey. Do we, Hal?" Her voice was friendly enough, but her cold eyes scanned Basma up and down like a metal detector. Hal shook his head. Basma thanked them with a weak smile and searched for someone else.

When she spotted a woman passenger pulling a small suitcase, she hurried over and asked if she knew of the restaurant. The woman shrugged and hurried off. Basma continued to ask people as the terminal filled with the early rush hour commuters on their way home. Some actually stopped to listen to her question, while others whisked on by as if she wasn't even there.

Then she remembered the time she'd misplaced the telephone number of Ridgefield Nursing Home and didn't want to trouble Mrs. Sadawi, so Abdel told her she could always get a number by dialing 411.

She wandered around a few minutes until she spotted a public telephone booth. She fished out two quarters and dropped them into the slot. The automated voice asked for the name of the district. Basma said Boston. The voice then asked if the number was for a residence or business, and Basma replied, business.

"What is the name?" Basma answered: Lay Hardin, and spelled out: L-a-y H-a-r-d-e-e-n. The automated voice said there was no such listing.

Basma insisted that there was, but the automated voice disconnected. On the verge of total exhaustion, she found an empty bench and sat down.

As time passed, it became increasingly hard for her to keep her eyes open. She just wanted to let go and slip into that wonderful haven called sleep. After, when she woke up, all of this would have been a dream. She'd be back at home in her bed, safe. The Ramadan dinner would be the next day and… and maybe she wouldn't say those things. Then, she wouldn't have to die. But, Shafal must have seen the gown. It wasn't where she'd put it. Was that the reason he gave her such an evil look when he first came home?

Well, she had left them… all of them. Now, for the first time in her entire life, she was completely alone… stranded in another State. The thought was so unnerving it caused a queasy sensation in her stomach. A horrible sickening feeling of dread came over her. What if the woman in the bakery was wrong and it wasn't Boston, after all, but some other city? What then? She broke out in a sweat. Her temples throbbed. When did she last have something to drink? Was it before the dinner? Where are the water fountains here? Got to drink something, never mind that it's Ramadan.

Against the heavy weighted feeling of defeat, she pushed herself to her feet, hobbled over to a food kiosk and bought an ice-cold Coca-Cola. The sweetness of the liquid flowing over her tongue revived her instantly. There were assorted bagels in a bin, freshly baked muffins on metal trays, and ready prepared sandwiches in plastic wrap laid out in a pleasing display before her. Yet, for some reason, she felt no hunger pangs at all.

Still sipping the drink, she continued to wander around the bus terminal aware of her absurd situation. How foolish was this? What was she thinking?

Then, out of the corner of her eye, she spotted something that restored hope. Just beyond the exit doors, a cab driver was setting a passenger's luggage on the curb. The passenger was reaching in his wallet and pulling out money.

Basma ran to the exit and out into the street. The driver was already back inside the cab when she reached it. She yelled through the passenger window for him to wait.

"Please, do you know where there is a restaurant called Lay Hardin?"

The driver, a man about her age, thought a moment, and then shook his head.

"Please, there must be a place here with this name."

"Lady, this is Boston. There are thousands of restaurants. Call directory assistance."

"I did, but the voice said there was no listing."

"Well, what do you want me to do if there's no listing?"

"There must be a place. Lay Hardin." The driver sighed and shook his head again.

"I don't know of any Lay Har— Wait. Do you mean Le like the French say it?"

Basma paused for a moment, not really understanding what he meant. Then she asked, "Is that different?"

"Well, it's spelled differently. It's umm… hold on. Yeah. Le Jardin, that new place. I read about it. I believe it's a long way from here. Cost you about thirty-five dollars."

Basma was so relieved she barely heard the price.

***

Le Jardin, as the white letters read on the hunter green awning, turned out to be a luxurious place, bustling with a mixed crowd of trendy young professionals just off work and a few much wealthier middle-aged couples. It was hectic. People came and went. Waiters and busboys alike moved about quickly, with purposeful, conscientious, expressions on their faces. Everyone was absorbed in what he or she was doing.

There were about fifteen people waiting to be seated when Basma walked timidly through the door. No one seemed to notice her even though she looked like a fish out of water.

She was far beyond exhaustion, pale and anxious. Nevertheless, her eyes widened in wonderment at the elegantly decorated room with huge vases filled with spectacular floral arrangements, at the contemporary glittering chandeliers, and at the people dining happily. She took in their sporadic bouts of laughter like breathing fresh air, and was revived by it.

She eagerly scanned the room with its wide black-slated staircase that divided the rear section.

A second level, encased in a brass and steel-slotted railing, led to more seating above.

The maître d' came toward the entrance to escort the next large group of diners to their table.

He caught a glimpse of Basma as she peered between the heads of two people. He frowned to himself then he beckoned to the boisterous group to follow him.

***

At the same moment, the manager's door on the upper level opened and Vincent Langois, elegantly dressed in a dark suit, his hair cut short, walked out followed by an attractive, distinguished older couple, also very well dressed.

Behind them was a man with an air of importance, glowing as if he were used to the limelight. Closely at his side walked a poised young woman with similar features. The last person exiting the office, a man closer to Vincent's age, locked the door and pocketed the key.

They all followed Vincent across the elevated platform to the far-thest end away from the tables. Standing along the brass railing, they had a perfect view of the entire restaurant.

The young woman turned and gave Vincent a flirtatious smile. He feigned shyness.

"It still amazes me how quickly this place took off," the older woman commented.

"When word gets out that the mayor dines here," the man with the key replied, patting the man on the back, "we'll be booked solid for years."

The older woman smiled and glanced proudly at Vincent. "I knew my son would succeed in something once he made up his mind." Vincent shifted uncomfortably, shoved his hands into his pockets and managed a half smile that really was more of a grimace. When she looked away, Vincent stared at her with animosity, wish-ing it were his real father standing next to her, instead of Phillip Crichton. He knew in marrying Phillip, who was a successful land-scape designer, his mother Dana was finally able to live the lifestyle his real father, the jazz musician, could never give her. To his mother, Dana Langois-Crichton, money was more important than love.

When Vincent looked around at the reflection of success, he and his partner, Gianni Fiore, were responsible for, he felt proud. He had wanted his own place for years and now, thanks to Gianni, that dream had come true. And he was determined to keep the Mob at a safe distance, this time. Gianni was cool, he knew how to deal with them—prop up their egos, but still keep them out. This place had to stay legit, that's why they pulled strings to get the mayor to come.

As Vincent looked over the railing at the busy lower level, re-calling the last few weeks of constant phone calls back and forth to the Mayor's office, he spotted Basma —a few moments before she spotted him. He was so astonished he did a double take. What the...? Blood drained from his face. Alarmed, his searched the restaurant suspiciously. His stepfather, Phillip, turned to say something to him and saw the disturbed expression on Vincent's face.

"Vincent, are you all right. Is something wrong?" he asked.

Vincent shook his head and swallowed hard, unable to speak. His thoughts were in a scramble.

Gianni inquired of the mayor, "You said there are some dishes you'd like added to the menu? Well Vincent is the one to…"

Vincent didn't hear the rest. He slowly turned his head back to the front entrance in disbelief.

***

Basma spotted him in that instant. They stared at one another, transfixed. How handsome he looked. Her facial expression registered a mix of joy, relief and then… confusion, when she saw he wasn't smiling back. She made an excited move toward him, but his stiff body language signaled disapproval. She halted.

He gestured for her to go outside. Her face dropped. For the first time she felt self-conscious, and then she turned and walked meekly back out the front door as more patrons entered. The maître d' returned just in time to see her leave.

***

Vincent stared off a moment pondering what to do.

"Look, I know this is sudden," he said, "but I just remembered something urgent that I forgot to take care of. So, why don't you all go ahead and have dinner and I'll be back just as soon as I can." He turned abruptly and began to file past them. Each watched him with bewilderment as he walked past.

Gianni couldn't believe Vincent—the more educated of the two—would actually leave him alone to entertain the mayor and his daughter. He reached out for Vincent's arm and gripped hold.

"Vincent, buddy… ah." His eyes pleaded. "Whatever it is, surely it can wait?"

Vincent, distant, barely looked up. "No! It can't."

There was a crescent moon hovering overhead, a cool breeze made the tree branches sway rhythmically and the muffled voices of jovial diners drifted out into the parking lot. Anyone would have called this a perfect romantic evening. Anyone, that is, except Vincent.

He walked quickly to his car, with Basma following shortly behind. He fumbled with the keys, jerked open the door, got in and slammed it shut. Basma slid tentatively into the passenger seat. She immediately tried to explain herself, but he flung up his hand to silence her. Disappointed, she clamped her lips together and stared at him, as they drove off.

After speeding along the highway in silence for several minutes, he turned off the road into a semi-lit, secluded area behind a closed strip mall, then turned off the ignition.

When Basma attempted to speak again, Vincent put up his hand once more and cocked his ear listening for something. Between the silence, there were only sounds of the occasional car zooming by. Yielding to the situation, he gave Basma the full force of his attention.

"What the hell are you doing here, huh? Are you out of your mind?" he yelled. "How did you find me? Did you go to the police?" Basma gazed at him, her cheeks flushed. When she finally tried to answer him, she broke down in tears. He rolled his eyes in disgust. "Did you tell anybody about me?"

She shook her head frantically and shouted through the sobs, "No!"

He let out a sigh of relief and rubbed his face roughly with both hands. "Everything has been going so well for me here." Almost too well, he thought. "Then I saw you and I thought, that's it. It's over… I'm going back to jail." He looked over at her. "I know what I did to you… wasn't right. It was selfish," he admitted. "But it wasn't rape. If you want revenge, you can claim that… but I'll deny it."

She barely responded. What in the name of God, was he talking about? Why did he have to use that word? She understood all too well what the implications of that word meant for a woman in her country. Violated, and therefore ruined, dishonored, unwanted. And for some, like her family, the specifics didn't matter. The mere touch of a man, suggestively, on the woman's shoulder would warrant the same punishment: death. For the woman, of course.

He saw her surprise. "So, if that's not the reason you—" he twisted his whole body toward her. "I mean, what are you doing here?"

First, she composed herself by wiping away the tears, and attempted once more to explain to him why she had come. He stared at her impatiently. She looked down at her hands and began fidgeting with the strap of her handbag. Now everything seemed totally absurd. She sighed.

"I don't know. I had to leave and—"

"Had to leave? Had to leave what?"

"My family."

Vincent peered at her as if she were unstable. "You left your family? She nodded. "Why? Why would you...? Wait. Not to be with me?"

She nodded again, this time managing a smile.

'Oh God!" he exclaimed to himself, and then addressed her with complete detachment. "Look, lady. There is no way that we—"

"My name is Basma," she cut in. "Basma Abseh."

"I don't care what your name is," he yelled. "You're out of your mind. You're insane." The more he realized what she had done, the more incensed he became. "You... you leave your family and show up here, without warning, and expect... what? What? What do you want from me?"

The unexpected anger was too much for her. She couldn't hold back the tears.

"Don't start that again."

She turned from him to wipe her eyes. As she did so, she caught a glimpse of the crescent moon in the indigo sky. Now in the silence, she could hear crickets. For a moment, her feeling of dejection subsided and she slipped into reverie.

"Remember that day when we..."

"Look, you're wasting my time. I have a business to run. Remember that? And there are people waiting for me. I'll drop you at..."

"I was dying! I was dying," she shouted. "And then the baby died." Her tone softened and she spoke as if in a trance. "I didn't even know that I..."

"What the hell are you talking about?"

"When you left me!" She paused to look over at him. He stared off. "You left me with a baby." It was sudden and it shocked him. He jerked his head around, aghast.

"What?" Basma nodded to assure him he heard correctly. "No! No. What about your husband?"

"No, I was only with you that way," she confessed. And then the words, finally set free, tumbled forth in a stream of consciousness. "It died. So much blood. But, if it had not," she continued, bitterly, "Shafal would have killed it, anyway... and me." Then she became sad. "But I didn't want to live without you. That's when I died. I didn't care about anything anymore."

Vincent's expressions shifted from amazement to remorse to indifference.

Basma continued, dreamily. "And Mrs. Jazeer... I couldn't believe she was braiding my hair..." She paused and then continued with attitude. "Then Shafal thinks he can help me get better. He brings my family to America and Aisha's killer to my house." Vincent's eyes widened with dismay.

She began to unleash a torrent of words and pent-up emotions. "My family? They kill people! They killed my cousin. Her blood was all over my... Sirhan did it. That's what they call honor. Killing children. Killing women. A woman's life has no value to them. Everything is honor, honor, honor! I hate it!" She paused to catch her breath and resumed as if in a daze. "He never showed any feeling about it."

"All right! That's enough," Vincent shouted, filled to the brim. "I can't listen to any more of this crazy, fucked up... It's... it's too much." He tilted his head back and let out a loud groan. "My God!" he exclaimed, loosening his tie. "Look, none of that is my fault. So... what do you want from me? An apology, or something? Is that what this is about?" She frowned, not understanding. "You want me to say I'm sorry? Is that it? Huh?" He reached into his pocket for a pack of cigarettes. It was empty. Frustrated, he crushed the pack and tossed it on the dashboard.

Basma pondered: whether or not she wanted to hear him apologize. Would it matter? Would it change anything? In that moment of silence, Vincent's suspicion returned. He looked at the large leather sack that she clutched.

"What's in that bag? A gun? Is it bugged?"

She hadn't a clue what he was talking about.

"Are you recording this?" he clarified, grabbing the bag away from her.

He rummaged through it, and spotted the purple silk gown. He paused. Then he held it up, recollecting. It had been an impulsive purchase. It came from a designer collection at Saks Fifth Avenue—the store his mother, Dana, used to work in when she was still married to his father. He had wanted to give Basma something special, something glamorous. But that day had an unexpected outcome. As his fingers stroked the sensual fabric, he found his mood shifting. After a while… a much warmer Vincent emerged.

"I had to get up here, fast. For the business," he explained, "And I… uh… didn't know how to reach you at that nursing home. I didn't know your name." He glanced over with a sheepish expression on his face. "Look, what happened was just a…" He stopped and stared, trying to figure out a way to explain his actions. "I wanted to be with you. That's all. You were different from all the women I'd met. And I couldn't figure any other way that we… I didn't know you were living in that situation. How could I?" He sighed. "Let me ask you something. Before you got into my car that day… did you ever… think about me?"

"Oh yes, many times," she replied, her face reddening.

"I felt it," he said, softly.

She reached over and placed her hand on his—he cupped hers—and for a while, it was the old Vincent/Bakery Guy, sitting next to her. He had never left. All that agony, that pain was just something she'd imagined. They were together again. Surely, everything would be all right.

They sat quietly as the crickets continued to sing and unseen cars whisked by. Then Vincent pulled his hand away.

"You can't stay. You know that" he insisted. "You have to go back to your family."

"No! No!" she cried, emphatically, "I cannot."

***

Back at Le Jardin, Vincent's parents and the mayor were eating their dinner while Gianni made small talk. Every few seconds, he'd look around for Vincent.

The mayor's seventeen-year-old daughter was too disappointed to eat. She pushed the food around her plate and occasionally looked toward the door as well, hoping to see Vincent stroll through. The only reason she had accompanied her father was to meet the gorgeous owner whose picture she had seen in the local newspaper's feature of this new up-coming establishment. She had caught Vincent checking her out a few times that evening. When their eyes met, he would smile back, shyly. She liked shy men.

His mother, Dana, put down her fork and dabbed the corners of her mouth with the white linen napkin. "I wonder what's keeping Vincent," she announced.

"Call his cell," Phillip ordered.

***

In the silence, the ringing was an invasion. It startled them both. Vincent pulled it from his belt clip, opened the car door and got out.

"Yeah?"

"Hey man, everything okay?" It was Gianni.

Vincent had completely forgotten that he had left Gianni with his parents and the mayor. "Yeah, yeah, it's fine," he replied unconvincingly.

"You've been gone a while. When are you coming back?"

Vincent looked at his watch and frowned. "Uh, soon, soon. Look, just keep them occupied, okay. Get the mayor talking. And G… I'm sorry about this… really."

"Well, man, what is the problem?" he asked.

Fed up, Dana, Vincent's mother, attempted to pull rank. She reached for the phone. "Let me speak to him," she demanded.

Gianni stared back at her, dumbfounded. "He hung up on me."

"Well, call him back!" she insisted.

"Honey, let it go," Phillip urged. "Whatever it is, I'm sure he's doing his best to handle it quickly."

Then Phillip inquired of the mayor if he liked sailing.

***

218

Vincent pocketed the phone and paced. Basma watched him for a moment, then got out of the car and joined him.

"Look, I have a business to get back to," he said, formally. "I told you there are people... Do you know the mayor of Boston is at my restaurant, right now, waiting for me?" He assumed a cocky attitude.

Basma stared back at him with a blank expression.

"I'll drive you to the train station," Vincent proposed, heading back to the car.

Basma didn't move. "They will kill me," she shouted.

"Oh, come on... don't be ridiculous!" He stopped.

"I told you what happened." She could feel his impatience return and knew he was unconvinced.

"Look, I don't have time for this. Make up your mind. What are you going to do?"

Anguished, Basma pleaded: "You have to believe me. I would not lie to you. They will kill me... you must help me."

Vincent gazed at her, curiously, and then smirked. "Oh really? Help you do what?"

"To be free," she replied, as if it were obvious. "Free of them." She moved in closer and added, unblinking, "And free of you!"

He returned her penetrating gaze, but turned sheepish again, as he comprehended what she meant.

"Why should I? There's nothing between us. I haven't seen you in months. You think I owe you, is that it?"

Basma didn't answer.

"Why?" Vincent asked nervously. "The baby?"

Her face said it all. He stared at the ground, sighed heavily and walked back to the car. Basma waited a few seconds and then joined him.

They sat quietly with Vincent deep in thought. This time his facial expression was so intense and distant that it frightened her. But all she could do was wait.

After a while, she stopped fidgeting with her handbag strap and glanced over at Vincent with a forlorn look on her face. She hadn't meant to disrupt his life, even though he had destroyed hers. She had thought he would be happy to see her. No, that wasn't actually true. She hadn't thought at all. Her situation called for immediate escape and Vincent was the only person she had ever been emotionally intimate with, therefore he was the one she felt closest to. But he was different now. Everything was different now.

Eventually, he turned to face her. She parted her lips. He leaned closer.

Her body tensed. He put his arm around her shoulders. She searched his face and found his expression ambiguous. Slowly, he unwrapped her head covering and unbuttoned the top buttons of her blouse. She looked into those alluring blue-green eyes, transfixed. He gently caressed her face and brushed back her hair with his fingers.

For a moment, Basma felt a little uneasy. A hint of danger passed across his face. She had seen it before and so she looked deeper. Trusting her heart, she closed her eyes and tilted her head back in complete surrender.

He observed the serenity on her face and the vulnerability of her bare throat. Without hesitation, his hands encircled her neck. She swallowed hard beneath his firm grip, as he kissed her eyelids… her nose… both cheeks. The scent of his aftershave was intoxicating. The heat of his breath caused a throbbing sensation in her loins. When he did speak, his voice was never more seductive.

"Maybe killing you would be the best thing for us all," he concluded.

And her eyes flew wide open when he finally kissed her lips.

CHAPTER 17

I t was one of those hazy summer mornings about a week and a half later, when a middle-aged couple hiking along the west coastline of Rhode Island came upon a woman's battered water-soaked purse on the river's edge. The woman opened the purse, dumping the contents onto the damp sand. She grabbed the wallet first and counted out $234.16. The man retrieved a passport amongst the pile and scanned through it. The remaining items were a toothbrush, assorted white cotton undergarments and a purple silk nightgown.

A few yards away from the purse, they spotted a woman's black loafer half buried in the sand. The man immediately dialed 911 on his cell, while his wife scanned the ocean for any signs of life.

In a matter of hours, a search and rescue team had formed made up of scuba divers, police with dogs, volunteers and people living in the vicinity. They combed the woods, searched along the riverbank and dragged the river looking for the woman in the passport photo. At one point, the dogs did pick up a scent and took off running. Everyone naturally took off in pursuit. But the dogs soon lost the scent of whatever they were chasing. By dusk, the group of exhausted policemen and volunteers decided to call it a day.

Since there was no sign of a struggle and her money and belongings were still in her purse, the police ruled out homicide. Finally, they reached the conclusion that the woman must have walked into the ocean fully clothed.

The passport made it easy enough to notify Basma's family.

When they had discovered her missing the day she left, Shafal was chagrined. He vowed to himself that he would do everything possible to find her and kill her with his bare hands if necessary. Abdel was surprised that she would actually leave, let alone not inform him. He knew she didn't have any friends that they didn't already know. So where could she possibly go? But he, Ahmed and Sumera were each resigned to the fact that she did leave and when she got settled, she would contact them somehow.

When the call came about Basma's suicide twelve days later, Shafal found little relief. And for the first time ever, Ahmed turned against his father.

"This is your fault! You drove her to it," he spewed at Shafal.

Abdel's fury was more diffused. No! It's all of them. They all drove her to it with their… their stupid… primitive… fucked up—" His anger imploded and he collapsed in tears. His accusations caused Sumera to run sobbing into the bedroom.

Osha, who was busy cleaning the bathroom at the time the call came in, didn't know what was going on. Disturbing sounds seeped beneath the bathroom door. She came out into the hall but didn't know which way to turn first. To her left, there were harsh voices and sobs coming from the living room. To her right, in Ahmed's bedroom, she could hear what sounded like Sumera in great pain. She decided to go to Sumera.

Pushing the door open slowly, she saw Sumera crouched on the floor rocking from side-to-side letting out ear-shattering cries of sorrow. Osha flung her arms around her aunt, asking what was wrong. But Sumera was so lost inside her pain, she couldn't feel Osha's hand stroking her head.

Moments later, Osha was relieved to see Uncle Khalid standing in the doorway. He looked taller now—with his chin raised slightly, as were his eyebrows.

"What is happening, Babba?" she asked with concerned innocence. "Why so much crying?"

His typical reticence calmed her instantly. Obviously, whatever happened was nothing she needed to worry about. As if to underscore this, Uncle Khalid came over to her, reached down and pulled her to her feet. Then with an overt look of distain at his sister, Sumera, weeping on the floor, he took his daughter-in-law's arm and led her from the room.

In fact, Uncle Khalid felt the assumed suicide was simply retribution and it solved the problem of having to handle it themselves. It was perfect, really, except he couldn't understand why they hadn't found the body. Perhaps the sharks had an unexpected feast. God is good, he thought.

When they entered the living room, Osha spotted Shafal and Ahmed absorbed in a heated dispute. Abdel was sprawled on the sofa smothering deep heart-rending groans into a pillow. Osha's waif-like body began trembling. Uncle Khalid immediately gripped her arm tighter, but it was not in comfort or support, but to warn.

Out of the corner of her eye, she saw her husband, Sirhan, his arms folded standing in the corner, away from everyone else. His lean angular face was drawn, but unlike the others, he did not appear sad, nor was he gloating. Sirhan, once again, was smoldering with rage.

***

Two major events occurred during the first part of the week Basma disappeared. One was the Imam referring to the dinner incident in front of the congregation at the mosque. He warned against allowing the admittance of any woman who disobeys her husband's commands and not only espouses incendiary ideas, but also entirely disrupts holy Ramadan to do so. Surely, to the Imam, an obstreperous woman of this nature would easily pollute the pious minds of their wives and daughters. He never came straight out and mentioned the woman's name, but word spread quickly that it was Basma Abseh. A few people already knew that the Abseh family had invited the Imam to their home for the first Ramadan dinner. It wasn't difficult to deduce from that information the identity of the woman who had inflamed the Imam. Even so, it was still difficult, if not impossible, for those who knew Basma to believe that such a docile, amenable person like her could incite anything.

The second major event that happened in that week was Shafal's decision not to inform the authorities in Queens that his wife had gone missing, because once they agreed it was simply too dangerous to bring in an outsider to kill Basma, Sirhan had volunteered to do it himself. He told Shafal he didn't care what the penalty was in America. She had insulted him and the family in front of the Imam, and, worse, she was an adulteress. A family had to protect their honor at all cost. Even in this "haven of the devil", called America, where no one cared about honor, or morality, he would restore his family's honorable position and he would be a hero again.

Recharged by a sense of purpose, Sirhan committed himself to the task by spending every day calling on the neighbors, and visiting local shops trying to pick up any leads on Basma's whereabouts. The mission seemed to enhance his already healthy self-esteem, his manhood and his purpose. Six days after Basma had left, inquiries about her had reached everyone in the community. As a result, for Sirhan, hearing that his cousin had actually killed herself added insult to injury. She had totally derailed his plan.

For appearances, the men arranged an informal wake for Basma at the apartment. On the table was an enlarged passport-type photo of Basma with a deadpan expression. Mr. and Mrs. Sadawi arrived first. Imani brought two bunches of flowers in varying shades of orange and put them in vases on each side of the unsmiling portrait. She recalled the radiance on that face the day they had gone shopping and Basma, carrying the most beautiful bouquet of orange tulips, announced her plans of opening a business. It didn't matter if she was serious or not, Imani thought, the fact that she had that idea, at all, was amazing. Oh, how happy she seemed then. Could that same girl kill herself? And why in Rhode Island? Why would she even go there? It made no sense.

Imani shook her head then walked solemnly over to Sumera, who was the only one weeping, and took her hand in hers and patted it. Sumera glanced up with doleful eyes and Imani realized Sumera didn't have her face covered.

Abdel and Ahmed sat near Sumera. Both sons looked so devastated by the loss of their mother that Imani couldn't bring herself to acknowledge them lest she fall apart as she had done the day she heard the news. So, she planted herself next to Azad, who was seated on one of the folding chairs beneath the window.

Around her, she noticed Shafal, Khalid and Sirhan mingling together. Although their expressions were serious enough, somehow, in spite of the sadness of the occasion, there was an air of aloofness exuding from them. That caused her to remember when Shafal first informed her that Basma had committed suicide—how dry and unemotional he had been about it. Her shock, followed by the well of emotion she had felt, underscored the irony of his detachment.

Osha came from the kitchen with a tray bearing mugs of hot tea and set them on a side table near the sofa and then returned to the kitchen, but not before Imani caught her casting a suspicious glance over towards the men. In that moment, she wondered if Basma had indeed killed herself. Recalling now what Azad had told her about the big fight in front of the Imam during Iftar, Basma's subsequent disappearance the very next morning, the ban from the mosque, then the suicide announcement—without a body—and Osha's suspicion, Imani began to consider the possibility that they had murdered Basma and hidden her body somewhere. After all, didn't Azad also say that Basma accused her cousin of killing his own sister in front of everyone? It was an honor killing. The very issue that made her blood boil. Now, it made sense. My God!

***

Kensasha had never been in Basma's home before and wished this first visit were more auspicious. Standing just outside the apartment, with a bouquet of white long-stemmed roses under her arm and balancing a cake box on the palm of her hand, Kensasha paused to compose herself. She rang the buzzer. Moments later, a short thin woman all in black, her face covered, opened the door with a warm greeting and ushered her in.

Imani got up immediately when she saw Kensasha enter, and hurried over to her. The two women hugged briefly. Imani then introduced Kensasha to Osha who bowed politely. Kensasha handed Osha the roses and cake, which Osha took into the kitchen.

Hooking her arm through Kensasha's, Imani led her over to Shafal who was flanked on both sides by two men who acted like his bodyguards. Each man was withdrawn and disinterested in what was going on. A couple, who had arrived a few minutes before, was still expressing their condolences. While Kensasha stood behind the couple, waiting to be introduced to Shafal, she used the moment to observe the others in the room. Her first impression was that beneath the general atmosphere of sadness and sorrow was an element of tension, conflict, blame. That was, of course, common with suicides.

The woman on the couch with her eyes closed must have been Basma's mother and, she surmised, the two younger men looking as though the world had just ended, must be Basma's sons. She recognized the man sitting near the window as Imani's husband, Azad, who rarely spoke. The other people gathered here and there were probably neighbors and friends.

The whole thing was so unsettling. Why would Basma run away and then kill herself? She could have at least tried to talk to someone about her unhappiness. She, herself, had long recognized that Basma's general disposition rarely shifted above apathy. Although she was very dependable—always arrived on time and did what she was instructed to do—there was no real interest in what was going on at Ridgefield or connection with anyone there. Nor had Basma talked about her family or herself, for that matter. In fact, the lunch date they had was the first time Basma ever said anything about what she thought. Even then, Kensasha felt Basma's beliefs were narrow, conditioned or insular. They were the politically correct thing to say, rather than an honest opinion arrived at after serious inner debate and contemplation. She recalled that back in the spring Basma started coming out of her shell and often exuded an uncharacteristic state of lightheartedness. Also, during that time, Kensasha had witnessed Basma smiling once or twice but then, suddenly, she reverted back, becoming morose, detached, unstable, and then the breakdown. Was she bipolar? she wondered.

She should have talked to me. I told her if she ever wanted to… Kensasha sighed to herself and turned back to observe the two men next to Shafal. Something she saw in the older man's eyes put her on guard. He was gloating. Now, why would he feel that? She glanced sideways to see if Imani Sadawi was also observing the two men. Instead, she found Imani entranced by Shafal and the man and woman who presently held his attention.

What Imani thought intriguing was the way the couple, Khadija and Tariq Tali, kept repeating how sorry they were. Tariq, in particular, looked so broken up over Basma's suicide, one would have thought he was responsible. He certainly appeared to be more grief-stricken about Basma's death than Shafal, Khalid and Sirhan put together.

Following Imani's example, Kensasha fixed her attention on Shafal. The more she studied him the more she felt a pretension in his whole demeanor. She perused his facial expressions and saw that he feigned grief—it was all a sham.

CHAPTER 18

By 2 a.m. that same evening, all of the people who had attended Basma's wake were in their beds for the night. Some were fast asleep, others tossed and turned before finally drifting into slumber. A few, however, lay wide-awake, staring into the darkness, their minds replaying every detail of the evening.

Two hundred and thirteen miles away, Vincent Langois calmly left his restaurant with a carrier bag and a New York City newspaper under his arm. After locking up, he got into his car, placed the carrier bag and newspaper on the passenger's seat. He took a cigarette from the pack lying on the dashboard and lit it, sucked the smoke deep into his lungs and watched as wispy, donut-like clouds drifted from his puckered lips. He promised himself to give it up, but not today. His eyes fell on the newspaper headlines illuminated by the moonlight.

MISSING QUEENS WOMAN BELIEVED DEAD.

There was a deadpan photo of the woman and the following text:

In a brief statement released today, Rhode Island authorities said they are convinced that a Queens woman, mother of two, whose passport and other belongings were found a week ago, must have walked into the river fully clothed, and was probably pulled under by the current. The coastguard promised to continue the search for the body a few more days. They now admit that they, too, thought it strange that her family never reported her missing…

Vincent smiled, pleased with himself and took a few more drags before starting the engine. Twenty minutes later, he pulled up in front of a three-storied townhouse on a tree-lined street. It was a quiet neighborhood of young professionals. He considered himself lucky to have found an affordable, nicely furnished one-bedroom apartment close to the restaurant. After the investors had put in their share, he and Gianni spent most of their own money on the restaurant's décor. It had to make a statement. Everything they had was riding on its success and already it was proving to be a great investment.

The rental was on the top floor. He leaped the stairs two at a time and was not even breathing hard when he turned the key to his apartment.

With the paper under his arm, he headed straight for the kitchen without turning on the light. He opened the carrier bag, took out a food container and put it in the fridge.

Strolling back out to the semi-darkness of the living room, he moved cautiously toward the white leather sofa, threw the newspaper on the stone and glass coffee table then sat down loosening his tie.

"It's done," he announced into the darkness. He sat quietly for a few minutes, and then slowly reached and turned on the table lamp. He glanced to his right. As light flooded the room, he saw Basma's face. She was stretched out next to him, asleep, wearing one of his sweatshirts. He put his hand on her leg and shook it. "Hey, did you hear me? It's done."

She opened her eyes, gradually. He leaned over, picked up the newspaper and pointed to the article. She saw the headline and clutched her chest.

"My picture is in the paper!"

"Yep. And now, phase one is complete. Pretty clever idea, if I do say so myself. Although, it did take them longer to find your stuff than I anticipated. I remember that area by the coast being more populated."

"Vincent, how did you know how to do that?"

"I guess you could say I learned from someone who did it for real."

He paused to reflect while Basma stared at him, not quite getting it. The gulf between their life experiences was palpable.

"Now we are in phase two," declared Vincent bringing himself back into the present. "How are you going to live? I'm not taking care of you."

"I did not ask you to. I will work," she replied, feeling insulted and hurt.

"Really? Doing what?"

She contemplated a moment. "I can find another job in a nursing home. Or maybe… computers!"

"You can work a computer?" he asked, doubtfully.

"No." Then, suddenly excited, she said, "But I can learn. I can go to school. My boys know computers very well."

Vincent got up and took off his jacket and tie. He strolled into the bedroom and hung them up. "The only problem is you can't get a job or go to school without a name," he said, his voice raised. "You need a new identity, a Social Security card. Stuff like that. I don't have those kinds of connections, baby."

She felt deflated. She couldn't think of anything to say.

He took out his wallet and laid it on the dresser.

"Did you eat?" he asked.

"Yes," she replied, with increasing sadness.

"What?" he pressed.

"Those long skinny things with white gravy," she answered, forlornly.

At that, Vincent strolled back into the living room, and responded mockingly, "Oh, you mean homemade angel hair pasta with truffles in a cream and white wine reduction with a touch of fresh oregano?"

She shrugged, still contemplating what to do. Then it suddenly occurred to her.

"Miss Lewis can help me! I worked for her. I will call her tomorrow!"

Vincent sat down coolly on the back edge of the couch staring down at her.

"You're supposed to be dead, remember?"

"I can tell her the truth. She will not tell my family. She will understand," Basma insisted, to reassure him.

He yawned. "It's your life… I'm going to bed." He got up to go, then turned back. "Hey… you've been sleeping on that couch since you got here. It's more comfortable in my bed. Come on."

Basma looked up at him, confidently. "I said I want to be free of you."

"I won't touch you. We'll just sleep."

She smiled at that. "It is me I am worried about, not you."

He leaned toward her, seductively. His voice softened: "So? What if something does happen? It's been a long time." She let his hand stroke her cheek. "It may be an even longer time before you get another chance."

Something in what he said caused her mood to shift. She became serious.

"To you, I am just for sex. That is all you want. That is all you ever wanted from me."

"That's not true."

She laughed incredulously. "You made me have sex with you…"

"I remember you liked it… a lot."

She flushed, and ignored his remark. "You threatened to tell my husband."

"Oh, come on! How many times do we have to go over this? You know I wasn't serious."

"You mean you would not have told my husband?"

"Of course not! How would that have benefited me?" Basma stared back. "It's the threat that's important. You know, like nuclear war. No one benefits from nuclear war. Ah, but the threat."

She pondered his explanation, like she'd done the day he bought the purple gown. It seemed so hard to believe that she'd suffered the fear of discovery, all those months ago when, actually, Vincent had no intention of exposing their affair. Still, she was unsatisfied.

"You don't want to be seen with me."

"You're supposed to be dead!"

"At your restaurant, you do not let any of your friends see us together."

Vincent shook his head, exasperated. "Where is this going? I just invited you to sleep in a more comfortable bed and now you're talking about…"

231

"Why don't you want me in your life, now?" she asked, with a hint of jealousy—recalling the young blond girl that was standing near him in the restaurant. "Am I too old?"

"What? No!" He ran his fingers through his hair then put his hands in his pockets.

She studied him, intently. He wouldn't make eye contact.

"Because I am Arab?" she probed. "Right? You think we are all terrorists?" Now he did look at her, appearing awkward.

He strolled off to the kitchen, got a cold bottle of beer from the fridge, opened it and strolled back to the couch and sat down beside her. He calmly took a sip.

"All right, let's deal with this." He placed the bottle on the stone coffee table. "Why did you really come here, after what I did to you?"

"Because I thought we..." She paused, letting his question sink deeper. "You think, because I did not marry for love, that I don't desire it, dream of it? You think because I lived a life without romance that I am dead inside? Well, I loved you," she said, earnestly, "I love you."

He didn't respond. Instead, he took another swig from the bottle.

Something inside of him hated whatever it was inside of her that made it possible for her to say those words to him. It embarrassed him, made him uncomfortable. Was she expecting him to say it back?

"You never really cared about me," she exclaimed, when he wouldn't acknowledge her. She shook her head, suddenly feeling self-conscious. "I have been stupid, like some... teenager."

Ego bruised, Vincent regained his voice. "Listen, baby," he said, leaning closer, "if I didn't care about you, you wouldn't be here now. And, your death would not have been faked!" He followed that with a cryptic smile. "So, stop all this bullshit. I'm going to bed." He stood, finished off the beer and slammed the bottle down on the side table, startling her, before heading to the bedroom

A good hour later, Basma lay staring up at the reflection of a streetlight on the ceiling, still mulling things over. She'd never been in such a fancy apartment. The kitchen was fully equipped with stainless steel appliances and granite counter tops. Unfortunately, it was rarely used.

Vincent had suggested she heat everything in the microwave. So she did.

Every night, he brought freshly prepared food for her from the restaurant. He called several times during the day just to check on her, and he always asked if there was anything she wanted him to pick up for her. She'd grown to trust him. Finally, she decided Vincent must have cared for her.

Kicking at the blanket until it slid to the floor, she got up leisurely, yawned, and tiptoed into the bedroom. His back was to the door. She crawled hesitantly into his bed, trying not to wake him. Immediately, sensing her presence, he turned to face her but she stopped him and snuggled in closer burying her face in his neck. The warmth of his skin and the scent from his aftershave caused that twinge in her lower belly.

"Umm," she moaned.

He lifted his arm over to touch her hip.

"No touching," she whispered. "Just sleep."

It was late morning when Vincent opened his eyes. Sometime during the night, Basma found her way into his arms. As a warm breeze sent the curtains billowing out, he watched her sleep. Still wearing the navy-blue sweatshirt and sweatpants he had given her the first night, she looked like any other woman. He slipped his hand down into her pants. She moaned. He kept exploring. She arched her back and her hips began to sway. He kissed the top of her head and her cheek. She peered out through half opened eyes at him. He grinned, flashing those perfect white teeth.

"Do you realize we can do this for hours?" he informed.

"Okay," she replied sweetly, moaning again with pleasure.

In his model kitchen—compliments of the previous owner—Vincent played chef for the day. He christened the professional-styled range by pouring pancake batter onto the griddle, while bacon sizzled in a frying pan next to it.

Basma bounced in, beaming, her step more assured. After her shower, she had taken the sea green shirt he had worn the previous day and slipped it on over her long brown skirt. She slid a bar stool away from the island and hopped into it.

"She is going to do it," Basma announced excitedly. "I will have a new identity. She knows people who can help me."

"Are you sure you can trust her?" he cautioned.

"Of course! And she's going to call Dr. Sethi. Maybe I will go to Eng-a-land and work with her." Vincent didn't comment. He used the pancake turner to scoop three perfectly round golden-brown cakes onto a plate and placed it in front of her.

"I can't believe I'm making you pancakes. This is a traditional American breakfast, you know."

"Umm, smells good."

He buttered the pancakes, drizzled real maple syrup over them, cut a piece and fed it to her.

She chewed for a second, and then frowned. "It is sweet!"

"It's supposed to be sweet, it's pancakes."

"Do you have some without the sweet gravy?"

Vincent was speechless for a moment. He pulled the plate to his side of the counter and prepared another plate of bacon and pancakes without syrup. This time, she buttered them herself and added the bacon to his plate.

"Very good pancakes. I like it." Pointing to the bacon, she told him, "In my religion, we do not eat that." He shrugged, took the pancakes with the syrup and extra bacon, and began to eat.

"So how long will all this take?"

"Don't worry, Vincent, in a couple of weeks I will be gone."

"That's not what I meant. I just… forget it." Irritated, he jammed another forkful into his mouth.

Basma reached over and touched his arm gently. "I am sorry."

He nodded to show he accepted her apology, and she felt the tension between them dissipate.

Suddenly, he put down his fork and gave her a curious look.

"So… who are these people you know that can get someone a new identity? I thought only the FBI could arrange that, especially in this day and age. I mean… for an Arab, after 9/11?" His curiosity had turned to disbelief. She understood why. She, too. was amazed and decided now was a good time to tell him all about Kensasha Lewis and her involvement with Dr. Neelam Sethi's crusade.

***

An hour before opening for dinner, several busboys were setting the tables. On the second level, William, the maître d, was absorbed in taking last minute reservations. Gianni was in the kitchen giving instructions to Michel, the chef, when the front door opened and in walked the detective.

He proceeded to scan the room. William spotted him and immediately notified Gianni. Before Gianni could get to the kitchen door, the detective entered. He flashed his badge quickly, and eyed the staff. Gianni smiled, awkwardly, and took the liberty of hooking the detective's upper arm.

"Let's talk outside here," he proposed in a congenial tone, pulling the detective towards the door. "I need my people to do their work."

The detective allowed himself to be escorted from the kitchen. Still grinning, Gianni let go of the detective's arm once they were in the dining area.

"Is there something wrong, detective," Gianni asked while continuing towards the front entrance of the restaurant. The detective reached into his pocket, and pulled out a clipped newspaper article with Basma's picture in it.

"I'm investigating the disappearance of this woman. Have you seen her?" Gianni glanced at the photo and shook his head. The detective scrutinized him a moment. "Are you sure? A cab driver says he dropped her off here."

"I'm sure I'd remember her if she was in this place," Gianni replied, with a smirk on his face. The detective peered around at the busboys and up at the maître d' on the phone and in the process of writing something down.

"What about him... over there?" the detective asked, pointing up at William.

Gianni followed his gaze and called out to William. The young man started. He looked down through the railing, nervously. Seeing Gianni and the man staring up at him, his eyes widened. He says something to the caller, hangs up the phone, and hurries down the stairs to join them.

"William, this is detective..."

"Slattery," informed the detective, abruptly, "Has this woman been in here?" He extended the newspaper clipping. William, wearing a white tuxedo jacket, black pants and bow tie, leaned closer and gazed at the woman's photo for a second. There was immediate recognition on his face.

"Yes, yes. She was here!"

"Do you remember when, exactly?" William put his hand to his temple and closed his eyes in thought.

"Uh, yeah, that was the night the mayor came in with his daughter," he recalled, excitedly. "It was crazy in here. We were packed."

Gianni was taken aback by this bit of information.

"Do you remember who she met here?" asked Slattery.

"Well, actually, she didn't meet anyone."

"She dined alone?"

"No. She didn't stay. I was busy seating other customers, but I remember seeing her by the door. I thought it was odd. Then she left. It was obvious she was in the wrong place."

"How do you know that?" Slattery asked raising his chin, while keeping his eyes level. The young man glanced over at Gianni and rolled his eyes at the detective's seeming naiveté.

"Well, see, we don't get those kinds of people in here, sir," William replied, with a slight air about him.

"What kind is that?" Slattery asked. William looked at Gianni again, this time for help.

"Arabs!" Gianni answered with distaste. "We don't have Arab clientele," he added with a boastful tone, unaware of his own crass assumptions. "This is a classical French restaurant."

Slattery grunted as if the comment explained everything. Then he scratched his head and asked, "Aren't there a lot of Arabs in France? Maybe she came here to meet a relative who works in your kitchen."

Gianni lost his patience. "Look, Detective…"

"It's Slattery."

"Detective Slattery," he resumed curtly. "We don't hire Arabs in this place, got it? Now it seems this woman made a mistake and walked into our establishment. When she realized her mistake, she walked back out. That's it. End of story. Now, we have to open in less than an hour. So…" Getting the message, the detective let out a sigh. It was obvious, with no other leads, Basma's trail ended here.

"Thank you, gentlemen," Slattery said, looking as though both Gianni and William reeked of a bad odor. He turned to leave just as Vincent entered through the back door.

On his way back to the kitchen, Gianni saw Vincent approaching and paused. Vincent, dressed elegantly, in a white silk turtleneck, brown tailored-jacket and trousers, had a curious expression.

"Who was that man?" he asked.

"A police detective," replied Gianni. Vincent stiffened. "He was asking about some missing Arab woman." The color drained from Vincent's face.

"Wh-what do you mean?" he pressed, trying to sound casual.

"Apparently, some Arab woman disappeared. The detective said she was last seen in here." Gianni explained, studying Vincent's face. Vincent remained silent, but his mind raced. "Strange, huh?" Gianni exclaimed, puckering his lips.

"Who saw her in here?" Vincent asked, shoving his hand into his pockets.

"William."

"Really? What exactly did he see?" Vincent probed, sounding a little too concerned.

"Not much. He just saw her standing by the door for a few minutes and then she left. That's it. She was in the wrong place," he elaborated.

"Yeah," confirmed Vincent.

Gianni spotted something on the table nearby that didn't meet his approval and adjusted it.

"So, William called the police?" Vincent continued, trying to sound nonchalant.

"No, no, it was the uh… cab driver," replied Gianni sensing his friend's undue interest. Vincent frowned, questioningly. "He drove her here. And when he noticed her picture in the paper, he went to the cops." Vincent nodded, then shrugged.

"Funny thing, though… it was the same night the mayor came… and you left us waiting." Vincent tried to pass this off, but was stone-faced. Luckily, Gianni misread the cause. "Hey, don't sweat it. I forgive you."

Vincent managed a rueful grin. Then he became serious, and much too concerned, all at once.

"So, do they know where she went after she left here?"

"Beats me," Gianni shrugged. "What do you care? It's nothing to do with us." He took a few steps toward the kitchen, turned back and patted Vincent on the shoulder. With a sly grin he added, "Hey, why don't you tell Michel not to put so much wine in the Bourguignon. He never listens to me, anyway."

***

The apartment was immaculate. Basma made sure of it. She was dozing on the couch after a day of scrubbing the floors, even though she knew Vincent did not approve of her cleaning for him.

"You're my guest," he had reminded her. But cleaning made her feel useful and it kept her mind off the things that haunted her, especially Aisha. Besides, she couldn't just sit all day leafing through Sport's Illustrated, Men's Health and Newsweek, she informed him. So, he bought her Cosmopolitan, Vogue and Vanity Fair. Her initial fascination with the clothes, the makeup and the jewelry soon turned into wondering what was the purpose of it all. It left her empty. Until, those other thoughts seeped back, obliterating everything else.

Vincent arrived home in an anxious mood. He walked hastily over to her and shook her. She opened her swollen red eyes.

"What's wrong? Don't you feel well?"

"I am fine."

"You don't look fine. Why the long face?" Basma sat up straight. At first, she seemed embarrassed—reluctant to answer. Then she decided to share what she had been holding back for so long.

"I miss Abdel, my oldest. I miss both of them, but I miss Abdel the most. I won't be at his wedding. I won't see his children." Vincent nodded, letting her know he understood how she felt. He considered what she was saying, and sat down beside her, slipping his arm around her shoulder.

"But, if you were really dead, you still wouldn't be at his wedding or ever have the chance to see your grandchildren, right?" Basma thought about that for a moment, but it couldn't shift her mood. Needing to address the matter at hand, Vincent removed his arm to face her directly. "Listen to me." His expression was grave. "The police know you came into my restaurant." To himself he said, "But thank God, no one saw us together.'" He took hold of her hand. "You must continue to stay inside here, understand? We can't risk anyone seeing you, now."

"But I must go to the shops tomorrow." There was a sense of urgency in her voice. "I need things to take." He let go of her hand and slipped out of his jacket.

"Forget about it," he replied. "Whatever you need I can buy it for you." Still talking, he unzipped his ankle high boots and took them off. "Just make a list and write down your size." She glanced away. He saw that she was uncomfortable with that and it puzzled him. "What is it? You don't want me to know your size?"

Basma shook her head and replied with a hint of shyness: "Some things only a woman can buy." Vincent stared at her.

"Like what?" he probed. Her shyness intensified as she searched for a way to explain. Then he smiled. "Ooh, that. Well…I can get that too. Did it for my ex many times. Not a problem" He squeezed her thigh, reassuringly.

Basma, however, was still uncomfortable about Vincent having to purchase all her personal items. But he read her well and knew it was critical that she took what he said seriously. He cupped her face so she couldn't turn away.

"Look, men here do it all the time," he assured her.

She dismissed what he said. "I wear a hat over my scarf, people won't notice that I'm…"

"No! You are not setting foot outside that door until it's time. Do you understand me?"

"I think everything is okay now," she persisted, stubbornly, wringing her hands. "My family thinks I am dead. It is in the paper. I need to go outside."

Vincent sighed in frustration. "Did you hear what I just said?" He grabbed her wrist. "A cop came into my restaurant tonight asking about you. Don't you get it?"

He stood up and began pacing the floor.

"I can't have my name and Le Jardin linked to your disappearance. And if what you say is true about your family, I certainly don't want to get killed because of you."

She felt a shiver down her back. Didn't he realize that they wanted to kill her because of him?

He stopped pacing and went back to where she sat, took hold of her hand and pulled her to her feet saying:

"I'm exhausted. Let's go to bed." He led her to the bedroom.

Suddenly, she halted and, with a clear, firm voice, said, "I think it is better that I sleep out here... alone... until it is time to go."

Vincent was thrown. He started to protest, but realized he was seeing a different side of Basma, one he'd never seen before. He let go of her hand and said,

"All right, if that's what you want. I'll get the sheets and..."

"No. I will get them," she replied.

CHAPTER 19

LONDON

Zafeera Hasni ran her hands through her shoulder-length ebony brown hair and finger-combed it back until she could grip every strand with one hand. Taking a thick rubber band from between her lips with the other hand, she managed to secure the unruly waves, all the while wondering how long she could continue taking days off work to come to this grungy bedsit and play detective—of sorts.

Sitting at the only table in the large rectangular room with muddy blue walls, she sipped a lukewarm cup of bitter coffee she'd purchased earlier from an Indian-owned deli a few doors away. She pined for the Starbucks near her home, or any gourmet coffee shop for that matter, but figured nothing of that sort existed within two miles.

Her white sneakers scuffed across the worn vinyl floor when she stretched out her legs and slouched, comfortably, in the vinyl-backed chair. No, this place certainly wasn't what she was used to.

She frowned when her eyes focused on the wedding photo she had placed on the windowsill above the kitchen sink. In the photo, a North African looking couple stared self-consciously at the camera. The bride's smile was false, she decided. Zafeera knew that lovely innocent face all too well. It belonged to her younger sister, Ghaybaa, who she hadn't heard from in almost two years.

Ghaybaa always smiled in that way when she was told to do something she didn't want to, but did anyway to ward off disapproval or reprimand. Consequently, Ghaybaa was the one always seen as agreeable, compliant, obedient—the perfect example of a daughter worthy of marriage. Unlike other daughters who disobeyed…

Zafeera took another sip of the vile coffee and glanced at the groom. His steely black eyes reflected a hidden arrogance—something brutish, fearsome, resembling cruelty—or so she thought. Perhaps that's only what she wanted to see. How could she really know what he was like if she had never met the man? She grew sullen at the thought, and then looked over to the futon couch where she'd laid a file folder. Everything that was known about the groom was in there. Everything. And nothing.

Her attention wandered back to the decade-old photograph and the sweet, charming face of the seventeen-year-old bride. Deception was impossible. Anyone who cared to look deeper would see the truth behind those eyes.

She remembered how Ghaybaa, as a child, had copied the baby pink hijab-styled scarf and pink denim jeans that became Zafeera's own trademark in high school.

Once Zafeera bought a dozen white tee shirts in medium and extra small, took cans of colored glitter and sprayed them randomly all over the tee shirts. Some in swirling motions, other times horizontal and vertical strokes were all she produced, yet it resulted in uniquely individual works of art that her fellow students coveted.

Ghaybaa had always requested Zafeera make her shirts with purple and yellow spirals. Zafeera accommodated by making an extra effort to design different patterns of the two swirling colors—anything to please the virtuous soul of her little sister, Ghaybaa.

Regardless of the uniqueness of the shirts and their desirability by others, the two girls could never show them off at home. Jackets buttoned to the neck secured their modesty whenever they left for school or until they returned home and were safely behind the doors of their male-restricted bedroom. Here, their two brothers and their father would never venture. Here, hidden away from the gaze of all but each other—they were free to wear such shameful attire.

And yet, they had considered themselves fortunate for having a father who permitted music in the house—and both girls took full advantage of that. Ghaybaa, in particular, had screamed excitedly when their father, Vasilis, presented her with a portable CD player and headphones, after she got good grades. The headphones soon became an appendage. Most nights the child fell asleep with them still on her head. As the family belief was that women should not play instruments, listening to music was the only balm that soothed Ghaybaa's aching desire.

On weekends and during long summer evenings in their parents' non-air-conditioned apartment, the girls made their own entertainment. In the privacy of their room, with music streaming from the CD player, the girls, wearing pink head scarves, glittered tees, pink denims and socks, performed to an imaginary crowd of screaming fans.

Zafeera could still hear the suppressed giggles her sister made as she leaped onto the bed, twirling unsteadily and strumming a hand-made cardboard guitar like a drunken rock star. Whenever it was Zafeera's turn, she'd get to her feet and begin strutting and prancing across the room like Michael Jackson. And, like clockwork, her sister's wide chestnut eyes reduced to slits, the paper guitar slid from her hands, and she would fall over backwards on the bed, her body trembling with gleeful joy. Then, Zafeera, too, would laugh, openly—in the safety of those four walls— behind the closed doors: the only place a decent woman was allowed to laugh.

Those sounds and images of her past triggered a deep inhalation. Her heart softened. Her body relaxed for a minute.

She redirected her attention to the groom once more, and a chill ran down her back when she imagined those heartless eyes fixed on that sweet loving face of her sister. She imagined his callous, insensitive hands groping her delicate skin's need for a tender touch. The thought made her desire to find them all the more urgent. Had something happened? She clenched her jaw and stood abruptly, bumping against the table. Carrying the coffee over to the sink, she dumped the remains down the drain and gave a stern look at the man in the photo hoping it would reach him somehow. Where are you?

Without another thought, she walked over to a tiny closet adjacent to the front door, yanked a fleece-lined denim jacket off a crooked wire hanger and jabbed her arms into rolled sleeves. She yanked her white tee shirt down over her hips, then she made sure the hem of her black jeans was straight, and her shoelaces tied. Taking an army green baseball cap from her pocket and placing it on backwards, she concluded her ritual.

She opened the door and stepped into a cold drab hallway, in desperate need of maintenance and where the smell of curry always permeated the air. Ironically, this time it whetted her appetite. It had been days since she had a home-cooked meal.

Door locked, she started walking toward the stairs. Behind her, a door flew open and a man rushed out dragging a coat. He leered at her when he passed and descended the staircase before she could react.

She halted when she heard someone wailing. It was a woman. Zafeera turned and followed the sounds. They led to an apartment near the end of the hall. The door was ajar. She peered through and saw a woman lying on a bed at the far end of the room.

Taking the liberty, Zafeera entered the apartment cautiously, making sure there was no one else around and went straight to the bed.

Surrounded by a chaotic mess of shattered lamps and tipped over furniture, she contemplated how to calm the woman, who appeared to be six or seven months pregnant with multiple bruises on her face, neck and arms. Some of the bruises were almost healed. Obviously, thought Zafeera, this was not her first beating.

"Do you speak English?" she whispered to the crying woman.

Startled, the woman looked up letting the heavy sobs die away. She stared at Zafeera for a moment and then managed to say, "No, I don't speak English," in north Levantine Arabic, spoken by Syrians and Lebanese.

Familiar with all Arabic dialects, fluent in her native Algerian, Zafeera was able to address the woman, who was no more than twenty, in her own tongue.

"You must leave this place, now! Do you hear me?" Zafeera commanded.

The Syrian woman stared up at the concerned face. The woman standing before her was dressed like a westerner with groomed eyebrows, no makeup, wearing a man's cap backwards. How odd to see her in this part of London where even teenage girls wore hijabs and abayas.

"Who are you? How did you get in?"

"I sometimes stay in a room down the hall. Just now, I saw a man leave and heard you crying. He must have left the door open."

Zafeera had a greater degree of concern and worry than the woman had for herself. The woman saw this and decided it was simply because Zafeera did not know the pressures her husband, Yusef, was under. He had a lot on his mind and she had been whiney. He hadn't meant to hit her.

"I will be okay. Because of the economy, my husband cannot find work and he is always agitated. Now the police are always harassing him since he got into this political group. He doesn't know what to do."

"That doesn't give him the right to beat you," countered Zafeera. The pregnant woman glanced away. A moment later, she wore an expression of steadfast loyalty.

"You should go. He will be back," she commanded.

"You need to come with me," Zafeera insisted. "Get away from him while you are still breathing, for God's sake." In response, the woman hunched her shoulders as if suddenly cold and began wringing her hands. Again, she looked away.

With the woman not budging, Zafeera reluctantly gave in and rose to her feet, stepping back on fragments of shattered cups. She felt relieved when she was finally out in the hallway. After all, it was late Wednesday afternoon, and she had a much more formidable foe.

NEW YORK

The first and only other time Basma had entered an American airport restroom was twenty-two years earlier. At that time, she marveled at how every stall had a door and how all were neatly lined up beside each other. The row of sinks, each with their very own soap dispenser. Of course, she didn't realize the third faucet on the sink was for dispensing soap, simply because, at that time, she wasn't aware that there was such a thing as liquid soap.

Shafal had already explained to her that in America hot water traveled through pipes into every home every day, all day. Everywhere there was hot water, he had said, so to have the cold and the hot water coming through a faucet in the restroom at an airport didn't surprise her. But she wondered what other type of water could there possibly be—warm water? Did they really need warm water, too, these Americans?

All those years ago, when Basma had seen a woman wet her hands then vigorously pump the other faucet, releasing a pearly pink viscous solution into her palm, she paused curiously, to watch. The woman then rubbed her palms together creating a rich sudsy lather. Afterwards, she rinsed it off under the two faucets, then walk over to a metal box hanging on the wall. She pulled out white rectangular paper, which had been neatly folded, and used it to dry her hands.

"My God!" thought Basma. "The soap in America is not only watery, it has a pretty color, and they are so rich here, they use a paper cloth just to wipe their hands one time and then throw it away!" She waited until the woman left before trying it herself.

Now, so many years later, when Basma entered the restroom, she noticed how it had changed. The faucets no longer had knobs—just a spout. At first glance, she assumed they were all broken. Then, as she had done twenty-two years earlier, she watched as other women simply held their hands under the faucet and, magically, the water came out! Instead of using the cloth paper, they held their hands beneath a different metal box on the wall and some kind of air came out.

Change. It was all about change. Everything here changes, how can you keep up?

When she came out of the stall to wash her hands, she realized that her appearance had changed, as well. The last time she was in the airport restroom, all the women stared when they first glimpsed her. Some let their mouths fall open. She recalled how one mother had to comfort her little girl who had burst into tears when she saw Basma draped all in black with only her eyes exposed. Apparently, the child thought Basma was a ghost.

Back then, a woman in full Islamic dress complete with face covering was rarely seen anywhere in the West. This time the women were only absorbed in washing their hands, or primping in front of the mirror.

Basma pumped white liquid soap into her palms and held them under the waterspout while marveling at the rich color of her new tailored suit.

Thanks to Kensasha, who did the final shopping, she now wore a dark violet jacket over a cream-colored blouse-buttoned up to the neck. Her violet skirt only reached to just below her calves, revealing flesh-colored tights. And for the first time, she had two-inch heeled black pumps—her choice. If she had known she would have to spend two days practicing how to walk in them without losing her balance, she would have settled for flats. Now, however, she liked how feminine they made her feel.

The reflection of her face in the mirror had also changed. Her eyelids were dusted with mauve shadow and her lips tinted with plum gloss. She had used Kensasha's black mascara to highlight her large brown eyes, and she had secured every strand of hair inside a satiny white hijab.

Basma picked up her purse with the Koran on top, which she planned to read for solace during the long flight, and stuck it under her arm. She then walked over to the hand dryer and held her hands underneath as the other women had done. Upon leaving, something made her stop and stare at herself. It wasn't just the makeup—she felt different.

Suddenly, and quite unexpectedly, Basma pulled the white satin hijab off her head, and finger-combed her long dark hair free. Then, just as impulsively, she grabbed the hijab and dropped it into a trashcan, and continued out the door.

Yet, her initial steps beyond the doorway were like crossing a vast frontier—an invisible gulf—not so much a cultural or religious one, but, rather, a huge psychological one. Because, on the other side of the restroom door, there were all kinds of men—strangers—who would see her bare head! What would they possibly think of her being exposed like that? How would they behave? A woman's hair was alluring—enticing to men. Oh, my God! How would she manage that kind of attention?

She braced herself, took a deep breath and slowly moved further beyond her imaginary border. Naked was her initial feeling. But as she took that second and third step, the dramatic reaction she expected from men when they saw her hair simply didn't happen. In fact, few of the men paid her any real attention at all. Those who did merely did so in order to circle around her to get to where they were going. For the most part, she was still invisible. This was a major shock.

***

Kensasha, who rejoined Basma back near the security gate, couldn't help but raise an eyebrow at the missing hijab she had bought for Basma. Nor could she imagine what Basma had wrestled with inside herself in that restroom to let go of her hijab. Covering, for Basma, was a symbol of so many things that had defined and shaped her life, until now.

Basma's eyes met hers in expectation of a comment, a disapproval. But Kensasha offered neither, deciding to allow Basma to take responsibility for the choice without knowing or caring, for that matter, what other people thought. So instead, she handed Basma a little gift bag.

"Now don't be afraid, Basma. Dr. Sethi promised to be at the airport when you arrive. You will love her. She's such a good person. And her house is filled with great literary works and paintings and—"

Feeling a wave of excitement, Basma uncharacteristically, gripped Kensasha's arm. "Thank you so much. I still cannot believe I am going to Eng-a-land.

"Well, I thought it would be the safest place for you under the circumstances, and you already have a job waiting."

Then, just as suddenly, Basma's excitement was clouded over by despair.

"I am afraid. It is so far away. I miss my boys so much my stomach hurts. You said they are very sad?" Kensasha threw her arm around Basma's shoulders to comfort her.

"Yes, and Imani was so upset, she was getting sick. I wanted to tell her the truth, but she still has to interact with your mother, and I just couldn't put her in that situation. It would be too dangerous for you. The boys are still grieving, especially Abdel. He moved out."

"Maybe I will call him and—"

"No!" Kensasha said forcefully, clutching her shoulders. "Basma, you can't do that. Don't you understand the situation? It's too dangerous. And if something happened to you because you contacted him, how do you think he would feel? Huh?"

The firmness in Kensasha's voice shook Basma out of her malaise, and she nodded that she understood.

"I told you I would keep you informed how they are, and I will. In time, they will heal."

"And Imani?" Basma's eyes widened, as she feigned cheeriness.

"Yes, Imani too, and your mother."

The cheeriness soon subsided and Basma looked fragile and disheartened again.

"Look, I know this is very difficult. I can't even begin to imagine what you must be going through inside. It's still hard for me to believe that I was interviewing those women to learn about something you knew about all too well, and worse, now you are in the same position. You were wise to run when you did. Shafal would have had you killed... I saw him... I don't doubt that for a second. But even worse than Shafal, is that cousin of yours! He's a mean one." Basma stilled, and glanced down. "But you know what? Now you have the chance to create a whole new life for yourself. And you won't be by yourself. You're going to meet so many courageous and committed people." Basma considered this a moment, and then appeared a little more hopeful. "Hey, don't forget you are going there to help other women in similar situations as you. And... you can talk about Aisha."

The wave of excitement returned, and Basma regained her confidence. Just then, Vincent rejoined them, looking every bit the successful restaurateur wearing a navy-blue designer blazer over a white linen shirt—no tie—his gold-colored hair dipping to just below his right eyebrow.

Kensasha acknowledged him with an uneasy smile. For the life of her, she couldn't figure out how Basma and the guy that kept Chappelle's female customers coming back for more, had hooked up. But it wasn't a stretch to assume he was the reason Basma was on the run in the first place.

To allow the couple the remaining time alone, Kensasha gave Basma a final embrace and a deeply meaningful glance. Basma smiled back warmly.

Kensasha turned to Vincent, bid him goodbye and walked away.

Only then did Vincent realize that Basma did not have her hair covered for the first time in a public place.

"Hey, where is your scarf?" he asked with astonishment.

"I do what I want to do now," she responded defensively. "I don't have to wear—"

"Okay, okay! I'm just surprised that's all. It's, uh, different."

They shared a tense moment, until Vincent remembered where he had just come from. He reached into the inside pocket of his jacket and pulled out an envelope containing certified checks in dollars and a wad of pounds sterling and handed it to her.

It was, totally, unexpected. She opened it and gasped, "So much money?"

Vincent shrugged, and said shyly "Well, you don't know how things are going to work out. So, that should hold you for a while." Basma was still stunned at the amount he had given her.

"I will pay you back," she assured him.

"I don't need you to pay me back," he said in earnest. "Besides," he added, teasingly. "It would take you twenty years to do that."

"I will pay you back," she insisted.

"Stop it! It's yours. Forget it," he exclaimed dismissively. "Anyway, what time is it? Remember, you have to pass through security."

Basma slid the envelope into her purse while watching him shift around nervously.

"The weeks went by pretty fast," he mused, smiling at her. "I was just getting used to having you around." He smoothed out her lapel. She continued watching him.

"Thank you, Vincent."

"For what?"

Her throat tightened. "For everything! All of it—every moment."

"I don't think you mean that" he reflected, glancing away. "What about the baby?"

His face blurred before her, as tears filled her eyes.

"Well, almost every moment." She grinned through the tears. "You made me feel things I… and you made me think… different thoughts. You and Miss Lewis."

He was puzzled, but he smiled warmly and pulled her to him, burying his face in her hair. Chagrined, he whispered, "Sorry about… the baby. I messed up. I really messed up there." He, slowly, released her, and taking hold of her hand, he continued speaking avoiding eye contact, to keep his train of thought. "Basma, it's not that I don't want you… you're a kind, beautiful woman. Its uh, it's just that… I'm a single guy and I… and I want to keep it that way. Do you understand what I mean?"

"Yes… me too," her tone was decisive.

"Okay," he whispered, glancing around. "I guess this is it."

Their eyes met. Her heart quickened when she noticed his were moist. He cupped her head in both hands and gave her a passionate kiss goodbye. When he released her, she swooned.

"I don't want to be free of you," she cooed, dreamily.

"You're going to miss your plane," he said, solemnly.

She stared into his eyes for a long moment.

"Goodbye, Vincent," she whispered, and walked away.

He watched her go; watched, as she struggled to keep her back erect, maintaining balance on those skinny heels. He watched, as people passed between them.

"Basma!" he called out, suddenly. She paused and spun around. He hurried to her and embraced her once again, tightly.

She finally broke down and sobbed in his arms.

"Listen," he said, "if… if things don't work out there and… I mean if you find yourself in a bad situation, you call me. Do you understand?" He pulled back looking deep into her eyes. "You call me… and I'll come for you."

Too overcome to even speak, she pressed her cheek firmly against his, and then continued her walk, unsteadily, toward security.

***

The whole world had changed forever since the last time Basma presented herself before passport inspectors. Sometimes change is motivated by horror and fear.

When it was finally her turn to stand before the inspectors, even the way they looked at her had changed. Where before, she was a curiosity shrouded in black, now she was viewed as a possible criminal. The female inspector's eyes bore into her as she held out her hand for the passport and ticket. Basma handed them both over avoiding the woman's eyes. Maybe it wasn't the smartest thing to do. The woman glanced at the passport and scribbled something on a piece of paper placed it inside and returned it to Basma—waving her through.

Several teenage girls traveling with a large group were right in front of her. They were ordered to put their shoes, handbags and belts into a large gray plastic bin and place it on a conveyor belt to be x-rayed. They didn't have this twenty-two years ago, Basma thought, as she followed suit. It was a relief to remove her shoes though—even if only for a moment.

After she cleared the metal detector, she grabbed the bin with her purse and shoes and was preparing to put them on, when another woman inspector intercepted her and asked her to step out of the line.

The inspector ushered her to another table and reached for her purse and gift bag. She looked in the gift bag with a solemn face then opened the purse and rummaged through it—ignoring the money. She stopped abruptly and pulled out a jagged piece of pottery. A male inspector walked up just then to stand next to the female inspector.

"What's this for?" the inspector asked, suspiciously.

Basma stared down at the bright colored glass beads that always looked like precious stones to her.

There was hardly a moon that night—just a sliver. She had remained in the car while Vincent walked to the river's edge carrying one of her black loafers and her favorite jumbo handbag. Under her breath, she had bid farewell to the purple nightgown that Vincent never had a chance to see her wear. Then her heart skipped a beat.

"No!" she called out to him. He didn't hear her, so she leaped from the car and took off down the sandy slope after him yelling, "I forgot something." When he stopped, she pulled the bag away from him and searched through it until she found what she was looking for: the shard of pottery.

"To remember," Basma replied to the inspector.

"What?"

Basma raised her head and looked at the woman with heartfelt eyes. "It was a gift," she explained. "It is very old."

The female inspector turned to the male inspector for approval. He gave the okay and she returned the wedge to the purse and handed it back to Basma. She reached for the Koran, flipped through, turned it over shook out the pages and handed that back to Basma. Then she waved her on to the male inspector.

"Can I see your ticket and passport?" he asked.

Basma obediently offered them to him. Opening the passport first, he gazed at the picture of Basma wearing the hijab and then at Basma standing before him bareheaded. He wasn't sure what to make of it. At that moment, she became overwhelmingly self-conscious and disconcerted, as he stared. She raised one hand to her head in a habitual desire to cover it.

The inspector returned an accusatory gaze.

"Aisha Langois?" he probed, reading off the name from the passport.

Immediately, Basma's eyes lit up and a child-like grin spread across her face. "Yes," she replied. Both security inspectors watched her curiously amused. They weren't sure she was all there, mentally. But the male inspector intuited that this Aisha Langois was not a threat to national security. He closed the passport, returned it to her and signaled her to move on.

Vincent had waited to make sure everything went okay with the passport. Basma took one last glance back to the other side of the security area just in time to see Vincent disappear into the crowd.

Now excitement along with conflicting emotions began welling up inside. Her new adventure had begun. She walked the long path alone to the departure gate. Smiling, as she turned a corner, she, immediately, collided with a Muslim woman who, ironically, was dressed in full abaya and veil.

The woman was with her husband and three other adult male family members.

In the collision, Basma dropped her gift bag. A book tumbled out and she bent down quickly to pick it up. The Muslim woman blurted out in Arabic:

"I am so sorry, so sorry." Her tone was, excessively, apologetic.

Basma stood bareheaded, aware that the Muslim husband and the rest of the family viewed her disapprovingly, sensing she was one of them. The smile left her face and just as impulsively, as she had done in the restroom with her hijab, Basma clasped hold of the woman's wrist to shush her.

Looking straight into the woman's eyes with a blend of compassion and wisdom on her face, she replied in Arabic, "It is okay. You have done nothing wrong," Basma assured her, as if relaying a secret message.

The woman bowed her head, and gave Basma a meek thank you. Basma released the woman's wrist, gave the men a subtle look of defiance and continued along the corridor to the gates.

Aware, now, of the gift bag Kensasha had given her, she reached in and pulled out a blank book-type journal with a beautiful brocade fabric on the cover. Basma smiled, took a few more steps and then turned back in time to see the distance between her and the veiled woman expand.

Part Three

CHAPTER 20

LONDON

Sometimes just roaming the streets of Brixton was enough to provide the information Zafeera sought. She didn't have to resort to questioning store managers or the occasional passer-by. Eavesdropping on the men outside the shops, and the women inside, gave her more insight than the answers to her questions ever did. The dynamics of interpersonal interactions between men and women intrigued her most. In that part of the city, it seemed as if the sexes belonged to two different races forced into cohabitation. Rules had been artificially devised for these people to follow, rules that went against the natural inclinations of an individual. As a result, there was an enormous suppression of energy and feelings— especially in the women. So many words unsaid. So many goals never attempted, or even dreamed.

What fascinated Zafeera most were the women who still covered their faces, like her mother did, though they were born in a democracy. How many of them did this willingly—without fear of criticism by husbands, in-laws, or the leer of angry, disenfranchised Muslim youths, like the ones who loitered in packs outside the council housing complex whenever she left?

She had made certain her jacket was zipped to the neck before she was out of the building, and, sure enough, there they were. Keeping her eyes focused forward, Zafeera walked slowly and confidently past the boys. They glared at her not knowing if she was Indian, Persian or Arab.

Nothing in her dressed-down masculine attire revealed a nationality or a religion. Sometimes they even wondered about her sex, but Zafeera's face and body were definitely that of a woman, and for that she felt proud—blessed, even. Never had she wished to be born male. What for? Her parents had fled Algeria in 1993 when a fundamentalist military organization came to power and imposed the Islamic religious law of Sharia which had become a contentious controversial issue for so many.

Sharia, a set of moral and religious codes founded on the words of Allah, and revealed both in the Holy Quran by the Islamic Prophet, Mohammed, and in the Sunnah, lays out the Prophet's exemplary way of life. Therefore, for Muslims, Sharia is God's law and like the Christian Bible, the purpose of these moral and religious codes is to help guide believers on the right path to a fulfilling life according to the will of Allah.

Sharia law addresses almost every area of a person's life, public and private, and it includes topics dealt with under secular law like crime, financial agreements, social dealings as well as personal topics like dietary restrictions, hygienic practices, plus sexual mandates which include the role of women in the home and in the world. Whenever there are difficult issues or questions that are not addressed directly in the primary teachings, a consensus of religious scholars and Imams can apply logic, or provide analogies, to impose Sharia law.

Through the centuries, however, different countries and societies developed varying interpretations of this law. Even within one country, modernists' views often clashed with traditional views, while fundamentalists—whose views were deemed extreme, especially in matters concerning women—clashed severely with the other two groups.

In her country, Algeria, the fundamentalists had control of the military in the '90s, and immediately defamed all just interpretations of Sharia and superimposed their own malignant ideology borne out of a pathological misogyny never witnessed before on earth. In no time, they had pressured the Algerian President to impose Sharia law. Under their version of the law, women were forbidden to work or attend school, and so all the women in the country, professionals as well, had to leave their jobs. All girls and young women were forced to leave their studies—give up their education—and stay at home. It was literally house arrest. The crime? Being born female, something alien—an "Other"—who needed to be cloistered or confined.

Women could only walk in the streets accompanied by a male relative and the burka was now mandatory. At first, whenever a woman refused to cover, the young men accosted her, hurling obscenities. The situation soon escalated and became deadly. All women were under attack.

Zafeera remembered the day a seventeen-year-old girl was killed for not wearing the hijab. That was the final straw for her father.

"We have barbarians among us," he shouted.

She knew he believed in hijab but not the slaughter of innocent women. By the time he moved his family of five to France, that atrocity had been repeated again, and again, until every woman was forced to succumb if she wanted to live.

Years later, her mother told them that the real reason their father left his precious homeland and sacrificed everything was so his daughters could continue their education. Whenever she found the girls slacking off, she would remind them of their father's sacrifice. But it had taken a long time for her mother to adjust to life in Paris.

"Too much freedom here!" her mother would yell out to show her disapproval of something the children did, especially the girls. Nevertheless, she and her sister, Ghaybaa, were finally home. Except for the head covering, to please their parents, the girls went everywhere and did everything the French children around them did—until puberty.

Looking back, puberty was a defining moment in her life. It was the first time their father had imposed stringent rules of conduct and a dress code in the house on her and Ghaybaa. Being boys, their two brothers were free to come and go as they pleased. Ghaybaa, being too young to oppose her father's demands, naturally acquiesced. Zafeera, on the other hand, felt his restrictions were punitive.

She always resisted.

Zafeera eyed a woman in an abaya carrying an infant. Her face was round with large light brown eyes. She watched the woman nuzzle her nose against the infant's cheek. The woman could have been Ghaybaa. They were about the same age. Her eyes welled up with tears. If only it were that simple: she could just walk down the street and run right into Ghaybaa happily smooching her baby.

Why had there been no contact? Why would Ghaybaa inflict such pain on her family? Was it that husband of hers? Why would he forbid her from calling her own mother?

Whenever she thought of her sister's husband, Fareed, the hairs at the nape of her neck stood on end. His background had been sketchy from the start, but their father was enamored by his scholarly assessment of Islam and the need to strengthen its image in the world. For a time, even Ghaybaa seemed taken in by him—that soon dissipated. But her father wanted him in the family. Ghaybaa was the only possible choice, because Zafeera was away at St. Andrews University in the United Kingdom finishing her political science degree. Besides, a forced marriage arrangement on Zafeera would have surely caused a war between father and daughter.

The woman and baby soon disappeared into the crowd leaving Zafeera with the ongoing pangs of guilt for not having been there for her sister. But it was all done so fast. When she found out, the wedding was already over. They didn't bother to wait until the end of the semester when she would have been able to return to France. This had pained her, too, until her older brother informed her, much later, that it was Fareed who wanted everything expedited. Apparently, he was needed in England for an important position.

Zafeera came to a standstill at a pedestrian crossing. People floated by her on both sides like a river's current. She searched as many faces as possible— women and men. How many times had she done that? How many times had she stood outside mosques waving the wedding photo asking if anyone knew them until they were sick of her? Once, a man did raise his eyebrow as if there was a hint of recognition. But he said he didn't know them.

The last phone call from Ghaybaa had come from Tower Hamlets council houses in Brixton, a district in South London.

"We are doing okay," Ghaybaa had said.

"I want to come to see you there," Zafeera offered, excitedly.

"No! It is better that we come back to France for a visit."

"When, Ghaybaa?" their mother interjected on the extension.

"Soon. Fareed said he will bring me home. He is very busy now with his new position and is always away."

"Have you registered at university, yet Ghaybaa?" their father had asked.

"My husband prefers I stay home when he is away. He sees no reason for me to take classes at the university because he wants to start a family." Both parents were silent. What could they say?

"I will write to you," she had said, and then hung up.

A letter did arrive every few months, but Ghaybaa, unlike Zafeera, wasn't a letter writer. Her letters were as unrevealing as the phone call had been and the tone distant, aloof somehow. But to allow two years to go by without one single communication with her own family was heartless, Zafeera decided, and so unlike Ghaybaa. Was this her way of punishing her parents for sacrificing her hopes and dreams just to have a man like that as their son-in-law? Zafeera needed a cigarette.

***

"You have to keep an eye on her in the beginning," Kensasha said. "Just until she's settled in. In a way, you have to treat her the same way as you do the others. She's a quick learner and likes to work, so feel free to immerse her right away. The more absorbed she is in the work, the less likely she'll panic and do something crazy."

"Since they believe she is dead through suicide, we have nothing to worry about," Neelam stated.

"Well… actually, the family wants the case to remain open until they find a body. Her husband, Shafal, suspects that she ran off with her lover."

"But I thought…"

"This is recent, Neelam," Kensasha informed. "Imani told me this morning. That's why I wanted to speak to you before you picked her up. Just don't let on to her about all this. We have to keep her spirits high."

"What kind of people are they?" Neelam inquired with alarm. "I mean will they hire someone to track her down, like some families do?"

"It's a possibility," said Kensasha. "But I'm not really sure. I don't know them. Imani would know. Though she's hardly speaking to the husband, she's so angry. I'll have to get back to you on that."

"Okay," Neelam replied. "Let's talk again tomorrow."

As Neelam set the phone down on her desk, she couldn't help but stare at the mountain of files, folders, legal books and unopened mail that blanketed the long antique table in front of the window. Ever since her return from New York, and the aftermath of the safe house tragedy, everything seemed to end up on that table.

She certainly had plenty of work for this woman, especially now that the push for an international summit was heating up. There was to be an alliance of ten different women's organizations. They would give a presentation before a body of officials who had the power to act. The alliance's agenda would be to demand all nations involved to start enforcing the laws they already have pertaining to gender based violence, or in some cases establish harsher sentencing for honor killings.

All countries must design new laws that would finally put a stop to the whole concept of honor killing, as well as all the other forms of familial, cultural and religious violence and insults toward a woman's humanity.

So far, the hardest part was getting the leaders of the organizations together on a conference call, let alone in a conference room. The alliance also needed to identify the officials in the countries where these crimes were most prevalent, and the alliance needed to have a name. The media, especially, would need that. However, the real test was identifying those subtle insults that had become a common part of the entire acculturation and socialization in most nations—like the belief that women are less competent than men; the belief that male characteristics are more desirable for leadership. Women in many parts of the world rarely challenged these beliefs, hence the lack of a substantial amount of them in leadership roles.

What made it all right for a woman not to have volition in her own life? This whole concept warranted further contemplation.

Neelam's cell phone buzzed and slid around the desk. She reached and flipped open the top. It was her driver, letting her know he was waiting near the magazine kiosk. Neelam told him she'd be right down then peered out the window. The weather had not deterred the media, nor those photographers hoping to get a photo to sell. The number of junior reporters outside of her office building had increased significantly since word spread of the Safe House Massacre, as the press called it. There was simply no way Detective Holmes could have kept that kind of news contained within a town like Taunton. At first, that was her major concern. It would cast a bad light on all her endeavors. Fear and suspicion could easily infect all the other places of refuge.

The irony of a safe house was that no house was safe for someone who was denied natural human rights. Did any of these cultures ever consider the rights of women when designing the body of *ethics*, the society would live by? It was in that moment she realized the chief issue here, the main argument, had to be about ethics.

The alliance of women would have to challenge religious and humanistic ethics, because, ultimately, those families believe that honor and rights are in the 'eye of the beholder' Reputations are volatile and subjective, based on what other people think. You can't build the moral foundation of a society or a family on the shoulders of one's reputation. Honor wasn't something to be subjected to the whims and opinions of people and political systems, nor must it be greater than a woman's or a child's life!

But how could the alliance defend the value of a human life before leaders who send their young men and women into battle? Why would tribal leaders or the militia care about a village girl's mutilated genitalia, when they themselves sanctioned the rape and slaughter of innocent men, women and children in their ever-raging civil and religious wars?

So, it was not only ethics that must be argued for, but a redefinition of honor and of individual rights in the face of nations that don't even have a *concept* of an individual identity. In these places, a man's sense of self was inextricably connected to his family's race, nationality, clan, religion or social group. Therefore, men also had no rights, identity, autonomy or world view separate from the family.

If there are men who truly believe a woman's sole purpose on earth is to bear their children, provide sexual gratification for them and to be subservient— not even warranting second class citizenship, because citizen status bestows some rights—then to those men, the very idea of 'women's rights' must be an *oxymoron*.

Once again, Neelam left the building through the side door. One would think those clever reporters would have figured that out by now.

***

Three international flights had arrived, forty-five minutes earlier, and now the passengers were filing out of customs. Some flights had been delayed so there were more people than usual waiting in the arrival area.

Neelam's eyes darted all around the crowd in search of the woman who would spend an indefinite amount of time living in her home and helping her with organizing the preparations for the summit—a woman with zero organizational skills, apparently, and no experience beyond putting folders in a drawer. A woman without a high school education, and minimal work experience. Imagine! All the same, Kensasha Lewis was very persuasive in her plea that Neelam take this woman on, specifically because she, like all the other women Neelam had vowed to protect, was on the run from her family.

Neelam saw students in jeans with backpacks slung over one shoulder rushing towards a chartered van; young couples with small children in tow searching for their loved ones, older couples with glowing faces clutching each other's hand for support as their dream vacation was about to begin.

Businessmen in crinkled suits overloaded with laptops, suitcases and briefcases struggled with their cell phones as they tried to hear their names being called by car service drivers. Lastly, there were those slender, fashion conscious women in short skirts and hi-heeled shoes pulling their designer luggage along—but not one woman wearing the hijab among them.

When that whole batch of passengers had found their connections and left the arrival zone, the only person left was a pale, frightened looking woman in an ill-fitting violet suit. There was no head covering, so Neelam assumed she wasn't this Aisha Langois, and looked away. Basma, on the other hand, recognized Dr. Sethi immediately, and for the first time since the plane had left the runway in Boston, she exhaled.

Waving with one arm and tugging at her suitcase with the other, Basma headed in the direction of the Indian woman with a colorful dupatta elegantly draped over her royal blue woolen coat.

"Hello!" Basma called, catching Neelam's attention.

One eyebrow rose slightly as Neelam surveyed Basma's attire. Clearly, the suit she was wearing was a few sizes too big, she wasn't used to wearing heels, and why was her head uncovered?

In the end, it was Kensasha who had done the shopping for Basma, bought all her personal items and decided on the violet suit. Basma had gotten much thinner in the five months after the breakdown and when Kensasha saw her again in Boston, there was no time before Basma's flight for her to travel back to New York, from Boston, to return the suit. Both Kensasha and Vincent had smiled approvingly when Basma first tried it on.

Since the two women had never actually met nor spoken on the phone, Neelam allowed the distance to close between them before making any gesture.

"How was the flight?" asked Neelam, formally, as Basma halted in front of her, slightly out of breath.

"Fine." Basma couldn't tell her that she had spent a third of the flight in the toilet with both diarrhea and severe nausea. All the confidence and excitement about having a new life that Kensasha inspired in her had evaporated as soon as the wheels left the ground.

The realization that she was heading thousands of miles away from everyone who meant something to her was absolutely paralyzing. She missed her sons the moment she left her house, but now it was Mrs. Sadawi, Kensasha Lewis and, of course, Vincent. In a strange way, she even missed irritable old Shafal who had plotted her death. After all, hadn't she been with him for twenty-four years?

Of more importance, what exactly was this new life where you leave everything you've ever known, change your name to protect your identity, and start over living amongst strangers, never to contact those very people you love most in the world? How would she overcome the agonizing guilt in letting her sons believe she was dead? Then, there was the psychological question: who was Aisha Langois? All Basma knew about her was that she was born, literally, when the airport security guard opened the passport, said the name and she nodded her head. That was the very moment it all became real—she had a new identity: her cousin's first name and Vincent's last name. Now, she was completely free to be whoever she wanted Aisha Langois to be. She could either recreate a mirrored existence in London of the one she just left, one that Shafal, her mother and her religious group had outlined for her, or she could act with her own volition, prompted from inner yearnings, establish her own values and follow them, even if they were the antithesis of everything her family and religious community believed in. Hadn't she already taken the first step when she escaped?

Even so, there was always responsibility intertwined with freedom. Someone had to bear responsibility for the consequences. There was no one to blame for her speaking out at Ramadan and no one else to blame for her running to Vincent for help. Why didn't she knock on Imani's door that night? She could have called Kensasha Lewis at a pay phone. Both would have understood the precariousness of her situation immediately. Instead, she acted on the strongest impulse of romantic love and ran to the very person who was the reason her whole life unraveled—the adultery, the lies, the pregnancy, her emotional crisis, and now her need to disappear.

On the plane, while others slept peacefully crossing the Atlantic, this burst of awareness brought both amazement and a tidal wave of existential angst. Here she was with all these consequences, and this new responsibility for her own life. What was the right thing to say or do? Who decided? Beyond the question of Aisha Langois was an even greater question: who was Basma Abseh? Was there ever a being, an identity apart from her family and upbringing? Should a person act according to moral duty or personal desire? Who gets to define morality? Shouldn't human freedom and experience be the pinnacle of life? What is life, anyway? Does it have a meaning? How would she find that meaning?

By the time the wheels touched the tarmac at Heathrow Airport, and they were pulling into the gate, the newly born Aisha Langois had already had an existential breakdown.

"What would you like to do first, my dear? I know the flight was long. We could go to my apartment and you can shower if you like and relax or we could go straight out to have lunch. Whatever you choose is fine with me," Neelam offered, wheeling Aisha's/Basma's luggage to the car.

"Umm... I... uh."

"Come on, my dear, speak up. I'm here to assist you today. Later, I will be telling you what I need you to do for me. But for today, my time is yours."

The driver hopped out when he saw them coming through the rear-view mirror. Neelam turned the luggage over to him and waited for Basma to answer. Basma's own indecisiveness made her feel hollow under the gaze of this powerful, effectual woman. Although food would have been the best choice since her throat was raw from the nausea and her stomach was growing queasy again—she really just wanted to lie down.

"Maybe I could rest for a while, then eat something later," Basma replied in a soft timorous voice.

"Is that your answer?" Neelam inquired as she opened the backseat door and gestured for Basma to get in.

"Yes," she replied, more softly.

"I can barely hear you. My dear, you have to speak up! Let me know what you want, for God's sake." Neelam gave the door an extra push shut. Basma jumped and began twisting the handle of her handbag around her fingers.

"I'll tell you now," Neelam continued as she got into the front passenger's seat, "I have very little patience. Didn't Professor Lewis tell you this?"

Basma remained silent, cowering in the backseat corner just behind Dr. Sethi. When the driver got behind the wheel, he did nothing to acknowledge her; he simply turned on the ignition and shifted into gear.

During the drive back to London, Neelam wondered, at first, if she'd been a little too harsh with Basma. Not one to coddle, she decided on a different approach. She'd act as a tour guide to put her new assistant at ease. For that reason, Basma had to struggle to absorb all the visual and logistical information about which town they were passing and the importance of this or that building.

Before long, her body succumbed to jet lag and her brain to psychological exhaustion. So that, by the time she climbed the stairs to Neelam Sethi's flat, and entered—what Kensasha had warned was a virtual oasis for intellectuals and artists—Basma's spirit had deteriorated into a will-less wimp.

Neelam led her to a bedroom and the driver brought in her bags.

"All right, make yourself at home. I'll leave you to rest for a couple of hours. Later, we can get some food and talk. Shall I bring you a cup of tea?"

"Yes. Thank you," Basma replied, this time more audibly.

When Neelam left the room, Basma removed her suit jacket and looked around for a closet.

There wasn't one, so she hung her jacket in a large armoire facing the window. She slipped out of her shoes and noticed the amazing relief of being free of those pumps, the pleasure of walking barefoot across hardwood floors. All she needed now was to stretch out on that queen-sized bed covered in a rich wine and green Indian motif comforter.

A door, open on the opposite side of the room next to the window, revealed an adjoining bathroom. Not bothering to take anything out of her suitcases, Basma went straight to the bathroom, slowly splashed her face with warm water, created a rich lather with the fragrant sandalwood hand soap and washed off her makeup. After patting her face dry, she took off the panty hose, rolled them into a ball and placed them on the edge of the sink to be washed later.

Just as she re-entered the bedroom, Neelam was crossing the room carrying a cup of tea and three biscuits on a tray. She sat the tray on the nightstand.

"Come, lay down," Neelam ordered, pulling back the covers like a doting mother. "I can see you are exhausted." Basma went over to the bed and climbed in, not bothering to remove her skirt. Neelam pulled the covers over her.

"Get some rest. You're safe now." Neelam adjusted the tray with the tea to secure its position on the table and left the room, closing the door.

Basma curled herself up and pulled the covers over her head. Her eyes hungered for a glimpse of Abdel and Ahmed. Would she ever see them again?

Excess saliva filled her mouth. The nausea had returned. Her body craved the security it found in Vincent's arms. The past week with him was both the happiest and the most painful. She had kept her resolve and slept on his couch until the last night, but finally allowed him to carry her into his bed. She smiled to herself when she thought about that. She couldn't imagine Shafal sweeping her off her feet and carrying her anywhere—not even out of a burning building.

Then she realized things weren't as final as she had first anticipated. Apparently, Kensasha planned to call weekly to keep her informed about Abdel and Ahmed, and Imani Sadawi. And what was it that Vincent had said? She could call him if things didn't work out. So, that part of her life wasn't completely severed.

Her body was just beginning to relax, when the face of her mother glaring back at her with disappointment jarred her, made her uneasy.

Would she ever be able to forgive Sumera for siding with the conspirators? A voice from deep inside of her gave an astounding "No! Never!" Soon tears started to flow. She had no mother now.

Across the room, a strong breeze rushed in through the opened window. The white net curtains billowed out and a bright ray of sunlight shot across the room and bounced off the gold trim border of the teacup and saucer. They glistened. Basma sat up and stared at the cultured arrangement. Besides the gold leaf trim, the tulip-shaped cup of real antique china was decorated with tiny hand-painted pink roses. A white doily had been placed on a matching plate beneath the cookies—no, she had to remember to call them biscuits, now. Next to the plate was an antique white linen napkin with lace trim.

Basma's first instinct was not to disturb the lovely setting, but Dr. Sethi was kind enough to bring it, so she reached for the cup and took a sip. The rich red color and bold flavor was unfamiliar to her, but she liked it. She carefully sat the cup back down on the tray and picked up a rectangular sweet with scalloped edges that smelled of vanilla and almonds. As she sank her teeth into it, she realized this was the first thing she'd eaten in a day and a half. Her eyes closed to experience the taste, exclusively. Delicious. Then came the awareness that she was now in this beautifully appointed bedroom in Dr. Neelam Sethi's home munching a biscuit. It was beyond anything she could have imagined—and it didn't matter where it would lead. She was here, now, and she was alive.

Finishing the biscuit, she took another sip of the tea to wash it down and noticed that her nausea had subsided. Being extra careful once again to set the cup softly on the tray, she turned over and laid her head back on the crisp white pillow. Somewhere in the flat, she heard a muffled voice. The sound comforted her as she drifted off into a deep, peaceful sleep.

Back in the living room, Neelam hung up the phone and poured herself a cup of chai. Then, she dialed Kensasha, who had just turned over and slipped into another dream when the phone rang.

"Good Morning! It's Neelam. I wanted to let you know that Aisha arrived safely and is now fast asleep."

"Oh, that's good news," Kensasha replied, her voice heavy with languor.

Not bothering to mince words, Neelam went straight to the point.

"She is like a little mouse, that girl. She looks sickly, and not at all what I imagined a personal assistant of mine would be like. I really don't think she is capable of this role, Kensasha. She can hardly—"

"Basma will be fine, Neelam," Kensasha interjected. She sat up and looked over at the clock. 5:18 a.m. "You know what Basma's been through. Just give her a chance," Kensasha continued. "That's all I'm asking. I know you're doing this for me, and I appreciate it—really, I do." She got out of bed and walked to the window. It was still dark out, but the moon's lingering glow illuminated rooftops.

"But the girl hardly says anything," Neelam countered, "and when she does say something, you can barely hear her and I am really concerned about that. I need someone who can talk to the leaders of these organizations, if necessary. How can she do that?"

Kensasha remained silent. During her stay in London, months before, she had suggested to Neelam how beneficial it would be for her to take on an assistant—especially given the state of Neelam's office, the constant phone calls, emails and meetings Neelam juggled daily. But Basma hadn't come to mind, then. The idea that Basma would be suitable came after she found out Basma was alive and needed protection from Shafal's wrath. Why not send her to London and let her help Neelam organize her office space and answer a few calls. Simple enough.

At last, Kensasha replied, "Basma is fully capable of answering the telephone and taking messages. Remember, she worked for me."

This time it was Neelam, who was silent. What could she possibly do if this mousey girl proved to be incompetent? Send her packing? Basma wasn't just any woman on the run that could be sequestered in a safe house for months on end, with the hopes of finding a suitable community to disappear into. Kensasha had arranged for her to come here, and Imani Sadawi knew the girl as well.

"Neelam, I'm so sorry you're disappointed," Kensasha said, returning to her bed.

"Well, I just wanted to let you know how I feel. That is all," Neelam explained." I will give her a few months. Okay?"

"That's fair," Kensasha complied with a sigh of relief. "I need to get back to sleep. I'll call to check in a few days and let you know if we have to worry about her family tracking her down."

"That will be fine, Kensasha. Don't worry yourself about what I said. Go back to sleep."

"I have a feeling she will surprise you, Neelam," Kensasha added, before saying goodbye.

Neelam set the cordless back on its base, looked across the room at the closed door of her guest bedroom and hoped Kensasha was right.

CHAPTER 21

P ulling her white silk blouse together to button, Zafeera glanced in the bathroom mirror at the flat-screened TV mounted on the wall in the bedroom. This was another one of her rituals—seeing which news stories were being fed to the public each day. Working for a news magazine meant as soon as she walked into her office, she'd encounter every co-worker talking about and analyzing the top stories.

She tucked the blouse down into a gray straight skirt and zipped it up. Black eyeliner was applied next, followed by a smoky lavender shadow, coral blush and, of course, her cherry lipstick. It was her way of showing her middle finger to the hardline Mullahs who frowned on such things.

Behind her, strong masculine hands caressed her shoulders, a head snuggled hers, a hard, toned, body leaned in pushing her up against the marble countertop. She shrunk away, irritated.

"All right, what's the matter, then?"

"Nothing," she said looking at her boyfriend, Mick Taylor's tall muscular reflection in the glass. Then, she picked up the hairbrush and began brushing her hair.

"Nothing? You've been ignoring me all morning!" he protested, standing beside her, tying his tie.

She gazed at herself and contemplated whether she should leave her hair down or sweep it up in a French Twist.

"See! You're doing it right now."

"Mick, I'm getting ready for work!"

"Well, so am I, you know."

French Twist. She reached into one of the stainless-steel containers lining her side of the sink for two long bobby pins, placed them between her teeth. careful not to get lipstick on them, and gathered up her hair.

Mick studied her. "You know, you do this every time you come back from that place."

Keeping her focus on her hair, she took the pins from between her teeth.

"Do what?" Then, before he could respond, she folded, twisted and secured her locks with skilled dexterity.

"Ignore me. Treat me like shit—like you don't want me to touch you." She turned around to face him and saw pain in his steel blue eyes. She moved closer and rubbed his arm gently.

"Mick, I… I." She couldn't explain it to him, or anybody. She didn't understand it herself. She just knew she had to do whatever possible to locate Ghaybaa. She lowered her eyes. "I'm trying to get out of here so I don't miss the Tube."

"Zafeera, I'm telling you now, you've got to stop going to that place. It's affecting you. It's affecting us! Are you any closer to finding them than you were five months ago? No!"

That hurt. She pushed past him, to the bedroom, threw open the closet door and took a pair of tall black high-heeled boots from their own cubby hole, sat on the bed and began putting them on as fast as she could.

Mick came in and sat next to her. "I'm really worried about you."

"Don't be."

Getting to her feet just as quickly, she picked up her suit jacket from the bed, slipped it on, grabbed her handbag from the dresser and went out to the hall closet. Slowly, Mick stood and followed her. She already had her coat on and was draping a blue pashmina scarf he had given her around her neck. With his hands in his pockets, he watched. She took her leather gloves from the side table near the front door and put them on. He leaned against the wall, and waited. She unlocked the door.

"I'll get my dinner at a pub tonight," he said finally, turning back toward the bedroom.

She knew what that meant, but just didn't have the energy or the time to smooth things out.

Outside, the pavement in front of the building was slippery. That, coupled with her lateness and the high-heeled boots, provided a perfect excuse for taking a taxi all the way.

In the middle of the back seat, staring out the front window, her mood softened. Mick was right. It was affecting them. She decided to call him and apologize. He didn't answer his cell—probably still pissed off.

Mick Taylor was a top investment consultant with a major company whose clients were mostly in the Middle East and Asia. He and Zafeera met when his company was profiled in one of her company's global finance issues, four years earlier. Her being tri-lingual made her a valuable asset—especially since one of her languages was Arabic. She was called in often to help with some of the interviews and translations.

The first thing that caught her eye when they met was his long sandy colored lashes and how they contrasted with his strong masculine jaw line. Soon he revealed a calm, exceedingly confident demeanor, even for a Brit. He smiled easily, unlike her. But what really captured her attention was the way he treated her: like a professional. Never patronizing, he saw her as an equal.

Mick was the first man she'd ever been attracted to, so naturally, she had no knowledge of discreet flirtation, or experiences in the art of seduction. Therefore, when the assignment ended, they gave their respective goodbyes.

A year after the story ran, a twist of fate brought them together again aboard a flight to Paris. Zafeera was on her way to visit her parents, for Mick it was business. They could only speak briefly during the flight since he was in first class and she in coach. Then, standing next to her at the baggage claim, he asked for her cell number. Now, two years later, she was living in one of the most fashionable buildings in West London with a man who loved and respected her. And she loved him right back. So why was she messing it all up?

***

The Good Eats café wasn't as crowded as it had been the morning of the massacre just three months earlier when Enid Statham had visited on Detective Inspector Holmes' recommendation. Yet the customers' conversations were still laced with fear, suspicion and shock that seven foreign-born women had been brutally gunned down in their peaceful, law-abiding town while many of them were fast asleep. Worse still, the police weren't any closer to catching the murderers.

At the counter, Holmes tried not to take what he was overhearing personally. He sipped his coffee and marveled at the consistency of Good Eats to serve up a great cup of coffee for over eight years. Still, each comment about the police not getting any closer was like a dagger jabbing at his competence.

That those responsible could still be somewhere in the vicinity was the unexpressed thought of many. Every newspaper had reported that the murderers were not terrorists, that the motive was merely familial revenge, yet the consensus remained the same: "Those people pose a danger to everyone around them and shouldn't be allowed to live next to normal people. Why, anyone walking down the street could've been killed by those madmen!"

Holmes took one last sip from his coffee cup, placed his money on top of the bill, and quietly left before having to fend off the question that drove the dagger deeper: where was the missing computer?

Outside, the cold damp air quickly seeped through his cardigan. He pulled his down jacket together and scrambled to get across the street to his car before a gust of wind could send him tumbling into a pedestrian.

Taunton, like most places in the world, managed to put its problems aside to acknowledge the change of season. Trees along High Street had already begun their transformation into autumn. Banners announcing the date for the harvest fair dangled across every intersection, and each breeze carried the scent of Christmas just up ahead.

For Holmes, the spirit of the season seemed a little dampened. Nothing occupied his mind more than finding that computer. It didn't matter that there may not be anything on it to help solve the case. What mattered to him was how the computer had been illegally confiscated from a crime scene by the very person he told could not have it.

Did she think he was a fool and wouldn't realize it was her?

He sat staring at the haze of dust on the windshield. It blurred the edges of buildings and people's bodies passing before him. A squirt of water and a few passes of the windshield wipers should be enough to make things clear again.

"What am I not seeing?" He spoke it aloud, as if doing so would present the answers more readily. Tapping nervously on the steering wheel, he recounted: "We searched the mother's house and we searched Mrs. Statham's. If there is anyone else, she knows and trusts along that route, we have no way of finding them without a list of everyone she's ever met."

After sitting a while in silence, he started the engine. On the drive back to the station house, he remained absorbed in the images in his mind.

What he reviewed was probably done hundreds of times since seeing it: seven bullet-ridden bodies soaked in blood.

Two of the bodies were in an embrace: a man and a woman. Funny how the media seemed to skim over the fact that there was a young man killed in the massacre.

"What was he doing there in the house with all of you women?" Holmes had asked the two survivors, one of whom was a child, but each acted just as baffled and refused to answer any more questions. How did they expect the police to do their job and find those responsible for this atrocity, if no one wanted to talk to the police? But this was his town, too, and he wasn't about to let it all fade away anytime soon.

CHAPTER 22

A mind that attempts to decipher complex issues involving women's liberation is not akin to a mind that preaches enslavement. Different hands stone the adulteress, while allowing her lover to go free. Very different minds sanction the removal of the feminine image from public view as if it were too hideous and deformed to be seen. Didn't the caliphs try to bar women from praying near the Ka'aba in Mecca? Political ideologies have always been used at one time or other to reinforce the repression of women in the world, and religion was brought in to ensure that the practice would persist.

Neelam laid down her pen, closed the yellow writing pad and lifted the teacup to her lips. It was cold. She hesitated a moment before deciding to get up and make a fresh pot lest it take her out of her concentrated thought on women and liberty.

It was all about fear: fear of women—in bed, out of bed. Why? Was it because man has placed his self-esteem, identity and his manhood on his ability to gain power over someone or something? Did he think he wasn't a man if he couldn't take control of things or people, or nature and subconsciously, God? Hence, the perpetuation of the myth that God is man-like or man is God-like, in the image of God?

Suddenly, she had a powerful urge to laugh out-loud, and her thoughts began to scramble. Time for some more tea.

After placing the kettle on the burner and lighting it, she opened the fridge to get the milk and noticed that aside from a dried-up samosa and a jar of Branston pickle, the refrigerator was empty. What would she feed that scrawny girl? Perhaps, dinner out... fish and chips? Then again, the girl might be too jet-lagged to go anywhere.

She opened a box of PG Tips black tea, she scooped out three heaping tablespoons full of the dried leaves and added them to the teapot along with four cardamom seeds. She began wiping off the counter while she waited for the kettle to boil. Slowly, thoughts of dinner gave way to a possible discourse for the next meeting.

In every popular religion, man has set himself up as the voice of God, the vessel by which God communes with the world. As if God only had the ability to speak through men.

Men in every religion have sought a way to gain power over God. Hadn't men taken it upon themselves to define God, create images of what God's physical appearance was likened to. Christianity chose an anthropomorphic image complete with a white beard. Even in those religions where anthropomorphism is forbidden, nevertheless God is assumed male. Allah certainly isn't thought to be a female spirit—nor is Jehovah, Yahweh, or Jesus Christ.

Yes, man has a whole corner on God. Men give God names. They are privy to what God wants of His people. They write stories about God. They act as secretaries by taking dictation of God's commandments. Men are the only ones allowed into His inner circle. They are His emissaries, His disciples, archangels and His chosen governors here on Earth. They are the ones He's chummy with. So enamored of men is God, that He allows or ordains the slaughter of women and children by men in His name, as mentioned in the Bible. Some of His male followers are so confused in their spiritual minds, they actually believe blowing themselves up along with countless other innocent people will make God favor them with an orgy of seven virgins! Or is it seventy?

The kettle sung out a high C. She turned off the gas, poured the steaming liquid into the cup and followed it with the last drop of milk.

Opening the sugar decanter, she saw that it, too, needed a refill. When was the last time she shopped? Who has time for such things?

Returning to the living room with her cup of very strong piping hot tea, she immediately sat down and began writing down everything she could remember thinking while waiting for the kettle to boil.

Then, more thoughts started to flow.

Men write the scriptures and say God was the real author. Men have devised every possible law and practice to keep women away from the inner circle of knowing, to keep women from discovering Truth for themselves. Every theological challenge or objection posed by a woman is harshly criticized, beaten down, laughed at or worse, ignored.

Why is it that in most religious text and political discourses, the female voice is either non-existent or it plays second fiddle to the male voice? Who constructed language to make verbs masculine or feminine? In everyday life, aren't women's voices drowned by the sheer number of channels men have access to? We know that in the Middle East, many women are muffled or gagged by black polyester hoods. Who really listens to someone without a face?

The ink stopped flowing. She got up to get another pen. Her stomach growled. She looked at the closed bedroom door and thought about the woman sleeping beyond it. Another one. Running. Another unfortunate woman marked for death.

The power over women's psyche is so pervasive and absolute in some respects, that even the most staunch feminist can be distracted by an ad for breast enhancement or find themselves buying pills that guarantee the shedding of 20 lbs. in two months!

She smiled to herself, remembering the half empty bottle in the bathroom cupboard.

Men have power over the interpretation of reality because they dominate the sources of information. What is important from day to day? Where should we fix our collective attention? On what? On whom? What's valued this year, and what isn't? What's in and what's out? A male-dominated media and political system decides. It's the world according to men—and most women follow those dictates without question. Even the original Big Bang Theory is a male construct—all through their eyes.

Well, what happens when you pull the curtain back, Ladies? Who is the Wizard of Oz?

Neelam stopped writing and took a sip of the hot tea. It needed more milk but she wasn't about to get up again, now. She kicked off her shoes and put her feet up on the coffee table, grabbing another pillow and placing it behind her back for better support. Feeling more comfy, she resumed writing.

First, men were just our fathers and brothers. Then, they became our husbands and sons. They appointed themselves Rabbis and Priests—Archbishops and Caliphs. The Ayatollahs, the Popes, and the Imams, the Buddha and the Christ. And, finally, that which gave Birth to All that Is, became known as God the father. By the time we realized they had become our oppressors, it was too late.

It was all quite clever really.

A brilliant scheme.

The ultimate takeover.

Absolute in its scope: the public sphere, the financial sphere, the intellectual sphere, the domestic sphere, the psychological and the sexual and, of course, women's bodies. Even the ethereal sphere of the Soul was compromised when women were barred from the temple and the synagogues.

Barred from prayer in public places.

Barred from learning sacred texts.

Barred from assuming leadership roles in most Orthodox congregations.

She paused. Could there ever be a serious woman contender for Pope?

We didn't give them power over us. They took it... slowly... over time.

Sometimes by force, other times sanctioned by social laws, codified by the religious myths they created.

The thoughts tumbled around incessantly and her fingers began to cramp. Gone were the nimble young joints able to capture an entire lecture in longhand. She tossed the pen and pad on the sofa and leaned back exhausted. I must remember to purchase one of those voice recorders, she thought.

Looking over at the pages and pages of scribble, she realized how far she had veered off topic. It sounded like she was advocating separatism. Even so, nothing in those pages could stop a father in India from strangling his own daughter for refusing to marry the groom he had chosen for her.

The strong tea warmed her, and the fresh jolt of caffeine seemed to stimulate her dulled synapses. As her body sank comfortably into the pillows, she stared at the suitcase sitting beside the bedroom door. A light went on in her head: Women's Liberty is not about men. It is about women. The forum should be targeting women; women from around the world must attend.

Unlike previous conferences where the scheduled speakers were leaders of women's organizations, professors, social activists, psychologists and political theorists, this forum will put regular women at center stage. We will let an audience of women hear other women tell their own horror stories, and then we will demand action in the respective countries in every possible way they can. Organize strikes, street rallies and protests on a mass scale to ensure that these abominable practices will end in this decade.

What new idea or strategy could be implemented that would cause a ground swell for real revolution?

First, we have to deconstruct the mind that thinks murdering a woman is preferable to living with some perceived slight against the family.

With that to consider, Neelam put down her cup, slipped her shoes back on and went to the closet to get her coat.

***

Languishing a while between silken sheets and feeling somewhat spoiled, Basma listened out. The flat was completely quiet. Had Dr. Sethi fallen asleep, as well?

Rolling onto her back and stretching both arms out to the side, she sat halfway up and surveyed her surroundings.

"I am in Eng-a-land," she whispered.

This wasn't a dream. Rising all the way to an upright position, letting the brocade spread slip down to her waist, she hugged her knees to her chest and rested her chin on them. Dual urges vied for expression. One was to leap from the bed and explore this enchanting house, the other wished nothing else but to dive once more beneath the covers and stay there.

Although she knew Dr. Sethi was a genuine person for sure, she couldn't think of anything to say to her. Whenever the woman looked at her, Basma's thoughts crashed into each other—nullifying them all.

There was a ringing outside the door. A telephone. No one answered it. She hurried from the bed trying to get to the phone before it stopped.

"Hello? Hello?"

"Neelam?" It was a woman's voice.

"No. She is not here," came the hesitant reply.

"And who are you?"

"I am Bas… Aisha… Langwa."

"Oh yes, of course. I forgot. So, where is Neelam? She said something about wanting to go out for a late lunch or early dinner.

Basma explained to the woman that she had been asleep and didn't know anything about the food plans or where Dr. Sethi was. The woman told her she would try to reach Neelam on her cell and hung up.

Basma laid the handset on the coffee table only just noticing the small piles of handwritten pages scattered around the sofa. It really was a fine room. She'd never seen so many books or bookcases as tall as these in her whole life. She strolled along the wall of shelves, letting her fingers glide over the spines of the ones within reach, as if doing so was, somehow, a sacred act. Hardcover. Paperbacks. Some leather-bound. Old, crumbling, ripped and stained—some brand spanking new. All of a sudden, she realized she had open access to all of them, and the freedom to read whatever she wanted without fear. What would Shafal say if he knew she had read all of these books? Was that even possible? Had Dr. Sethi read them all?

She imagined herself sitting in the overstuffed chair Kensasha talked about, with stacks of books at her feet. Which one should she read first? Could you read more than one at the same time?

Ninety minutes later, she heard a key turn in the lock and the front door open. Footsteps. Something smelled good. Basma went out to see. Neelam came in carrying three brown paper bags, followed by a woman who carried two shopping bags and a white square box, the kind they put cakes or pies in.

"I hope you are hungry, luv," Neelam said as she disappeared into the kitchen. Raising her voice, she added, "I brought us Fish 'n Chips."

The tall slim woman set the shopping bags just outside the kitchen door and placed the white box on an antique Japanese sideboard. Then she glided regally toward Basma, with her hand outstretched.

"I'm Enid Statham. We spoke on the phone earlier."

She wore a brown suede jacket over a vanilla cashmere turtleneck. Her slacks were brown tweed, and gold brooch-styled earrings accentuated her straight blond hair. Basma glanced away, shyly, as she took Enid's hand and squeezed. It was a firm, solid grip, not at all like the limp-grip one Enid had anticipated.

"I don't know what Neelam is talking about," she ventured. "You seem capable enough." The meaning did not go over Basma's head.

"Here we are," Neelam announced as she brought in a tray laden with batter-coated crispy fried cod and haddock and a heap of chips, English-style fried potatoes.

They each found a place on the L-shaped sofa amongst the yellow papers, and Neelam informed Basma that the salt and the bottle of brown vinegar were to be used for seasoning.

While they munched on pieces of cod and haddock, Enid perused the yellow legal sheets—every inch covered with words. She picked up random sheets and read here and there.

"A bit inflammatory, that!" Exclaimed Enid. "Do you really feel this way? About men, I mean?"

"It is all true."

"Well, some of it may be, but..."

"Show me what isn't."

"I'm sure there's... I mean... I don't profess to be as smart as you, Neelam, but I don't feel this way and I doubt if the majority of our supporters will either. It's quite harsh, you know, and I really don't see how espousing all this hatred toward men will help get us an international hearing."

"Hatred? I don't see it as hatred, Enid—just presenting the facts. History. Current events."

"I think a lot may disagree with your version of history. I think you have to tone it down. Don't you?"

"Well… Yes, I suppose so," Neelam sighed. "But I must tell you, it was a wonderful purging and has lifted my spirits quite a bit." She chuckled. "Maybe this is exactly what the forum needs to be—a catharsis for women, eh?"

"That will only make things worse for the people we are trying to help, won't it?" Enid countered.

"Just joking, my dear. But it would be a healing experience, don't you think?"

Enid grinned "So, how will you present all this in a 20-minute speech? We have to let other organization heads talk as well, don't we?"

"I'm sure I will have something more suitable when the time comes. Don't worry," Neelam assured her.

Basma watched the two women during their exchange, and recognized the deep level of trust and respect they had for each other. She imagined them having the same for her one day. She didn't mind not having their attention. It gave her the space to observe and to be with this new self. It was an experience she was enjoying, immensely.

"Aisha!" Neelam called out.

She jumped.

"Must you be so skittish?" Both women stared at her, but with curious eyes. "Do you like the fish and chips?" Neelam inquired. Basma nodded enthusiastically. Her plate was nearly empty. "Tell us what happened to you," Neelam urged. "Kensasha only told me your family thinks you are dead and if they find out you are not, they may try to find you and kill you. Why is that?"

Basma leaned over and put her plate on the coffee table, picked up a napkin and slowly wiped oil and salt from her hands—all the time wondering exactly where she should begin.

CHAPTER 23

T here are people fortunate to have only sheep to count in order to fall asleep. Zafeera lay awake in the bedsit counting how many times the front door in the hallway slammed, how many footsteps thumped on the metal staircase in the middle of the night. In the distance, a dog was missing his master, and an infant a warm breast.

The couple down the hall had argued most of the evening until they ran out of steam. Soon that disturbance was replaced by teen boys loitering, outside, with hip-hop as the soundtrack.

She didn't believe futons were designed with women in mind. Wasn't it illegal to turn off the heat before 10pm? She doubled the blanket and was glad she had kept her socks on. A woman like her should be out dancing with her man on Friday nights. Mick was probably fast asleep by now—in their warm, plush bed with silk sheets—missing her.

The cold dreariness of the following morning could easily be dismissed when sitting in the Cozy Bear Café near Brixton Station. The restaurant had become her escape from that stark, drab furnished bedsit she rented, and it could be counted on for serving up a decent breakfast at a reasonable price. The coffee wasn't bad either.

Between forkfuls of egg on toast with fried potatoes, Zafeera thumbed through the folder on Ghaybaa's husband, reading and re-

reading the same papers and documents she'd read several times before. She had enlisted her journalist colleagues at work in gathering
everything they could find on him—most of which was incomplete.

Along with a picture taken for his driver's license in Paris, the
document stated: Fareed Al-Akbar Messood was born in a small
province north of Cairo, educated at the University of Cairo majoring
in engineering and political theory, and had worked for five years in
Cairo for a large construction firm until he was hired to work on a
project in Dubai. From there, he went to Saudi Arabia and Pakistan
to work before settling in Paris.

She knew that her father, Vasilis, was introduced to Fareed at the
mosque. Whatever conversation the two men struck up must have
impressed her father.

After years of odd jobs to feed his family, Vasilis Hasni now ran
a successful home contracting firm with fifteen employees. Was it the
prospect of working together in construction or Fareed's political
stance that fueled the connection? Knowing her father, it was probably Fareed's political views on France's relationship with Algeria—
its former colony—or, even better, Islamic fundamentalism in pre-
sent-day Algeria. That was surely something to get her father both
riled up and stimulated.

Vasilis continually resisted falling into step with modern France
and, like many older immigrants, remained cloistered in a mindset
and in traditions thousands of years old. Many of those traditions
needed salvaging—needed to be integrated, then the whole of society
would be enriched. Paris and other cities around the world had already experienced a cultural transfusion with the influx of North
African and Middle Eastern immigrants. Just the same, not all infu-
sions were without harmful side effects.

From the first phone call that Ghaybaa made after her wedding,
Zafeera felt unease. There was something about Ghaybaa's voice.
What triggered alarm for Zafeera was not what her sister had said, it
was what she hadn't said.

After breakfast, the park was Zafeera's next stop. The bleakness
of the morning had now transformed into a sunny Saturday afternoon. More people braved the cold crisp air.

Mothers from Bangladesh and the Caribbean mingled in their respective groups: two here—four over there, like coffee klatches—while their exuberant children ran, skipped, jumped, giggled, fought and cried together. In other neighborhoods, these women would have been the nannies minding other people's children. Zafeera was relieved to see that wasn't yet the case in Brixton.

The initial strategy was to start walking east and just circle the entire place asking every Bangladeshi woman if she recognized the people in the photograph. Many of the women were so engrossed in their conversations with each other, or distracted by Zafeera's masculine attire, they barely looked at the photo. When they did look, however, they just shook their heads and resumed their conversations.

She had covered two thirds of the park when a toddler darted out across her path, tripped and fell to his knees. The sudden tumble frightened him. On instinct, Zafeera, moved quickly to help the squealing child to his feet. His mother rushed over, along with a few other women.

After lifting the child in her arms, she thanked Zafeera, as did the other women around her.

Remembering why she was there, Zafeera took out the wedding photo and the photo of Fareed from the folder and showed the pictures to the women asking if they recognized the couple. The women encircled her and studied the photos.

After a while, one of the women said: "The man used to go to our mosque near here."

"Yes, I remember him," said the mother patting the child, who was now just whimpering. "The Imam favored him."

Zafeera felt her heart leap and the adrenaline rush through her. Six months canvassing the entire county it seemed, and finally recognition.

"Didn't he have some group?" a third woman asked.

"He wasn't from Bangladesh," stated the first woman.

"The girl is not from there, either" added the mother.

"No," Zafeera informed them eagerly. "She is Algerian and the man is Egyptian, but he was working many years in Pakistan. That would give him more rapport with your Imam and the other men at the mosque. He probably speaks Urdu."

Considering this, the women nodded.

"Can any of you remember the last time you saw him there, approximately?" Zafeera asked. They glanced at one another.

The woman with the child was more forthcoming: "Maybe one year. Why are you asking about them?"

"Because that's my sister and I... our family has not heard anything from them in almost two years," Zafeera explained. She looked longingly at the wedding photo, and then added, "I think she's in trouble. I have to find her."

With her head reeling excitedly and her hands stiffening from the cold, she thanked the women and quickly left the park the way she came. Now she had to decide if she should contact the Imam of that mosque, once again. He was the first person questioned when she arrived in the neighborhood. He declined to give her any information.

Squeezing her fingers into a ball in her pockets to keep them warm, she walked back to the bedsit with a feeling of hope she had not felt in a long time.

As she put her key in the door, the image of the young woman down the hall came into her mind. Her husband had fought with her until way after midnight. Zafeera hadn't seen the woman since the last time she stayed in the bedsit two weeks earlier. She tossed the folder on the table, then went and knocked on the woman's door.

Sounds of movement could be heard inside and feet shuffling across the floor, but it took a while before the young woman answered.

"Yes, who is it?" she asked, wearily, in Arabic.

"I live down the hall. I came here to help you a few weeks ago. Do you remember?"

"Please... go... away!" Her voice sounded like she was having difficulty forming the words.

"Are you all right? Can't you open the door?"

"No! I am sick."

"Look, maybe I can help in some way," Zafeera insisted. "Do you need something from the chemist? I can go for you." For a moment, there was no response. "If you are sick, why don't you open the door?" Zafeera pleaded. "I can help you." Again, a long pause, then she unlatched and slowly opened the door.

The very first glimpse made Zafeera's stomach churn. The young woman's puffy blue and purple face was barely recognizable. A gash on her bottom lip looked infected and both eyes were blackened.

Zafeera didn't need to see the rest of her body, which was draped in a hooded black robe, to know there were bruises everywhere. Miraculously, the woman hadn't miscarried.

Not bothering to ask the woman to leave with her, Zafeera just threw an arm around the woman's shoulder and literally pulled her out of the apartment.

"You are coming with me now, do you hear me? Now! Your husband is crazy! He will kill you sooner or later." The woman resisted a little but now seemed relieved to have someone concerned about her. "Where is your family? I can take you to them."

"No, no. They will be very angry with me."

"Angry with you? Why? Your husband did this to you."

She halted "Please, I have to go back. I have to go back." There was panic in her voice, but Zafeera ignored her pleas.

Grasping hold of the woman's arm, she continued walking to the front door. "Look, I am not letting you go back there. Do you understand? I am taking you some place safe, where he can't get to you ever again. Do you hear me? You must think of your baby, now." Tears began streaming from the woman's bloodshot eyes. Her body, weakened from all the punches, finally submitted to Zafeera's pull. "I am Zafeera Hasni, by the way. What is your name?"

"I am called Salima."

"Cover your face, Salima. People will talk if they see it.

The two women walked out of the building, slowly, hoping not to draw attention. However, the teen boys that usually hung around the street corner couldn't help but notice Zafeera, wearing her flipped baseball cap, walking with a woman in a burka. One of boys said something to the others then grinned and pointed.

Deciding to cut across the street before reaching the boys, Zafeera had no idea how she could get the woman to a shelter without the privacy of a car or taxi. Brixton wasn't an area where taxis passed frequently and, clearly, the woman was too weak for the long subway ride.

Maybe she should call Mick. They could wait in a restaurant until he came for them. But her intuition was telling her to get the woman out of the neighborhood as soon as possible. A second later, Zafeera flagged down a car and told the driver that Salima was pregnant and having contractions—she needed to get to a hospital immediately. It was easier than she expected.

At the hospital, Zafeera wanted to pay the man for helping, but he waved them off. They walked steadily toward the entrance of the hospital. Zafeera looked back to see if the car was out of sight. When it disappeared in front of a bus, she took Salima's arm and hailed a taxi.

The Maubry Women's shelter was fully prepared to take in battered women who also needed medical attention. They kept nurses on staff and their doctor was a call away. Discretion was the most cherished of all the policies. Like the safe house, the women's shelter protected the identity of all those who were victims of domestic abuse. This was almost three quarters of all the women there. Many came with their children. Those who did were usually relocated after a few weeks to larger facilities, until they could be relocated out of London.

Both the weekend manager, Adelaide Hughes, and the staff of five, surrounded Salima. They carefully inspected the mess her husband had made of her face to see the extent of the injuries. With Zafeera translating, Adelaide Hughes promised Salima she'd do everything she could to make sure it would not happen again.

"We really protect our women here," Adelaide assured Salima.

"You don't have to worry about anything now," Zafeera added for reassurance. "No one knows where you are. You can stay here as long as you need to. They will take care of you."

"We need both of you to fill out some papers," Adelaide informed then, addressing Salima, "And after, you will need medical treatment. So, let's get started." Zafeera explained all this to Salima and helped her with the forms. She told Salima that in the days to come, it would be decided if charges should be pressed against her husband and someone would go to the apartment and retrieve her personal belongings for her. She accompanied Salima into the treatment room. At first, Salima was reluctant to allow photographs to be taken of her injuries. Soon, she yielded.

Finally, Zafeera waved goodbye to the very tired, frightened young woman as the nurse went to work applying antiseptics and gauze to her face and orderlies readied a clean bed for her to sleep.

Now, Zafeera had no desire to return to the bedsit and possibly run into Salima's husband. Her next strategy with Fareed could easily be planned at home where it was clean, warm and comfortable. Right now, she just needed time to walk and reflect a bit before getting into another taxi. Salima was safe; that was most important.

Her good deed done for the day and feeling especially pleased with finding out Fareed had definitely been in Brixton a year ago, she walked back out into a still sunny brisk afternoon with a triumphant smile on her face.

CHAPTER 24

S
o far, Basma hadn't felt at all like an assistant with Neelam insisting on cleaning the plates herself the night before and then
preparing breakfast, as simple as it was: toast with marmalade
and a hearty pot of chai.

"Aisha, I've decided, we're going to do some 'fun' things today,
as I know the upcoming week will be very hectic. First, I'll show you
around the neighborhood. Then we'll go shopping along the Portobello Road because Saturday is the best day to do that. You can pick
up whatever you need and later we can have dinner out. I'll tell you
now I don't like to cook—except when I'm entertaining. So, better get
used to takeaway and restaurants."

Basma found herself nodding, reluctant to reveal her own love
of cooking.

Minutes later, she was staring at the skirts and sweaters in her
unpacked suitcase. Each had been neatly folded and put there by
Kensasha. The skirts, a chocolate brown, a dark navy with pale gray
pinstripes, and a charcoal black one, each had a matching sweater
that contained enough colors to mix and match. Still conservative in
length, the styles were in keeping with a contemporary cosmopolitan
city like London. Regardless of which combination she chose,
Kensasha wanted Basma to look as if she fitted in easily with the kind
of women who surrounded Dr. Sethi. She chose chocolate brown.

There were also a number of hijabs in different colors. Basma reached for a golden yellow one, and draped it over her head then went over to the mirror. How familiar. How comforting it was. Her defiant act in the airport restroom of throwing the white satin hijab in the trash seemed so long ago and almost pointless now. Here, beyond the scrutiny of a husband, without the dictates of a group—free of condemnation by the Imam, she could either wear it or not. She chose to wear it.

Tucking the ends of the yellow fabric inside her coat, yet allowing some of her hair to show, she walked out of the bedroom and joined Dr. Sethi at the front door.

Neelam, with an Indian shawl of lambs' wool elegantly draped around her shoulders, characteristically raised an eyebrow, but added a slight grin. She did not comment on the head covering, instead she said, "I suggest you wear those gloves as well," glancing at the black woolen gloves sticking out of Basma's pocket. "The weatherman predicted frost in the air."

On the way, Neelam pointed out where to buy milk, fresh meat and fish, warm baked bread, where to find the chemist/pharmacy, the dry cleaners and the nearest Underground station.

"We can buy fresh fruit tomorrow," Neelam announced.

To reach Portobello Road Market, they rode the District Line from West Kensington to Notting Hill Gate, during which Neelam taught Basma how to read the Tube map and to understand London's different train lines, especially the Circle Line which was most important for getting to and from her office.

Basma's excitement at being in the new city was often curtailed by her overwhelming insecurity. At first, being with Neelam Sethi wasn't much different from being with Imani Sadawi in that both older women treated her as one would a daughter-in-law. They were protective, instructive— but, at the same time, not as forthcoming about themselves as they would have been if she were a daughter. This, in turn, caused Basma to maintain her own usual reticence, all of which reflected the same psychological and emotional isolation she'd experienced most of her life. But after three hours of perusing antiques at the south end of Portobello Market, milling through crowds, looking at crafts in Tavistock Piazza, then hunting through all the ethnic clothing stalls along its north end—where Dr. Sethi consistently pulled out colorful summer dresses and hats holding them up to Basma saying, "This would look lovely on you, Aisha," or "Why don't you try on that skirt for fun," Basma found herself laughing. The most memorable moment of the day for her was making Dr. Neelam Sethi laugh, as well, by putting a red floppy hat with a bird-feathered band over her yellow hijab.

They returned home just as the streetlamps flicked on—cheeks rosy, feet sore, stomachs rumbling—carrying plastic bags full of Indian-styled blouses, beads and scarves for Basma, and a contemporary hand-blown glass vase, in ruby-red and sea blue, that Neelam could not resist.

***

Bare, pale green walls, one caramel leather chair and green tweed industrial carpet were the only items of color in Neelam's office. Perpendicular to Neelam's desk, eight piles of stuff managed to block out what little light that side of the building received. Neelam's office seemed to be the antithesis of her magnificent, colorful flat. Here, where order was most important and expected, chaos reigned. Neelam pointed to the towering stacks.

"See what you can do with that. I'm at a loss. The cabinets are full. There's no space for a new file cabinet." She pushed the start button on her computer. It hummed. "I have about twenty calls to make and I need my chai."

Standing in the middle of the office, Monday morning, wearing an aqua Indian tunic with matching hijab, Basma stared at the work before her, feeling a sense of usefulness. At last, here was a problem she could solve.

As Neelam turned her attention to returning phone calls and writing emails, Basma began to sort items into specific groups utilizing the floor and windowsill. She prepared labels and made-up new folders. One batch was for Neelam to determine what to keep and what could be discarded. What she needed now was two-dozen plastic file bins. Preferring to get as much done in one day as she could, Basma asked Neelam for directions to the nearest office supply store. Fifteen minutes later, hand-drawn map in her purse, Basma set off on an errand, alone, in London for the first time.

As she exited the front door of the building, a small TV crew was just coming up the walkway. She saw the split-second shift from excitement to disappointment on the face of the female reporter upon realizing Basma was not Dr. Sethi. Basma glanced away, slightly embarrassed, then solemnly headed toward her destination, eager to prove herself competent and reliable.

***

The offices of In Our Time magazine, were located three miles north of the City, London's major financial center. Besides covering the financial arena, the magazine reported on all political and social conflicts from an unbiased, multicultural perspective—so they claimed. In addition to Zafeera Hasni, they employed Benjamin Ubiatu, a Londoner of Nigerian decent, Carla Ruel from Jamaica, two Russian men, two Hindus, one Japanese and one Sikh. All the important editorial positions, and decisions were made by their predominately British staff.

The magazine had a large female readership primarily because of spotlighting women in business, and women who took the Road Less Traveled as that feature was entitled. Not only had previous issues profiled a female archaeologist, an American female army general and a female captain of a cruise liner, but also Dr. Neelam Sethi and her ardent quest to end familial and cultural violence toward women.

Regardless of what the top story was, however, Monday mornings at the publication were particularly hectic. It seemed as if every employee in the office had skipped a wholesome breakfast and opted, instead, for triple espressos because their chatter was amped up in volume and speed as each relayed every detail of their weekend, embellished to such a degree they rivaled the magazine's published articles.

That Monday morning was no different. The central room with sixteen journalists was abuzz. All of the ten mounted 40" TV monitors were on and tuned to news channels across Europe, Asia and the Middle East, some in closed caption.

Like Zafeera, most of the editorial staff had either listened to the radio or watched the early morning news shows before they arrived at work. The top story reported by most media agencies at that time was about a prominent financier arrested for embezzlement. However, the lackluster reporting of the event by the anchors on the prime stations failed to capture much attention and did not suspend anyone's preoccupation with their own weekend that had just passed.

Like her colleagues, Zafeera also reflected on the events of her weekend. She had already downed a large latte and had her second in her hand when she breezed off the elevator, hair flowing, alongside Benjamin who like her was often the last to arrive. They chatted cheerfully and then departed to their individual cubicles.

To get to her desk, Zafeera had to weave her way around people staring at the TV monitors. She was surprised at how captivated everyone was by the financier's arrest. Weeks before, there had been speculation of his involvement. Good thing In Our Time had failed to get an interview with the man two years earlier. She set the coffee on her desk. When she lifted the strap of her bag over her head and began to unbutton her coat, she heard someone say, "Oh! How awful!"

"What's so awful about it?" Zafeera called out. "You don't think the rich can be just as greedy and dishonest as anyone else can be?" Several of her colleagues standing nearby looked at her, puzzled. "Well, they are," she added.

"What are you talking about, Zafeera?" Manesh inquired. "These were not rich people." He pointed to the monitor over her shoulder. She turned and looked up.

First, she saw the bold text: Breaking News, then a police officer being questioned with patrol cars in the background and spectators behind a barricade. It was looped footage with a reporter narrating.

"As you can see, this neighborhood has been shaken by this terrible tragedy," the reporter said.

The looped footage repeated a clip where an on-site female reporter posed questions to the crowd of spectators: "Did any of you know the woman?" Some people shook their heads others simple stared into the TV camera.

A psychologist weighed in. "This is more common than people realize," he said. "There isn't a place on earth that hasn't experienced a tragedy like this. I can't tell you how to prevent it from happening again."

Even Dr. Neelam Sethi was seen giving a comment about the situation. "It is insidious. But the real cause is fear."

Zafeera watched and listened grabbing at bits here and there but still didn't understand what had happened until the loop repeated from the beginning and the reporter announced:

"As we've reported, an hour ago police were called to an apartment building in Brixton (insert of live footage from the apartment building) after neighbors reported a domestic disturbance and cries for help."

Zafeera's body stiffened when she saw the building. The reporter continued: "They discovered the battered body of a woman who has now been identified as Salima Al Halabi. The 21-year-old Syrian immigrant was seven months pregnant. Her head had been crushed with a blunt object. Police are now searching for the husband, Yusef Al-Halabi."

Zafeera clutched the back of her chair for support. "No! No! No! No! No, no, oh nooo," she moaned, tears blurring all other images. Nausea gripped her. She slammed both hands on her desk hard and collapsed in the chair burying her face in her arms.

Stunned and confused by her outburst, everyone turned and stared.

Benjamin rushed to console her. He was only a few feet away when Zafeera leaped to her feet, grabbed her purse and tore past him to the elevator. She banged on the button repeatedly, then hopped aboard before Benjamin and Manesh could reach her.

***

"WE CAN'T FORCE PEOPLE!"

"Well, you should! Someone in her condition should not have been allowed to leave." An emotional Zafeera began using her hands to get the point across. "Je ne comprends pas. Je ne comprends pas!"

"Look, women do this all the time. They come to us for help, we give them a bed and free food, a place to shower, free medical treatment if they need it, and, in some cases, money, and still some go right back to their abusers. For many, this place is a revolving door. We are privately funded. We do our best, but people have the right to come and go."

What could Zafeera say to that? All she could see was Salima's bruised and swollen face looking back at her as she waved goodbye on Saturday.

Outside, reporters had already begun congregating once investigators learned that Salima had entered a women's shelter, days before the murder. When Zafeera left the building, a few reporters rushed to her shouting questions.

"Who are you?"

"How long was she here?"

"Why did you send her home?"

Behind Zafeera, the shelter went into lockdown. The unexpected onslaught of people with microphones and cameras directed at her eroded her last bit of self-assurance and certitude. She pushed past them without uttering a word, jogged a few blocks in heels before she was rescued once again.

Safely inside a taxi, she phoned her editor, Bill Sutton, and apologized for running out so abruptly, explaining that she had known the pregnant woman on the news who'd just been murdered. Sutton gave her the rest of the day off, so she returned home, crawled into bed with all her clothes on, telephoned Mick and told him what happened.

"Sorry to hear that. How are you holding up?" he asked.

"I'm in bed."

"Probably the best place. I'll come home early."

"No, eh... eh." She hit the pillow in frustration.

"It's okay," Mick said comfortingly. "I know when you're very upset, you forget English. Well, at least you tried to help her."

After a few more words of encouragement, Mick hung up. Zafeera went to the medicine cabinet for a Panadol to stop the splitting headache that had started soon after leaving the reporters. Now, what would settle her stomach?

She spent the rest of the morning pacing around the apartment going back over Saturday with a hundred maybes. Maybe it was her fault—maybe she should have minded her own business. Salima had pleaded with her to go back. This was a woman afraid of her own parents!

Why didn't she go back to the shelter on Sunday, just to keep Salima company, or help her make decisions as to what to do next. Let her know her options. No one at the shelter spoke Arabic and Salima's English was miniscule. Maybe she was dreadfully lonely there. If she hadn't gotten involved and taken Salima away from her apartment, maybe her husband wouldn't have gotten angry enough to kill her. Maybe Salima and her baby would still be alive. Oh God!

By 4 o'clock, the start of the evening rush, Zafeera had filled an ashtray to the brim and emptied a box of Kleenex. She got up to dump the butts and wads of tissue into the trash. While standing at the bathroom mirror, she noticed the smeared eyeliner and used cotton balls and almond oil to remove what was left.

By the time Mick arrived home with Indian take out, she had already taken a hot bath and was stretched out on the couch with her arm across her eyes. The TV was off. Mick put the food down on the coffee table.

"My stomach is a mess," she announced.

"Got to eat something," he replied.

"Do I?"

He sat next to her and kissed her on the lips. "Ugh! You smell like a chimney."

"Cannot help it."

"Sure you can. Everyone's stopping."

"I'm not."

He kissed her again and feigned a cough then clutched his chest. For one second, she grinned.

"See, I'm more in danger than you are. Second-hand smoke."

She punched his arm lovingly and he took her into his arms and rocked her.

"I'm not going to work tomorrow."

"I understand. Just rest. Let it all go for a while."

"Oh, no. I can't do that," she protested. "I'm going back to Brixton. To the bedsit."

Mick was astounded. He let go of her. "Why? Why would you want to go back there now? The police are combing the area for her husband. That building is a crime scene. They'll question you."

"So, they question me."

"Well, you can't tell them you—"

"Why not?" she interrupted, "They'll find out soon enough. I signed documents at Maubry's."

"Okay then, wait until they make the contact," he urged. "This doesn't concern you."

"Of course it does. I took her to the shelter, Mick. I saw what he was doing to her and it wasn't the first time."

"What?"

"It's not important. I need to be there, not way on the other side of town in a million-dollar condo high above it all."

"This is your home, not that place. Remember?" She pushed past him and got up. "There's nothing you can do to change what happened to that poor girl," Mick persisted. "It's unfortunate. But it's not your affair."

"She was a woman—a Muslim woman, Mick, how is that not my affair?"

"Zafeera," he pleaded.

"I left my file there. I never do that. I have to get it," she insisted, and then turned and walked to the bedroom closing the door.

***

With two large shopping bags in hand, Basma took her time getting back to the office that day, hoping the news crew would have finished by then. They probably wanted Dr. Sethi to talk about the organizations coming to the first meeting, she thought. Meanwhile, she was having fun being out and about on her own in London. Dr. Sethi had given her money for the office supplies, but Basma decided not to use any of it. Already Dr. Sethi had done so much for her and she hadn't even made tea yet. She needed to give back, and, at last, money certainly wasn't a problem.

The night before, she had counted $6500 in the envelope Vincent had given her. It made her dizzy—euphoric. Like a schoolgirl, she wanted to burst from the room, run to Neelam and divulge everything she had left out about Vincent on Friday night. Although, at the same time, she felt Dr. Sethi would probably not understand any of it.

All of those afternoons with Vincent in motels would have to remain a secret—just like the money. It was their secret.

Many of the stores along the high street were bustling with foreigners. She found each shop interesting enough to draw her inside. One shop was devoted entirely to candles of all colors, shapes, sizes and fragrances; she found it intoxicating. She bought two for herself and two for Dr. Sethi.

The Italian shoe store carried heels so high, she couldn't let go of the salesgirl's arm.

Passing up the window with women's lingerie that reminded her of the purple gown Vincent had given her, she couldn't resist the store that only sold stationery. She found herself wandering from table to shelf, captivated especially by mini-sized boxes of envelopes embroidered with gold and floral designs and imagined composing a note to Abdel and Ahmed, then mailing it in one of those tiny envelopes. It would be a secret message that only they would understand. Something to take away their pain, something that would reveal the truth: their mother was alive!

***

Brixton was a wonderful potpourri of ethnicities—mostly from the Caribbean. Like most of London, it had a mix of style and taste. But, from the moment she stepped off the Tube, Zafeera felt an energy shift. A polarization had occurred. The ease with which people related to each other just a day ago, had dissipated.

Some of the people passing whispered to each other when they spotted her.

Media trucks populated one entire block south of Salima's apartment building. When Zafeera turned the corner approaching the building from the west, she saw patrol cars blocking both ends of the street. Two officers stood guard at the entrance.

She had no plan. So, feeling self-conscious yet displaying an air of controlled determination, Zafeera walked right up to one of the officers on guard and asked, "Have you found him yet?"

"No, miss, we haven't," the officer replied. "Now please step back."

"I live here," Zafeera informed. "I was staying with a friend when I heard."

"Oh, I see," said the officer. "Did you know the victim?" Zafeera wasn't expecting that and didn't know if this was the right time to be questioned. "I saw her twice, but I can't say I… I may have some information. Who can I contact about this?"

"If you have any information, I suggest you go straight down to the station."

She nodded, and then proceeded on to the front door.

"Wait, miss. I need to see some I.D. with this address on it." She had nothing in her possession with that address since she didn't actually live there. She pondered a moment and then reached into her pocket.

"All l have is this key to my room. It's on the same floor as… Salima's apartment. Someone can escort me."

Trained to be overly cautious and suspicious, the officer eyed her as if she might be a conspirator before signaling another officer to stand in his place. He beckoned her to follow him in.

It was hard to imagine that three days ago she and Salima had rushed out through those same doors to supposed safety—now Salima's dead body was lying on a slab somewhere. How did that happen?

All the way up the stairs, she replayed every detail over, and over, again. This time, every word echoed more loudly.

"Here is my room," she told the officer, pointing to the door on her right. The officer stopped and waited until she'd opened it and went inside.

"Merci, Officer." He nodded and left.

Once she closed the door and saw the folder just where she'd left it, fresh emotions began to stir. There was the all too familiar grief accompanied by uncontrollable guilt.

Opening the folder, she wondered if Fareed ever beat Ghaybaa. Could he do that? A wave of heat that began in her stomach radiated up to her head. She swooned. Did he do that? Is that what happened to Ghaybaa?

Tears spilled down her cheeks. Something very bad must have happened.

She couldn't stay there; couldn't even sit down for a moment. She needed to walk. What she really wanted was to find Salima's husband. That's what she had really come for.

The officer who had escorted her into the building was talking with two men when she exited and didn't notice her leaving.

Walking west taking quick steps, within fifty seconds she was at the corner and around it. The only ones who noticed her were the teen boys perched on a parked car amongst the spectators directly opposite the entrance. These were the same four Bengali teens that had congregated on the northeast corner on Saturday afternoon, when she left with Salima. The boys glanced at one another, and then without saying a word, they followed her, moving as one unified whole: one mind and one, intent.

The streets to the north were empty. Crossing another street, she headed in that direction. Besides a few flats, there was a hardware store, a storefront tax solicitor, two stores for rent and an active community center, frequented mostly by Bengali and a few Arab Muslim men.

Zafeera reasoned that if the husband were hiding inside the community center, the men most likely wouldn't talk to the police, since any one of them could easily be in the husband's position. If the doors were closed at this time of the day, it probably meant he was in there.

She slowed when she was a few meters away. The center was closed. She paused in front of the usually busy doorway and listened. Not a sound. She took out her phone, got the operator to connect her to the Brixton Police Station and suggested to the officer who answered that they get over to the center because the husband was just spotted going inside. She put the phone back into her pocket and continued walking, deciding to go up a few more blocks before doubling back in time to see the police arrive.

All of a sudden, she heard footsteps behind her. She glanced over her shoulder and saw four teenage boys moving closer. She walked faster, but felt no fear. They overtook her and continued on their way—as if she were invisible.

She didn't want to walk too far and miss the husband being escorted out. She imagined him resisting, a scuffle ensuing and the police beating him into submission. Can't miss that!

They grabbed her at a passageway between two commercial buildings and pulled her towards the rear. At first, she didn't realize what had happened. One boy covered her mouth with one hand and clasped her tightly around the waist with the other.

"You need to mind your own business, bitch."

"Yeah, keep your nose out of other people's shit," added an older looking boy.

Imitating the Jamaican and African youths in the neighborhood, these Bengali teens' whole style and swagger was a mix of what they believed was tough and cool. Their mannerisms were copied from too many American B flicks and music videos.

She gave a hard elbow jab to the one holding her.

"Ow! You, bitch," he yelled, this time in Bengalese and loosened his grip on her. She tried again, but was punched in the stomach by another boy, knocking the wind out of her. Her knees buckled. She slid to the ground coughing.

The air echoed with laughter. Two of them grabbed her by her jacket collar and dragged her to a door with a broken pane. Feeling her strength return, she jerked and clawed, opening wounds with her long nails. But that didn't stop them. It was four strong teenage boys against one woman. No contest.

Another boy, who looked eighteen, kicked open the door. They practically threw her inside. She landed face down on a dirty concrete floor. A whiff of damp mold, mixed with dried urine, and a glimpse of broken beer bottles violated her senses. She rolled over on her back and lay there staring up at the teens. Each boy was fixed on an item of her attire. There was a pause, a moment when each seemed to contemplate his next move. The one she elbowed came closer.

"You think you a guy, bitch, that you tough? We'll see how tough." He reached down and pulled off her 'offending cap.' Then, he dropped to his knees next to her and put his hand on her breast.

In seconds, her fingers gouged his eyes. He screamed and fell backward. Another boy tried to touch her breasts and she rose up on her elbow and kicked him in the groin. The remaining two boys leaped on her, cursing and punching her wildly in her head, face, breasts and stomach, but she clawed, kicked back and spat at them with equal fury.

At one point, she grabbed a handful of hair from the older boy and yanked with such force a clump came out. He fell away from her, holding his head. Straight away, the uninjured one was joined by the one she had kicked in the groin. Each grabbed hold of an arm and yanked her to her feet. Her legs buckled. One boy let go. The other spun her around, and hurled her across the room into a stack of crates. Then, all four came after her, pulled her up by her clothes, and flung her to the other wall. She landed up against the second stack of crates and collapsed to her knees.

She felt the warmth of her own blood oozing from her nose and lips. Probably just lost a few teeth. Yet, in the midst of it all, she was determined to fight back. Unless she lost total consciousness, she was not going to let them rape her. They'd have to kill her first.

Then she saw it: one half of a beer bottle laying inches away. Did she have the nerve? The stomach? A second later, the only guy so far unscathed strutted over, squatted beside her and lifted a clenched fist, his contorted face dark and ominous. Was she ready to die now in a dark abandoned building? She grabbed the broken bottle, swung fast in a circular motion opening a deep gash across the side of his face. He shrieked out, hysterically, when he saw the amount of blood dripping all over his chest and dashed from the building. Another boy held his crotch and wiggled out right behind him, followed closely by a third who stumbled along, intermittently stretching his arm out, for guidance. The older boy, his bald patch reddening, kicked Zafeera to the ground before taking off after his mates.

She wasn't sure how long she had lain there doubled up in excruciating pain, going in and out of consciousness with every part of her body throbbing. She was unable to stand and could barely see there was so much fluid around her eyes.

Thank God for cell phones.

* * *

CHAPTER 25

T he chai was much too sweet, but Neelam didn't say a word. She just sat at her desk sipping it like it was perfection. With the recent call from Kensasha confirming the fact that Aisha's husband was unforgiving and hoped she was really dead, Neelam realized how fortunate Aisha/Basma was, to be in London. And she realized her own good fortune to have her as an assistant. Organization through color coordination—that was what Basma had created for her.

Green file bins were assigned to hold all matters concerning the safe houses: locations, names of the women, contacts for all the service providers and the code sheet with the names of British citizens in various aspects of government who secretly used their connections to help them.

A duplicate of everything involving the safe houses was also on Neelam's computer and password protected—minus the actual names. After the safe house tragedy, it had been decided not to put people in danger by having their vital information on a computer in case it wound up in the wrong hands. But who would bother with a row of colorful bins lined up right out in the open, opposite the entrance? They practically screamed: "Look at me."

By far, the best thing was that Basma had given everything a disguise. The safe house labels read "real estate". She had taken it upon herself to go to a bookstore and study the various elements of owning property and then labeled the different sections accordingly: brokers, loan companies, managed properties, contractors, workers, best locations, inspectors, electricians, and legal advisors.

Information for the proposed forum was not coded, since all of it would be passed on to the media, in time. Still, Basma had placed the papers dealing with the forum in magenta-colored bins and then put miscellaneous office papers and bills in white bins, in between the green and magenta. Everything was perfectly alphabetized into a simple yet creative system making Neelam very pleased, indeed.

"Have you checked your email?" Basma asked, opening the mail and designating a specific pile for each correspondence. "I spoke to a Mrs. Kurtami, yesterday, and she said she would email you a few more officials identified in Jordan, Pakistan and Saudi Arabia that we should contact."

Neelam nodded and turned to her computer screen, then looked back at Basma.

"Aisha!" she called out. "Why don't you come over here and check it for me?"

Basma froze. Other than glancing over the shoulders of Kensasha at Ridgefield or Ahmed and Abdel's at home, she'd never touched a computer.

"Come, come," Neelam beckoned, as she cleared a spot on the desk for her chai.

"I have more mail to open," Basma protested.

"Do them later," Neelam ordered. "I want you to be able to do this on your own. Now come."

She hesitated, hoping Neelam would become impatient and say forget it. But when she saw that wasn't going to happen, she laid down the letter opener and went over to Neelam.

"Here, you sit. I'll show you what to do."

With Neelam standing over her, Basma stared at all the strange symbols before her not having a clue what they were.

"All right, then. See that earth icon in the center of the screen?" Basma nodded.

"Put your hand right here on the mouse. Yes, that's it. Now, I want you to put the arrow there over the earth icon and click on it twice very quickly and it will take us to the Internet."

After Basma clicked, they watched the hourglass a few seconds before a new window opened up, revealing all the top stories for the day, the weather forecast, how many days before Christmas, ads for weight loss products and the most frequently watched videos on YouTube.

Neelam's attention first went to the Top Stories link. She searched the list for anything that might be of interest to her or her work, but other than a suicide bomber in Iraq, the only other item that caught her eye was: Brixton Attack Woman Leaves Hospital.

"Now see that area up there? I want you to highlight it by dragging the cursor."

Neelam went on to casually explain the concept of a web address, ISP and hosting while logging onto her email account. Not once did she ask Aisha/Basma if she knew how, or why she didn't know how, to use a computer.

By lunchtime, Basma had practiced logging on four times, and learned how to open the file attached to an email from A. Kurtami of the Asian Women's Rights Initiative or AWRI.

***

Two weeks in Intensive Care with fractured ribs, a sprained back and ankle, whiplash, two missing back teeth, possible liver damage from all the kicking, and six broken fingernails. It meant she was in worse condition than Salima had been the day she took her to the shelter.

All four teens, between the ages of fifteen and eighteen, were captured and jailed within twenty-four hours of the attack. They were charged with attempted rape and aggravated assault.

Once the authorities learned Zafeera was the woman who had also brought Salima Al-Halabi to the Maubry shelter, they looked into a possible connection between the teens and Salima's husband. Apparently, the husband was discovered holed up in the back room of a social club based on a tip from a woman with a French accent. It had been all over the newspapers. It vindicated her with Mick, though he still wouldn't forgive her for ignoring his warnings and going back to that neighborhood. Nor could he leave her side. She had to get mean with him to get him to leave her and go back to work.

Limping, and still black and blue all over, it was a pleasure to be back home. Mick had the housekeeper come in every day to assist her. But all Zafeera demanded was cigarettes and that was the one thing Mick told the housekeeper not to get her.

Days slipped by. She couldn't go back to work. And, she would have to testify at the husband's hearing—perhaps the boys' hearing as well, if they continued to plead not guilty. Before long, every time the housekeeper arrived, the TV was on and it stayed on until Mick came home in the evening.

Here and there, as the case approached trial, television stations ran stories on other female victims of domestic violence. It was reported that the number of women who go to shelters and then return home, only to be beaten, shot, or stabbed to death, was staggering. Zafeera found herself becoming obsessed with it all.

She began to order books and documentaries on this type of violence and devoured them. She learned that it wasn't restricted to any specific ethnic or religious group but was happening everywhere. In places without protective shelters, women ran to neighbors or family members and those who opened their doors had often been injured or killed by enraged spouses.

She reread the interview In Our Time had done with Dr. Neelam Sethi, who had exposed the practice of honor killings to the British media. Each morning, as soon as Mick left for work and until he returned home, Zafeera's eyes were glued to the TV or reading a book. When the housekeeper brought lunch, Zafeera barely noticed. Mick often returned to find a half-eaten sandwich or cold bowls of soup and dried-out rolls.

It was never the separation of men and women, in her culture, that she took issue with—it was the inequality of attitude and position. Women were always in the back of the hall, in another room, up in a balcony, or off to the side. Separate living rooms. Invisible: hidden behind walls or dark veils—faceless and voiceless. On the periphery. Wasn't that a perfect description of women's status in the entire world? On the periphery?

Almost breathlessly, she told Mick what she had read or what she watched each day.

"In the Congo, soldiers are raping women and then mutilate their vaginas and uteruses with rifles! The women who live through it are hospitalized for months and can never have children and suffer unbelievable physical and emotional pain. Hundreds of thousands have been raped like this, and you can't imagine the reason one of these so-called soldiers gave: It's for good luck", so they can win a battle! I've been wondering all day: what kind of men, do this?

"Remember those Serbian soldiers who raped two Muslim sisters, nine and eleven years old, in the nineties, and then the soldiers set both girls on fire? Why?

"An American soldier raped a fourteen-year-old girl, in Iraq recently, then killed her and her whole family. I don't think he was the only one there who has done that. It seems that raping and killing women and children of the supposed enemy is a common strategy in war. No one's exempt.

"Pakistani women are having acid thrown in their faces by their husbands, and girls who ignore or refuse a man's advances are having acid thrown in their faces as well. They are disfigured for life. These are not rare events, Mick. I saw the films. I saw how many women, more than a hundred every year. It's unbelievable that men can do such things."

Mick listened and became just as horrified, but all he could do was to let her talk. Eventually, she began to wind down and allowed him to hold her until she fell asleep. But, the following evening, it repeated.

"I saw this film about all the thousands of women in the border towns of Mexico that are murdered, mutilated and buried in the hills. They don't know who is doing it or why.

"Wife beating is like you say, 'A tip of the iceberg.' You don't want to know what happened to thousands of women in my country, Algeria, in the 1990s—it's too gruesome, too horrific.

"And in South Africa, men have raped babies as young as six months old. Do you know why?"

"No, Zafeera, I can't even imagine why," Mick replied, almost irritated.

"Well, I will tell you why. Are you ready for the answer? You have to be ready."

"Actually, I don't think I want to know."

"Too bad. I'm going to tell you: To help cure AIDS!" Mick stared back.

"Men with AIDS think raping babies will cure them. Babies! Mick. Babies!"

He shook his head, dumbfounded by it all, and by her absorption in it.

"Do these people have a soul?" she asked. "I don't think so. You know what I think, Mick, I think there is a virus rotting *le cerveau*—the brain— of the men. This virus is rotting away the power of reason and logic, and the part that is compassionate and empathetic. Both of these qualities are imperative for civilization. These qualities are at the foundation of our humanity—what it means to be human. Yes? I believe there is something in men that struggles to keep the primitive animal urges from gaining total control. Maybe it's a hormone, or a gene," she surmised, "The human gene, or the "human hormone". Maybe it is spiritual, like maybe the 'God gene'. It makes you not only aware of yourself, but makes you feel worthy of life, worthy of love and worthy of truth. It makes you feel the life in other living things, and you want to honor and respect that life, and have honor and respect for whatever created that life.

"My theory is maybe this hormone or gene is starting to mutate. People are now being born with smaller amounts of this hormone or a mutant form of the gene. It explains a lot, no?"

Mick stared back at her, then rubbed his face and let out a groan. She was, actually, waiting for a response. Instead, he got up and went over to the small bar near the entertainment center and poured himself a Scotch then came back and sat down facing her.

"All of these stories are terrible, I agree. It makes me feel sick to hear them. I don't know how you can watch these things all day. But haven't these awful things been happening in the world from the beginning? Horrible stuff, this, but nothing new, I don't think. I mean, how do we know if it's worse now than in the past, or better? We can't know that, can we?" He sipped his whisky coolly, and continued. "My concern is you. I mean, this is all you've been on about for weeks. Before this, you were obsessed with finding your sister, which is fine and all, but it doesn't explain renting some crappy room in

Brixton. What was that all about? And now, you're consumed with all the sick shit men do to women, and want some input on my part. Well, I don't know what to say. I'm not like that! I would never, ever, do any of that to anyone, man or woman. I don't know any man who would do that kind of stuff."

"I'm sure there are men in your office who have done things to women that may surprise you," Zafeera said, dismissively.

"How can you say such a thing?"

"Because all of these horrors were carried out by ordinary people! Husbands! Brothers! Sons and fathers did these things! Despicable things. Soldiers did them, students did them."

"Soldiers aren't ordinary people," he countered. 'They are trained to kill."

"What about fathers and brothers who kill their daughters and sisters for family honor? Remember the Safe House Massacre?"

"Yeah, yeah." He downed the remaining Scotch and got up for a refill.

"You need to watch some of these films, Mick, then you will understand why it upsets me," she explained.

"Honey, I understand being upset, but you're getting too emotionally involved in things you can't change. It's making you sick. What's the point? Let it go. I'm sure there's something better to watch."

Wanting to be a model patient and please Mick, Zafeera turned her attention to more pleasant films, romantic comedies and thumbed through more positive, uplifting books. Despite all of that, before long, her mind drifted back to the dark moldy storeroom where fists and boots pummeled her body, where twisted, menacing faces glared down at her with extreme hatred, for no reason. And, to the two things that still left her puzzled and intrigued: first, she never thought to scream for help. And the second was the delirious satisfaction she had felt fighting without restraint—scratching, kicking, and biting like a wild woman releasing her own fury, her own rage— wanting to do the same to Salima's husband and to Ghaybaa's.

In the six weeks it took Zafeera's body to heal, she became aware of something inside of her changing. Mick's supportive words and tender caresses had failed to assuage the burning desire she could no longer deny.

One Saturday morning, Mick had gone out to get breakfast for the two of them. He returned to find Zafeera dressed in brown cargo pants, tee shirt and sneakers with her hair pinned up, standing at the window staring out across the Thames. She hadn't set foot outside of the apartment since returning from the hospital.

"I got some great stuff for us from that French place you love. And I made a special trip to get your favorite Turkish coffee." He set the bags on the dining table, took the coffee out first, and walked over to the window and handed it to her. "Why are you dressed like that, again?"

"I'm going back in."

CHAPTER 26

After three weeks without a single word, Zafeera finally returned Mick's calls by asking him to meet her for lunch in the City, the global economic center of the world, complete with its own police force. It seemed a fitting place.

Always elegantly dressed for work, Mick chose one of the best restaurants where he would be surrounded by his colleagues and his competitors. Familiar terrain. Zafeera arrived dressed in gray baggy safari pants, a new denim jacket, with her cap turned backwards like a teen thug.

"Darling," she said after they embraced, and their order was taken, "remember your friend's wedding in Newcastle where we stayed in that hotel near the lake?"

"Ah… yeah. Why?"

"There's farmland ten miles west of that hotel, about 200 beautiful acres, with lakes and hills, all green and lovely." Her eyes lit up as she described it to him. He leaned over.

"Zafeera, why haven't you returned my calls? You could have at least called me at Christmas. My parents kept asking me about you. I felt like a fool because I practically had to lie. What are you doing in that goddamn place? What's all this secretive shit? You know, I was, actually, going to call the police. Look at you, you've got to stop all this craziness."

"I'm not crazy. Listen, I need you to do something very important for me."

"Where were you at Christmas?"

"I need you to buy that land for me." Before he could react, she put her hand on his. "You wanted me to stop being obsessed with things I could not change. You were right. So, I decided to try and change those things."

"Is this about the attack? You were offered counseling, Zafeera, and you refused. And then, you leave home, again—a lovely home, I might add—to live in some impoverished neighborhood, and walk around dressed like a gang banger and doing God knows what. I don't hear from you for weeks, and then you show up expecting me to, just, buy you two hundred acres of land?" He stared at her, exasperated. "You don't think that's being crazy? It's absurd! You don't need two hundred acres of land, Zafeera. Nobody needs two hundred acres of land, for Christ's sakes!" The forcefulness of his tone caused heads to turn. "You've really changed," he continued. "I just don't get you, anymore. Are you having a breakdown?"

"Of course, you don't get me... you're a white man."

"Meaning?"

She stared at Mick with disappointment, and wouldn't answer. Wasn't he supposed to be her soul mate, the one person who could understand her, even when she didn't understand herself? He hadn't even tried to make the effort.

Just as the waiter brought their order, she got up coolly and walked out.

Twelve days had passed when a large envelope was hand delivered to her Brixton address. It was the first. Since she wasn't expecting anything, and hadn't given the address to anyone, she cautiously tore a strip down the side and pulled out the thick document. It was the deed in her name for 200 acres of farmland in the Lake District near Newcastle-Upon-Tyne. A note attached read:

From the white man who loves you. M.

Her eyes watered. Her heart leaped. And her first impulse was to call him immediately, thank him and remind him that she loved him too, and tell him why she wanted the land. Yet, for some reason, she didn't, and she didn't know why. Mick had always been loyal, and he genuinely cared about her. It was something she realized during the summer they had spent in Devon. Stretched out side by side on the beach, he had asked her about the phone call she had received earlier that morning.

"They want to come here to visit."

"Do they know about us?"

"Yes. But they don't know we live together."

"Oh, is that a problem? I mean, your father won't kill you, will he?" He smiled, half-jokingly.

"No," she laughed, and then grew serious. "He'd kill himself."

Mick bolted upright and looked down at her trying to read her intent.

"Does that mean you want me to marry you and make you respectable?"

She sat up too. "Is that a proposal?"

"If you want it to be… yes."

First, she smiled with pleasure, satisfaction, and relief, all at once.

Then her smile faded slowly to contemplation and her eyes lowered.

"Hey, you still with me?" he joked.

She smiled, again. "I don't want to marry now. Maybe someday, but not now."

"What about your father?"

"I am not Ghaybaa."

***

The first ad appeared in an Algerian newspaper noted for its moderate stance. A second ad was taken out in a Palestinian paper. Both read:

PUBLIC NOTICE

> For Women Only! Are you looking for adventure? Ready to leave your ordinary life behind and make a real difference in the world?
> WILA needs you.

Ex-soldiers. Professional body builders. Athletes.
Ex-police officers and victims of rape. (Yes, that's right). Ex-felons okay.
We will train you to be fierce. We will train you to be strong.
We will train you to WIN.
Send letter to P.O. Box 9408, in Marseilles, France.

The Palestinian and Israeli newspapers carried an additional ad:

American, Indian and Japanese women!
WILA needs women technophiles, engineers, and pilots.

The following week, a notice appeared on a public website:

Attention former female CIA operatives, WILA needs you.
WILA needs your expertise, your connections
and your commitment.
The time has come FOR ALL OF US TO UNITE FOR VICTORY.
You know who the enemy is. We will NOT be defeated.
Your identity will be protected at all times.
Contact us now: wila@gmail.com

The ads lit a firestorm of media attention and set off a national security alert in the countries carrying the ads. Who was the enemy? The last thing the world needed was another rogue terrorist cell.

Who could be bold or stupid enough to put something like that on a public site with all the fear surrounding terrorist affiliations? Surely these people realized what would happen, became the debate.

"Who is WILA?" became the most searched topic on all the search engines, with four million hits, but no one came up with anything more than references to the obscure newspaper ads and a post office box in Marseilles. Yet that was all it took. Before long, hundreds of thousands of people all over the world were now reading the ads originally posted in the foreign papers.

Following the media blitz, P.O. Box 9408 began to receive an unprecedented onslaught of mail and international focus. It was almost too much for the small postal station to handle.

Hundreds of letters arrived daily from women and a few men. Many were sent out of sheer curiosity about WILA.

As was expected, the supervisor of that postal region was instructed by both French Intelligence and the local authorities to notify them as soon as the renter of the box came to pick up the mail. Never had his station received such attention. The international press had reporters on the scene every single day hoping to be the first to get a photo of the renter of P.O. Box 9408. Bags of letters were then stacked in the largest postal bins they could find and stored in the back of the station, with more bags added each day. No one came.

Each night, it was reported on all the international TV news networks that the stacks of mail accumulating in a Marseilles post office remained unclaimed. Ten days later, mail was still arriving for box 9408, when a rumor began to spread about it all being a hoax. There was no WILA.

Immediately, the number of letters arriving for P.O. Box 9408 dwindled as rapidly as they had begun. The supervisor of the Marseilles post office depot, at the center of it all, contemplated disposal of the hundreds of thousands of letters sitting in bins at the back.

In addition, not one woman, anywhere, reported receiving a response from their email. So naturally, the media gradually turned their attention elsewhere, and CIA offices and outposts around the world began to relax. Shortly thereafter, the whole thing became nothing more than great comedic fodder for late night American talk show hosts.

Then two interesting things happened: first, an intriguing website appeared and, second, the postal supervisor in Marseilles got a telephone call from a woman claiming to be the renter of box 9408.

Speaking fluent French, she instructed him to forward the mail via cargo ship to a dock in northern England and not to inform the authorities of her call. The renter of the box told him the station was under surveillance by WILA. Payment was wired to him and, for his own safety, he did exactly as she had instructed.

The website, like the newspaper ads, solicited 'women only' and hinted at some agenda involving secret missions. Naturally, millions of women logged on out of curiosity, but had to become members with a legitimate email address to gain access to certain pages.

However, further details about WILA, and what they were up to, continued to remain a mystery.

CHAPTER 27

After reviewing the notes of her intended talk, Dr. Sethi placed her pink index cards on the table in front on her and patiently watched as women filed into the hall and took their seats. This was their third meeting, but the first one held outside of Dr. Sethi's flat.

As Basma had once seen Kensasha do, she tapped the heads of the microphones that the four panelists would use. The sound reverberated a little too much, so she signaled to the sound technician at the side of the room to bring it down some.

She was pleased to have found a meeting room large enough to seat 150 people where a sound person was also provided. She scanned the audience and smiled. Over a hundred women were present, including the presidents from six of the ten women's organizations, who were due to speak. Not a bad start. She saw Amanda Kurtami, from the London branch of Asian Women's Rights Initiative, sitting to the left of Dr. Sethi and Enid Statham, while all the other panelists for the night, sat on the right. All they needed now, besides the approval from the U. N., was a name.

When the lights dimmed, friendly chatter faded into respectful silence. Basma took her seat at the far side of the front row just as Neelam, the first to speak, stood up and put on her glasses. Basma felt her heart pounding. Neelam began speaking, her voice calm and controlled.

"God, power, violence. Ladies! Why would you even *want* to follow a deity that sanctions the oppression, in any way, of one half of humanity—women, by the other half—men? Why do you worship God in fear? When did fear become an attribute? Fear and violence are what men use to obtain power and control. It is, and has always been, a weakness, a defective program– so to speak.

"The fundamentalist version of *all* religions is about nothing but forced sexual oppression under the threat of death—social and/or physical, and certainly spiritual. Violence does not belong on the path of human evolution! Violence and actions motivated by hatred can only destroy. Never *heal*. Never create.

"Ladies," she said, peering over her glasses. "I believe the Power that is of God can only *transform*. Don't you see? God doesn't need or require violence, fear or the separation of His people, Her people or ITs people to obtain obedience or submission—if obedience and submission is what It truly wants of us. Violence is of a very low vibration. As is hate. It's animalistic.

"I believe the Power that is God, Ladies, is within YOU." She smiled, placing her hand on her heart. "It causes you to breathe, to feel both pain and joy. It gifts your body with the ability to be a vessel for new souls to come through and experience this magnificence called Life on Earth. The Power that is God is all encompassing, all-inclusive. IT is fullness and IT is complete. IT needs nothing. IT is *Everything*." She paused to let that sink in.

Removing her glasses, she continued with a firmer tone.

"The Power that is God doesn't need marauders running about with AK-47s, hand grenades or unmanned drones blowing up and laying waste the beautiful bodies that IT created and into which those spineless men cannot breathe life!

"And I believe the Power that is God does *not* require your *obedience*. It requires the expression of your *true Self*. It does not need you to be a watchman of others, but an observer of your Self. Nor does IT need anyone to 'spiritually police' you.

"The submission that all great spiritual teachers, gurus and prophets talk about cannot be ordered. That submission cannot be demanded. It is impossible. That submission, if it's going to happen at all, happens automatically—whenever a human being takes the journey inside of herself and comes face-to-face with that which created all of this. Then, one cannot help but drop to one's knees, so to speak." Her eyes glistened. "For, you see, the Power that is God is the Power of *Profound Love*—palpable love that engulfs you and washes away all your doubts, all your hatreds and all your fears. It is the purest form of Mother Love exalted to the highest level imaginable. It is truly a Love Divine," she said with growing passion. "It seeps into every cell of your being and you, in turn, will feel that love for all life, and for all of your life. Then you will understand what it means to be Human.

"Don't all of you feel this to be true in your hearts? Why then, do we submit to a patriarchal concept of a God that needs fear, intimidation, favoritism or punishment to control our minds and every aspect of our lives and make us feel inadequate, ashamed or filled with sin?

"Ladies, I think it is time you reexamined this male concept of God. Or even better… Ladies, let's create our own idea of God. Write our own Bible. Our own Torah. Our own Bhagavad-Gita. Our own Koran. Why not?" Neelam asked in conclusion.

The silence in the room was palpable. Slowly, the corners of Neelam's mouth curled into a grin. Tiny flecks of light danced in her eyes.

In the front row of the audience, Neelam saw one woman in black hijab, toss her head back and begin to laugh out loud. Then, the woman leaped to her feet and began applauding. A few other women, roused from their deep contemplation, also stood up and began clapping, followed by more and more women. The unexpected monologue left them inspired, motivated—if not overwhelmed.

Still, some women were not so quick to applaud. They felt the speech reeked of heresy, blasphemy or, was it anarchy? Whatever it was, it frightened them.

After a long while, the applause subsided, and the audience took their seats. Neelam felt pleased for receiving such a response. There was also the feeling of gratitude because she really hadn't planned to say any of that. She eased gracefully back into her chair, relieved now of so much of the tension that had led up to the speech. Her stack of pink index cards remained conspicuously untouched.

But, before the next panelist, Amanda Kurtami, rose to her feet, the woman in the front row of the audience who had laughed, stood up again. Neelam noticed that besides the black hijab on her head, the woman also wore an olive green short-sleeved tee shirt stretched tightly over muscular arms. Her shirt was tucked and belted into taupe cargo pants. The look was an arresting blend of submission and physical mite: the hijab and the pumped body.

"I commend your efforts, Dr. Sethi," the woman said sincerely with a heavy French accent. "You have truly captivated all of us with your insight and your earnest commitment to stop the violence toward women who are not fortunate enough to have been born into families that love them or into a world that respects the female. But to think a world forum on 'honor killing'... which is not happening everywhere, by the way. To think a forum... will somehow... put an end to these age-old practices is naïve. The cause is a viral infection... a disease in the soul of men.

"You think lofty words—no matter the sincerity behind them, will reach the malignant ears and heal the calcified hearts of such people—dare I call them people? At best, it will draw the attention of a few journalists, maybe a TV network, which may, perhaps, cause a little embarrassment for some leaders here and there. But to actually believe your words will affect those hardened fundamentalists you mentioned, the ones who influence people throughout the Middle East, or Asia and the North of Africa, the ones who are blinded to a woman's humanity, is worse than naïve—it is utter stupidity!"

Gasps resounded throughout the audience. Neelam's face reddened.

"You have no idea what you are dealing with, do you?" the woman continued. "I respect you and agree with what you said, but the problem is way beyond religion and tradition. Dr. Sethi, you said it yourself: men need power over things. A wise man once wrote: 'No matter how poor a man is, no matter what brutish ways make up his character, he is expected to marry whoever he chooses and do whatever he wants with her. And, any female offspring is seen as both a liability and a bargaining chip.'"

"And yet," replied Neelam, confidently, "real power comes when, instead of dancing to the abstract discordant tune of his parents or community, a man follows the pure dictates of his heart and honors his wife and children by always being there for them, respecting each of them—supporting their hopes and dreams as much as he does his own."

The woman smirked. "Abstract discordant what? The only way to stop these atrocities is for women to be cast in an entirely different light, Dr. Sethi. Before we can even decide to continue to share our lives with men or continue to give birth to their children, we must finally take the one action women have avoided down through the centuries. And the time is now!"

"What on earth are you on about?" Neelam asked, irritated now at how this unknown woman had so skillfully insulted her. The woman turned slightly and reached for her coat on the empty seat next to her. It was a camouflage jacket. She casually slipped it on as she answered.

"For women's total liberation in all areas of their lives, the only viable solution, Dr. Sethi, is not more speeches or a march, or another set of resolutions and legislations from a United Nations ruled by men, but the action WILA alone plans to undertake."

More gasps resounded, as the women in the audience reacted to the name WILA.

"And what is that?" Neelam demanded authoritatively, feigning her knowledge of WILA.

The woman coolly reached into her pocket and pulled out an olive-green baseball cap and placed it securely over her black hijab, thrust her hands into her pockets and replied:

"A battle to the death, Dr. Sethi. A *battle* to the death!"

Her tone sent shivers up and down several spines and, for the second time that evening, the audience was stunned into silence. Dumbfounded, Neelam stared at the woman, fervently searching her mind for a clever, yet sensible, retort. And then, mimicking what Dr. Sethi herself had done earlier, the woman's mouth curled into a grin—but her expression was devoid of warmth. Her cold brown eyes darted around to various women seated within the audience, giving them a signal with her head. Next, the woman in the baseball cap strolled, calmly, up the aisle and left the building.

One by one, all of the women she had signaled stood and began handing out leaflets to the other women seated around them. After that, they simply followed their leader's path up the aisle and out the door, leaving Neelam Sethi and the audience in a rapt awe.

***

Basma was the first to snap back, and read the flyer that had been handed to her.

Who is WILA?
The Women's International Liberation Army.
What do we want?
Our objective is to take out any misogynistic regime that uses violence and intimidation to silence women.
To restore the basic dignity and rights of women to pursue education, gain skills, practice a profession, make a living for themselves and their children, marry and divorce freely, and walk the streets of the world fearlessly, without harassment and without a veil if they choose.
We have no religious, political or national affiliation.
We are of many religions and no religion.
We belong to every nation.
We speak many languages, but have One Voice.
Our battle will have been won only when women fully share social, economic, political AND religious power in their respective nations and cultures.
We invite you to participate in the coming Battle.
Help us achieve our goal by offering any technical and medical skills you may have. Right now, we especially need strong women skilled in explosives, firearms, flying helicopters and operating satellites.
Access to any of these would also be highly appreciated.
We accept donations to our cause in any amount.
To contact us: send an email to wila@WILA.org.

Well, there it was, finally. Evidence that WILA was real, crazy, dangerous, and that they may actually be out to sabotage everything Neelam and her new Women's International Alliance attempted to do.

Enid left her seat next to Neelam, picked up one of the flyers and read it. Handing the paper to Neelam, she waited for her colleague's reaction.

"An army? Satellites? They can't be serious," Neelam responded, incredulous, passing the flyer on to her fellow organizers at the table.

"That woman seemed deadly serious to me," Enid replied, glancing at the empty seat the woman had occupied. "Was she their leader? Imagine if she was... I know lots of photographers would have killed to get a picture of her. It would be worth a small fortune, wouldn't it?"

Amanda Kurtami leaned forward to address Neelam. "Enid is right," she said, looking out into the audience. "I wish at least one of you would have used your cell phone to capture what she said."

"Well, no one knew who she was, did they?" distinguished guest MP, Sabrina Coulter-Todd, commented from the audience.

"And we still don't," Neelam added, levelheadedly.

"She mentioned WILA," pondered Amanda, sounding a bit intrigued.

"That doesn't mean she's their leader or has even met their leader. Do we even know there is one leader?" Coulter-Todd asked.

Enid rested against the table, folded her arms across her chest and stared once more at the empty seat. "I wish someone from the press had been here tonight. Talk about free publicity."

"Ladies, that is not the kind of publicity we need," Neelam countered. "I'm totally against violence and that woman was talking about battles. You heard her. And that flyer talks about explosives! Look, now we have lost our focus. I think we need to adjourn this meeting."

Basma got up reluctantly and watched the panelists gather up their speeches, index cards, laptops, and pens. There was a somber quality in their ritual. The expression she saw on Dr. Sethi's face was indecipherable. She knew Dr. Sethi had counted on this meeting to be the one to really draw in the members and galvanize them into action. Theirs wasn't a task that could be pulled off by a few good women. But one million, acting in concert, could. Maybe the next meeting would bring them closer to that goal.

***

Adrenalin pumping, Amanda Kurtami wasted no time. Immediately after leaving the building, she called her husband. He, in turn, called everyone he knew. And before she pulled out of the parking lot, a text had been forwarded to everyone in her contact list. The rest of the night she sat in front of her webcam describing what had happened— down to what the 'woman' looked like and posted it on the web, then she typed up a long email and sent it to the 100,000 women in her organization.

MP Sabrina Coulter-Todd's cool exterior belied the thrill she had putting a call to the Guardian newspaper informing them of the incident before she could get her coat on. She continued to feel this persistent excitement the following morning, while sitting amongst fellow Members of Parliament, of being at the forefront of something important, having attended Dr. Sethi's meeting.

Some might have thought it ironic if they knew that she had agreed to attend only because her barrister, Terrance Statham, pressured her into lending her support to his wife, Enid.

Basma had become too absorbed in Dr. Sethi's radical speech and the seeds it planted in her own consciousness, that most of what the woman in the audience had said escaped her. She sat on the side of her bed for the remainder of the evening, unable to put her mind to rest.

For Neelam, ironically, it was the first time since the massacre that she doubted herself, her cause, and the whole concept behind a world forum: where civilized human beings listened to other human beings proclaim publicly their humanity and right to live. Will the world ever change?

She quietly closed the door to her bedroom and sunk down into her bed. Only hours earlier, her body had felt rejuvenated, alive, buoyant with hope, and possibility. A Member of Parliament had called to say her schedule had opened and she would be attending. Then, Amanda Kurtami, of AWRI, agreed to give a short speech at the meeting. It had all fallen into place. And now…

Exhausted and dismayed, she turned off the lamp. All the mind's incessant questions, examinations, and reviews came to a sluggish halt as she tried to sleep—all except one:

Who was that woman?

***

Whether it was her intention or not, Zafeera's appearance at the third meeting of Neelam Sethi's forum committee spurred an even greater media storm of speculation than any of WILA's ads ever did. That was because of two factors: first, a Member of Parliament had been present and, second, she uttered the words, "battle to the death." Everyone wanted to weigh in on what that meant. Blogs and chat rooms all over the Internet were abuzz with: 'Were the words literally or figuratively expressed?' 'How do we know if that woman was the same person who ran the ads?' 'Should we give this story any credence at all?'

MP Coulter-Todd was called by the Associated Press and asked whether she thought the Security Services (MI5 & MI6) should be on alert. In all of the years that she had been a Member of Parliament, she had been ineffectual in being heard when it came to matters that the majority of her colleagues supported and she opposed. On record, she was known to be the one to give in to popular sentiment. She played it safe but flaunted the prestige of the job. Consequently, it was understandable why she was both flattered and hesitant in providing her views to the AP.

However, given the anti-government protests triggered by the global financial crisis brought on by the pandemic, the persistent terrorist attacks still plaguing the world, and that woman's last words: "a battle to the death," Sabrina Coulter-Todd finally went out on a limb, for the first time in her life, and said,

"Yes, I believe all the National Security Services should be on alert."

Zafeera caught a glimpse of a newspaper headline over the shoulder of a passenger on a crowded southbound train, the following afternoon, and read some of what was being said about the incident. She was unfazed. Everything she did, as far as she was concerned, benefited WILA and the media's views or involvement no longer interested her. Dr. Sethi's speech touched Zafeera, no doubt. She thought about it most of the night. Her theory about God and love may be true, but has it stopped people from doing horrible things? No. Did her speech contain practical, concrete solutions? No. How can you fight evil with lofty ideals?

Basma spent the day fielding calls from news organizations that only wanted Dr. Sethi's account of what happened concerning that woman.

Neelam, herself, was peeved not only at how that woman's appearance had disrupted such an important meeting, it completely eclipsed the whole concept and purpose of the forum committee in the media.

When one of the reporters couldn't get Neelam on the phone, he asked Basma if she were present at the meeting and to describe the 'mysterious' woman. Seeing nothing wrong with that, at first, Basma did her best to give them what they asked for. When asked for her name, she wavered, wondering if someone would come to take her picture like they were always doing to Dr. Sethi.

"I am only an assistant," she informed the reporter on the phone.

"Yes, madam, but I need a name before I can use the story. I won't publish your name, but we do need to have the name of our source in our own records." Her throat tightened.

"Do you need my picture too?" she inquired, with apprehension.

"No, madam. Your name is sufficient."

"My name is Aisha Langois."

***

Green frogs perched on the rim of a blue pond. A mother and father wearing broad smiles held the hands of their two children, a boy and a girl, in front of an orange house with a red chimney. Tufts of green grass populated the bucolic setting. Thick yellow spikes, like inverted sugar cones, extended from the circumference of a yellow disc suspended high above the red chimney. Intermittent patches of cobalt blue looked as if the eight-year-old artist had added it as an afterthought. Colorful pushpins secured the drawing to the wall, along with twelve similar ones around the classroom. Behind the teacher's desk, Zafeera let her eyes focus on the drawing and, for a moment, the innocence and simplicity of childhood overtook her.

Like the convention hall in a Paris hotel donated to WILA the previous week, Zafeera now had the use of a schoolroom in South London on weekends, where she could interview more applicants and decide whom to recruit.

At the Paris hall, in response to ads for medical personnel, IT specialists, and engineers, about eighty women, mostly Turkish, Iranian, Korean and German, dressed in casual business attire, had shown up. It was assumed that at least six of them were probably there only to spy on the proceedings and report back to some authority, but Zafeera had no way of knowing if their superiors were other women's organizations or branches of foreign governments.

For the Paris group, Zafeera went over the packet of documents WILA sent out to each applicant, answered their questions, and had each of them explain why they wanted to be involved. Now, she needed a different type of woman, and the women walking into this schoolroom definitely fit the part: bomber jackets, studded belts, construction boots, muscular tattooed arms and a few facial scars. She expected ex-military, former wrestlers, big biker women, and truck drivers to be tough looking, but these women were hardcore. Some looked as though they only dined on medium-rare steak, and whisky.

Their ages ranged from mid-thirties to late forties. Each appeared in excellent physical condition. If chosen, these women would be the ones living on The Land. The ones to be prepared for combat. The real Women's International Liberation Army.

The idea of a women's army came to Zafeera one sleepless night, just days after her return to the rented bedsit. She envisioned a secluded place, much like a high-tech health retreat, where soldiers could be trained in mixed martial arts, advanced fitness, along with military strategies and how to use the latest weapons.

Zafeera was taking out a stack of applications from her briefcase when three more women walked in and found seats. She glanced up. Two she recognized from their photos: Inez Munoz and Vellanova Sanchez. They had fought as teens with the guerrillas in El Salvador and were experienced with explosives. The third one, tall, with dark mocha skin, smirked at the child's chair and opted for the desktop, instead. Her purple kinky hair, styled in a Mohawk, faded jeans with the knees cut out, an excessive amount of Native American silver and turquoise jewelry around her neck, wrists and fingers, caught everyone's attention. They watched, enthralled, as she flamboyantly unwrapped the lilac scarf from around her neck and unzipped her black studded leather jacket. She propped her feet up on the desk in front, rested her forearms on her knees and proceeded to study Zafeera as if she had x-ray eyes.

Unperturbed, Zafeera continued sorting through the applications, placing the ones with photos attached to the right and those without to the left. This process would go differently than in Paris. She would not ask them to explain why they wanted to fight. When she had everything laid out the way she wanted, she got up from behind the desk. Wearing her now customary uniform of camouflage pants and cap with brim to the back, she positioned herself near the center of the group, two feet from the Mohawk woman. Securing her hands, characteristically, into her pockets, she began.

"I appreciate all of you taking the time to be here. I know there are those of you who have flown in from the United States, Central America and Israel. I apologize for the uncomfortable seating, but we are fortunate to have use of this primary school during the winter break. It's been a lengthy process for you, I know. A lot of forms to fill out, writing about your experiences as women. Some of you sent in videos, which was very helpful.

"Before reviewing the documents we sent, and before answering any of your questions, I want to tell you what qualities are most important in becoming a part of WILA."

As if rehearsed, all the women sat straight up in their chairs. The Mohawk woman cocked her neck forward.

Like Neelam Sethi, Zafeera had spent a lot of time mulling over what she would say, particularly to these tough no-nonsense women—women with whom she would normally cross paths. Woman who had life experiences she did not share.

"What WILA requires most from you, besides your passion and willingness to sacrifice your life, is your total respect and loyalty to each other." Their eyes withdrew from her, briefly, to settle on who-ever was sitting nearby.

"I hope none of you are here for your country, your race, or your religion," Zafeera continued, "because what we fight for is beyond all that. Our battle originated long before the idea of a country or a race. Our conflict began before ways of worshipping God were given a name. You must be here only for yourself as a woman.

"All of our missions will be to assist and rescue women. Some of those women will be Muslim, Buddhist, Christian, some Jewish or Hindu. There will be atheists among them, African and Chinese, Arab, Persian. Some won't be very bright, some illiterate, and some will be college professors, intellectuals and artists and some will have dark skin. But all will be women, so you must respect all of them as you do yourself. If you cannot do that, if your ties to your race or your religion are stronger than your ties to your womanhood, you should leave now. WILA is not for you."

Taking her hands out of her pockets and folding them across her chest, she paused to give each woman a chance to digest what she had just said—to examine their own feelings and make a choice. The last thing she needed was an Israeli woman hesitating in a battle to save an Iranian woman. Or an American subconsciously sabotaging efforts to help a Pakistani or North Korean woman. That's not what WILA was about.

No one got up to leave. But, reading their postures, she noticed over half of them leaned back in their chairs. Those who did not sit back, she decided, weren't sure where their loyalties lay. She made a mental note to reject all of them.

Having no chair to lean back on, the Mohawk woman began to rock back and forth and Zafeera had no way of determining what that meant. She turned to the desk and looked through the photos, selecting the women who now leaned back in their chairs and placed their applications in a new pile, creating a third pile. The women watched closely when Zafeera picked up the stack of applications without photos and began calling out the names on the form. As each woman answered to her name, Zafeera placed their form on the newly created pile or returned it to the bottom of the photo-less pile.

"How do you feel about ex-cons?" The woman with the purple Mohawk asked testily before her name was called.

"Depends what for," Zafeera replied.

"Armed robbery. Assault."

Everyone's attention turned once again to the Mohawk woman, who seemed to be enjoying herself.

"Have you ever killed or injured anyone?" Zafeera inquired with a business-like tone.

"I did some serious injury to my boyfriend once." She grinned and got a few laughs.

Zafeera nodded, then fixed her gaze on Mohawk woman. "During the training, we will be sharing the same living quarters. I am sure everyone here wants to do that with people they can trust."

"Hey, I don't steal from folks, ya know?" Mohawk woman said, glancing around at everyone.

"What kind of place did you rob?"

"Just a small bank and a liquor store. That's all. No people."

"But a person owned that store and people kept their money in that bank," replied Zafeera matter-of-factly. Looking around self-consciously, Mohawk woman replied,

"Yeah, but it's insured. The liquor store was insured too."

Zafeera folded her arms again and went back behind the desk.

"How many of you would feel totally comfortable leaving your possessions around..." She paused and addressed the woman with the purple Mohawk. "What is your name?"

"Angela," the woman said, proudly. "Angela Johnson. I feel I was named after the great black revolutionary, Angela Davis." She grinned.

"...around Angela?" Zafeera continued to the rest of the women. No hands went up. Angela's head dropped to her chest. She was visibly hurt.

Suddenly, with a grunt, she leaped off the desk, and stormed towards the back door, slinging and shoving aside every empty desk or chair in her path like a tornado. In the doorway, she paused, her voice shaking.

"I scraped up every penny I had to come here. Every fucking penny, and I did not steal one cent. I don't steal from people!"

A minute later, a loud bang echoed through the halls as the front door of the school slammed shut. The remaining applicants began mumbling to themselves and each other, continuing the commotion.

This was something entirely unexpected and out of order. How should she handle it? On the forms, there had been several questions about the law, committing crimes and being arrested. On her enlistment form, Angela had left all of them blank.

Ignoring what had occurred, Zaferra waited patiently for the women to settle back down so that she could let them know what they were in for when they arrived at The Land.

Fifteen kilometers from the nearest hamlet, situated amongst lush rolling hills and meadows blanketed in heather, bordering a small forest containing dozens of streams, The Land was a feminine version of an army base: nine prefabricated, single-story buildings with five of them designated as semi-private barracks. Each soldier would have their bed and night table, closet and chest of drawers separated from their platoon mates by a decorative partition. A provisional cafeteria, with shades on the windows and round wood dining tables, a coffee shop, clinic and Laundromat had already been set up, thanks to the enormous financial contributions secured through the website. Donated books for the library, however, were still in boxes, as well as all the brand-new computers and flat screen TVs donated for the computer and media rooms. In time, Zafeera hoped The Land would become more self-sufficient by producing its own fruits and vegetables.

Once she regained their attention, she calmly continued, "I've received a profuse number of suggestions in ways to train a women's army. Since we are battling an ideology, as well as men, we must not become what we are fighting against. Many visionary women have offered suggestions on how we can differ our strategies and use powers innate to us as women. All of these suggestions seem valid enough, but they take time—years, in fact—and the world needs us now.

"The preparations we have settled on include familiar techniques like Karate, Chi Kung, Tae Kwon Do, and weight training. As women, we must strengthen our upper body to be able to carry heavy artillery.

"One of you has suggested a Native American ritual for spiritual cleansing and fortifying called Sweat Lodge. I did do some research on it and I believe it would be very helpful for all of us. But we must have an experienced Native American to guide us—someone who has earned the responsibility of leading such a ceremony. It can be dangerous I am told, so I sent out emails for someone to come and host it. I have not yet received a reply.

"Other techniques you will be experiencing are sensory deprivation and transcendental meditation. Both are designed to heighten your consciousness and awaken psychic powers."

This part brought a chilly stare from everyone.

"Why do we need psychic powers to fight a buncha guys?" asked a muscular American in her forties with a craggy face and stringy, shoulder length blond hair whom Zafeera knew to be a former wrestler named Cat Murphy.

"Because no matter how much we build up our muscle mass and no matter what type of guns we carry, a lot of the men we will face are much bigger, stronger and more vicious than we are. They have had years of combat training. They sleep with their weapons and probably all of them have been in some type of major conflict before.

"We have to utilize a force superior to their physical strength. You have seen Tae Kwon Do masters, and students of Aikido and Chi-Kung fling people twice their size across a room, haven't you? A master sensei can stop his opponent without even touching him. I want you to have this ability."

"Stuff like that takes years to learn as well," Cat Murphy called out, cynically.

"It used to," Zafeera responded with a patient understanding tone. "But not anymore. Since the intelligence branch of many governments are always searching for more powerful, more effective methods for their special forces, some have assembled top instructors to devise more efficient ways to teach using sound. One of our instructors, in fact, worked for the KGB. Russia was highly invested in researching the powers of the mind."

"Well, it looks like that didn't do them much good," Inez, the El Salvadorian, added with a smirk.

"You damn right," Cat said leaning over and extending her palm to Inez. Inez slapped it and they both snickered. An Israeli looking woman slumped down in her chair and began fiddling with the cuff of her weathered brown bomber jacket. Another woman became transfixed by the children's artwork on the wall.

Zafeera's first instinct was to be defensive. She had imagined that they would be excited about what was being offered. WILA intended to have an elite army trained in the most sophisticated methods of self-defense in the shortest amount of time. Perhaps, she had assumed too much. After all, these women had no idea exactly what they were getting into. They certainly didn't know who <u>she</u> was. Besides each other, she was the one person they most needed to trust—to believe in.

Unable to loosen up, however, Zafeera continued. "Another important reason that I want you to have these skills is because, in spite of what has been said all over the TV and the Web, and even what the WILA website implies, we do not want to actually kill anyone." The women stared back at her with surprise and dismay.

"Whoever heard of an army that doesn't want to kill anyone?" Vellanova exclaimed, disappointedly. "That's what an army is. That's what soldiers do, man. We fight and kill people."

"Yeah, that's right!" Inez called out, nodding her head. Several other women nodded in support.

"That is what 'male' warfare is all about," Zafeera clarified with a forceful tone. She began gesturing with her hands. "WILA strives to set a new model, a new precedence in warfare." Cat Murphy frowned and looked away. "Okay, I know you are all probably here to get out your aggression against men. But, if you read everything carefully in your packets, especially WILA's mission statement, you will have realized this is about justice and human rights. We are not going to attack a unit of soldiers to kill them. What purpose would that serve? That's not our goal. Yes, you are asked to sacrifice your life, if necessary, and yes, you may have to kill in self-defense, if there is no other choice. But you will have many different weapons in your arsenal.

"I think as you go through the training that we have designed for you, new ways of seeing will open up for you. I see there are twenty-eight here today. In total, we want to start with fifty.

"Next week, I will have another interview session and continue until we have fifty women. If you are chosen, you will receive further instructions for what to bring, and the time and place for pick up."

After answering a few questions, Zafeera thanked them for coming and mentioned that in the years to come WILA would need more and more recruits, so those who are not chosen this time around may still be a part of the combat branch of WILA in the future.

Overall, it had gone pretty well, Zafeera decided, as she packed up the women's applications to leave. When she reached for Angela Johnson's application amongst the rejects, the image of her purple Mohawk filled Zafeera's mind along with the distress on Angela's face as she bolted from the classroom.

Zafeera sat back down and began to read. There, on the page, beyond the hardened façade was a woman's gripping story of abandonment and abuse—of strength, determination and what the Americans called balls.

Her beginning was not atypical for an African American. She never knew her father. Her teenage mother had little time for a needy, sobbing infant, so she put Angela in a dumpster not far from the city housing complex where she lived. When no one had come forward to claim the baby, Angela was turned over to the Child Protection Agency. Over the years, Angela lived in eight different foster homes before the sexual predator son of one of her foster parents came into her bedroom one time too many. She stabbed him in the leg, and took off with nothing to live on the streets of Chicago.

During those years she, along with other runaways, discovered all the churches that provided food and clothing for the homeless and hung out close by.

She wrote that: "All of the runaways, especially us girls, were solicited day and night by pimps and johns alike. They didn't care that some of us, like me, was only fourteen. We found packets of crack and heroin mysteriously appearing in our pockets or backpacks daily. Some of the kids thought they had died and gone to heaven, but after a few months on crack, they looked like hell. Before long, they were selling for a local dealer."

Strong enough to resist the drugs and the selling of her body, she succumbed to the charms of a 'curly-haired-sweet-talking' 22-year-old thief. With him, she escaped the desperation of Chicago's south side, only to land in the squalor that was the South Bronx in '86. Under his tutelage, Angela Johnson learned the art of persuasion, commonly known on the streets as: hustling. He used her in all kinds of schemes to separate people from their money. But she, herself, never actually took anything from anyone.

Then came the fateful day her boyfriend wanted to hit the 'big time'. He wanted 'real' money, not nickels and dimes. The liquor store was the test run.

Because of her age, Angela's job was to just walk in and start picking up bottles of liquor to distract the owner away from the cash register. Before he realized what was happening, her boyfriend had leaped over the counter, opened it and had a wad of bills in his hand. They laughed for days after.

Her boyfriend was so revved up by the robbery, he wanted another, bigger fix. "Why don't we hit a bank? We'll be set for life."

Sentenced to ten years, the first two in a juvenile facility, and then in a State Penitentiary, Angela's real nightmare began. In prison, she had to literally fight for her life. Being slashed by rejected admirers motivated her to take up kickboxing, and she became good enough to win a few of the matches held at the prison for recreation. Her newfound self-esteem led to wanting a better life. She enrolled in a GED program—to get a general equivalency diploma—for inmates and pursued a career in fitness, but had problems getting hired anywhere when she got out because of her prison record.

"I hooked up with some guys at a club and started to DJ private parties and weddings. Hustled my way onto a few music video sets and got paid to assist with the sound. Now I work with a production company and I still DJ for private parties.

"I stay fit by keeping up with my kickboxing and it's been real cool. And I feel blessed to have a chance to go further and belong to something like WILA that would give me a bigger purpose in life than just my own survival. Thank you. Signed: Angela Johnson."

Zafeera laid the paper down and drummed her fingers on the desk. Her eyes wandered up to the drawing on the wall, again. She focused on the hands of the children enclosed securely in the hands of the parents: a mother and a loving father. All smiling, while a frog croaked, a babbling stream flowed to the front door of a home and overhead a brilliant sun shined. Mohawk Woman's application was transferred to the accepted pile.

The rawness of the wind had chapped Zafeera's lips by the time she reached the Underground at Chapel Hill. Now, the two other things that had to be sorted out were finding a private, secluded location to meet and interview the two women respondents who claimed to be former CIA and Secret Service employees, respectively, and whether she should have dinner with Mick on Valentine's day.

CHAPTER 28

T oday, she would tell him everything. Whatever happened afterwards was entirely up to him. She wondered if he'd show. Brixton certainly wasn't his part of town. It was too real, maybe, too reflective of the multiculturalism into which every cosmopolitan city had evolved. Or maybe he just felt uncomfortable rubbing shoulders with people whose yearly income was only a fraction of his bonuses. Anyway, the Cozy Bear was her restaurant of choice. Maybe she was being unfair to him, insensitive. After all, he came through for her by buying The Land without asking any questions.

On her second cup of coffee, she signaled the waiter and asked the time, then rechecked her cell phone. He was fifteen minutes late. She added another teaspoon of sugar and stirred while glancing at the door.

Customers were already lined up outside for tables. Inside, the service people carried piping hot plates piled high to every table but hers.

Well, whether he showed or not, there was no turning back for her now. Rather than weakening support for WILA, her "battle to the death" statement—quoted repeatedly in every newspaper, blog and TV discussion about WILA—had caused a surge in volunteers. The WILA network was expanding in leaps and bounds with minimal effort from Zafeera, and little opposition so far. Obviously, it was an idea whose time had come. How many other women had had the same thoughts? Based on the kind of respondents WILA received, quite a lot.

Two ex-pilots sent their resumés and an African American female retiree from NASA offered herself as an expert and consultant in Radar and Satellite technology.

There was also a surge in donations from wives of very wealthy businessmen from the Middle East and Southeast Asia. Women who didn't have access to their husbands' fortune wound up selling their expensive jewelry and sending the money to the private bank accounts set up for WILA in Switzerland and the Cayman Islands. Four different attorneys had suggested the idea of having the accounts in these specific countries, mainly for the privacy and the neutrality they offered. Zafeera hadn't even considered beforehand how she would handle the funding. She was deeply moved by all the support, but maintained an even keel because the task ahead was daunting.

In days, the first group of women recruits would be arriving at the pick-up point in north London and climbing aboard a bus to the land. It would be their basecamp for the duration of their contract. The majority had signed on for three years.

Where was he? Was this his way of getting back at her for disappearing at Christmas? How childish! She checked her phone to make sure the battery hadn't died. It was fine. No text message, either. Twenty minutes late.

Her waiter, a cherub-faced college kid, sporting spiky blue hair with dark roots and wearing black nail polish, glanced over each time he brought an order to another table. Outside the building, the line grew as it usually did that time of day.

Her coffee cup was empty. If she ordered another one, she'd be up all night. Herbal tea wasn't her thing. She drank a little of the now lukewarm water hoping that would suffice.

Both ends of the Cozy Bear café had large flat-screened TVs, but her chair was positioned so that the monitors were behind her—so she moved it to one side to watch while she waited.

The closest monitor was airing a music video channel. As she tuned into the beat, her head started to bob, and her fingers began to tap the table in rhythm. It helped to loosen her up and brought her focus back into her body and her present surroundings. Her worries about taking on the enormous responsibility of leading an international army, advised by so many high-powered career women, on an audacious and aggressive mission to restructure the power of women on earth, had kept her up at night. Now they began to subside. Thoughts of "how many WILA soldiers would die?" turned into "how many women can we save?" Her concern about the pain she had caused Mick also subsided because tonight he would understand what she had been creating.

Another artist's video came on and she watched a new female band hop and leap across the screen.

"Oh Zafeera, I am so happy. I was talking to my teacher and she said there are music schools where I can learn the guitar. Maybe I can make a CD and be on the television. I'm going to be famous, Zafeera. Everyone will come and see me. How do you make a CD?"

Light beams flickered from Ghaybaa's eyes as she shifted from Darja—the Algerian Arabic—to French. They had just crossed one of the busiest boulevards in Paris dodging cars, as they loved to do. Not looking where she was going, Ghaybaa nearly tripped up on the sidewalk from excitement.

The sun was bright that day, and Ghaybaa's book bag was sliding down her arm. Zafeera caught it before it hit the ground and pulled her sister's arm back through the straps and fastened the belt around her waist.

Having already completed her Terminate—the final year of secondary education in France—and having passed the test, Zafeera wanted to spend as much time with her sister as she could, before leaving for university. But Ghaybaa was too absorbed in the prospects of becoming a recording artist to discuss anything else.

A few times a week before Ghaybaa's classes recessed for the summer, Zafeera made a point to meet her after school so they could walk home together like they had done years before. It was a time when Ghaybaa was full of expectation for the future. Fourteen then, she was convinced she'd be able to reach goals far beyond any woman in their family had ever imagined. Already she had dreams none of her Algerian ancestors ever had. That was what bothered Zafeera most; they were just dreams—fantasies. Of course, they were all possible for a French girl, a white girl—but not for an Algerian girl.

"How will you go to music school?" Zafeera finally asked, pulling her little sister back to reality, as they walked.

"I will talk with Abbun—père. You can too. Yes?"

"I do not think our father will pay for that, Ghaybaa. I do not think he will let you go."

"I will tell him I must go, and he will have to let me go. I want to make music, Zafeera. It is my life!" Pulling her close, Zafeera rested her chin on top of Ghaybaa's head.

"If music is your life, Ghaybaa, then you have to go for it. I will talk to father as well." However, she never took the opportunity to talk with their father.

Mick eased around the people at the door and entered the long dimly lit cavernous room with rock-like walls, tables made of recycled concrete and all of it balanced by bamboo wood floors. An eclectic mix of upholstered chairs and sofas gave the place a homey feel. The kinetic atmosphere was the result of the median age being twenty-eight—give or take a few years. At thirty-nine, Mick had to be the oldest customer—and the only one overdressed. However, unlike the clientele in the West End establishment he had picked to meet Zafeera, no one in the Cozy Bear Café looked twice at his King's Road cashmere overcoat and black Italian designed suit.

When he stopped to look for a host or hostess, the spikey-haired waiter waved to get his attention. Once Mick saw him, the waiter pointed to Zafeera whose back was now turned away from the door. Mick recognized her green cap and nodded to the waiter and then lifting his briefcase toward his chest, he weaved his way through the narrow spaces between tables.

Sitting almost motionless, Zafeera's eyes seemed to penetrate the glass she was holding, unaware of his approach. He dropped the case beside her chair, leaned over and kissed her on the cheek whispering: "Happy Valentine's Day."

She smiled and breathed a sigh of relief before looking up at him.

"I am so sorry, darling," he began while taking off his coat. He glanced around for someplace to hang it up and realized that everyone had their coats on the back of their chairs or folded next to them if they were on one of the sofas. Frowning, he carefully draped his coat over the back his chair and sat down.

"I know this is inexcusable, but one of my overseas clients is having a serious financial crisis and wouldn't let me off the conference call. When it was over, I just grabbed my coat and rushed to get a cab. I figured I'd call you from the cab. But, as soon as I found one, his partner called, and I was literally talking to him all the way here."

Everything he said sounded completely excusable except the 'darling' thing. He had never called her 'darling' before. There was something insincere about that word.

"You're here and that's what counts." She handed him one of the menus. "Let's make the waiter happy and order quickly." Using light from the candle to scan the menu, he frowned again.

"Why did you want to meet here? We could've had a candlelit dinner at home. I could have prepared something or ordered something for us."

"The food here is very good. It's one of my favorite spots. I wanted to share it with you. And I wanted to talk about some important things and," she added, with a hint of a smile. "I know you won't cause a scene in a public place."

"Cause a scene? Why do you think I would do that?" He paused for her to reply. Then: "Wait. Are you breaking up with me on Valentine's Day?"

The waiter appeared. "Are you ready to order?"

Zafeera told him they needed a few more minutes and then suggested a few of her favorite dishes to Mick. Totally distracted now by the suspense her remark generated, he just threw up his hands and told her to order for them both.

When the waiter returned, Mick added a bottle of wine for the occasion, then leaned in and put his hand on top of hers.

"You don't seem as intense tonight as you did the last time I saw you, so whatever you have to tell me can't be that bad."

She decided it was best to hold off saying another word about it until they finished eating.

The warmth of his hand on hers was comforting, but his blue-gray eyes reflected a glimmer of fear that triggered a surge of empathy inside her and a reluctance to do what she needed to do.

"I know I have been selfish. I know I have done many things that look crazy to you. I want to explain myself tonight and to let you know what the land is for and what my plans are." She spoke slowly and deliberately. "I am not trying to break up with you because you have done something wrong—you have not. You have been wonderful. Really. No man would have put up with his girlfriend spending most of her time in a dreary room on the other side of the city without some kind of ongoing communication. I left my job and then asked you to spend nearly a million pounds on property you don't want or need. And you did it... for me... for my mission."

"What mission?"

The waiter brought the wine and two wine glasses and set them on the table. Mick caught a glimpse of the black polish on the waiter's fingernails and then stared at Zafeera as if the polish underscored her bizarre behavior.

"Open the wine," she coaxed, gesturing at the bottle. "I need some, too."

Mick pulled out the loosened cork and poured the burgundy liquid into her glass as she watched.

"What mission?" he repeated. Her lips parted. Should she tell him now? Blurt it all out? Get it over with? The appetizers came just in time.

"Let's eat first," she suggested.

Two empty wine bottles later, Mick paid the check and they left. Light-headed, he appeared relieved once they were outside in the brisk air. He immediately searched up and down the street for a taxi as they strolled. Zafeera put her arm through his.

"We don't need a taxi right now. My place is a few blocks from here. I thought..." The dismissiveness in his expression and his continued search for a cab provoked her to say: "Maybe we should end it right now. If you can't even come up to my flat, if you can't even stand to be in the neighborhood that you know I have been staying in, then I do not see any reason to share..."

"I'm sorry. I thought we would go back home and..."

"No, you could not have thought that." Her voice was firm, detached.

He lowered his head sheepishly, and said, "Lead the way."

***

A different group of boys were loitering in front of the entrance when they arrived. This time, Mick, not Zafeera, was the target of their curiosity. He pretended not to see them by fumbling in his coat pocket just as he passed them. His eyes widened at the graffiti-laden murals in the hallway. He held his nose, but the stale pungent aroma of curry still made him gag.

When they were right outside the door, Zafeera took out her key to open it and then she paused and turned to reassure herself that Mick was truly there. He was really standing behind her, ready to walk into her… command center? Secret haven? Padded cell? No one had ever crossed that doorsill but her… until now.

She stepped in first, moved to the side and then beckoned him to enter. As soon as he was in all the way, she closed the door and they stood in the dark for a moment. She flipped the switch and the room materialized instantly before them.

"What the…?"

He couldn't finish. Every surface was covered with stacks of paper and books. Makeshift file organizers, boxes and shopping bags of mail crowded every corner and lined every wall. On the wall nearest the kitchen table was a white jumbo writing board. Zafeera had used black, red and blue markers to draw diagrams and write out lists of names, items and countries. Some things were circled. Questions were noted with an asterisk. On the wall above the futon couch, she had taped a large map of the world with pushpins marking certain areas and countries. He saw her laptop flipped open on the kitchen table. The only window in the room was facing a brick wall. She hadn't bothered to hang curtains.

Zafeera saw the stunned look on his face and took his briefcase from him, set it down by the side of the entrance, reached for his hand and led him over to the futon, like a child There was only a small clear patch.

"Sit here." Completely flabbergasted, he sat down obediently, expecting something to crawl out and bite him.

Taking off her cap and unbuttoning her jacket, she began. "Mick, do you remember the heavily publicized news story about P.O. Box 9408?"

He barely heard her he was so shocked at the condition of the place. She read his face, the eyes, the expression, all said, you're out of your mind, completely bonkers, I've lost you.

She removed a pile of letters and folders from one of the chairs to the floor, and then pulled the chair close to the futon and sat facing him. She reached out for his hand, squeezed it and tried again with more force.

"Mick! I need you to listen to me."

His eyes, opened wider than normal, finally met hers. "What did you do to your hair?" he asked, astonished.

"Listen to me! Remember that story on the news about P.O. Box 9408 in Marseilles and the enormous volume of mail arriving in response to an ad?"

He nodded slowly while staring at her hair.

"And do you remember all the fuss about wanting to find out who rented the box and now the latest obsession over WILA and a mysterious woman that came to Dr. Neelam Sethi's forum meeting?"

"Yes, yes. Of course, I remember—the media won't let us forget it."

She smiled, then just came right out and said, "I am the woman they are looking for. I am the founder of WILA."

If he was shocked at the condition of the room and the color of her hair, her claim of being at the center of one of the most publicized news stories in recent history was absolutely, downright stupefying. He couldn't get his head around what she was saying.

"I am collaborating and consulting with thousands of women right now all over the world," she informed him, eagerly. "And, on Friday, I will take fifty women soldiers to the land that you bought me. They will be trained for combat by top mixed martial arts instructors who will make their bodies their most deadly weapon: hands, legs, feet, head, and psychic abilities." She paused to give him a chance to speak.

"Is this a joke?"

"No, Mick. This is very real. I told you I would stop worrying about what I could not change. I have created what I believe will make a change: an army of women soldiers, like mercenaries, but we will only go into a place where the women are abused and in danger, and the legal system for them is corrupt, or controlled by fundamentalists or nonexistent. We have already been contacted by hundreds of women begging for our help. Violence towards women is increasing and we are determined to stop it."

"You really are insane. You can't just walk into a country and start shooting people because you don't like the way they treat women. What kind of laws are you following?"

"WILA makes its own laws. Laws that are partial to women not men."

"I see," he said, disappointed. He pulled his hand away from hers, opened his coat and slipped out of it. He went over to the heap of boxes and scooped up a handful of letters. All were addressed to P.O. Box 9408. It was true. Everything she was telling him was true. Letters were postmarked from all over the world. But most of them seemed to be from India, Middle Eastern and Central American countries.

"First of all, I still don't see how you can possibly do what you said. And, even if you do get in and start shooting up the place—then what? Say you managed to survive. You can't stay there.

"What happens after? Are you going to have a massive airlift? Or overthrow governments and kill off the religious dictators? Once you leave, Zafeera, everything will revert right back to the status quo. It's happened before. You're trying to change something that has been this way for thousands of years—and you want to use violence? How original." He tossed the letters carelessly back into the box, but his sarcasm didn't deter her.

"Women in military jobs have contacted me. WILA is a network. My closest advisors are former CIA and MI5. We have technicians, a medical team."

"Zafeera! Listen to yourself! This is madness! Do you really think intelligence agencies and security forces are going to just sit back and let you play Rambo? You've watched too many Hollywood movies. Your ads just attracted all the crazies out there. I don't care if they really are from the CIA or MI5, they're still loony to want to be a part of... whatever this is. You can't trust these people.

"I remember those films you watched. I know there's a lot of horrible shit out there, but there's no war on women! And even if there was, what makes you think you—of all people—can lead a fucking army? You're not a fucking soldier, Zafeera, you're a journalist for... an inconsequential business magazine!" he shouted, reproachfully.

Sound gave his words mass and density. The repressed anger from all the months she had ignored his calls turned his words into weapons that pricked, slashed and, finally, crushed her. Salty tears burned her eyes. She clenched her teeth, but couldn't stop a few tears from spilling down her cheeks.

As if suddenly becoming aware of the gravity of what he had said, Mick asked, "Where's the loo?"

CHAPTER 29

Neelam had just sent an email response to a woman named Claudia Velasquez who was heading a campaign to bring global awareness about Guatemala—a country of only fifteen million—where thousands of young women were being raped and murdered every year.

Claudia had sent Neelam a manila envelope containing her letter and several newspaper clippings and very disturbing photographs. In her letter, Claudia wrote:

"Each day they find the bodies of at least two women who have always been raped, first. Quite often, the victims suffered extreme torture before they died. Many of the bodies have been mutilated—cut up and heads cut off. None of the murders have been investigated. No one arrested."

Her letter stated that police, lawyers, and even the judges were either too corrupt to do anything, or, in most cases, too afraid to do anything—lest they or a member of their family became a target.

She said that her own daughter, Mema, had become one of the victims. Mema's body was found dumped near a shallow stream. Her throat had been cut and she had been raped. Witnesses said that they had seen a man pull her into a car and drive away. She was just a block from her house, when she was taken. Mema was thirteen years old.

The organizers, a group made up of mostly Guatemalan women, hoped to be a part of Dr. Sethi's International Forum. They believed this would give them the amount of media attention necessary to shame the law enforcement personnel in their country into doing their job. Claudia wrote:

"To avoid having to investigate murders of women, the police tell the reporters the victim was probably a prostitute because she was outside in the street instead of in the house. A number of the murders never reach the papers.

"We know that your forum is about women who are killed by their families. But here, in Guatemala, we don't even know who is killing us. Maybe these killers are fathers. We know they are sons of someone and brothers and husbands of someone. In this respect, they are our family. Women are raped and mutilated by a member of some other woman's family."

Neelam felt sick to her stomach after looking at the graphic pictures and reading the articles. She decided to leave the office for what she hoped would be a long walk to catch a breath of fresh air. It was early evening and a March wind unraveled her shawl. While returning it to her shoulder, her phone rang.

"Neelam? Where are you? Get to a TV right away!" It was Enid, sounding frantic. The urgency in her voice almost sent Neelam into a panic since she was already in a highly emotional state.

"What's happened? I'm not in the office."

"Get in front of a TV, now! Go to a pub! Whatever. I've got to go."

If there had been a pub next door to her office, she wouldn't have known. She turned on her heels and practically ran the five blocks back to her office and was totally out of breath climbing the two flights of stairs. Basma was busy at her own new computer trying to type using two fingers, when Neelam flung the door wide open.

"Aisha! Quickly, turn on the TV!"

In a second, Basma was up pressing a button on a television mounted near the window. Neelam grabbed the remote off the ledge and punched in a news channel.

A building in flames covered the screen, then the image dissolved to an aerial view of multiple buildings in flames. Inserts in the lower right of the screen showed footage of police cars on fire. Neelam gripped her chest.

"Where is this? Where is this? Oh God, not another terrorist attack."

Basma stared, speechless. The images cut to what looked like government buildings splattered in red paint. Neelam realized, then, that it wasn't England, but perhaps southern Europe. The screen image split and a male reporter with a Spanish accent began describing in English the initial panic that had occurred when bombs exploded in all the buildings, simultaneously.

"People were awakened all over the city. Everyone I interviewed said they thought it was a terrorist attack. And, as you can see, one of the buildings was a criminal courthouse, and two of the eight buildings targeted were police stations. Behind me is one of ten police cars that were set on fire." The camera zoomed in on a patrol car in flames and a few bystanders flinging rocks at it.

"Why are they throwing rocks at the police cars?" Neelam wondered aloud.

The images changed again and she saw what looked like dead bodies wearing uniforms strung up on lampposts at major intersections and bridges next to white bed sheets used as banners. Again, the camera zoomed in on the sheets, each with a different quote. Meticulously printed in large letters using black magic markers, the words were subtitled in English across the screen:

In Guatemala, we have monsters. They rape young girls every day.

They mutilate our daughters, our sisters, our wives and our mothers—every day!

Who can find the monsters? Who will destroy the monsters?

The blood (written in red and smeared) of our daughters, our wives, our sisters and our mothers, runs in the streets while corrupt judges take hush money and buy big houses.

In Guatemala, police are only little boys pretending to be policemen. They don't do their job but they cash their paychecks.

In Guatemala, women are not valued.

In Guatemala, there is no justice for women.

When the camera cut to a close-up of the dangling bodies with thick rope around the necks, Neelam saw that they were not real bodies but effigies—dummies. She breathed a sigh of relief.

The reporter on location in Guatemala, addressing a news anchor in the London studio, then referred to another incident that had also taken place less than an hour before.

"A local television station, here in Guatemala City, received a phone call telling them to have a camera crew waiting outside their building in fifteen minutes because something was going to happen. A crew was dispatched. According to reports, a blue truck pulled up, and a dark-haired woman wearing brown cargo pants, a bright blue tee shirt, and workman's gloves jumped out from the passenger's side. She went around to the back of the truck and banged on the panel."

They played the footage of what occurred. Neelam sat down on the edge of her desk transfixed, as it cut to the truck the newscaster had just mentioned.

The corrugated door was raised and two more women wearing the same identical cargo pants and blue tee shirts, but carrying assault rifles, jumped out. One of them went around to the front of the vehicle to stand guard. A fourth woman with blonde, stringy hair and a rifle slung over her shoulder, leaped from the back gripping a chain, which was attached to wrist cuffs of a sneering shirtless man in his twenties.

As hundreds gathered holding up their cell phones, and the TV camera rolled, the man, identified by the reporter as a possible gang member, jumped down, followed by six other loathsome and contemptible-looking creatures—supposed gang members, in their teens and twenties, with angry or bored expressions. All of them were linked together with heavy chains around their necks, and each was shirtless.

The woman who had come from the passenger's side of the truck climbed into the rear and pushed a ten-gallon barrel to the edge, followed by a covered plastic five-gallon bucket which she dragged to the edge. One of the rifle-toting women went to help the first woman, who appeared to be the leader, take both containers off the truck. Next, she rejoined the blond woman who was guarding the chained men.

The women raised their assault rifles and pointed them at the men.

"Get down on your knees," they ordered in unison.

The men sneered, not budging. In no time, the blonde-haired woman bashed the leader in the face with the butt of the gun. Blood spurted. The crowd gasped. A few applauded here and there. The gang leader dropped to his knees. Slowly, the other men dropped down one-by-one, their expressions changing from contempt to apprehension.

More TV crews and people descended on the area when the spectacle went live. Police sirens could be heard in the background. The blonde woman who hit the gang leader shouted in Spanish for the people and the cameramen to stand back.

The barrel was opened. Basma sucked in her breath as she watched the screen. Two of the women poured the contents—a dark, blood-red liquid—all over the men.

The men screamed out in disgust and fell over.

The women shouted at the camera. "This is the blood of our daughters, our mothers and our sisters that these monsters have spilled."

"We will cut you into pieces and feed you to the dogs," one gang member shouted as he writhed and flailed around in the viscous liquid.

After, the second container was opened, and the women shouted in unison: "This is what these monsters are!"

Two women lifted the large container and splattered a thick, lumpy, brown sludge on the men that caused them to jerk, gyrate, howl and spew in absolute horror. Hundreds of people scattered, clasping their hands over their noses, but the cameras kept rolling.

Finally, patrol cars descended on the scene. Police officers bolted toward the truck, weapons drawn. All three women with assault rifles— the one standing at the front of the truck and the two at the rear, cocked the guns simultaneously and aimed them straight at the police. At the same time, the leader returned to the rear of the truck, pulled out another assault rifle and a small brown bag. She walked threateningly towards the camera then trained her gun on the gang members. Instantly, everything came to a halt. The men stopped gagging and lay still, eyes fixed steadily on her rifle.

The leader moved right up to the TV camera and said:

"Our men have failed us. They can no longer protect us. It took five women two weeks to do what the police could not do in five years: capture these murdering pigs. Women, you must fight back. We will train you to give rapists and murderers of women what they deserve."

She put the strap of the rifle on one shoulder, and opened the small paper bag and carefully pulled out a transparent plastic bag and held it high. "Be warned! This is WILA justice!"

People stretched their necks to see what was inside. The TV camera zoomed in on the contents.

"My God!" Neelam shouted. It was a severed penis. Basma cupped both hands over her eyes. Waves of shock and awe rippled throughout the crowd in Guatemala City and the live TV audiences.

Lifting her rifle again, the leader turned and threw the bag at the foot of one of the police officers nearest the camera. He jumped back as if it were a bomb.

Next came WILA's dramatic exit.

All four women quickly stepped back towards the truck, rifles still aimed. One leaped up into the rear of the truck, while the remaining three continued aiming their weapons. Once there, she trained her gun back on the police and the blonde then climbed aboard and pointed her rifle. Next, the leader withdrew her weapon and marched around to the front of the truck where her front guard stood with her weapon fixed on two police officers, their hands in the air. The leader signaled to her front guard to get into the cab of the truck.

Then she got in herself, just as the vehicle moved forward.

Neelam realized that a fifth woman must have been in the driver's seat, all along.

The police stood their ground, aware of the TV cameras on them. The patrol cars blocking the truck began to reverse. But, not fast enough. The truck increased its speed and plowed right through the roadblock, banging up the fronts and sides of four of the police cars as it sped away.

Basma began to breathe again. She looked at Neelam, who was still staring at the screen. "Do you think that those are the women who came to the meeting?"

Neelam was too stunned to reply. Her head was spinning because the envelope from Claudia Velasquez had only just arrived that very morning.

In addition, as if to compound the matter, the TV report cut to another stunning incident that had occurred in another part of the world.

"Now this video was sent to the Associated Press just hours ago," the TV anchor announced. "Our sources in Iran can now verify that Iranian Television reported that sixty-five women escaped from a prison in Mashhad, Iran, three days ago. Mashhad is the second largest city in Iran and close to the Turkmenistan border.

"Now if you watch the video, you'll see that it was filmed by someone who was not a prisoner because it shows, clearly, that person entering the prison, talking with prison guards and personnel. If you look at the direction of the eyes of the guards and the people at their desks, clearly there is more than one person entering. The person filming doesn't say much. Also, judging by the degree of shaking, as they move, this must have been a hidden camera.

"Okay, now watch closely and see what happens just as the guard opens that third gate. We can hear a scuffle and the camera swings back to capture two men lying on the ground, either unconscious or dead. There's no blood and no gunshots are heard."

Basma stared hypnotically at the jittery images. It made her feel as if she, too, were moving alongside them as they ran quickly down a hall and turned. She continued watching.

Another guard intercepted them, and words were exchanged. The prison guard didn't like whatever they told him, and another scuffle ensues. The guard was coerced into a room and did something to a panel with knobs. When the guard started to yell out, someone off-screen knocked him in the head. At this point, the filming stopped. Then it resumed, showing two prison guards at a service entrance insisting that these people were going the wrong way. When the guards realized that these people wouldn't turn back, they became aggressive. Three women in full chadors—black, head-to-toe cloaks worn by Iranian women—stepped forward into view, lifted their arms simultaneously and pointed assault rifles at the prison guards who then opened the gate.

One woman turned and waved her hand. Immediately, a large group of women in chadors moved swiftly up the corridor. The guards were ordered through the gate first. Beyond were two laundry trucks and two food service vans. Female inmates were hustled quickly into the back of the vehicles. The prison guards were blindfolded and forced into a food service van.

The videographer got into a car along with four other women and continued filming as the vans drove away.

"It seems that whoever these people are," the studio anchor continued, "they want a lot of media attention."

"Yes," replied the reporter in Guatemala, "and I think the penis-in-a-bag did just that." The studio anchor nervously brushed over the comment and tried to look serious.

"We are trying to understand why the video was sent days after the prison incident was reported, and my only guess is that they wanted it shown at the same time as the Guatemala City attack," the reporter extrapolated.

Neelam snapped out of her stupor and phoned Enid telling her about the envelope she'd received from a Claudia Velasquez.

"Do you have a phone number for her? Why don't you send another email then call me back after she responds?"

"All right. I will do that now." She reached for the remote and clicked off the TV.

***

The Land turned out to be exactly the oasis Zafeera had described, complete with wild flowers, hidden streams and rolling hills blanketed in heather. The women who were not out on an assignment spent the afternoons learning how to plant and tend the vegetable and herb gardens. Some of them preferred strolling through the forests, fishing on the lake or researching in the computer lab and in the small reading room with hundreds of donated books.

Alternatively, if they were so inclined, they could shut themselves inside the soundproof room used for meditation and silent contemplation. That was what Zafeera and fifteen other women from the Mashhad mission chose to do that very day. It was a chance to discharge the negative images from the TV report and focus on nature's beauty, their own health and wellbeing or whatever brought them joy.

Zafeera sat on a pillow, eyes closed, legs crossed Indian-fashion, focusing on her breathing to quiet her mind and connect with her inner self. The wellbeing part was easy to experience at the Land with Tai Kwon Do, yoga and Chi Kung classes incorporated into self-defense strategies like kickboxing, morning and night. For beauty, all she had to do was look at her surroundings, not just all the greenery, but all the women who were now also committed to WILA. Even so, Zafeera was having a very difficult time with the joy part. Everything about the Iranian experience kept replaying itself in her head, though both missions had been a success.

What the camera didn't record, but what women rescuers saw was the sheer surprise, fear and reluctance to leave, that the female inmates felt, not understanding who was beneath the chadors. However, it just took an assault rifle pointed at their captors to inspire trust in their liberators.

What is also missing from the film is the punching, scratching and biting the two prison guards had to endure from the inmates in the back of the van. Many had been raped, assaulted and blatantly humiliated by these very men.

Also, the people who watched and the Associated Press who aired the footage were ignorant of the fact that half of the offenses these women inmates committed involved either drug abuse or murdering their husbands. The other half of the women had committed sexual improprieties, specifically: pre-marital sex and adultery. The latter group was awaiting execution.

As further news of the escape unfolded, Iranian TV falsely reported that the escapees were all violent members of an anti-Islamic organization with ties in the West.

The vans traveled ten miles and stopped on a deserted street. One of the women jumped out of the first van and opened a gate of an abandoned factory. The vans drove through. The bruised prison guards were transferred to the trunk of the car and later released in a suburb of Tehran.

The Latina women, Vellanova and Inez, had come up with the Guatemalan plan to bring wider attention to the issues that Claudia Velasquez had told them about. Every WILA soldier with a drop of Latino blood volunteered for the assignment. But Vellanova and Inez were experienced guerrilla fighters and thought it best to work with a small team. Cat Murphy, the only non-Latina in their unit, was chosen for her imposing physical frame. In the end, Zafeera decided to entrust these women with her ideas and message. She had let go and allowed Vellanova Sanchez to lead the team and, judging by what she'd seen, she had executed a brilliant strategy with fierce professionalism.

After the initial live broadcast, the event was repeated on all the TV stations in South America, as well as other parts of the world.

Guatemala's president pleaded with the international community to help him find these women. But native Guatemalan women assailed him for it.

WILA's website crashed because of the astronomical number of hits it received in one day—mostly from young teen girls in Central America, wanting to enlist.

Still, Mashhad was what dominated Zafeera's mind now. Mashhad was WILA's first mission, and she wanted to show the other women who volunteered for it that she had the necessary courage and resolve to lead. It had gone smoothly for the most part, but it still was a dangerous mission. At any time, one or all of her soldiers could have been killed or worse: caught, raped by police, tortured and locked up—forever.

It had taken a little over three days to smuggle the sixty-five women prisoners out of Iran and safely into Turkmenistan. Each freed woman had a choice to stay, but their other options would have been living on the streets or putting their families in danger if they contacted any of them for assistance. All the women rescued chose to leave their country where they had little to look forward to, except subhuman treatment, brutality, solitary confinement and filthy conditions—without great prospects, even if they were paroled.

What moved Zafeera about the Mashhad mission besides setting the women free was having the opportunity of teaming up with a former Algerian Freedom Fighter, Hassiba Djebar and an ex-Israeli soldier, Jonina Halevi, to strategize. The two women never left

Zafeera's side from the moment they entered Iran until their arrival back at the factory.

Mick popped into her mind for a second. They hadn't spoken since the night in Brixton when she revealed everything to him. Now she wondered what his reaction would have been when he saw the footage.

She would have given anything to have the impressive military power necessary to free women from Iran's dreaded Evin prison—women whose only crime was to demonstrate against the regime. Wouldn't that be a major blow to its perverse judicial system and how that system navigated what many called the 'convoluted, gender-biased labyrinth' of Sharia Law? She thought about the interview she'd read with a former Basiji Militia guard at Evin prison. He said that according to Iranian laws, a virgin could not be executed. So, in order to execute the condemned virgins, who have spoken out against the regime, prison guards are given the 'coveted' assignment of 'temporarily marrying' the condemned via a 'wedding ceremony' in her jail cell the night before the execution day. After that, the guard could perform his husbandly right to deflower her, thus ending her virgin status. In other words, a prison guard/husband raped the condemned girl and then she was executed the following morning.

It was one humiliating atrocity after another. The more people pushed against the walls of social and religious oppression, the more the hardliners pushed back, it seemed—and women bore the brunt of that force. Sharia Law was always cited and used to either legally force women into submission or incite peer pressure so the Western-polluted Muslim woman found herself ostracized by other 'more Islamic' women.

The situation had grown so complex and had deteriorated to the point that one could never know what god-fearing modest women really believed. Conditioned to hide their faces and bodies, many women masked their true convictions, as well, to protect themselves, their families and to protect their precious reputations—which had become so fragile.

It wasn't unheard of that devout women, who spoke their pious platitudes the loudest in favor of Sharia law or the validity of religious restraint, actually harbored opposing views deep inside. These women were often allowed extra privileges in society for their devotion, which they used to improve their families' situation and guarantee protection. However, late at night, when everyone in their households were fast asleep, it was these same obedient, observing and pious women who were logging onto WILA's website and blogging. There—free to express all the pent-up rage against the injustice and inequality they and their sisters faced—these women had become the most vocal about how to dismantle the patriarchy.

It was several of these types of women, each unaware of the other, who informed WILA of how their own respective countries were becoming more oppressive than Saudi Arabia was for a woman.

Apparently, in one of these countries, Syria, less than a year before, a group of men—all outsiders—had gained the ear of some of the clerics and mullahs by criticizing them for not having a firmer hand in enforcing religious values, the ear of the President, and in punishing those who did not adhere to the policies. This group accused the theocracy of becoming like the infidel men in the West who expected other nations in the world to envy them and adopt the Western ideologies which was, clearly, a taint on Islam and true believers.

Calling themselves *"Les Vrais Guerriers de Dieu"*—God's True Warriors, these foreign nationals led by a Syrian, tried to inspire the Mullahs in secular Syria to have a greater vision for the currently-destabilized country—one in which any new president who wanted to give more rights to women, would not get the support he needed to accomplish that.

The bloggers wrote: For months there have been political and religious attacks, daily, in the theocratically controlled newspapers, of our troubled President and anyone who supports him. It has spilled out into the streets and there are fights daily between the military and anti-government protesters who say they want democracy. Then, about four months ago, with all the confusion in the larger cities, Les Vrais Guerriers de Dieu began to invade small areas in the villages, clandestinely, and set up control by fighting with police there. Overpowered, the police were given a choice to join them or get shot. They joined them.

'Now, every village is under siege with their version of Sharia law—and the women whom they feel have violated those laws have been arrested and put in jail. Many single mothers who are widows or whose husbands have run off, had to go out to work or to buy food. Even so, the police have arrested them for being outside, alone, with no male relative accompanying them. Like the Afghani women under the Taliban, we too have become prisoners in our homes."

Zafeera rolled her neck around to stretch the tight muscles that threatened a headache—so much for silent contemplation. Perhaps a shot of wheatgrass juice, and raw vegan zucchini pasta with cashew nut cheese, would do the trick. Angela had raved about it.

She rose quietly and left her comrades in their own perpetual struggle to reach Samadhi, that state of consciousness, beyond mind, where one experienced true bliss. Although few people had ever actually achieved this state of being, the effort had its own rewards.

Outside, the crisp air carried the promise of spring. Zafeera crossed a shaded walkway lined with plants just beginning to bloom. Passing the prefabricated building that housed the fitness room and boxing gym, she peeked in. There were only a handful of women inside working out.

With such warm weather for March, she assumed many had chosen to hike, and those 'hardcore fitness buffs' were jogging around the 200-acre property, instead.

A whiff of wheatgrass filled her nose, as she reached the makeshift raw foods café, causing her to halt and do an-about-face. Health was not at all what she needed. What she needed was a strong cup of Turkish coffee and one of those luscious homemade steak and onion pies they made in the cafeteria.

Almost tasting the rich brown gravy, she hurried over to the cafeteria, found it unusually crowded, and every conversation that reached her ears was about the severed penis.

***

Claudia Velasquez couldn't recall the last time she had felt so exhilarated. Oh, the taste of revenge! She could not tear herself away from the television set. Her phone kept racking up messages, but her eyes remained glued to the screen all day. Remote in her hand, she smugly surfed the news channels, analyzing their coverage and spin.

How foolish the law enforcement personnel looked, trying to answer the reporters' questions after the incident. These were the same men and women who had been completely indifferent just months ago when she had begged them to do something about the killings. Now look at them.

Eventually, it was nature's call that pulled her attention away from the box. When she returned, she picked up her phone and scrolled the call log. One number, in particular, caught her eye, and she listened intently to the message.

***

"Well, what did you tell her, Neelam?" Enid demanded. "Surely you can't let people who use these violent, sordid, outright criminal tactics associate themselves with us. We already have ten organizations involved. We don't need any more of these people with their—"

"Yes, yes, I know. I just—"

"You just… what?"

Any other day, Neelam would have been home at this hour. Outside the window, the mid-March sky resembled blue ink. Her knee ached. She rubbed it then stretched out both of her legs. Each had grown stiff from sitting at the computer handling emails, writing letters and making phone calls.

It was only yesterday that she and Enid had received news from Kensasha that the United Nations had not only agreed to the Forum, but had given them a date. Her subsequent time had been spent digesting it all. Having put so much energy and focus for the past eight months into creating a coalition of women, and petitioning the U.N. department overseeing violence issues against women, the fact that both had been accomplished left her and Enid uncertain what to do next.

Neelam had written a long to-do list and given a copy to Basma before turning in for the evening. The remainder of the night, however, she spent staring at the ceiling and jotting down more things to add to the list.

Receiving Claudia's package from Guatemala, coincidentally, the very next morning with the explicit photos, her request to make a presentation at the Forum, if it was given the go-ahead, then the TV spectacle— all on top of her having to inform the leaders of the coalition, and arrange when all ten, plus their deputies, could meet to plan and strategize their next phase—had only added more pressure on Neelam. Then there was the fluttering of her heart that she neglected to mention to Basma or anyone.

"I told her we will try to fit her in—give her ten minutes," Neelam replied, hesitantly.

"What? Oh Neelam! Why?" Enid admonished. "I wish you would have at least consulted with the rest of us first. This is supposed to be about honor killing, and specific cultural violence that families orchestrate against their women and girls. You know very well what happens when too many issues are thrown on the table, nothing gets—"

"Is it really too many different issues, Enid," Neelam cut in with renewed confidence. "Or, various symptoms of the same problem?"

"I understand," Enid continued impatiently. "But my concern is for the women and girls in our care who are in danger from their family members! These are the people we've tried to help for the past six years, we owe it to them not to shift the focus to all the other kinds of violence women face in the world."

"You are right. But I think that Mrs. Velasquez's presentation will shift the focus of violence against women from being labeled an Indian, Middle Eastern, or African problem. It is in the Americas, too. We know in the United States there is an inordinate amount of domestic violence and sexual assault, and the same in England. This violence is everywhere."

Enid decided to let it go for the moment. Already this Guatemalan issue had consumed more time than they had to spare. "Does Aisha like her new flat?"

"I haven't had a chance today to ask her, but I am sure she does."

***

Her shoes came off first. It had been a full day, with that TV drama and an escalation of things to do, now that the Forum was certain. A frazzled Dr. Sethi still had plenty of letters for her to mail. And now, Basma was walking into her very own place, a one bedroom flat with a galley-style kitchen on the top floor of a two-family semi-detached house.

She could've taken a bus that would have left her off a few blocks from the new apartment, but the advantage of taking the Underground, besides its closeness to the post office, was the speed in which she could arrive home.

In the five months Basma had stayed with Neelam Sethi, she had often found herself surrounded by women with whom she had nothing in common. Women who, whether married or not, mothers or not, had taken control of their own lives, made their own money, women with personal and political power. They were the kind of women who knew how to set goals and had no doubt they could achieve them. Every one of them had impressed her and made her want more.

In five months, she had learned the basics of using a computer and discovered that she not only had an aptitude for it—but also enjoyed it. Wouldn't Abdel be proud?

Neelam had taught her how to make lamb curry vindaloo and green pea and potato samosas during the Christmas Holidays. They exchanged gifts, even though neither of them was Christian.

At the age of thirty-eight, she had a bank account for the first time in her life. She had managed to read four books in that time—often turning out the light at the crack of dawn. New worlds, and new possibilities suddenly lay before her.

One morning, she woke up and realized she wanted to have a place of her own. Not her family's, not her husband's, not a room in Dr. Sethi's beautiful loft, but a home of her own. Perhaps with sea blue walls in the bedroom and bright yellow sheets on the bed that she picked out herself.

At first, Neelam assumed she had said something or had done something to offend Basma, or had said something that crossed boundary lines. After all, they did work together and live together. But once Neelam recalled Basma's personal story, it helped to clarify Basma's need to create something of her own.

Then it took Enid to come up with the idea of letting Basma move into one of the safe houses that wasn't being used. There were pieces of furniture already in the flat. Basma could fix it up whatever way she chose. She already received a livable wage out of the forum budget, now that she was a part of the organizing committee, so they charged her a nominal rent.

The walls had not yet been painted that sea blue she dreamed of, but her sheets were lemon yellow with white lilies. She discovered a shop that only sold bed linens and picked them out without having to get anyone's approval.

On the very first evening alone in her own place, Basma, had celebrated by buying fresh orange tulips for the small round bistro table she used to dine at, and placed another multi-colored bouquet on her nightstand.

As she sat on the couch with her fish and chips take out, she put her feet up on the coffee table, and read late into the night. That simple activity had given her immense joy and satisfaction.

In the time that she stayed with Neelam Sethi, Basma began wearing silk Indian scarves draped over her head. Sometimes she chose a floppy hat and other times she chose to wear nothing on her head at all. Whatever the impulse was that day, she followed it, and everything fell into place. It was magical. She felt perfectly aligned with her surroundings, the people she encountered, whatever she chose to do.

Shoes by the door, once again she relaxed with the convenience of a prepared meal. Tonight, it came from a Turkish restaurant across from the Underground. Using her own plates and silverware, she sat at the table enjoying an aromatic cuisine that reminded her of jagged mountains and goats bleating in the distance. She thought about the women who had walked into an Iranian prison and walked out with most of its female inmates.

When she had finished eating, she leaned back in the chair and a thought slipped into her mind, out of the blue, and took center place: Why not go to school? Get an education like Neelam, Enid and Amanda Kurtami have. Know what they know. Was it even possible for an adult here in London to go to High School? Is it called High School here? Of course, she had no papers, no provable background—no documents besides her passport and visa—which soon needed to be extended. How could she even consider going to school when Aisha Langois had been born just six months ago?

Though the idea was a good one, there was no way it could happen for a person in her situation. Could she pay someone to teach her? Vincent had given her money. It was a comforting thought to realize there was an alternate path to every goal—if you really want it. She took that idea to bed with her.

Nevertheless, when the lights were out, deep inside beneath the comforter, there was always something gnawing at her. Sometimes it was just the familiar bad dream: Aisha's murder, or Sirhan's freedom. Sometimes it was subtle, and she fell asleep right away. But other times, she had to fight to keep it at bay: that agonizing desire to see Abdel and Ahmed, just one more time.

CHAPTER 30

To Zafeera, it made sense for WILA to slip into the largest town. Her hands, cold and clammy, began to shake like never before. Five minutes to go. The target was easy. A one-story warehouse with barred windows on the northwest and southwest corners. It was a wide, flat structure made of cinderblock and mortar with a corrugated iron roof. Situated at the edge of the city, the makeshift prison for women had no other buildings within a fifty-meter radius. Eight policemen patrolled the prison. The plan was to approach it from the west and be in and out in seven minutes.

The Mashhad break had gone brilliantly. But, Zafeera had not, actually, gone inside with her team—easier to network, solicit, set goals, coordinate, and strategize than it was to take up arms, crawl in the dirt and do battle. Wasn't it easier to imagine ramming the butt of a rifle in the enemies' faces—feeling their skulls crack, blood spurt—than physically doing so?

Now, the churning and fluttering in her stomach was causing a burning sensation in her chest.

Beneath the dark fabric, perspiration formed on her forehead, nose and upper lip. What if she had to pull the trigger to save someone? Or herself? Could she? Would she? These men weren't teenage boys with fists and sticks, but policemen and rebel soldiers with guns. This wasn't a rundown storage facility in Brixton. This was another country thousands of miles away geographically, and centuries away ideologically—a country that had taken WILA weeks to infiltrate.

She glanced to her left. A statuesque Swedish woman with just a tiny slit in her niqab revealing pale blue eyes nodded. Behind her, seven more women, all properly covered in full chador, were on heightened alert. Nine other WILA soldiers waited inconspicuously in cars and non-descript vans positioned fifty meters away from each side of the building.

One more full breath… in and out. Okay. Here we go.

With speed and urgency, WILA advanced towards the warehouse. Yelling at four police who stood around the front-loading dock, the women demanded the right to visit with their daughters and sisters who had been unjustifiably imprisoned.

These officers were no easy pushovers. They had no trouble shouting for the women to disperse right away or they, too, would be thrown into the prison. Unperturbed, the women continued demanding to visit with loved ones. The ruckus brought a captain out and he ordered the women to leave, as well. Nevertheless, they stood their ground. He ordered the other officers to take them into custody, immediately, and lock them all up with their corrupt daughters.

With weapons pointed in their faces, the nine WILA soldiers were viciously manhandled and prodded with guns until they were through the rusting metal doors of the warehouse. Each end of the loading dock housed a structure used for offices and toilets. Without doing paperwork of any kind, the WILA 9 were herded into the dimly lit main open area that acted as a mass jail cell. Nearly one hundred women were sitting or lying on mattresses on a filthy floor, or huddled against the walls weeping, sobbing, rocking back and forth, or staring off into space. The air was oppressively hot and thick with sweat and body odor, as well as bodily waste. The five toilet stalls in the huge space, formerly used by workmen, were not equipped to handle a hundred women. Nor was the ancient plumbing system.

As soon as the police slammed the doors shut, locking them in the cell, WILA revealed their weapons beneath their robes to the prisoners, and Zafeera shouted in Arabic that they were here to rescue them and ordered them to quickly move away from the eastern wall. Too surprised, too sick or too tired to react fast enough, seven of the soldiers actively helped women out of the way where necessary. An eighth soldier had already begun planting the explosives on the wall with thick putty. When she had finished, she nodded at Zafeera who whispered, "Now," into the headset of her cell hidden by the veil. Seconds later, an explosion was heard in the distance, as a car was detonated fifty meters from the front entrance. Three police officers jumped into their jeeps and took off in the direction of the blast.

Two minutes later, the explosives blasted a massive hole in the rear wall of the warehouse.

"Out! Out! Go now! Now!" the WILA soldiers shouted.

As women charged through the jagged opening, leaping and stumbling over crumbled bricks, running for their lives, four startled police ran out the front with their guns drawn. Two went to the right and the other two circled the building to the left to see what had happened.

Outside, the women found themselves facing a bright blue sky with a wide stretch of barren land extending to the horizon. Vans and cars with open doors waited, and more WILA soldiers kicked into action as a trained rescue team, quickly ushering the prisoners into the vehicles— though not quick enough. Police came from around both corners shouting at them to stop, simultaneously firing their guns—causing mayhem and downing women here and there.

Now, for the first time, WILA was challenged to use its weapons. Aiming only to wound, as trained, they took out three. Unfortunately, when the fourth officer shot an older woman who was not so agile getting over the shattered brick Vellanova, the leader of the Guatemalan team, leaped out of one of the vans, raised her assault rifle and shot him to death.

After the wall had exploded, Zafeera and her other two soldiers ran to the cell door to hold off whoever came in. When the last policeman rushed in and saw what was happening, he began to unlock the cell. As soon as he saw three women rushing his way, he pulled out his weapon. Immediately, the women stopped in their tracks and dropped to the ground.

"Who did this? Who did this?" he shouted. They shook their heads in unison. He ordered them to get up and beckoned them out. They passively obeyed.

Once outside the cell, Zafeera turned around and said, "These women know nothing, I was trying to help them. Release them and I'll tell you who hired me to do this."

He glared at her, then at the other two. Without responding to Zafeera's request, he marched them to an office and locked them in—not bothering to search them for weapons because, according to his religious beliefs, it was improper to touch a woman he was not related to, a belief he and his comrades on the night shift often forgot.

As he rounded the back of the building, he spotted six women and one policeman, dead, while three of his men moaned in pain. Rescue vehicles and cars were speeding off northeast and southeast leaving a cloud of white dust swirling behind them.

Infuriated, the policeman left the wounded men lying on the ground, pulled out his walkie-talkie as he stared in amazement at the gaping hole in the wall and yelled for the other police to return immediately.

Climbing through the ruined enclosure the policeman walked past soiled mattresses, head scarves, a few pairs of shoes, broken bits of soap, used metal plates, paper cups, plastic spoons, and balled up wads of paper. Finally, he phoned for medical assistance.

The locked office had no windows. Three of the walls had a desk facing into the center of the room with telephones on each. Under different circumstances, the phones would have been useful, but Zafeera still had her cell phone, and knowing that she and the other two women were still armed helped to assuage any fear.

Trained to keep silent, each of them squatted like statues up against a space along the walls, hampered a bit by the excessive fabric of their chadors.

Listening intently for any noise or voices that might signal danger, they were poised to react.

Zafeera eased her cell phone from the pocket of her cargo pants, and began texting while glancing up, cautiously, at the door.

Twenty minutes passed. Their limbs grew stiff. Feeling pins and needles, Zafeera was the first to stand up. She stomped her feet and walked around in a small circle to get the blood circulating once again.

As her other two comrades watched, she strolled over to each of the desks, perusing the papers, and nonchalantly studied the framed documents and pictures on the walls.

In the distance, they could hear a car engine and voices.

She took in a deep breath. In a minute, the police would burst through the door. She cocked her ears. Her eyes jotted around the room and landed on a photograph, behind the desk opposite where she stood. It was of five men in traditional clothes. Slowly, she advanced toward it. When she was two feet away, she stopped and caught her breath.

"What is it?" the Swedish soldier whispered in English, ignoring the rules.

Too overcome to speak, Zafeera just stared at the photograph.

Outside, the voices grew louder, and seconds later, they heard a key in the lock. The other two women sprung to their feet, and shook their arms and legs, then gripped their weapons beneath the chador.

The policeman, who had locked them in the room, entered, followed by three of his men.

"Tell me who you are? Who is your leader?" he demanded.

Zafeera turned away from the photo. "I already told you if you let these two women go, I will tell you what you want to know."

Once again, he stared at them, this time appearing both humiliated and angry.

"Take them!" he ordered, pointing to the other two women.

With a subtle exchange of glances, the women were removed from the office.

He turned back to Zafeera. "Who did this?" he repeated.

Feeling that the game had shifted once again in her favor, Zafeera pointed at the picture. "Who are these men?"

"Who did this?" he shouted, ignoring her question. "If you don't tell me, your friends will be executed right now."

"They are not my friends."

"You do not care if they die?"

"Of course I care. Anyway, they don't know anything. I said I will tell you what you want to know, but first I must know who these men are."

Curious now, the police officer walked over to see whom exactly was in the photograph. Then he stared back at her suspiciously.

"You don't know who that is? How is it possible that you don't know Les Vrais Guerriers de Dieu?" The startled look on her face made him more curious. "Who are you? Where do you come from? You are not from here."

"I must speak with this man!" She pointed to the man standing to the right of the man in the center.

"He will not speak to you, you are a woman!"

"But I am also family. He is married to my sister."

***

As soon as the two WILA soldiers stepped outside the office, they were handcuffed, shuffled out of the building, and ordered into a jeep and driven to the main jail ten miles closer to town that did not provide sections for women.

Upon arrival, one policeman escorted the women inside, and a second removed their handcuffs. Before the second policeman could re-pocket the keys, he received a swift karate blow to the stomach. The first policeman had his weapon knocked to the floor and got a sharp jujitsu kick to the groin.

The WILA soldiers dashed from the jail, with other police in hot pursuit. The two women split up and headed straight onto a busy street cutting through passageways where women circulated. Dressed like the other women in black, faces covered, it was easy for them to get lost in the crowd.

***

An hour later, Zafeera was blindfolded, thrown into a jeep, and taken on a forty-five-minute ride to an adjacent town.

Led from the jeep into a compound, her blindfold was removed, and she saw a woman in a burka standing before her. The woman ordered Zafeera to remove her niqab. She complied. The woman stepped forward and ordered her to open her chador. Zafeera, hesitated, but the prospect of seeing Ghaybaa again made her take a chance being defenseless. Slowly, she unhooked it at the neckline and spread the robe open with both hands. Startled, the woman jumped back. There, dangling on a two-inch leather strap crossing her body was a FAMAS rifle. The woman shot a wild glance over Zafeera's shoulder at the policemen who had brought her in, then back at Zafeera.

"You must remove your weapon!" the woman ordered. Alarmed, the policemen rushed over and cocked their own weapons.

Under their red-faced glare, Zafeera released a latch on the strap and let the gun crash to the ground. A policeman immediately picked it up. The woman studied her for a moment, then turned and headed back across the courtyard of the compound toward a building that may have once been government offices. The policeman, holding her gun, ordered Zafeera to follow.

Pausing outside ten-foot-high double wood-paneled doors, the woman directed Zafeera to go through, and then she left.

Inside, there was an ornate desk, an oriental rug, leather office chairs, and large empty wooden bookcases, all gathering dust. When she heard footsteps approaching, she lowered her eyes, bracing herself to face the man she'd spent the past year in London trying to find.

A door to her right opened. A tall, thin figure with a thick, black, wiry beard entered wearing the traditional attire of a cleric. He encircled her like a panther and she could feel his eyes dissecting her. Suddenly, he came to a standstill right in front of her. When she lifted her eyes, she was met with the coldest hate-filled stare imaginable— it was almost lethal.

She was taken aback. Not because of his venomous glare, but because he was not her brother-in-law, Fareed. Instead, he was the man who had stood in the center of the photograph at the prison.

Shocked and disappointed, she wondered why they had brought her to this man instead of Fareed. Her hopes of being reunited with her beloved sister faded and she resigned herself to whatever they had planned.

Then it dawned on her. He must be Syrian-born Amir bin Al-Mutabi, forty-nine years old and the leader of Les Vrais Guerriers de Dieu. His actions were the reason WILA was asked for help. He was the most powerful and feared man in Syria, right now, and he was fully prepared to become its new leader—as soon as the president stepped down.

Amir bin Al-Mutabi was determined to put Syria back on course toward a true, pure, self-sufficient Islamic state under religious rule. All trade and investments from the West would be outlawed and he would align with Iran to fortify his nation from the claws of western economic and cultural imperialism.

Mutabi saw her surprise, but rather than give her an explanation, he proceeded with his own agenda, believing a government-led militia sent the women.

"What kind of men would give a woman a gun?" He pronounced "woman" as if he were talking about something depraved.

"Probably the same kind that coerced that young Palestinian mother in Israel to strap bombs to her body and blow herself apart on a bus full of people," Zafeera replied, meeting his eyes with equal loathing. And for a brief second, he seemed unsure what to say next. Still, his interest was piqued. He folded his arms.

"You think blowing up a prison to let vulgar, offensive women escape has the same honor as fighting to free Palestine?"

"No, not at all. I don't think blowing up a busload of people has any honor, no matter who does it, or the reason they give for doing it. I simply meant that the men who give women guns usually do so to have them die for causes and situations the women, themselves, had no part in creating."

Mutabi paused, digesting the full meaning of what she had said. At that, Zafeera knew she was in for a fight. Before her was a powerful, influential man who not only embraced the belief that men were somehow superior and had a kind of divine ownership of women, but had seduced the clerics into enforcing even more oppressive rules and regulations over the domestic sphere. The effect always impacted women's rights and behaviors more than the men's. In this case, specifically, many women had found themselves arrested and imprisoned in a filthy warehouse for months without legal representation or visitation rights, simply because they wore their head scarves in a way that exposed a few inches of hair at the crown, or they preferred wearing colorful floral-patterned hijabs; they may have dyed their hair—which was, supposedly, against Sharia law—or worst of all, if they were young or Christian and did not want to cover their heads at all.

"So, the President and his army have become so weak, they give women dangerous weapons and make them risk their lives by going against God's word. Do they even show you how to use it?" he smirked.

"No man sent me. The Women's International Liberation Army rescued those women who were unjustly imprisoned. And, yes, I do know how to use that gun," she replied, smugly. The look of astonishment on his face delighted her.

He turned and walked over to the desk, and sat behind it, as if needing a prop to enhance his authority. "What is this… army?" The increased distance from him gave her some relief.

"WILA is a network of women whose sole purpose is to free other women from male tyranny." She knew this would incite him. She began to walk around and gesture with her hands as she continued, feeling ready for battle. "We have women emailing us from three continents describing the horrible conditions they are forced to endure because men can't wage war with each other without raping or killing women and children. You know: those places where women are not granted the same legal rights as men, where women have found themselves at the mercy of a corrupt system?

"As a matter of fact, right here in this beautiful country, right now in the twenty-first century, women have been forced from school, from their work and ordered to stay in the house or they will be arrested? I believe some confused, distorted religious babble was cited to justify it. Well now, we are tired of it. And, the Women's International Liberation Army has declared war on all of that."

It was a mouthful, but she wanted to get out as much as she could while she had the chance.

Ironically, if she had been a man, she would be dead already. He looked amused and bemused.

"Women?" he spewed. "Women are declaring war on the holy laws? On the world? On God? On me?" he scoffed. The latter seemed to irk him the most. From her vantage point, it was as if she had spoken to him in a language that could never be translated adequately for his comprehension.

With smoke almost pouring from his nostrils, Mutabi stood up and came toward Zafeera in a threatening manner, and in that instant, the door opened and in walked Fareed.

***

Why they had left a city like Paris to live in Brixton, Ghaybaa had often wondered but Fareed made it clear in the first week of their marriage that his decisions were not to be questioned. She also learned very early in their marriage that Fareed was a man with secrets and insecurities—both very dangerous for a wife.

Fareed had originally met Al-Mutabi in Saudi Arabia and found that, much like Ghaybaa's father, shared his conservative views about religion and tradition and the importance of keeping both pure. Like Mutabi, Fareed believed that once men loosened their grip on their women, moral decay would eventually set in, leading to the collapse of the family and the country, like in America, and, finally, civilization itself.

Ghaybaa did not know that in Fareed's mind, western secularism was the evil proof of what happened when women are allowed to do as they please, dress as they please, and have sex when they please with whomever they please. In the evil West, women worked alongside men, they took jobs from men, and learned what should only be for men.

She and her father did not know that Fareed never intended on allowing his wife to attend a university, in spite of his promises. That was one of the reasons he moved Ghaybaa to England and away from her family. The other was because he heard that Mutabi had become associated with a mosque in Brixton and was making a name for himself.

What Ghaybaa did know was that Mutabi had enormous power to get a lot of the men in the mosque fired up for just about anything. She had witnessed once-gentle husbands turn into browbeating intimidators who treated their wives as the enemy.

Away from her family, from Zafeera, away from the beauty of Paris, unreachable by phone, no TV, forbidden to read anything other than the Koran, and living with a man who had little to say to her, Ghaybaa found her solace in music.

Without a job to earn money to buy the latest MP3 player or an iPod, Ghaybaa took some of the grocery money Fareed had given her and purchased a cheap CD player at a flea market one Saturday afternoon, along with a couple of old CDs. On her way home, she took a route through the park. It was early autumn, warm—the leaves were already golden yellow, brick red, burnt orange. She found a park bench, put on the headphones and spent a good hour listening to songs that instantly took her back to her childhood in France.

That day, music once again lit up her spirit, quelled the loneliness and rekindled her desire to be a performer. As she hummed to the melodies, her long slender fingers tapped to the beat of the drums and curled around the neck of an imaginary guitar.

From that day on, every chance she got, Ghaybaa took off to the park or wandered through the stalls of the outdoor markets listening and humming to music.

Despite that, her evenings with Fareed were becoming unbearable. He spent more time at the mosque than at his job at a local repair shop so, naturally, he was let go. Enraged, he threatened to burn down the shop. Then he directed his anger toward Ghaybaa, imposing more restrictions on her. Now, she was only allowed to go to the Laundromat, two blocks away, on Mondays, and her shopping was restricted to Thursdays with him accompanying her.

One evening, he came home in a particularly dark mood and discovered Ghaybaa at the stove moving her hips to a song on their small digital radio.

Horrified by what he perceived as wicked behavior unbefitting any wife of his, he forbade her from ever doing such a thing again. And, to ensure she didn't, he sold the corrupt device. Subsequently, with no radio, Ghaybaa cleaned the house with her headphones and the CD player attached to a belt.

At the Laundromat the following week, she continued listening to her music and imagining herself playing while sheets, towels and socks tumbled before her in the dryer.

She took up smoking in the hall, so the smell wouldn't be in the apartment.

It was during this period that writing to her family became a chore. She felt that all they wanted to hear was how wonderful her life was with Fareed, how interesting to live in London, and that there was a baby on the way. None of which was true. When she thought of another life growing inside of her, she couldn't breathe. Because of that feeling, she had nothing in common with the other wives and mothers in the complex. Not fluent enough in English to connect with the British locals, who, in reality, she had more in common with, and not having a husband who asked her what she thought about or how her day went— Ghaybaa resorted to… writing songs.

She filled three notebooks with passionate lyrics about fairytale romances, loss, believing in dreams, and just about anything else that came to mind. Up-tempo beats, Algerian-style ballads, pop, rock, and hip-hop were all blended together to create a style uniquely her own. She stored the notebooks in her old school backpack along with her CD player and thirty-four CDs. The backpack became the center of her entire existence—her own treasure chest—her reason for being.

It all came to a head in a matter of days. First, Fareed announced that they were moving to Syria as soon as he could secure visas. Then she found out she was to become a mother. Two days later, a problem arose with the electrical system in the mosque and Fareed went home to fetch his tools. Since it was Monday, he happened to look into the Laundromat as he walked by. Ghaybaa did not see him enter because she had her eyes closed and her headphones on, humming to music. Incensed that she had disobeyed him and was still listening to one of the most corrupting forces on the planet—music—out in the open for all to see, he grabbed her arm, scaring the life out of her.

Without saying a word, he pulled her to her feet, yanked the headphones off, threw them on the chair and ordered her to go home immediately. Red-faced, she said that the clothes were not ready yet.

"Don't worry about the clothes!" he yelled.

The incident caught everyone's attention. Heads turned as Fareed pushed Ghaybaa towards the entrance. She swung around to get her CD player and backpack, but he gripped hold of her harder and shoved her out with force.

"My bag! I have to get my bag," she insisted.

Fareed let go of her and went back for the backpack but left her CD player.

The two blocks back to the apartment were the longest she'd ever walked. The thought of turning around and just running—running as far away from Fareed, and the suffocating future with him in Syria, that was to be her life—did occur to her. Unfortunately, she wasn't brave enough.

What followed was a blur, a bad dream. Fareed slammed the door shut, dumped her bag on the kitchen table and then raged again, and again about evil music and disobeying him. She remembered that he talked about sending her back to her parents, which would cause them shame and dishonor. He had mentioned needing a wife who was worthy of someone like him. Then he grabbed the backpack from the table to sling it across the room and she gasped.

Curious. Spiteful. He unzipped the bag and shook out its contents. As the books and CDs fell to the floor, Ghaybaa rushed over and swooped up her notebooks, clutching them to her chest, protectively.

Fareed flung the empty bag to the side, and asked to see the notebooks. She told him they were just silly words of a schoolgirl. Believing her, he directed his attention back to the CDs, and began stomping on them in a cool, deliberate manner. As she watched, her eyes filled with tears. So, he stomped harder, crushing the plastic covers and scratching all the discs. Nevertheless, for some reason, that wasn't enough. He grabbed the books from her arms, and began ripping the pages out in pieces like a madman.

Frantic, Ghaybaa clawed at the books trying to stop him, but that only made matters worse. A man like Fareed would have seen this as demeaning—a challenge to his authority as a husband. He dropped the books and began slapping her in the face with both hands—one after the other. Then he tore off her head covering and slung her across the room. She hit up against the edge of the coffee table before landing between it and the couch. She remembered him charging after her, pulling her by the shoulders, shaking her, and yelling at her about obedience and about how he was trying to save her from all the evils of the world and asking why she doesn't understand this.

With her still on the floor, Fareed got his tools and ordered her to have his dinner ready when he returned from the mosque.

When all the screaming had died down, the silence was deafening.

Ghaybaa lay on the floor staring at the ceiling for a long while before she remembered the laundry… and her CD player. She imagined herself entering the Laundromat and finding the CD player still on the chair. With her swollen face and bruised body, she would fold the towels, neatly, and return home leaving the CD player for someone else to enjoy. Later, they would have a quiet dinner and not speak a word about what had happened.

The last thing Ghaybaa remembered, before crawling across the room, selecting a razor-sharp sliver of hard plastic from the ruined CDs and slicing open both of her wrists, was that her beloved sister, Zafeera, never made it to her wedding.

***

When Zafeera's eyes Fareed's, her chest rose and fell with a sigh of relief and her heart sped up with anticipation. Now, at last, she would see Ghaybaa again. The thought filled her eyes with salty tears and she wasted no time.

"Where is my sister? I want to see her now!" Fareed and Al-Mutabi exchanged glances.

"So, you are the one Ghaybaa talked about. You are more shameful than she was."

"Was? What do you mean: was? Where is she? She left you?"

"She's where you will be very soon," Mutabi replied calmly. Zafeera searched his face. A sense of dread came over her. She turned back to Fareed.

"Did you hurt her?" she demanded, her lips quivering. "Did you? Did you hurt my sister?" she shouted. Both men took offense by her insolence, but Fareed chose to bait her.

"She was not fit to be the wife of a true believer," said Fareed. "She never did her prayers. She never—"

"What did you do, throw her in a cell because she wouldn't get on her knees five times a day? Huh?"

"She was stupid," he continued, ignoring her question. "Maybe insane." He tapped the side of his head. "Like you. She had the devil inside her."

"Devil? Ghaybaa? What are you talking about? She was—"

"Possessed by evil! He had to do it," Mutabi added. "The music took her soul."

"Answer me! Where is my sister?"

"She is dead! She was possessed by the—

In one split second, rage had propelled her through the air so swiftly, neither man had a chance to react. Targeting Fareed, she went straight for his eyes and gouged so hard she drew blood. He screamed out in anguish and grabbed hold of her wrists to yank her hands away. But she kneed him in the groin. He let go, doubling over. She went in for an all-out assault: hitting, punching, and kicking. For a moment, she was back in that dark, damp storage room.

A stunned Mutabi reacted with shouts for assistance. Instantly, the doors burst open and the room filled with police—guns drawn. It took six policemen using extreme force, to subdue the vengeful Zafeera long enough to get a humiliated Fareed up off the floor and out of the room to safety.

"Take this disgusting creature and put her in a cage where she belongs—a very small cage. Tomorrow she will become rat food like her sister."

Adrenaline still pumping through her veins and tears still streaming down her cheeks, Zafeera shook herself free long enough to yank Mutabi's long black beard with all her might. He slapped her down, but she lurched towards him from a kneeling position and sent him sprawling against the empty bookcase. The police pounced on her like flies. She twisted around violently, and got caught up in the fabric of her chador.

Handcuffs restored, they dragged her away, but not before hearing an infuriated Mutabi command: "I want everybody to watch. Everybody!"

CHAPTER 31

With nothing over her eyes, Zafeera was hoisted into the back of a dusty pickup truck like a sack of potatoes. Four policemen with rifles climbed in behind her and the truck zoomed down the driveway and out past a checkpoint.

Lying face down, nose running, saliva drooling from the corners of her mouth, her body was jarred by every bump in the road. Feelings of failure and immense despair reached so deep, she began to lose consciousness. Ghaybaa was dead. It had all been for nothing. All those nights in that horrible dingy bedsit hoping to run into her, to save her, and all the time Ghaybaa was already gone. She had slipped right through their fingers.

The policemen guarding her were silent. They were aware that this woman had physically attacked Mutabi, so looked forward to seeing her before a firing squad.

A mile from the compound, the pickup truck encountered a mule-driven wagon with a broken axle blocking the road. The rear of the wagon was filled with crates of eggs and two women were unloading the crates and stacking them carefully on the side of the road.

The truck slowed and inched towards the wagon. With rocks lining both sides of the road, passing them would not be easy. The driver made a hard-left turn in order to squeeze around the wagon. When the truck was perpendicular to the wagon, the two women spun around, flung open their black cloaks and pointed assault rifles at the truck.

One rifle was trained on the police in the rear, the other on the cab.

"Hands in the air! Now! Now!" one woman ordered, in Arabic. Startled, the police raised their arms, reluctantly, watching for an opportunity to overtake them.

The second woman walked to the side of the truck, waving her weapon.

"Stand up!" she shouted in English. "Come on, stand up now!" Out of her purview, one of the policemen stood and took aim. A bullet from behind him grazed his ear and his weapon dropped to the ground.

"Zafeera! Zafeera! Are you all right?" she called out.

On the bottom of the truck, surrounded by the muddy boots of the uniformed men, Zafeera heard her name in the distance and struggled to sit up. She had no idea what was happening. The woman rushed closer, peered in and saw Zafeera moving. Relieved, she ordered the policemen to get out as she climbed up. Each of them hopped down with their hands in the air, obediently, aware there was another gun pointing at them behind the rocks.

Zafeera held out her hand for extra support as the woman helped her to her feet. She saw a dark brown hand grip hers, firmly, and she could see warm moist eyes through the slit in the veil.

"Take your time. I have you," a familiar voice said reassuringly.

As soon as both women were off the truck, an old car sped out from behind the rocks and stopped a few yards in front of the wagon. Another woman got out and walked towards the group.

With her clarity and sense of purpose restored, Zafeera ordered the men to take off their rifles and lay them on the ground. When they had complied, she picked up two of them and headed for the waiting car, nodding in appreciation to the first woman who diligently watched the two police at the front. The third woman from the car picked up two more rifles and pointed one at the four men. Finally, the woman who had helped Zafeera waved her rifle at the men, ordering them to back away from their truck. When they didn't move fast enough, she jabbed one with the nose of her gun making them even more infuriated. Then, she ripped off her covering and threw it at them. All four policemen jumped back startled, then they stared, mortified, at a beautiful, tall black woman with just a strip of purple kinky hair down the middle of her head. Angela 'Mohawk' Johnson laughed at them and then picked up their remaining weapons.

With just a smile, the woman behind the wheel handed Zafeera a bottle of cool water, which she guzzled before the brake was off. Behind her, the three remaining WILA members ordered the six policemen to lie face down on the ground. As the car pulled away, Zafeera glanced in the side mirror in time to see her team pummeling the men with eggs.

But, before the scene faded altogether from view, Zafeera was sure she heard six distinct gunshots.

***

They re-entered Turkey on four different buses. Zafeera and twenty WILA soldiers spent a week decompressing in local non-descript hotels before traveling by rail to France.

Worse than finding out that Ghaybaa was dead was telling her family. Her mother collapsed and was inconsolable. But it was really her father, Vasilis, who took it the hardest. He immediately blamed himself for arranging the marriage knowing, in the end, Ghaybaa had just gone along with his wishes. Both of her brothers threatened to kill Fareed, but Zafeera pointed out it wouldn't bring Ghaybaa back.

That night, she laid awake in the room she and Ghaybaa shared as children, listening to her mother sob and wail. Unable to sleep, she went into the sitting room and logged onto WILA's website.

Already, video footage had been uploaded of the Guatemalan incident, the Iranian prison break and the Syrian warehouse explosion complete with the freed inmates being helped into vans and the police opening fire, hitting some of them. And the last post was Zafeera's rescue.

By documenting as much as they could, and posting it online, WILA had control over what was seen and what was reported about them.

She clicked the play button on the rescue clip. The camera's vantage point was high up on the rocks, with a full view of the truck, wagon and she getaway vehicle. The time counter read twelve minutes. She fast-forwarded the tape towards the end, and then clicked play again. The car she had been in at the time disappeared off the left side of the screen while the police had eggs thrown at them.

Angela seemed to enjoy humiliating the men by laughing, while the other two WILA soldiers stopped to disagree about something. During the moment that they argued, one of her soldiers could be seen gesturing up at the camera. At that point, the video portion went black and then gunshots were heard. The implications, greatly concerned her, the possibility sickened her. There was absolutely no reason to kill those policemen. That was not what WILA was about. How were any of her soldiers with guns different from men who used violence to deal with every confrontation? If any of her soldiers killed again, in upcoming conflicts, how would she determine whether, or not, it was in self-defense? She would have to come up with a way to address this complicated issue before the entire group when she got back to the Land.

Right now, she desperately craved a cigarette, but her father didn't believe women should be allowed to smoke. He had no idea who Zafeera had become, or what she'd been up to during the past year, let alone the last six months. All the same, Zafeera chose to respect her father's beliefs while staying in his house. Ever since her initial provocative full-page ads had appeared in foreign newspapers, which had received a deluge of responses, and her reported appearance at Neelam Sethi's first meeting with the women's coalition, Zafeera had gained a cult-like following amongst teenage girls in France, Romania, Macedonia, South Korea and Lebanon. Girls who said she was the first role model who wasn't a pop star, and they needed someone they could relate to and aspire to be like. A few thousand of these girls emailed WILA regularly, and created Facebook pages to connect with each other.

The internationally televised Guatemalan and Mashhad missions guaranteed that every day more people would be logging on to WILA's website, which, in turn, linked to various other websites across the world that also called for an end of repression and violence against women, websites complete with their own videos and strategies. Employing a full-time staff of IT specialists who utilized the full power of the Internet, social media sites, forums and Twitter, in no time, WILA.org became the central coordinating hub of information about this new, organically evolving, International Sisterhood, complete with associated events, mission statements and goals outlined.

Consequently, women were being informed at lightning speed about various levels and masks of oppression all around them—like a matrix—and how they could liberate themselves, starting with their own consciousness.

She was informed that colleges in the United States were reporting an increased enrollment in Women's Studies courses. In Italy, college students were suddenly developing an interest in the papacy and all its treatises on women, while South Africa, France and New Zealand had an increased demand for classes in self-defense.

At that moment, Zafeera decided WILA should create their own branded self-defense techniques that could be learned by girls as young as seven. In the first few months of WILA's inception, new lectures and workshops on women's issues were held across America, creating a greater sense of community than the earlier women's liberation movement of the '70s in the United States, which had marginalized women of color while focusing too much on sexual freedom and equal pay.

Women's needs, empowerment, and sexual harassment became the topics most talked about in the churches.

And, true to form, an anti-WILA movement, started by ultraconservative women, sprung up across America, Mexico, China and Brazil, with scathing magazine articles, blog posts, and demonstrations about the dangers of militarizing women. Many believed that the CIA and the Department of Homeland Security were behind the Anti-WILA movement.

***

Zafeera yawned and continued staring at the computer screen. On any given day, WILA's general inbox contained the usual five to six hundred emails, many of which had already been handled by the admin staff housed in South London. Her private screen name account was only known to a select few. When she entered her password, she discovered several hundred of her own emails that needed sorting through. Much too tired and still grieving the loss of Ghaybaa, she decided to just scan the addresses and subject line. One unknown address had sent her almost twenty emails since she'd last logged on five weeks ago.

It was from a man insisting that they meet—that he wanted to 'help WILA' and had 'very important connection'. He included a private cell number and said she could call anytime. Each subsequent email provided a little more information about his connections. He said he had the finances she needed and access to other important services no one else could offer her. Suspicious and intrigued, she called the number.

The man's voice on the recording sounded like someone fluent in many languages, therefore, she could not determine his nationality beyond a British education. She left a message without leaving her name. First, she wanted to know what city or country he was in and, second, how did he expect to meet with her.

He responded by email the next day telling her he could meet in whatever city she desired. She wrote back asking why should she trust him and how would she know this wasn't some kind of setup to trap her into a picture or worse, to capture her.

An hour later he wrote back reminding her that he had her private email address that only a few people knew, therefore, he must be very close to a trusted colleague of hers. She pondered that for a moment, and then telephoned him. He answered.

Since she was in Paris, she suggested they meet early evening at the Fontaine de l'Observatoire in the Jardin Marco Polo, which was south of Jardin du Luxembourg.

"Yes, I am familiar with the park and think that is a perfect place to meet."

"I will be wearing a baseball cap and dark glasses," she informed, feeling somewhat excited. It gets very crowded there. How will I recognize you?"

"I will find you," he replied, confidently.

The day had started with a brilliant blue sky, which balanced the gray gloom in the house. Without a body to mourn over, Ghaybaa's death could easily be dismissed as a lie.

"Maybe she is still alive," her mother said in hope. But death was the only explanation for not receiving one letter, or phone call, in almost a year.

No one had the strength or the appetite to eat the breakfast Zafeera had prepared. By late afternoon, the house began to fill with friends and neighbors. Buxom women in flowing black abayas brought homemade favorites that sat drying out on the table.

Men gathered in the living room and the women congregated in the cramped dining room. Her brothers' friends went straight to the boys' bedroom to listen to music.

By the time early evening rolled around, the sky was as gray as her mother's face.

She told her father she had to meet a business associate and would be home late. He asked what kind of business required her to dress like a boy. She avoided an argument by giving him a warm embrace and dashing out quickly.

She arrived at the Jardin Marco Polo ahead of schedule and walked to the southern end. She stopped about forty meters away, thinking she could spot the mystery man before he saw her.

The threat of rain had emptied half the park and about twenty people lingered around the Fontaine de l'Observatoire. Tourists were always easy to spot. They were the ones posing happily, despite a few clouds overhead.

She wasn't the only woman with a cap, it turned out, but she was certainly the only woman wearing a cap over a headscarf, and sunglasses.

Looking up at the top of Jean-Baptiste Carpeaux's sculpture in the center of the fountain, she gazed at the globe supported by four women— each representing the continents of Asia, Africa, Europe and America. The sculpture's reference had been a favorite of hers in her art history class: women supporting the Earth.

She moved closer glancing at everyone who passed.

After a while, a man in his forties approached her from the right also wearing dark glasses and dressed like an Ivy League professor. His dark olive skin and the closed top button of his light blue shirt screamed Indian, Persian or, maybe, Arabian, like herself.

With a look of complete surprise, he bowed formally, but did not offer his hand.

"I hope you haven't been waiting too long. We had to get special clearance."

"Special clearance?"

"Yes. For my plane."

"You have your own plane?"

"Of course."

He studied her face, her cap and quickly glanced down at her pants and sneakers with added curiosity. "I expected you to be…"

"White?"

"Yes," he smiled, a very beguiling smile. "Your accent is…"

"Was it my accent that made you assume I was white, or was it who I am, and what WILA is?"

Another beguiling smile, this time revealing bleached white teeth.

He started walking and she fell in comfortably alongside him.

"I know this is rather awkward for both of us," he said. "You see, I cannot give you my real name and you, obviously, cannot give me yours. So, what do we do about that?"

"Let's not worry about that just yet," Zafeera responded. "I want to know how you can help WILA."

"I can do several things. But after watching the films on your website, I know what you are trying to do right now requires a more realistic strategy, better supplies, equipment and much more than fifty troops. For a start, I can provide you with one thousand trained men to help the fight."

"Are you crazy? We don't want men! WILA is for women only. Our entire purpose is to empower women, and show that we are, fully capable, to fight our own battles. Save ourselves! Obviously, you do not understand us at all." She shook her head. "This was a waste of my time."

"Perhaps you are right, I do not understand. But I want to understand. I admire you very much." Zafeera slowed and looked over at him. He removed his sunglasses, and she saw he was honest. "Please. I can get you the very best artillery, and I can assure you the latest survival equipment, heat sensors, shields, protective clothing, and military vehicles."

"How much?"

"Nothing."

"Oh, I see. You prefer other forms of payment."

Appalled at the suggestion, he quickly tried to clarify.

"I am a very rich man. I have everything you can possibly imagine. I want nothing from you but your success."

That only increased her suspicions. How could he possibly want her success, when every opportunity he had in life was based on him being better—more deserving than she—because he was a man? Her success... WILA's success would put an end to that.

He saw this on her face. "I love my wife," he said earnestly. "She is a stunningly beautiful, highly educated woman who is unable to do anything with that other than shop and attend lavish parties, secretly, and only when we are abroad. At home, she stays cloistered behind marble or enveloped in her many black sequined cloaks. If our circumstances were different, she would probably join your fighting forces, too. I am doing this for her."

"Where are you from?"

"I cannot tell you that."

"Why? What could I possibly do, if I knew?"

"I am not sure. But I think it is best for everyone if you don't know that... yet."

"I have no way of protecting myself if I say yes to you."

"So, you are saying yes to my help?"

"For the equipment and the military vehicles—those things, yes."

He thought for a moment. "You know, except for you, and perhaps your own soldiers, no one has to know that most of them are men. They can all wear the burka."

"That is absurd! If they were captured... or killed, it would be humiliating for us."

"No... no, wait. If anything like that happens, if any of the men are shot, they would be carried off and handled by women. That is the custom. You know that. So, if your women soldiers take the bodies as soon as they can, no man will ever see them."

Zafeera was silent, contemplating this. She'd still need to work out how and where they would combine forces. The Land was a dojo, army base and sanctuary for women only. Every woman there was handpicked. How would she handle a thousand men? She couldn't.

She explained the concept of the Land to him as best she could and he found it fascinating.

He suggested that the male troops be used only for combat type missions or when numbers were needed as a show of force. Moments later, her stomach growled.

They ate at Les Papilles on Rue Gay Lussac. She had a glass of wine. She told him about her encounter with Al-Mutabi and watched his eyes nearly pop from his skull. They laughed.

"Men like Mutabi can never see themselves on the wrong side of anything. He's already marked you for death. If you don't take him down, you will always have to look over your shoulder." She nodded, considering what he said and poured herself another glass of wine. Then out of the blue, he offered to fly her back to London.

At first, she thought she had mentioned London inadvertently. Then she realized she hadn't.

"How did you know I live in London?" She saw his face flush when he realized he had slipped up. Was this, some kind of, entrapment? Panicking, she started to get up from the table.

"Please, Zafeera!"

Astounded, she dropped back down in the chair heavily, with her mouth open. "You know my name? All this time, you knew my name?"

"Yes, I am sorry. I had to know whom I am risking my... I had you investigated. I know everything about you that is necessary."

"How? Nobody knows I created WILA. I mean, no one you know about, except the women themselves and even some of them in the network don't know my real name. I know none of them would betray me."

"I assure you, your identity is safe with me. I just needed to protect myself, you understand."

"But who are you? Where's my protection?" she glared back, aggressively.

"All right!" He threw up his hand. "You can call me Bashi."

"Bashi?"

"Yes," Bashi said.

"And that will protect me?" Zafeera asked, doubtfully.

"Maybe. Now listen. In a few days, I will prove to you that you have my genuine support. Tonight, I want you to post whatever supplies you need on your website and I will get them to you."

He took out a diamond studded cell phone from his breast pocket, placed a call and said, in Arabic, "I am ready."

Leaving the waiter two days' pay as a tip, Bashi escorted her out.

Right in front of the restaurant sat a sleek white Rolls Royce with darkened windows. The chauffeur got out and opened the door. He gestured for Zafeera to get in. She hesitated, feeling confused and, quite frankly, dumbfounded.

"Go on. It is late. He will take you home."

She shook her head, but found her body inching closer to the inviting cocoon of the car. The tan leather seats were soft like lambskin. Bashi closed the door behind her, and watched until his chariot sped off, merged into traffic and disappeared down the Champs-Elysées.

Was this really happening? What an amazing evening, Zafeera thought. Fortunately, it was late when she arrived back at her parents' home. The streets were deserted except for a passer-by here and there—no one she knew. She got out of the gleaming white, yacht-on-wheels, and watched it drive away. A person in that neighborhood could live a whole lifetime and never glimpse a Rolls Royce, let alone ride in one.

What did it matter anyway? His "stunningly beautiful, highly educated" wife was still a prisoner of her culture and tradition. She was his trophy, and he was hers. Money defined them. Yet somehow her husband's wealth could not buy her personal freedom.

Zafeera tiptoed into the bedroom and stretched out on Ghaybaa's bed, to reflect on the mysterious Bashi. Could he be trusted? Should she let him get involved with WILA? It was impossible for her to be decisive one way or the other.

Before falling asleep, she emailed Bashi to inform him that she decided to wait until she got back to the Land before posting what she needed, that way she could discuss everything with her advisors.

The new day brought less gloom in the house.

On her way to her parent's room, she spotted her mother sitting on the couch in the living room, shoulders hunched with sorrow, her hands folded over a book on her lap. A few neighborhood women, Zafeera did not know, sat silently nearby.

Zafeera nodded at the women, knelt before her mother, and clasped hold of her lifeless hands. She kissed and rubbed them against her cheek and her mother lifted her head enough to focus her weary eyes on Zafeera. Feeling the pang of guilt, Zafeera wondered what the women were thinking. That she didn't have to meet that man, Bashi? She should have stayed with the family and mourned. But hadn't she mourned enough? She'd had already been mourning Ghaybaa for the past year.

It was, definitely, time for a cup of strong coffee. Zafeera gently let go of her mother's hands.

They dropped down heavily on her lap making the book—a notebook—fall to the floor. Zafeera picked it up for her and peeked inside. French? Her mother didn't understand French. Then she recognized the handwriting. Page after page was filled with song lyrics. Verses and choruses were neatly marked.

"Where did you get this, Mama?"

One of the women went over to the computer desk, picked up a large empty manila envelope and handed it to Zafeera. She checked the postmark. It had been sent six days earlier without a return address. But it was obvious to her it came from Fareed. So… he had a conscience after all.

Overcome and anxious to read it, Zafeera returned to her bedroom shutting the door.

Crouched in the corner, eyes gushing, Zafeera finally found Ghaybaa amongst the words. Ghaybaa's own way of seeing—of feeling— was written within them. The things she cared about, her pain, her loneliness. Her deep hunger for things she could never have and her longing for things she could not identify. All revealed there on the page: a whole person and a personality:

> *The only things I have of real value now are my words—*
> *written in solo.*
> *Without censor. Without care if they will be liked or not.*
> *My words are me, pure and simple.*

*Unleashed from some deep torrent ocean of desire and carried to
the surface of my mind by tiny subs of inspiration,
Captained by frustration.
They are me—my words. It is all that I am.
My body is not mine. I did not design it,
I don't take much part in its nourishment, regeneration or repair.
Now my husband owns it.
Does what he wants to it.
My Life is not my own, parents have mapped out the course for me
and still others navigate it (in spite of my dreams and longings) to
their own island.
At any given moment, a storm can brew up and tear my life apart.
So, how can it be my life?
Did I create the storm or direct its course?
At any given moment, an impetus within me compels me to eat,
drink, speak, favor one color over the other; to like this music— not
that music.
This fashion—not that one.
Why?
But my words are my own. They are me.
They question who I am. What is life anyway?
I can hate or love with my words.
And if some fire came and burned the paper on which they are
written—
Then the Ether will carry them into eternity,
or scatter them in time.*

Ghaybaa's lyrics, like all authentic art, were her catharsis, the balm that healed her, a magic carpet promising new lands and new possibilities. And when Zafeera had reached the final page, nose red and swollen, her heart ached for more and her ears craved the melodies that would have truly given those words wings.

CHAPTER 32

NEW YORK

No one was happier about the forum on honor killing at the United Nations, than Imani Sadawi. She was the one who had pushed Kensasha to go to London and meet with Dr. Sethi. And it was she who had hosted the women's group where Neelam Sethi first spoke in America.

Imani, like all the other women in the coalition, had written countless letters in the hope of getting a hearing. The rejection letters always referred to the conferences on violence against women that had already been held in Beijing and Mexico, years ago, where new propositions and legislation had been passed. They also cited the most recent event held at Manhattan's Lincoln Center.

One rejection letter, specifically, had caught Imani's eye, because it included a reprint of, a previously, public statement:

"We are very aware of all of the situations of violence women are faced with in the world today. We have done extensive research into the causes of this violence, especially rape—which has reached epidemic proportions, already, in this decade. I personally believe it is a perversion of the mind—men's minds. There is no dignity in it no matter who does it.

"Rape is also a type of discrimination that stops women from fully participating in all areas of society and fulfilling their potential both as women and as human beings."[1]

The letter had been written by a newly appointed director of the United Nations Committee on Violence against Women and Girls, and went on to give an analysis on patriarchy and cited it as the prime cause behind all violations of women's right as if this was some new revelation. Quoting some document in the letter, the director said that for real change to occur, nations had to take another look at how their society was structured and re-evaluate all the relations between men and women.

"We now believe that only through a fundamental restructuring of society and its institutions could women be fully empowered to take their rightful place as equal partners with men in all aspects of life."[2]

Great! Imani thought. But until we can restructure society fundamentally, what do we do right now to stop the next child from being killed?' Frustrated and downhearted, she called Kensasha, right away, and began to read her the latest rejection letter. But Kensasha stopped her abruptly, saying she had received the same exact letter, as did every other petitioner that month.

Imani did not realize, at the time, that ever since Kensasha's initial return from London, she had set her mind to making Imani and Neelam's dream come true. She would get them a public platform, to expose to the world, customs, she, too, found utterly deplorable. And she was determined not to let another bureaucrat, no matter how eloquent, dissuade her. Instead, she resolutely smoothed out her copy of the same letter, got four pushpins and tacked it to her wall of rejection letters, which happened to have been juxtaposed to her vision board with the women's forum as its central objective. For those reasons, she couldn't possibly give up.

Shortly afterward, Imani, Enid and Neelam finally settled on a name: The Coalition to Stop Domestic Terrorism Against Women and Girls, and the new director at the United Nations, Heidi Schecter,

---

[1] Actual United Nations public statement—posted on the Internet—based on research studies on causes of escalating violence toward women and girls, internationally.
[2] ibid

received a special delivery parcel from Professor Kensasha Lewis. In it were the audio interviews that Kensasha recorded of the young women, in Dr. Sethi's charge, just weeks before they were all murdered in the Safe House Massacre, along with Dr. Sethi's essay identifying Gender Terrorism. Their forum got the green light.

***

Prior to the forum's start date, Kensasha booked hotel rooms for Neelam and Enid at a new boutique hotel on Second Avenue and 44th St, a few blocks from the U.N., then called around for the best group rates and forwarded the information to the presidents of the ten women's organizations who were participating.

That June, one week before the Forum, members and designated speakers of the ten participating organizations based in the United Kingdom, France, Spain and Sweden began arriving in New York City in order to visit as many media outlets as possible, hang posters, pass out fliers, meet the U.N. Director and hold last minute rehearsals of their PowerPoint presentations in the actual conference hall.

Wasting no time, Kensasha, Neelam and Enid headed straight to the United Nations' new conference building after breakfast, and met with the director, Heidi Schecter, a petite woman with short gray hair and clear blue eyes, who escorted them to the door of the conference room where the forum would be held. Then she went off to get personnel who would be assisting with the technical and personal needs of the presenters.

They walked in and stood staring in silence. Enid was the first to speak.

"I imagined a much larger space," she said.

"You mean like the general assembly hall with leaders from all the nations of the world present and accounted for?" Kensasha asked, laying her briefcase on a chair.

"Well, yes," she said, sounding disappointed. "I guess that is what I had imagined. How about you, Neelam? What did you imagine? Don't you think this is rather small?"

Neelam looked around the hall. Of course, it wasn't General Assembly Hall, but it could easily hold about three hundred people with standing room. The fact that they were granted a hearing at all was satisfying enough for her. What was important wasn't the size of the hall but who would attend. Would they have the attention they desperately needed? Thousands of correspondences and RSVPs didn't guarantee anything.

She wiped her forehead and removed her purple silk jacket. "If there are people sitting in the rafters, I do not care. As long as we do our part, and motivate the people who have the ear of those in power, it will be fine."

The hall had three main doors and three aisles leading to a podium and raised platform and it was equipped with three enclosed booths containing state of the art audio-visual equipment.

"Hello! Sorry I'm late. Couldn't get in touch with my contact at Time magazine." The auburn-haired Thai woman with a slight London accent scanned the hall as she walked toward the others. "Not very big, is it?"

"I've been vindicated," Enid exclaimed and took a seat.

Kensasha laughed and said, "That's what we were just talking about." She offered her hand to the woman in her mid-40s. "I'm Kensasha Lewis. Are you Amanda Kurtami of AWRI? We spoke on the phone."

"Yes, I am." Amanda took her hand. "It's good to finally meet you. Last night at dinner would have been better, but I had to meet some of our members at the airport. Now I'm wondering if this hall can hold everyone."

She turned to Neelam, who was putting on her glasses to examine a procedural document the director had given her. "We may have to reserve a third of the seats don't you think, Neelam?"

Neelam hadn't been listening. She was exhausted from packing, from preparing for the trip and from traveling. She was concerned that everyone scheduled might not get a chance to present. She was worried about the advocates that had already begun congregating outside the U.N. even though the Forum was six days away. Will Aisha be all right, on her own? She wondered. Who set the thermostat so high on such a hot day?

"Neelam!" Startled, she looked up. All the other women were staring at her.

"What? What is it?"

Before anyone could respond, Imani Sadawi arrived in her regal manner, adorned like an Egyptian goddess, a long sheer black iridescent scarf loosely draped on her head, a colorful Moroccan-style dress ending at her ankles, high-heeled sandals and large gold earrings that swayed with her every move. She introduced herself to Amanda Kurtami and nodded at Enid Statham whom she had met at dinner the night before.

Heart racing, she was so excited to be there, Imani immediately took charge, oblivious to the size of the room. She reminded them that it was important to have all the presenters with media materials meet at the hall the day before the forum was to begin. She suggested they each have specific areas to oversee so that everything ran smoothly. No hitches.

Moments later, the director came back with a team of nine U.N. employees experienced in multimedia presentations. After everyone was introduced, the designing phase began. The director stayed as long as she could to provide pointers and make her own suggestions. She, as much as the others, wanted the forum to be a success. Her department had notified diplomats as well as the standard notifications to leaders of government but, so far, had received minimal response.

Hours into the planning, and after poring over different program designs, Mrs. Sadawi noticed a name that had not been inserted in the first two drafts of the second day's events. Suddenly, there it was.

"Who is Claudia Velasquez? I don't recall seeing that name before. Which organization is she with?"

"I don't know. I… uh, haven't seen it, either." Kensasha reviewed the names of presidents, and the names of all the members, in the ten organizations, who would be attending, but couldn't find a Claudia Velasquez written anywhere.

Enid kept silent. Claudia Velasquez had been a point of contention between her and Neelam. She waited for Neelam to illuminate the situation, but Amanda Kurtami beat her to it.

"Wasn't she involved somehow with WILA and that Guatemalan incident? Remember? Everyone was talking about it."

"But what does that have to do with this forum," Kensasha inquired, addressing her question to the three ladies from London. "Who wrote her name here?"

Neelam finally owned up. "She only wants ten minutes."

"What does she expect to say about honor killing or dowry deaths or female infanticide that no one else will say? We have thirty-three speeches listed already."

"I don't think it will be about those things, but she asked, and I said okay."

"Tell her it is not possible, there are too many people already and that will end it," Imani ordered.

"I will do no such thing!" Neelam countered. "I told her she could speak at the forum. And that is that. There is no need to make more of this than is necessary. I feel we need to expand our focus and take it off just the poor from our countries, Imani. You didn't see the photographs she sent me, but I assume she will bring copies with her."

Imani certainly wasn't used to anyone talking back to her, not even her husband.

"You are talking about photographs and we are saying anyone presenting a different cause at this forum will dilute the whole purpose of it. All our intentions will be blurred into hundreds of other problems out there. What have we been working to stop for the last year? Honor killings."

***

LONDON

There was no need for Basma to go to the airport with them. Waving goodbye as the black taxi pulled away was painful and frightening enough. Instead, Basma went to the office to check the mail. Everything was in perfect order. Even so, without phone calls to be answered or made, without a stack of letters to file, there was little else she could do. Neelam always handled her own correspondences.

Basma made herself a cup of chai then sat behind Neelam's desk hoping to get the same view of the world that Dr. Neelam Sethi did.

What on earth would she do for the next ten days, alone in London? Finding a tutor may be the first thing. Now how exactly would she go about doing that? The Internet?

She could visit one of the safe houses; talk to the women, bring books and magazines to them. Tell them about the forum. Yes, that was a great idea. Okay, one day filled, nine more to go.

Her bedroom needed painting. That could take up a full day. Maybe two days since she knew nothing about painting and would have to buy all the supplies and read up on how to do it.

She didn't finish her chai. It wasn't nearly as good as Neelam's.

Kensasha would meet them at JFK airport.

It wasn't so long ago that Kensasha, who had shopped for her, had traveled to Boston and then seen her off to London.

Basma locked up the office and walked out onto the busy thoroughfare. It was past noon and she simply had no place to go. A strong wave of melancholy overtook her. Every single day for the past eight months, the forum had been on her mind. Now that it had become reality, she could not attend. She could not be there amongst the most important women in her life: Kensasha Lewis, Mrs. Sadawi and Dr. Sethi, witnessing the manifestation of something she had been an integral part of, because she, Basma Abseh, alias Aisha Langois, was dead.

She wandered the streets with all kinds of impulses pulling at her. Being able to make one's own choices in life was a heady experience for someone who had previously had no choice, or always needed someone else's approval before going anywhere, buying or doing anything. It was like being a perpetual child, never achieving the gift of independence adulthood brings.

Once again, amidst a sea of people, the angst that had overwhelmed her on the flight to England resurfaced. The notion of freedom for any woman in the world took on a whole new form, a new dimension when there were multiple choices—all with their accompanying consequences— and she was on her own.

For Basma, there was no longer a husband around to dictate what, how, why, who or when. There were no neighbors scrutinizing everything she wore or did. No family honor to hold dearer than her own life. Her precious sons were now men. She had $6500 in the bank under her new name. She earned enough money to pay the rent and still have enough left over for utilities and food. It wasn't a lucrative income, but to her it was more than she'd ever had.

Living on her own, she could choose to eat or not. Choose to pray or not. Follow Islam, Christianity, become a Hindu, a Buddhist or Jew… or not. Choose to be with a man… or not. She was the first of her tribe, the first in her family to become an *independent* woman.

All along the high street, there were always interesting shops to explore, different cuisines to sample: a bakery here, a perfumery there. Her new discovery was just up ahead. She recognized it the moment she saw it by the tingling in her body—the sudden feeling of anticipation and mischievousness. How many times had she walked past it while others rushed in? Wasn't this a place for the un-believers? The infidels? A place forever forbidden to all the women in her family, because of its immense power to influence, inspire and corrupt? But now…

She walked up to a window, not caring who saw her, and gave them what they asked for. A few minutes later, in the cool darkness a completely new universe seemed to unfold. As the images passed before her, tears filled her eyes. When the music played, she felt her heart expand, her body rise toward the sky. She was swept off to de-lightful realms of fantasy previously unimaginable to her, and she never wanted to return.

Sitting there, alone, in the last row of a movie theater, Basma Ab-seh finally found happiness.

THE MIDDLE EAST

Same day

The demonstration had taken five weeks to organize, and an-other three weeks to get all fifty soldiers from WILA over the Syrian border and assimilated, inconspicuously, into the social milieu.

Five women's organizations based in Syria had come up with the idea to protest the closing of women's colleges in the districts con-trolled, primarily, by Al-Mutabi's militia. It was the same place where district leaders thought it okay to imprison women who did not follow the strict dress code the Mullahs, under pressure from Al-Mutabi, imposed. The prison break several months back had inspired many women enough to want to capture the ears of the Mullahs.

Hundreds of emails had been sent and flyers distributed announcing the time and place. Waving signs and posters, several hundred women of varying ages and economic standing showed up in the walled courtyard of one of the colleges—its hallways and classrooms vacant. But the long-silenced courtyard was now abuzz with anticipation and hope.

Every woman had arrived in black burkas or abayas. Many faces were covered. WILA, with the help of their own black chadors, easily blended with the crowd—including thirty of them who carried assault weapons.

After intense discussions, Zafeera thought it best not to use male troops, as Bashi had suggested, since this was a peaceful gathering. Getting her women in and out of Syria safely was all she had asked of him and so far, he had delivered. Phone calls to the right people at the right time and they found themselves crossing borders like the nationals.

Zafeera, the only woman wearing a baseball cap over her hijab, paced nervously as she recalled the last time she had been in that city. Quick flashes of the steamy hot warehouse, the despair on the women's faces before they were set free and Al-Mutabi's deadly stare popped in and out of her mind. "If you don't take him down," Bashi had warned, "you'll be looking over your shoulder for the rest of your life." Worse, still, was hearing Fareed's voice calling Ghaybaa evil and the sickening feeling she had in her stomach when he told her Ghaybaa was dead.

The organizers had a little podium erected for the occasion and had arranged for an independent news crew to travel from Damascus to film it.

The first person to speak was a teacher. She talked about how rewarding and fulfilling teaching had been for her, how much she loved her students and how devastating it was to see the school closed. She told the crowd how she had tried to hold classes in her home for some of the girls, but when this was discovered, she was jailed for several months. Other teachers shared similar experiences, often becoming emotional— on the other hand, the suspended students shouted about losing their civil rights and being denied the same education their brothers received. The students stressed how important an education was in helping them become independent and self-sufficient, how it was helping them learn skills that would have made them employable enough to contribute to their family and society.

Fifty minutes into these speeches, police motorcycles, vans and jeeps began to arrive outside the perimeter. The sounds muffled the speeches inside. When no police actually appeared inside the courtyard, the women, determinedly, pressed on. Some of them appealed to the Mullahs, specifically, to reinstate their legal rights to an education.

Widowed mothers, who originally came just to observe, began shouting about the loss of their jobs when all women were banished from the workforce and how they were now unable to provide for their children.

Finally, Zafeera stepped up onto the podium. It was the first time she'd stood before people who weren't enlisting. Whispers circled the crowd as they speculated who she was. She clarified that she no longer needed to remain anonymous. Mutabi and Fareed already knew who she was.

"My name is Zafeera, and I am the founder of WILA and I want you to know that WILA is here to support you."

At first, the crowd gasped. Then, they began to applaud and whistle and wave their placards feverishly. The startled news crew zoomed in with their camera, for a tighter shot. Cell phones could be seen in use everywhere.

"Listening to all of you," Zafeera continued. "I am reminded of just how absolute these oppressive laws are. They target and restrict every aspect of your life. Just being here, today, outside and talking about these injustices requires courage from all of you. I want you to acknowledge and applaud the women who took it upon themselves to arrange this demonstration."

The crowd applauded.

"Those of you who have been to our website know what we stand for is the total liberation of women. That means social, political, and religious liberation."

The crowd whistled and cheered.

Meanwhile, four hand-trucks containing metal trash bins were wheeled a few yards from the podium by WILA soldiers and arranged in a circle.

Volunteers stepped from amongst the demonstrators and began directing people to back up and a fire was started in each of the bins.

WILA soldiers lined up on both sides of the podium facing the audience.

Minutes later, the religious police in full riot gear began filing through the two corner entrances at the south end of the courtyard opposite the podium and lined up along the sidewalls. A jolt of electricity rippled through the crowd. Cell phones were raised and used as weapons by documenting whatever the news cameras couldn't and emailing it to family and friends who weren't present.

WILA soldiers gripped hold of the weapons beneath their robes.

The news crew, from Al Jazeera based in Damascus, zoomed out for a wide shot.

Demonstrators moved closer to each other creating a massive shield and braced for an attack. Beyond the wall, more news vans descended on the area.

Zafeera tapped the mike. It echoed. The crowd turned back to her.

She continued. "A few months ago, many of you suffered the humiliation of being arrested for wearing a colored scarf on your head or dying your hair or for some other violation of an unjust law. A law made specifically to rob you of your personal freedom and dignity.

"You were criminalized for doing a fraction of what all women in a free society do every day. This demonstration today is to show our solidarity and to make a stand against those who deny women a public face and who want us to be silent and invisible!

"We invite you to participate if you are not wearing your burkas, your abayas, your hijabs as a choice, but to obey. If you are not wearing hijab because of religious motivation, but out of fear—fear of being arrested, fear of being abused by your husbands, your fathers, your brothers—then participate! Do you cover out of fear of what others may say? Fear of being attacked and stoned to death by men who, God forbid, see there is flesh underneath? Isn't it easier for cowards like Mutabi to deny rights to the faceless and the voiceless?"

The demonstrators caught their breath when she mentioned Mutabi and Zafeera could feel the daggers from the row of religious police—all Mutabi's men.

She nodded to one of the volunteers and the fires were stoked. Next, two WILA soldiers walked out of the crowd to the smoking barrels, yanked off their hijabs and cast them into the burning flames. The onlookers gasped. Next, the two removed their abayas—the long coatdresses worn over their tee shirts and jeans—and tossed them in, as well, then walked back into the crowd.

The first teacher who spoke, moved to the flames next and pulled off her face covering and threw it in, then boldly unhooked her abaya, balled it up and threw it into the can. Sparks flew. In an instant, more teachers followed suit, some removing only their face covering.

However, when young students came up to the flames and took off their headscarves and the long robes covering their fashionable jeans and high heels, they made a dramatic display of it. Hundreds of other people watched in disbelief, while cell phone cameras clicked away.

No one found out who gave the order, but suddenly, the religious police moved in and began attacking all the demonstrators and, of course, the women fought back. The WILA soldiers tore open their robes and used the nose of their rifles to hold some of the police at bay. A lot of women got trampled in the melée.

Then shots were heard at the southeast gate. The melée ceased in that instant, when people recognized Al-Mutabi flanked by seven of his bodyguards with their weapons drawn.

Mutabi immediately ordered the police back in line. Then he looked on in disgust as if the women's presence alone was an affront to him.

Sparks from the burning robes shooting into the air caught Mutabi's attention. He began to walk in the direction of the podium to get a closer look at what was happening. Demonstrators rushed to either side as he approached creating a center path and he glimpsed their bare heads. Although, what really captured his attention were the flaming trashcans and what appeared to be garments strewn on the ground around them.

When he realized what was happening, he stopped and shouted, vehemently:

"I want every woman in here who has done this lewd act arrested."

"Did you patch up the wall yet?"

His head followed the direction of the voice, and he spotted Zafeera glaring back at him. His eyes widened in stupefaction.

Before he could respond, she stepped forward boldly, her head tilted up in a show of defiance. Keeping her eyes on him, baiting him, she tore off her abaya and flung it in the flames.

Once again, the demonstrators gasped. A subtle ripple of fear vibrated through the crowd.

She took off black-lace gloves and threw them on the ground, then stooped to untie her combat boots knowing every eye was on her.

She kicked them off and taunted him wearing her camouflage pants, army green tee shirt, and cap over a black hijab.

At first, Mutabi was dumbstruck at the spectacle, unaccustomed to defiant women. He stared at her with absolute loathing.

Finally, as she walked toward him reveling in the abhorrent expression on his face, she tore off her cap, threw it down, then unwrapped her hijab and flung it at him while shaking free her flaming-red dyed hair.

Mutabi's face appeared to swell and his eyes darkened. Zafeera beckoned him to attack her—craving another opportunity to fight him, this time in front of women. Everyone was dumbfounded.

Zafeera advanced, closing the gap, flaunting her freedom by strutting, stretching her arms wide and tossing her head—the long red mane swinging side to side—and dancing to music only she could hear. It was a bold, fearless, dramatic, and very flamboyant performance—which she had put on many times before in the confines of a child's bedroom to an audience of one.

A captivated crowd watched as she bopped and kicked her legs up as she'd seen her favorite artist do. She strummed her imaginary guitar all the while beckoning Mutabi closer, hungering to sink her nails into his flesh.

What was Zafeera doing? Vellanova wondered. This was not part of the plan. She looked around at her comrades. Each woman stared at Zafeera, poised to act upon command. Instead, Zafeera seemed to have forgotten their mission, entirely, and was out for her own personal vendetta.

He had called Ghaybaa rat food—said she was possessed by evil—he and her cowardly husband, Fareed. Where was Fareed? Zafeera wanted to finish him, too.

The TV camera crew eased through the crowd and zoomed in so that only Zafeera and Mutabi with his bodyguards were in the frame.

As Mutabi stood his ground like a stubborn bull, leering at her, Zafeera tossed her red mane and inched closer. Each held the other's gaze with equal loathing.

Zafeera took another step closer to Mutabi, playing her air guitar. She continued to provoke him, as everyone watched, stupefied.

Why won't he attack me? I want to fight him, she thought.

Cat Murphy spotted one of his guards grip his weapon tighter. She clutched her own.

"Attack me, you bastard," Zafeera muttered in Arabic. Mutabi still didn't move one inch. He just glared back.

Vellanova was just getting ready to leap out between Zafeera and Mutabi, to end the standoff when, all of a sudden, the air surrounding Zafeera stopped circulating.

Zafeera blinked, knowingly. Oh no! A split second later, Mutabi exploded. He spun around to his men and shouted, "Shoot her!"

Before WILA could react, before they could lift their weapons, the bodyguards opened fire, and, instead of Ghaybaa's fits of laughter, all Zafeera could hear was the hail of bullets that seemed to rip her flesh, forcing air from her lungs. She collapsed to the ground.

And, for the longest, agonizing, moment, everything was surreal. Too shocked to scream, no one uttered a sound. Even Mutabi's men who had pulled their triggers seemed visibly surprised that they had truly done it.

With horror, Angela, Cat, Inez and Vellanova rushed to Zafeera, calling out her name. Inez checked her pulse.

"Oh my God, oh my God, she's dead!" Angela screamed. "They killed her! They killed Zafeera!" No one moved, not even Mutabi.

Cat, Angela and Vellanova carefully lifted Zafeera up into their arms and carried her bullet-ridden body out of the schoolyard.

Inez remained behind to oversee the aftermath.

The next person to react was an old woman. She came out of the crowd, walked to the smoldering ashes, and with a show of disgust, took off her black robe and threw it in the fire and walked away. Seeing that, another woman instantly followed suit by discarding her robe and hijab, unceremoniously. Mutabi watched them, confounded.

In no time, about seventy women moved somberly to the bonfire, and began stripping off their robes and scarves and throwing them into the blaze.

For Mutabi, that was the final straw.

"Kill them all!" He commanded the police at the top of his lungs. His men lifted their rifles and took aim. WILA, weapons drawn, moved between the police and some of the demonstrators.

"Shoot! Shoot!" Mutabi commanded, red faced.

"But… but these are our sisters!" one policeman protested.

"And our wives," another called out.

Red with fury, he shouted again. "Shoot them, now, I said!"

"I won't kill my mother!"

Infuriated that his own men had disobeyed his direct order, Mutabi drew his own gun and pointed it at the crowd of women. Just when he pulled the trigger, one of his own bodyguards shoved him hard causing the bullets to sail over the women's heads, shatter a window in the vacant school, and Mutabi to stumble to the ground.

A WILA soldier walked up to the fallen leader and whispered, "Game over!"

Outside of the school walls, under the watchful eyes of more TV cameras, Zafeera's body was carefully carried to a van.

Distraught to the point of hysteria, Angela spun back around, pulled off her blood-stained chador, and began waving her rifle, shouting,

"I'm gonna kill every one of those fucking bastards, those pieces of shit."

Cat Murphy grabbed hold of her, but Angela was out of control and fired the rifle in the air. People screamed and scattered. Vellanova climbed back out of the van and along with Cat quickly subdued Angela by reminding her who she was: a member of WILA.

They pushed her into the van and took off, with photographers in hot pursuit.

CHAPTER 33

"**O**h God! Oh God!" Angela moaned as she stroked Zafeera's head.

"Por favor, Angela!" Vellanova pleaded. "We have to think."

Cat swerved the van around the cars streaming towards them, ignoring one-way streets and traffic lights. Her primary concern was getting them as far away and out of sight as fast as possible.

"How are we going to get her out of the country? We can't use the buses, now."

Angela's cell rang first, and then Vellanova's.

Vellanova answered hers. It was Inez and the rest of the unit wanting to know what they should do now.

The demonstrators were pouring from the courtyard and merging with the people in the streets. The police, still reeling from nearly massacring their own mothers, huddled in small groups watching Mutabi's bodyguards form a tight barrier around him as he walked, defeated, from the yard.

"Make sure all of the women demonstrators are safe even if you have to escort them home," Vellanova commanded.

"There are too many of them," Inez said. "And some of our soldiers aren't feeling well. 'Zafeera is gone! What does it matter now?' they are saying."

"It matters very much," Vellanova said. "We will continue everything as planned. Maybe we will widen our scope."

"But how can we do anything without all the help Zafeera had from all those people. They will know she is dead. The funding will dry up. We are finished. It's over!" Inez persisted.

Vellanova glanced over at Zafeera's limp body shaking from the movement of the van, then at Angela's dazed expression and wondered if what her comrades were thinking was true. Was it all over, just like that?

***

Bashi received the frantic phone call from Vellanova explaining what happened, and asking for his help. He dispassionately expressed his condolences then dispatched one of his helicopters to pick them up.

Zafeera's body was flown back to London and remained in a funeral home while the local magistrate notified Mick Taylor as the owner of the property known as the Land.

A haze of gloom descended over the Land, as each woman reflected on what WILA had meant in her own life the past five months and realized the dilemma they all faced.

Angela Johnson took Zafeera's death personally. When she wasn't storming about the place promising revenge, she was resting her head in a fellow mourner's arms. Her sorrow stemmed mostly from her tearful night of shame following her stormy exit from the classroom interview, and the call she received the following afternoon when she was so depressed, she couldn't climb out of bed.

"I read your letter," Zafeera had said, "and see you have determination to make a better life for yourself, and though your life has been very hard, still you want to contribute something to the world. I like that. And... I like your fire. You never had a real family to love you, to guide you and to protect you, like so many women in the world. But now you do. Angela, welcome to The Women's International Liberation Army."

Mick was heartbroken, angry and bewildered, but he took full responsibility of getting his girlfriend's body back to her family in France, all the while wondering how he would explain her death to them. Sickened at the thought, he had no intention of going anywhere to see the body. Everything was arranged over the phone with the help of the man called Bashi.

There was so much pain inside, Mick couldn't possibly allow himself to feel it, not all at once, or else he believed he'd die, too. For him, grief was like ocean waves. It rumbled to the surface, cresting, crashing, turbulent at times, sucking him under, and then it ebbed. Often his grief came quite unexpectedly, right in the middle of a business luncheon, and he'd miss half of what was said.

He hated her. Missed her. And had grossly misjudged her. For days, he thought of nothing but her. He had scoffed at her newfound crusade. Her death was his punishment for not trying to understand.

***

Feeling a call to arms, Tracy Blunt had given up her job as a Fleet Street broker to work exclusively for WILA as an office manager and live at the Land.

She sat wondering if she could get her old job back, while sorting the personal mail addressed to the women. Amongst the letters, was a small package addressed to WILA. It startled her.

Oh my God! We've been discovered, she thought.

No one who knew the address would send anything addressed to WILA, unless their intention was to expose them, or bring them down.

Tracy ran into the supervisor's office with the package. A half hour later every woman on the Land was sitting or standing shoulder to shoulder around one of the TV monitors, while Tracy Blunt placed a DVD into the slot on the DVD player and pressed play.

When the image faded in, they saw a serious-looking Zafeera, sitting on a couch staring at them.

There was instant excitement, but they were soon silenced the moment she began to speak.

"Hello, my brave soldiers. If you are watching this, then I guess things didn't go as planned and I did not return home with you. I was aware of this possibility—knowing Mutabi—and I do not want you to waste your time mourning for me. Remember, our mission continues beyond the absence of any soldier.

"Moving forward, it is time for your training to graduate from physical training into discovering the powers of your mind. Next month, a master of the secretive MindTech Training School, Sunji Tanaka from Japan, will come to the Land and begin to teach you. I see a future where the weapons of patriarchy will become obsolete against the forces you will harness within you, and the power you will be able to unleash with your mind. Until that time, my dear comrades, you must respect all life, including the men you fight. Take a life only if there's no alternative.

"As you all know, the WILA advisory committee in France, analyzes data and hotspots of violence against women, to determine which countries next need our assistance. However, the advisory committee has left it to me to choose my successor. I have arranged for Vellanova Sanchez to take my place. But remember, you must all work as a unified whole, as we have always done.

"I am very proud of what we have already accomplished in such a brief time. Let the world know that WILA will not stop until every woman on Earth is safe and free to evolve, and all the temples and monuments to patriarchy, hiding in the feminine mind, have been crushed and scattered, and become just a bad dream from our collective childhood."

As the image faded to black, the women continued to stare hoping there was more, hoping to see Zafeera's lovely, sincere face one more time.

After a while, Cat Murphy turned to Vellanova, who seemed as surprised as everyone else. "Did you know about this... arrangement?"

"Uh... No," Vellanova mumbled, still staring at the screen. "Zafeera never even hinted that to me."

***

In Syria, after much debate, SANA—the Syrian Arab News Agency—along with Al Jazeera news network released the story. Spinning it in their favor, the government-controlled television news networks reminded the audience that the pro-government police force stood down and that Al-Mutabi, who was plotting a coup, was now horribly disgraced.

The story was gradually picked up by the BBC and other news outlets in the Middle East, and then reported on local stations throughout the European Union. Nowhere was it mentioned that the real heroes were the women of Syria who fearlessly took back their power that toppled Mutabi's plans and, simultaneously, made the mullahs realize they were on shaky ground.

***

On the second day of the three-day women's forum at the United Nations, the video of the entire incident in Syria was posted and seen around the world. It aired on all the major TV networks. And people in New York's Times Square stopped and watched it on the huge three-story video monitors. Ironically, it was Zafeera's filmed assassination that finally showed the face all the news agencies in the world had been willing to pay a half-million dollars for, and every person wanted to see.

As the news spread around the world, teenage girls of every religion across America dropped to their knees sobbing for their fallen idol in the same way their counterparts were doing in the United Kingdom, France, Rumania and Iran, as well as India, Pakistan, China and other parts of the world.

Overnight, talk shows throughout Western Europe and America found women celebrities to express what Zafeera's death meant to them.

"She had a vision that will never materialize now. No woman in history has created a women's army to protect all women and connected so many women from every nationality."

Literary journals solicited articles from intellectuals and mystics philosophizing about her archetypal role in society and the meaning of her meteoric rise and sensationalized death, and news magazine shows featured guest politicians speculating what the Muslim world would do now.

In Our Time magazine, anticipating mega sales increases, planned to re-print articles to which Zafeera Hasni had contributed and planned to publish a special issue devoted to their former colleague, which would contain interviews she had done during the years she worked for them. Her closest colleagues: Benjamin Ubiatu and Manesh Singh, who had originally helped her gather information about her brother-in-law, Fareed, were chosen to oversee the issue.

The evening the video first aired in Times Square, Jim Cantrell, a host of a show on the Entertainment News Network, commented:

"You know, we've never seen this kind of outpouring of grief except with a pop star. It is really amazing when you consider that none of us knew who she was."

"You're right, Jim," Brittany Malor, the co-host of the show, noted. "Ironically, she was the first international celebrity without a face or a name! And by far the most surprising and unexpected condolences have come from Abdullah Bashar El Faisal, the son of a Saudi Prince."

***

A week after Zafeera's death, Islamic extremists issued statements accusing the Women's International Liberation Army of being formed and funded by the United States government to destabilize the Muslim world. The United States countered that WILA was made up of renegade covert operatives, funded by Al Qaeda to distract the West from its war on terror.

The outrage on both sides increased and overflowed like a tidal wave.

It was a ground swell for the women in Iran, Jordan, Lebanon, and Kuwait who united in support of the Syrian teachers and students and took to the streets. Feeling threatened, fundamentalists in all countries, mostly men, held their own protests. The shouting matches turned ugly. Peacekeeping forces were dispatched to these regions to curtail the violence. People died.

The British Prime Minister urged the President of the United States to be cautious, so as not to arouse anger from the American women who also supported WILA and have them retaliate.

"On top of everything else that is happening, Mr. President, we don't need a gender war," the Prime Minister warned.

Then a rumor spread that Zafeera wasn't dead, after all. Instantly, tee shirts were printed up and sold on the streets and across the Internet and, as usual, somebody got rich from it.

In the weeks following her death, WILA put aside their mourning and resumed their training and mission. Soon after, there were reports of sporadic gunfire heard in the villages of the Democratic Republic of the Congo.

It was Angela Johnson, who had insisted WILA help the Congolese women.

"Every day they risk their lives, risk being raped every time they go to buy food or just to a well to get water," she informed Vellanova. "Shouldn't they have protection, too?"

Soon after, photos popped up on the Internet of an Amazonian-like black woman with purple Mohawk hair, leading groups of armed Congolese women. In addition to the women carrying Russian-made assault rifles over their shoulders, a news reporter said, "Many of the women were also carrying water on their heads, and had their babies tied across their bodies." The question then posed by the U.N. Security Council wasn't "How can we help?" Instead, they wanted to know: "Who is supplying the weapons?"

Sadly, it was Zafeera's violent death that generated unprecedented media focus on the Women's Forum, primarily because Zafeera's first publicized appearance was at Neelam's committee meeting, several months earlier, and all the media attention that event had caused.

CHAPTER 34

O n the first day of the forum, attendees were shown video clips of women talking about being sentenced to death by their families because they had refused an arranged marriage, or had been raped, and how they escaped only to live in constant fear.

The attendees heard real stories of women and girls as young as five years old who were not so fortunate and had met their death at the hands of a brother, a father or a cousin. The sheer volume of video footage and photographs gathered and submitted by the women's coalition telling comparable stories shocked the predominately female audience—since many of them had never heard of honor killings.

At 3:30p.m., four women marched into the conference hall, spoke to an usher, and then proceeded down the side aisle left of the stage.

Neelam, along with Enid and Imani, sat with the other presenters. Kensasha, Amanda Kurtami and members of the organizations who had just submitted the footage were on the stage carrying on an in-depth discussion of what had been shown and answering questions.

One of the four women went straight over to Neelam and whispered:

"Excuse me. I am Claudia Velasquez. We spoke on the telephone. You remember?"

"Of course, I do," Neelam replied. She shook Claudia's hand, then glanced back, awkwardly, at Imani who was seated directly behind her.

"Can we talk outside?" Claudia asked intently. "I need to ask you a favor."

Neelam hesitated before getting up, and leading Claudia and the other three women out a side exit near the stage.

"I know you said I could present tomorrow, but something has happened, and I need to be back in my country by tomorrow morning. Can you let me present today?" At first, Neelam was stunned and just stared at them.

"How can I possibly do that?" Neelam responded, dismayed. "The program has already been set. We end today at 6 p.m. and we are already running behind. You know how these things go. I'm sorry. Besides you know this is a forum on honor killing, and I've already gotten myself into a bit of hot water with my colleagues for granting you a ten-minute slot tomorrow."

Claudia looked around at the women who accompanied her. They were clearly disappointed. "We came here just for this. It can't be for nothing. We don't have a lot of money. Por favor! There are women counting on me to show our video here. You promised us. Por favor!" she pleaded.

Before long, Neelam yielded and led Claudia to the video room and explained to the technician that they were modifying the program a little. She told Claudia to be prepared to speak right after the current presenters finished, which would be in fifteen minutes.

"And remember, just do ten minutes. All right?"

Claudia, busily taking out the materials she brought, answered with a slight nod.

Returning to her seat, Neelam avoided eye contact with both Enid and Imani and told the next scheduled presenters that they would go on in about half an hour.

When Kensasha and the others had concluded the Q&A, Neelam leaned back and braced herself. Claudia walked onto the stage, introduced herself and began a brief introduction about the many forms that the hatred of women can take. Then, she signaled for the video to begin.

Lights dimmed, the screen went black and, slowly, the images and sounds faded in.

Seeing the faces of disfigured young women in Afghanistan talking about how it feels to have acid thrown at them because they tried to go back to school, the audience gasped. They saw acid-attack victims from Pakistan—women who had been maimed by rejected admirers or angry husbands—and they were appalled.

With horror, the audience heard Congolese women talk about being raped by soldiers, young boys really, and then having their genitals and uteruses mutilated with the barrel of a rifle and of lying in a hospital bed for six months in agony. The same type of footage that got Zafeera so fired up. One woman talked about being unable to ever conceive a child now, and of being in constant pain whenever she urinated.

"Men say it's because of the war," the woman said. "We say men always have a good excuse to attack a woman."

From Iran came a clip of a woman who talked about being badly beaten by her husband and his family, believing it brought them shame when she joined a women's group to protest the government.

Many attendees were dumbfounded by a woman in a burka talking about being beaten in the streets and jailed by police after begging for food, because she was in public without a male relative as her escort. She said her husband had been killed in the war with America, and in her country, women are not allowed to work, so she had no food for herself or her small children.

A caption across the screen read: There are many women and children starving in Afghanistan because of this custom.

In the final clip, they were nauseated to hear women from Central America, Algeria and Pakistan with photographs and newspaper clippings talk about how women in their country are raped, killed and then decapitated to spread fear.

The lights came on again. Overloaded and distraught, several attendees left the auditorium.

Although, there was nothing in the films that Neelam hadn't already heard about, it was seeing it all at one time and hearing the voices of real people that moved her as well. She too, found herself feeling overwhelmed with anguish. This problem is insurmountable. How on earth did we think we could stop all of this? she wondered. It is too much. It is just too much.

Claudia returned to the stage briefly and said, "I have lost my 13-year-old daughter to the same kind of brutality and hatred. Please help us stop these demonic acts." Hands went up for questions, but she hurried off. This created a commotion in the audience. At the same time, a dispute erupted amongst the organizers because Claudia's presentation took the forum's theme in an entirely different direction. 'Why was that shown?' some presenters asked. And to top it all off, no one knew who would go on next, since the video portion of Claudia's presentation had run for 44 minutes, clearly pushing three scheduled presenters off the program entirely.

The fallout was directed at Neelam Sethi and Imani Sadawi who were listed as the program coordinators.

With about twenty people mobbing her—practically shouting their questions, and the U. N. Director, Heidi Schecter, approaching to inquire what was going on—Claudia Velasquez pushed her way through, quickly thanked Neelam and disappeared.

The director went to the stage and asked everyone to please settle down. Once she had everyone's attention, she made an announcement.

"That was the final presentation for this evening. We apologize for not being able to accept any more questions at this time. There is plenty of literature outside at the tables that you can take with you. Remember, we have two more days. See you tomorrow morning."

The disgruntled presenters rolled their eyes at her, Neelam and Imani in turn.

"Look, what else can we do?" Amanda asked calmly. "It's been a long day. Let's all go out to dinner and the committee will work it out by tomorrow." Amanda turned to Neelam and saw she was already on the verge of tears, having made so many people angry, and not having a clue how she'd resolve things to everyone's satisfaction.

Like her, many of the presenters had traveled from the United Kingdom. But a few had come from France and India and they had looked forward to speaking at the United Nations. Now there was no guarantee that they ever would.

Amanda persuaded Enid to help get the coalition members out of the auditorium into taxis and on to the designated restaurants for an early dinner. Kensasha and Imani accompanied a downhearted Neelam back to her hotel and ordered room service. Neelam was too upset to eat. Once again, someone had unexpectedly disrupted her carefully planned event. Even so, she spent the rest of the evening trying to salvage the program.

Early the next morning, feeling somewhat better, Neelam ordered breakfast and placed a call to Basma to find out how she was getting on alone in London.

"What? You bought painting supplies?" Surprised, amused and somewhat relieved of her worry about Aisha/Basma, Neelam leaned back against the headboard, stretched out her legs and began to flex and extend her ankles as a brief exercise. "Are you going to do the painting yourself?"

"Yes," Basma replied confidently. "I am reading the instructions now."

"So, you are getting on quite well by yourself. That is good," Neelam responded rubbing her arthritic knee.

"How is everything there? You sound tired."

"I am tired. I've been up all night trying to fix the schedule. Remember that woman, Claudia Velasquez from Guatemala? She sent that letter and those photos."

"Yes, I remember," said Basma. How could she forget? The photos had upset Dr. Sethi, so much.

Neelam explained to Basma what had happened the previous day with Claudia.

"I am sorry to hear that you had to cut the program. Congratulations, anyway, for working it out, even if people are angry with you. The most important thing is that you are all there. The forum is now happening."

Neelam nodded as she listened to Basma's reassuring words and noted, to herself, how much more mature Basma—Aisha—sounded.

After the call, Neelam took a quick shower and laid out her clothes. Her breakfast arrived, and she poured herself a cup of tea, clicked on the TV with the remote and removed the silver cover from her plate. She searched the tray for the honey she had asked for.

On the television screen, the same images had just begun screening on the monitors in Times Square. Neelam stopped and stared as a familiar face filled the screen. Addressing a crowd of women, all waving placards in the air, was the woman who had so boldly insulted her at the meeting. This was a televised footage of Zafeera's impending assassination.

At the place in the video where Zafeera, now with long, bright-red, hair, was fired upon, Neelam clutched her chest and collapsed.

Curious to hear if anything else was mentioned about the forum, Kensasha, also, clicked on the television and saw the same footage. She quickly dialed Neelam. No answer. She tried repeatedly without getting a reply. Concerned, she contacted the concierge and had them go up to the room.

Hours later, with Dr. Neelam Sethi in NYU medical center in serious, but stable, condition, the forum had lost its leader and keynote speaker. Neelam Sethi was the one person everybody in attendance most wanted to hear from. Her name and reputation were what drew the media. She had put her heart and soul into preparing her speech and the reality that she would not be able to deliver it was devastating to her. And a waste, Enid thought, remembering the hard work Neelam had done in an effort to make the ideas more concrete than her original abstract, philosophical, essays.

Kensasha telephoned Basma about Neelam having suffered a heart attack.

Basma immediately became distraught.

"Basma! Please listen to me," Kensasha called out. "You have to be strong for Neelam. She's had a lot of pressure and it affected her health. She must rest, to get better. Don't make her worry about you, too. And I don't want to worry about you either. Do you hear me?"

Basma swallowed hard, wiping her runny nose, then replied in a barely audible voice, "Okay."

For a good half hour after, Basma sat at her computer in Neelam's office, immobilized. Her mind raced. Her thoughts grew dark. Oh God, what if Neelam… It was too horrible to mention. Her entire life now revolved around Neelam Sethi. She came into the office that day specifically to hone her computer skills, to be a better assistant for Dr. Sethi. Already, she had learned how to research any topic and was finishing up an instructional on paint primers when she received Kensasha's call.

Without another thought, she shut off the computer, grabbed her handbag and bolted from the office. The bank was a good six blocks away.

She made a frantic dash to it—arriving just as they were about to close.

A few thousand dollars should do.

Ninety minutes later, passport and suitcase in hand, Basma was in a taxi on the way to Heathrow Airport. Having an affinity with cab drivers, she asked him to take her "to a plane that goes to New York right away". It was a unique request and he did his best to oblige.

At the counter of British Airways, Basma explained to the woman at the counter why she did not have a ticket.

"I must go to New York now. It is an emergency!"

The last-minute ticketing price left her agog, but she had enough to pay in cash. Eight and a half hours later, Basma's plane touched down on the tarmac of John F. Kennedy Airport at 10:30p.m. EST.

As she passed through New York customs, it was as if her whole life in London had been a dream. Now, she was wide-awake trying not to remember the life she had escaped from that July night.

With confidence, she handed the customs officer her passport. He scrutinized the photo of a sad, unsmiling woman in a full hijab, then glanced up at bareheaded Basma wearing a short sleeve dress, her hair fluffed out hanging below her shoulders, and nodded approvingly. She gave him her brightest smile and he promptly returned her passport.

Like most places, New York City had its own unique smell and energy. Its vibrancy recharged the hopes and possibilities of many people. With the Statue of Liberty just beyond its shore, New York was a city that affirmed Life, because it enabled all races of people, with varying characters, to make a niche for themselves. Still, New York could also deflate, intimidate and, sometimes, humiliate, anyone who dared to negotiate its pedestrian thoroughfares or its corridors of business, alone.

425

Fortunately, Basma never knew any of this. Once through customs, she went straight to the nearest pay phone and, using the quarters still in her wallet, she dialed Neelam and Enid's hotel and asked for Enid Statham's room. No answer. She waited another fifteen minutes, watching passengers claim their luggage and ride away in cars, vans and limousines.

Unbeknown to her, one terminal away, her cousin, Sirhan, now employed as a cabdriver like Shafal, was helping a woman pull her baby's stroller from the trunk.

Basma tried again, still no reply. Reluctantly, she dialed Kensasha's cell, and braced herself for Kensasha's reaction. To Basma, the phone seemed to ring forever. Finally:

"You are where? Are you out of your mind? Why would you do something like this?"

"I... just wanted to be with... I..."

"You see, Basma? You're not thinking clearly. Need I remind you that many people took risks to give you the freedom to create a whole new life for yourself? Neelam has been singing your praises for months, and now you are back here in New York City at the airport? A place flooded with cab drivers! Shafal may be just beyond the door, Basma. Any one of those drivers may recognize you as either that missing Queens woman, or Shafal's wife from the mosque, or both. Did you even think about that?"

"No. I am sorry. I... please don't be angry with me. I just want to help. I can stay in the hospital with Dr. Sethi."

"You cannot stay in the hospital, Basma! Besides, your presence here will only upset Neelam even more. I don't want her to know you're here."

Basma clutched the receiver. Had her impulsiveness put her in a precarious situation that could threaten the health of the very person she most wanted to help? An overwhelming and terrifying feeling grabbed hold of her. She had no place to go. When she left her home in Jackson Heights, she knew she could never return there. Now what?

Fuming and wanting to get a little distance from all the emotions kicking around inside of her, Kensasha told Basma to call back in ten minutes. She needed to think.

"Remember, ten minutes. Now, don't wander off anywhere! Stay where you are." The phone clicked off abruptly.

Basma leaned in closer to the phone pushing her face into the corner of the booth so no one could see her, wishing for a pair of dark glasses. She stared at a clock on the wall above a shuttle service counter. The hands seemed frozen.

After ten minutes, she redialed.

"All right," Kensasha said, sounding more like the woman Basma was used to. "The important thing is to get you safely away from the airport and cab drivers. I want you to locate the hotel shuttle counter, and take whichever shuttle that's leaving next. Make sure it's going to a Manhattan hotel. Once you know which one, call me again and I'll arrange for an Asian or Russian car service to bring you to Enid's Hotel. She will meet you there and you can stay with her tonight."

"Thank you, Miss Lewis."

Without saying anything further, Kensasha hung up.

As instructed, the Chinese driver delivered Basma safely to the lobby of the hotel where Enid sat waiting.

Enid smiled with relief, and rushed straight over, throwing a friendly arm around Basma's hunched shoulders. "This is quite a surprise, Aisha. Whatever made you...? Oh, don't cry! Come. Let us go upstairs. You must be exhausted."

CHAPTER 35

S hafal hurried up the floral bordered pathway of the Sadawis' four-bedroom house and begrudgingly slipped his rent check into their mailbox, as he'd done every fifth day of the month for the past twelve years. Yet, never had he resented giving these people his hard-earned pay as much as he did today.

The U.N. Forum that Imani had helped to organize and had devoted all her time to, so diligently, for the last few months, spat in the face of his values—not to mention being an all-out assault on the Rahim family. This is why he no longer spoke to her. Azad obviously told her everything that Basma had said during the Ramadan meal, and still she went right ahead and enlisted most of the women at the mosque to assist her in promoting an event that condemned exactly what Basma's cousin had done. Why would Imani do such a thing?

Now, with Azad away in Egypt, taking advantage of the fertile ground of business opportunities that the Arab Spring, and its recent political upheavals had excavated, Shafal really had no reason to make physical contact with his landlords at all. If he could afford to live elsewhere, he would.

He managed to reach the end of the path, cross the street and get into Ahmed's waiting car, before Imani entered the kitchen for her morning tea. By the time she was dressed, and ready to leave for the final day of the forum, Ahmed had already dropped Shafal off at the Long Island City garage to get his cab.

Following his normal routine, Shafal put a dollar into the ancient, no-frills coffee dispenser, and pressed "Black with Sugar". He placed the lid on the cup, got into his cab and headed for La Guardia airport to pick up the early morning arrivals.

Today promised to be another long hot one with his shift ending around 6 p.m. At that point, he'd return the cab to a Brooklyn garage where Sirhan would continue driving it through the night shift.

Pulling up behind a white limousine at the American Airlines terminal, Shafal turned on the radio and waited accompanied by the sounds of planes landing and taking off in the background.

He reflected on all that had happened and found it hard to believe that he originally thought to bring just Sumera to America, believing Basma would get better having her mother around. Instead, Sumera wanted to bring an entourage! Now Basma had disappeared—supposedly dead—and two of them were still in his house.

That Khalid. The mere thought raised his blood pressure. Nowadays, Khalid seemed incapable of doing anything other than eat, sleep and critique. And Sirhan was one of the most ill-tempered, unfriendly human beings he'd ever come across in all the years he'd lived in New York—worse than any American passenger. The man rarely speaks, he thought. He has no interest in anything—except, perhaps, making money. Of course, that's understandable, considering he had three wives back in Yemen, a considerable number of children, and with the country on the brink of collapse.

Shafal sighed, lifted his coffee from its holder and sipped.

It was all her fault! How many times had he sat in this cab and imagined seeing Basma, and having the opportunity of running her down... or folding his hands around her throat and just squeezing until her breath was no more? For all the shame and humiliation, she caused him, choking was too good.

***

At first, Kensasha thought it best for all concerned to leave Basma in Enid's room until they were ready to return to London, whenever that would be. Then, feeling a little more forgiving, she thought maybe Basma would be useful at the forum.

429

Instead of bringing video, some presenters in the women's coalition brought actual survivors of honor killing attempts to speak.
They needed someone who could interact with these women, meet
their needs while they waited to go on stage, someone with a sympa-
thetic manner.

The following morning, though jet-lagged and bleary-eyed,
Basma found herself walking with Enid to the grand corridors of the
United Nations. It was hot and sunny. They passed throngs of young
women of varying religions and nationalities waving signs and banners as they shouted. Basma assumed this was usual.

After passing through the security checkpoint, Enid led her into
the crowded conference auditorium where the last day of the forum
was already underway.

The lights were dim, as they walked down the side aisle. The audience was watching an Indian woman report how she fought off her
in-laws who had dowsed her with kerosene.

The coalition had expected the auditorium to be filled to the rafters on its final day, because Dr. Neelam Sethi was scheduled to give
the closing presentation that news reporter, Courtney Goodman, had
successfully created a substantial buzz.

The organizers, with the assistance of the director, had invited a
significant number of diplomats, ambassadors, journalists and policy
makers representing India, a few countries in the Middle East and
Africa. And the video of Zafeera, playing again at Times Square,
proved to make the evening standing room only.

Neelam's heart attack the day before, however, left organizers
scrambling to find someone to replace her, someone of similar stature
who supported their cause and was available at such short notice. So
far, they were out of luck.

Sitting amongst the presenters in the front row, Kensasha was
involved in a discussion with Amanda Kurtami and the U.N. Director. Basma spotted her immediately, and felt somewhat relieved. Still
smarting from how forceful Kensasha had been on the phone, Basma
slowed and fell in behind Enid. Fingers looped in the strap of her
handbag, she waited anxiously for the moment when Kensasha
would turn around.

Enid stopped, and as the gap between them closed, Imani Sadawi, who had been standing against the wall with arms folded listening to the woman on stage, glanced nonchalantly at the person who had just come up behind Enid Statham.

"Mrs. Sadawi?" Basma exclaimed. Imani blinked, assuming the low lighting impaired her vision. Then she realized it was true. Shocked beyond belief, her legs buckled. Enid reached out to grab her. But Basma rushed into Imani Sadawi's arms. Instinctively, Imani squeezed Basma tightly, and then broke down sobbing with joy. Distracted, people in the audience nearest them looked around to see what was going on, but soon turned their attention back to the stage.

Confused and dazed, Imani tried to comprehend the miracle.

"I see you two know each other," Enid commented curiously.

For a long while, the two women stayed locked in the embrace, both weeping—though for different reasons.

Imani was the first to pull away when she realized this wasn't some miraculous coincidence—that Basma was not only alive, but had found her way to the convention auditorium!

Trying her best not to distract the audience, she waved to get the attention of the presenter sitting closest to Kensasha. The woman nudged Kensasha who finally looked around. Imani could only glare at that point. The degree of pain she had suffered this past year believing Basma was dead, was, at times, unbearable. Yet, Kensasha never ever said one word to ease that pain.

She held Basma at arm's length and looked her over.

"No more hijab?"

"Sometimes. If I feel I want to."

"You look lovely. Where did you go? My husband told me what happened. Why didn't you come to me?"

"You were not there. I left on the first night of Ramadan."

"For Kensasha's?"

"No. A friend in Boston."

"Oh, I didn't even know you had friends in Boston." Basma smiled, awkwardly. "You know, I never gave up hope… never. But surely you know you are still in danger being here?" Basma nodded, reluctantly, not wanting to discuss it after her dispute over the phone with Kensasha. Instead, her eyes lit up excitedly.

"How are my boys? Did they marry yet?"

"I'm sorry to tell you that no one really knows where Abdel is. He just ran off. Maybe Ahmed knows, but he has not told anyone."

"Oh," she responded with sadness. "And my mother?"

"She went back to Yemen, with that young girl. They may be in a refugee camp. We haven't heard from them. But those other two are still in the house," Imani informed, turning up her nose. "Oh, that vile uncle of yours. I'm sure Shafal wishes he hadn't brought them over. I don't think they will ever leave." She sniggered, knowing Basma understood the irony.

They stared warmly into each other's eyes recalling a different time. Imani Sadawi was the first person that had taken her shopping in New York. You cannot stay in the house forever, Imani had scolded that day. You're coming with me… now!

Basma smiled to herself, inhaling slowly. This was the woman who had insisted she learn to speak English and pressured Shafal into letting her. Imani Sadawi was the person who had also gotten her the job at the nursing home. One could easily believe Imani Sadawi was her real mother, not Sumera.

"Maybe we should go outside and talk," Imani suggested. "It looks like we are disturbing people."

"Miss Lewis wants me to help out. I think I should stay in here."

"Then let's find you a seat, until she's free."

Imani had started to search for a seat for Basma when Enid came up, pulled her aside and briefly informed Imani what she knew of the situation.

With a hurt expression on her face, Imani exclaimed, "I couldn't be trusted to know these things? What more surprises are there?" Enid shrugged and led Basma through a door at the back of the stage.

Inside, presenters and the women they brought to tell their stories sat or stood around in small groups. With expressions Basma knew well, the abused women acted as if their bodies were fashioned from porcelain, and any sudden, sharp movement would shatter them. They cowered against walls, huddled in corners, stared into space. They bore the scars of battle on the outside and inside. Yet, somehow, these women were the brave, courageous ones. They chose to speak, to expose their abusers and display their wounds—not hide them.

432

"This is Aisha Langois," announced Enid. "If you need anything, just let her know and she'll get the message to us. All right?" A few of the women nodded back. Turning to Basma, she continued, "Okay, Aisha. Just sit in here for now. As you can see, there are plenty of things to drink." Enid gestured toward a table behind Basma. "If we run out of ice, just come and let me know. I'll stay close by. Are you feeling better?" Basma nodded. "Good! Kensasha will come to see you as soon as she's finished. They're discussing whether the audience should be informed of Neelam's hospitalization. If so, should we tell them now or wait until the time she is scheduled to speak. We don't want people leaving early. Amanda's due to go on just before her."

"Did you speak with Dr. Sethi today," Basma asked.

"Yes, we all have," replied Enid. "Kensasha told her that we spoke to you. She calls one of us every half hour, checking in. But the doctors want her to relax. They want us to disconnect the phone service, now. And, we had to make sure she got into a private room, so she wouldn't see a TV set. It could cause another attack. So that's why Kensasha was so hard on you." She patted Basma on the back. "Go and have something to drink. Get acquainted with everyone. Oh, and have a sandwich, if you like."

***

One after the other, they came out into the spotlight when they received their cue—eighteen women and girls. Their ages weren't important. Standing exposed, center-stage, facing an audience that was now filled with prominent ambassadors, diplomats, and Emirs, each speaking in their native tongue, they testified.

As Basma watched from the sidelines, she was captivated. She gave each woman a gentle embrace when they came back to the holding room, and noticed that a huge burden seemed to have been lifted from their shoulders. Basma had just embraced a young girl with lacerations all over her face and arms who'd survived a knife attack by her brothers, when she heard a voice behind her say:

"Can you forgive me?" Basma spun around and saw Kensasha Lewis.

Eyes filling up, she smiled and timidly walked to Kensasha, glancing down.

"Yes? No?"

Basma nodded.

Kensasha knew that would have to suffice, and gave her a quick hug. "Imani was right, you look lovely," said Kensasha with a smile. "And, very fashionable, I notice. Healthy."

Basma flushed and inadvertently reached up to adjust her non-existent hijab.

Shaking her head, Kensasha said, "Still can't receive a compliment, I see."

The last of the eighteen women came back into the holding room leaving the final presenter to give a closing statement.

Kensasha sighed and looked away, dissatisfied.

"What is wrong?" Basma inquired.

"Everything!" replied Kensasha. "Neelam's health is getting worse because she's upset that she can't be here. People from the press are asking where she is. The director is threatening to make the announcement right now. I know people are going to walk out, when she does. Amanda's feeling apprehensive about her own speech now. She doesn't want to be last. What else? The ruckus outside is escalating. More people are congregating because word got out that leaders from India and Syria have arrived, you know, and some people think there are women in the audience from WILA. Maybe some are, I don't know. Anyway, it's just... it's... and they keep showing that horrible scene from the video over and over, and it's not helping the—"

"Which video?"

"You know, the video from Syria of that woman." Basma stared back, shaking her head, still not understanding. "The video that caused Neelam's heart attack!"

Basma was oblivious, she hadn't a clue what Kensasha was referring to. She had spent the past week in a very different world: searching the Internet for a private teacher, buying paint supplies, which she stuffed in the corner of her bedroom hoping to pluck up the courage to take on the job, and indulging in her first passion, ever: going to the cinema.

"You haven't seen it?" Kensasha asked, puzzled. "How is that possible? It's everywhere. The one where they show that woman being shot to death? The same woman who came to Neelam's meeting and created that ruckus.

You were there. You met her, too."

"She is dead?" Basma cried out, cupping her mouth in disbelief.

"Yes!" Kensasha confirmed, dumbstruck "Where have you been? Everybody is talking about it. Didn't you see all those people outside, when you came in? The video is being shown, right now, in Times Square. Women are leading riots in France and in Algeria where her family emigrated. Her poor family… it's a shame."

Heidi Schecter entered, interrupting them.

"I'm going to make the announcement now," she said, a bit harried. "Do you want me to tell the audience Dr. Sethi is in the hospital, or that she had an emergency, and had to leave, and apologizes for not being able to give her, much anticipated, address?"

"As I said before, I think you should wait until after Amanda Kurtami from AWRI gives hers. But, if you must, do it now, tell them the truth," Kensasha insisted. "Remind them what the purpose of this forum is about. Surely, after what they've already seen here so far, they didn't return today just because of Neelam's celebrity."

Basma, like Neelam, and so many others, was overcome by the news of Zafeera's death. Zafeera had stirred something in her, too, that she'd only just come to realize. It was something Zafeera represented. For that reason, Basma slipped away to have a quiet moment alone.

Across from her was a table where, earlier, platters were piled high with sandwiches, fresh fruits and chocolate chips cookies. There had been bowls of pretzels, bottles of water and cans of soda set out in groups and a full dispenser of freshly brewed, coffee. All that remained was an apple core wrapped in a soiled napkin, and a scrap of dried-out rye bread. The dispenser was empty and on the floor beneath her chair, someone had left a few pages of their speech written in Hindi. Here and there, lay a discarded, pink or white, cue card. At last, the forum that Mrs. Sadawi, Miss Lewis, and Dr. Sethi worked so diligently, to create, was concluding.

Moments later, Enid and Amanda entered. The director informed them what had been decided.

"I think the best thing to ensure that most people stay, is to have Amanda on the stage with you," Enid suggested. That way, when you finish, she'll be ready to take them on a visual journey, describing exactly what outcomes we want accomplished, if this Forum is taken seriously enough for real sustained action, to be implemented, across the board."

"Are we all in agreement?" Amanda asked.

Apparently, Basma wasn't.

CHAPTER 36

"N o Basma, absolutely not! I can't possibly let you do it. That would be suicide!" Kensasha warned. "We've tried so hard to keep you safe. There are hundreds of people out there. Your face will be everywhere. Shafal and that cousin of yours will know you are not dead!"

"Maybe that is good," Basma replied, gripping Kensasha's hand for reassurance. "Then they will know I did not kill myself because of them, and my boys will know their mother is still alive."

"It won't matter. They can't protect you. No, I won't let you!"

"You know... I have been afraid all my life. Every day. Afraid of what Shafal will do to me, if I say the wrong thing or do the wrong thing. Sometimes I have been afraid of my own thoughts. Can you imagine that? I know fear. Every woman who spoke here was risking her life," she added, gesturing around the room. "Why should I be any different?" Kensasha shifted her eyes away, unconvinced.

"Basma, I apologize for saying this, but you can barely speak one-on-one, how are you going to speak in front of a room full of people and video cameras?" She saw a wave of trepidation engulf Basma, as if she hadn't considered the audience. Kensasha assumed this would be the end of it.

"Miss Lewis," Basma said, after a moment. "Dr. Sethi has been so good to me and... and, I must do this for her. I must read her speech, speak her words to those people out there. And what happens to me after," she continued with earnest, "…if they find me. It's okay. I know now what it feels like to be a woman… free."

***

In the Brooklyn taxi garage, Sirhan snorted at the TV images of the melée unfolding in midtown, as the three-story monitors at Duffy Square milked every pixel.

Uptown, Shafal cut across three lanes of traffic on Second Avenue to pick up a couple—his last fare of the day—before making his way to the Brooklyn garage.

Once the couple were inside, Shafal eyed them contemptuously through the rearview mirror, as they decided where they want to go.

"The Olive Garden on Seventh," the woman said.

At the United Nations, Amanda Kurtami stood to the right of the stage, and watched the facial expressions of the audience shift from concern to disappointment, when they heard the director announce that Dr. Neelam Sethi was hospitalized, because of the recent event in Syria.

"Although Dr. Sethi never knew the identity of this woman," the director went on to say, "she, like many other women, respected Zafeera Hasni's courage. In lieu of Dr. Sethi, following our final presenter as scheduled, her personal assistant, Aisha Langois, who helped with putting on this forum, and whose own life experience encapsulates the very theme of this forum, has volunteered to read Neelam Sethi's keynote speech. Ms. Langois was also present at the now infamous meeting where Zafeera Hasni made her first known public appearance as a member of the Women's International Liberation Army."

There was a scattering of hushed reactions when the audience heard the name.

The director glanced at Amanda and began an introduction that chronicled Amanda Kurtami's achievements—both personal, as a victim of sex trafficking, and now as President of the Asian Women's Rights Initiative headquartered in London—that had helped thousands of Asian women, stranded there and abroad, find justice.

***

Immersed in heavy traffic, Shafal dropped off his passengers on Seventh Avenue and forty-ninth street, flicked on the off-duty light and tried to proceed south.

Surrounded by megawatt neon lights, 300-inch digital screens and over-the-top billboards, his cab managed to creep another block before getting caught up in a frenzied crowd made up of theater go-ers, tourists, onlookers and young women of different ethnic groups shouting, squatting along the curb or waving make-shift signs. Some of the girls were crying as if their whole world had fallen apart. They shook their fists at police who, in turn, were trying to maintain order.

Shafal eased his foot off the pedal when, a throng of pedestrians flooded the streets and encircled cars. A man in a business suit tapped at his window. Shafal shook his head and points up at the off-duty light. Frustrated, the man gave the window a hard slap. Shafal double-checked that his doors were locked and turned up the air con-ditioner. He sneered and shook his head at the spectacle being played out before him, then contemplated making a dash for a slice of pizza.

***

At that very same moment, on the other side of the world, on a busy boulevard populated mostly by men going about their day, three rowdy teen boys joke and playfully punch one another, as they saunter past a school yard. Up ahead, they can see a group of girls, high school age, leaving the building. Engrossed in conversation, two of the girls, dressed in identical black hijabs, tee shirts and camou-flage pants, start walking towards them.

Excited, the boys prepare to harass the girls as was common in that town.

However, on this day, the three boys stop in their tracks as the girls get closer. And, without uttering a single word, the boys simply stare, as the girls proceed passed them.

Creating a similar reaction from other people up and down the boulevard, the girls continue their jovial banter, while the bright ruby red curls of their hair, dangling outside their hijabs, dance in the breeze. On each of their tee shirts—sparkling eerily when struck by the rays of sunlight—are bold purple iridescent letters that read:

Zafeera Lives!
… in me.

***

As Basma sat in contemplation behind the stage waiting her turn to speak, knowing full well that this decision could cost her her life, she opened her purse and pulled out the old wedge of pottery from long ago. Running her fingers along the rough edges and across the colored glass stones, she recalled those days when forbidden, alien concepts like liberty and choice sauntered brazenly past the most pious of thoughts: "Remember to keep every strand of hair corralled."

She recalled all the years she had navigated the world cloaked in a long black shroud as if mourning her own womanhood. But all that came after, many years after, her family's antiquated beliefs about honor led to the nightmare that would haunt her dreams for the rest of her days. She was only eleven then.

A light tap on her shoulder signaled that her turn had finally come.

Returning her attention to the present, she slipped the wedge back into her purse and with trembling hands, quickly gathered up Neelam's neatly printed cue cards that Kensasha had given her. She stood up a little too fast and her purse tumbled to the floor. She picked it up and carefully placed it on the chair.

Heart pounding, she walked out into the assembly.

Straightaway, flashbulbs went off almost blinding her. Beyond the glare, there was an outstretched hand. She reached for it, grabbed hold and, with legs shaking, was led to the stage.

Outside, the shouts and chants surrounding Shafal ceased. The crowd converges into Duffy Square, and, for a moment, Shafal was only able to move his cab another few yards before being forced to a complete standstill.

People stopped, staring transfixed at a giant TV screen.

Shafal leaned forward, peering up through the windshield to see what had everyone so captivated. It was the live CNN broadcast from the United Nations.

Shafal saw a woman moving across the screen.

Unlike the other presenters, Basma had to ascend the steps alone.

In the audience to her far left, she could make out men in crisp white robes customary for Saudi Arabia, men wearing the grand boubou of Africa, and men in designer suits.

When she glanced to her right near the front, she was greeted by the reassuring faces of Imani Sadawi—who nodded proudly at her—and Kensasha Lewis, who managed to smile while dabbing at her eyes.

Shafal's body stilled, his mouth gaped open, his eyes narrowed, then widened with shock, bafflement and pure outrage.

One irrational impulse later, he leaped from the cab, darted blindingly across Broadway, jogging east to the U. N.

Heart pounding, he reached Sixth Avenue. He tried to flag a cab. All were full.

The center sections had been reserved for the dignitaries, Secretaries of State, representatives from major human rights groups, and, to everyone's amazement, here on the last day, most of them had come.

Along the aisles stood the ordinary women. Women who represented a good sixty percent of the countries on Earth.

Huffing and puffing, face dripping with sweat, Shafal made it to Fifth, and then Madison. His legs weakened, but they kept going—fueled by rage.

Not far away, in a Brooklyn cab garage, an incensed Sirhan leapt to his feet spewing, "No! No!"

Basma stared apprehensively at the first three rows directly in front. Because, there sat a few of the most feared and outspoken mullahs and imams, revered rabbis and ministers—representing Islamic, Judaic, and Christian communities worldwide.

Dr. Sethi should see this, Basma thought. It's more than she ever could imagine.

Now on the verge of collapse, Shafal stumbled across First Avenue, and entered the U.N. grounds. He fought to catch his breath. His heart pumped blood so rapidly it blurred his vision. If it gave out, so be it. He still wouldn't stop until he got his hands around Basma's throat.

A few yards away, a security officer saw a disheveled, elderly Arab man, with a near-crazed demeanor, staggering across the plaza, avoiding security protocols. Alarmed, the officer immediately tackled the man to the ground.

With newfound grace, Basma glided to the podium and lay down her cards. With newfound confidence and self-esteem, her eyes met the audience with a depth of compassion rarely seen in such settings. And when she opened her mouth to speak words that would be transmitted around the globe, her back was perfectly straight, and her head was *unbowed*.

The End

EPILOGUE

D espite the media spectacle, the women-led riots and marches around the globe, and the mystery surrounding WILA and Zafeera's assassination, it was the faces and stories of ordinary women, together with Basma's powerful and heartwarming delivery of Neelam Sethi's closing address, that garnered the most meaningful attention, inspired the deepest emotions and left the most lasting impressions on all who attended that day.

The women and girls who spoke at the forum about the horror of being marked for death by one's own family, or having acid thrown in their faces by their husbands, helped turn the tide of domestic violence against women, and allowed the light of human experiences to cut away the chains and begin the erosion of patriarchy.

Authorities, under the scrutiny of the heads of offending countries, arrested male family members for attempted murder, and imposed life sentences. Those convicted of honor killing were given the death penalty. The resulting financial hardships forced people to seriously reevaluate that abhorrent cultural practice. Simultaneously, the women and girls who spoke out became local heroes for all the other women fearing such a fate.

Over time, Neelam Sethi's forum at the United Nations and the closing address—which had everyone talking—came to be recognized as the watershed moment. It prepared the ground for her New Philosophy of Women to be put forth in a treatise.

In the year that followed, women's rights became interwoven with international law. Countries with the highest number of human rights abuses against women were fined heavily and forced, under threat of severe sanctions, to adopt legal mandates and implement practical methods of enforcement, to ensure that women were afforded the basic rights and privileges of a human being in any respectful society.

Aisha Langois/Basma Abseh obtained an order of protection from her husband, cousin and uncle, that guaranteed their arrest should anything happen to her.

Rumors continued to circulate that Zafeera was still alive.

And Dr. Sethi's published work: A New Philosophy for Liberation Manifesto, helped to shape the global consciousness about women, that reflected in the United Nations' decision to declare honor killing, dowry deaths, female infanticide, acid attacks and female genital mutilation as Gender Terrorism.

But the remaining victories took decades to achieve and were not the result of bloodless battles, or peaceful negotiations, because the ranks of the Women's International Liberation Army swelled to 372,000 actual soldiers who continued Zafeera's Hasni's aggressive military campaign to rescue women and girls from "misogynistic savagery," as they called it.

Like all spiritual warriors, WILA took the oath Zafeera mandated after the irresponsible death of the Syrian police officers: "To only take a life to defend a life—a woman's, a girl's or my own."

Highly proficient in the most progressive mixed martial arts combat skills, with Vellanova Sanchez at the helm, WILA implemented sophisticated war strategies aided by hacking into the advanced satellite technology of Skynet 5.

Targeting rogue nations, these young women warriors faced violent clashes with brash young fundamentalists, rebel soldiers in the Congo, Columbian drug lords, and the Taliban. However, the women recruited by WILA—post Zafeera, as they became known—were truly fierce. Undaunted, they threatened rapists, serial killers and pedophiles in the United States, with castration. Not surprisingly, these offenses saw the sharpest decline because everyone remembered the "penis-in-a-bag" incident.

And, finally, with their oil reserves in great decline, the long-tolerated country of Saudi Arabia—deemed the last bastion of ruthless patriarchy—saw their most malignant form of institutionalized misogyny on the planet, Wahhabism, crumble.

—K. L., 2036

***

"Now hold on, everyone can't speak at the same time," Neelam scolded, playfully, from her hospital bed, the day after the forum ended. Her room was blanketed with get well cards, floral bouquets and the eager faces of her team.

Imani took the lead and recapped what had happened—minus Shafal's detention by police, Basma's Restraining Order, and her own very emotional conversation with Abdel. She preferred mentioning that Prince Abdullah Bashar El Faisal and his stunning wife, Leila, were spotted in the audience.

"You know, that was a very brave thing for you to do, Aisha," Neelam said, after. Basma, who was sitting on the edge of the bed, beamed back. "And, I am very, very proud of you. We all are. What a courageous girl you are, risking discovery like that. When we get you back home safe and settled, I will throw you a party. Imani and Kensasha, you both must come, too, okay?" Kensasha nodded, eagerly.

"And, I will make the food from my country," Basma offered, excitedly. Neelam reached out, and Basma took her hand.

"Who would believe that this shy girl—I mean, woman—could read in front of any audience, let alone one including distinguished, prominent figures?" Neelam teased, glancing over at Kensasha and Enid with a twinkle in her eye.

"And to do it with such passion—in English!" Kensasha added, with astonishment.

"But I made mistakes and my legs were shaking."

"Oh, that doesn't matter! I've made mistakes, too, when I spoke in front of people." Neelam comforted. "It was the way you delivered it that, obviously, generated such praise, Aisha."

"Yes," Imani agreed, and added, "She is full of surprises."

Kensasha moved in closer to Basma and whispered, conspiratorially,

"I just received a text from Vincent." Basma's eyes widened and her face lit up even brighter.

"Who is Vincent?" Imani inquired, feeling left out—again.

Basma just lowered her eyes and smiled, demurely.

*

YES, VICTORY CAN BE achieved. Neelam Sethi and Zafeera Hasni's goal to make every woman's dream of true liberation and genuine physical safety, a reality, is possible. But in the months that followed Zafeera's death—as a wary Vellanova Sanchez sat in the rec lounge on The Land, listening to the original soldiers proudly recount their earlier Iran and Guatemalan victories to each group of new recruits—she was keenly aware that a newly-formed, all-male, Global Security Task Force had just been commissioned by the United Nations to seek out and destroy WILA.

And she knew that, regardless of WILA's humanistic agenda, the real battle to achieve complete liberation for ALL women on Earth, had only just begun.

Author Bio

American-born LESTINE has lived in London, with stays in India, Germany, Switzerland and Greece.

A former professional singer, long-time meditator, holistic healer, director, producer, she graduated magna cum laude from the CUNY Graduate Center with a Baccalaureate degree in Creative Writing and Documentary Filmmaking. She attended NYU.

UNBOWED is LESTINE's first novel, based on her original screenplay. Another controversial novel, plus a sequel to UNBOWED, is in the works.

She resides in New York City.

LESTINE can be contacted through lestineauthor@yahoo.com

We invite you to write an honest review of this work and post it on Barnes and Noble or Amazon. It would be greatly appreciated.